Q1

MW01005737

"Obstetrician Clara Raymond in *Quality of Care* loses a patient and author Elizabeth Letts sends her heroine on a journey to face the repercussions of that loss, emotional as well as professional. This novel is intense, fast-paced, and almost claustrophobic in its coincidences. The lost patient was married to Clara's ex-boyfriend, and the horse farm that Clara flees to is owned by her father's longtime nemesis. Clara hides her identity as she tries to uncover the story of her father's professional demise and other family secrets. Letts vividly renders the detail of workaday routine, whether on a hospital obstetrics floor or a horse farm. Her heroine's work, in turn, engages the reader. Clara's closeness to unfolding events captures the emotion in this drama-rich story. We experience with her the remembered horror of a near-fatal accident, the fear of professional ruin, the lingering disbelief and grief of losing a patient."
—*The Washington Post*

Nurse/midwife Letts's debut, about a woman forced by tragedy to search for her past, is a winner....Deeply moving and emotional, Letts's novel shows the foibles of humanity and answers the mystery of Clara's past. The characters are alive, enigmatic, and realistic—the backbone of superior women's fiction."
—*Romantic Times*

"A haunting tale of loss and redemption." —Sara Gruen

continued...

ELIZABETH LETTS

Family Planning

NAL
ACCENT

FICTION FOR THE WAY WE LIVE

NAL Accent
Published by New American Library, a division of
Penguin Group (USA) Inc., 375 Hudson Street,
New York, New York 10014, USA
Penguin Group (Canada), 10 Alcorn Avenue, Toronto,
Ontario M4V 3B2, Canada (a division of Pearson Penguin Canada Inc.)
Penguin Books Ltd., 80 Strand, London WC2R 0RL, England
Penguin Ireland, 25 St. Stephen's Green, Dublin 2,
Ireland (a division of Penguin Books Ltd.)
Penguin Group (Australia), 250 Camberwell Road, Camberwell, Victoria 3124,
Australia (a division of Pearson Australia Group Pty. Ltd.)
Penguin Books India Pvt. Ltd., 11 Community Centre, Panchsheel Park,
New Delhi - 110 017, India
Penguin Group (NZ), cnr Airborne and Rosedale Roads, Albany,
Auckland 1310, New Zealand (a division of Pearson New Zealand Ltd.)
Penguin Books (South Africa) (Pty.) Ltd., 24 Sturdee Avenue,
Rosebank, Johannesburg 2196, South Africa

Penguin Books Ltd., Registered Offices:
80 Strand, London WC2R 0RL, England

First published by NAL Accent, an imprint of New American Library,
a division of Penguin Group (USA) Inc.

First Printing, March 2006
10 9 8 7 6 5 4 3 2 1

LIBRARY OF CONGRESS CATALOGING-IN-PUBLICATION DATA:

Letts, Elizabeth.
Family planning/by Elizabeth Letts.
p. cm.
ISBN 0-451-21759-4 (pbk.)
1. Nurse practitioners—Fiction. 2. Women's health services—Fiction.
3. Separated people—Fiction. 4. Pennsylvania—Fiction.
5. Secrecy—Fiction. I. Title.
PS3612.E88F36 2006
813'.6—dc22   2005022659

Set in Goudy
Designed by Ginger Legato

Printed in the United States of America

For Ali

ACKNOWLEDGMENTS

This book would not have been possible without the help of many people. In particular, I'd like to thank my editor, Leona Nevler, and my agent, Anne Hawkins, for inspiration and gentle guidance. For thoughtful questions, thanks to Tova Sacks.

For being my best reader as always, thanks to Ginger Letts. For keeping me sane through the writing process, many thanks to Tasha Tyska. I'd also like to thank all of the wonderful people at Backspace, and especially Karen Dionne and Chris Graham, for giving us a space to hang out and a place where any question is welcome.

Thanks also to the many people who supported *Quality of Care*, especially Kaye Teloquin at Buckhill Books in Lititz, Pennsylvania, and Joe Draybak at Chester County Books and Music. Thanks for making a local author feel welcome.

For inspiration, and for keeping me laughing, thanks to Mary, Casey, Fran, Diva, Maritza, Carmen, Damaris, Hepzibah, Anna, Lilliana, Lucy and everyone else—who can tell you that nothing in this book is as outrageous as real life.

For advice about Spanish language and cultural issues, thanks especially to Carmen, Eileen Cruz Coleman, and Marta Pineda—any mistakes that remain are entirely my own.

For her wonderful information about images of the Madonna, thanks to art historian Laura Hendrickson.

And as always to Ali, Joey, Nora, Hannah, and baby Willis, thanks for letting me do my thing.

Now, at this time, there were no roses in the New World, and it was the middle of December. But when the Virgin placed her hand on the earth, roses suddenly grew and bloomed in moments.

—FROM THE LEGEND OF THE
VIRGIN OF GUADALUPE

One

Charlotte Hopper was good at keeping secrets. That's what she did all day—collect up women's secrets. She knew who got pregnant and who didn't. She knew who was cheating on whom, and sometimes why. But when she felt blood trickling down her leg as she stood in the exam room talking to Darla Beckwith, she knew she had kept one secret too many. It was one thing to hold on to her patients' secrets. Something entirely different to hold on to her own.

Darla Beckwith was seated on the exam table, her blue eyes round with sincerity. She was wearing a too-big T-shirt with an arrow pointing down toward her abdomen that said, BABY ON BOARD.

"And I just know I'm pregnant," Darla said. "I feel sick all the time, I get dizzy, and my boobs hurt. . . ."

"Darla," Charlotte said, glancing down at the big red minus sign in the chart, "you said that you had a normal period two weeks ago."

"Well, one of my girlfriends said she got her period every time. Right up to when the baby was due."

Charlotte pulled her pen out of her lab coat pocket. In the slot labeled DIAGNOSIS she wrote *pseudocyesis*, imaginary pregnancy. She flipped back through the notes for the previous few visits. It was always the same story.

"Darla. Your pregnancy test is negative. You are having normal menstrual cycles. I am certain you are not pregnant." Charlotte studied Darla's round face, wondering if she was flat-out crazy or just above-average dumb. Darla was twenty-five, according to her chart, but she looked much younger, especially swimming in that huge maternity T-shirt.

"But my girlfriend told me her pregnancy test came out negative until they did a blood test."

It would be much easier just to order a blood test than to sit here and argue with her. But the blood test cost money, and this patient had no insurance. She couldn't approve a blood test that the patient clearly didn't need just because the patient was nuts.

Charlotte felt like sitting down. She was tired, and her back was starting to hurt. She looked at Darla Beckwith's chipmunk face. Suddenly the exam room, the linoleum floor, the sink, the countertop, the exam table zoomed out of focus, then zoomed back in. Charlotte grabbed the edge of the countertop to steady herself. *What was with her?* Well, she knew what it was, actually. The same thing that was the matter with half of the girls she had seen that morning—just not with Darla Beckwith. She blinked twice, eased up her grip on the counter edge, and tried to imagine ahead of time the way her voice should sound—soft and supportive.

"Darla, I know how much you must really want to be pregnant."

"Oh, I do. I do. That's all I want in the world."

"And you will be, Darla. You're young. You're healthy. How long have you been trying?"

"Three months," Darla said earnestly. "And I'm starting to feel the baby move."

But Charlotte grimaced. She felt a sharp pain in her abdomen. She gripped the counter edge again. She blinked. Could feel sweat beads popping out on her forehead.

Darla saw the grimace. "You don't believe me, do you?"

It was right about then that Charlotte felt the blood trickling down her leg. She wasn't sure it was blood when she first felt it.

"Thank you, Darla," she said. "You can just head out to the window. They'll check you out."

Charlotte could hear Darla protesting, "But I need a blood test. Everything makes me nauseous. My girlfriend says . . ."

Charlotte headed out of the exam room door, passed the new girl, *what's-her-name*, in a hurry, and pushed her way into the bathroom. She stared at the thin red line rolling down her leg. She sat down on the toilet, wiped, looked at the tissue. Bright red blood. Her heart started beating fast. . . . *No, not blood . . .* Charlotte took a deep breath, tried to calm herself. *Now think. It may be nothing. Maybe just a little spotting.*

Pain again. A thick band of pain, dull and sharp at the same time. *Don't let there be more blood.* Then she wiped again, but this time there were only a few pinkish strands mixed with mucus. She felt her heart rate slowing down a little.

She was almost two months along, and somehow the moment had

never come to tell her husband, Charlie, that she was pregnant. Now, holding a bright red piece of toilet paper in her hand, she thought maybe she should have tried harder to find the right time. She sat for a moment longer, slumped on the porcelain, pressing her forehead against the cool white surface of the sink. She should have told him, and Charlotte, who was prone to feeling guilty, thought that maybe keeping it from him was part of what was making this happen.

She wiped one more time: this time, nothing. She stood up, washed her hands, splashed water on her face, and then ran her fingers through her faded brown pageboy. She took in the puffy skin around her eyes, the creases that were starting to appear between her brows, the Guatemalan beaded earrings from the fair-trade store in Wayne. She picked up a little of Arecely's mango hand cream that was sitting on the bathroom sink, and she smoothed it on her hands, breathing in the scent, then unlocked the door and went back out.

The new girl (*what was her name? Right. Mary Louise*) was standing in the hallway, waiting for her to emerge from the bathroom.

"Do you need me?" She saw Mary Louise draw her head down between her shoulders.

"Well, if you're busy, I . . ." Mary Louise spoke so softly that Charlotte could barely hear what she said. She was an older woman, but she seemed completely new to medical office work.

"Actually, I . . ."

It was Mary Louise's second day on the job, and there was already an office pool about whether she would last through the day. They were all on eggshells, hoping she wouldn't quit like the last two new girls had.

"I'm sorry," she whispered.

"Don't worry about it," Charlotte said, trying to keep the impatience out of her voice.

"I just can't remember which papers go in the chart. Is it the white paper and the blue paper, or the yellow paper and the green paper?"

"Don't worry, Mary Louise. These papers confuse everyone at first. You're doing fine."

Finally, after a few moments, she managed to break away. That was the thing about Charlotte. She had a hard time saying no to anyone. Some people thought that was one of her strengths, but she knew that it was more of a weakness. She punched the numbers of Dr. Goodman's office into her keypad, trying to steady her trembling hand.

*　　*　　*

There was a fluttering heartbeat on the ultrasound. Charlotte could see it, and for just a brief moment, she felt a surge of joy, but then the joy started to seep back out of her as Dr. Goodman pointed to the screen and in a matter-of-fact voice told her the problems: an irregularly shaped sac, a slower-than-average heartbeat. For now the pregnancy was still viable, but the outcome was far from clear.

"I'm going to run serial betas," Dr. Goodman said.

Two blood tests two days apart. The HCG hormone should double every day. If it didn't then she might be losing the pregnancy. She didn't want to cry in front of Dr. Goodman. She sucked in her breath and looked out the window, afraid that if she spoke her voice might crack.

"So . . . what should I do?"

"You can go home and rest if it makes you feel better," Dr. Goodman said. "But it isn't going to change the outcome one way or another."

Charlotte could feel a single tear escape from her eye. She wiped it away, hoping she wasn't going to start sobbing full-out, there in the office. That was the kind of thing that happened to Charlotte. One minute she was calm, and the next minute, she was a sobbing mass of wet Kleenex and runny nose. Dr. Goodman laid a hand on her arm. "I know this is hard, but at this point, all you can do is wait and see."

Of course, as a women's health nurse practitioner, Charlotte already knew all this, but when she was the one sitting on the exam table, her knowledge and training didn't seem to help.

It was always hard not to be struck by the difference between Dr. Goodman's office and the place where Charlotte worked. Dr. Goodman's office was in a new office complex in Westville. Inside the waiting room, there were pleasant upholstered sofas, a fish tank, and an air of calm.

El Centro, where she worked, was just two miles away, but the distance from Westville to Londondale seemed longer. After she drove past the new shopping center with the Starbucks in it, the businesses along the highway started to change. Now ramshackle homes, tractor sales, and little Spanish markets lined the highway.

El Centro de la Mujer/The Women's Center of the Greater Londondale Area (everyone called it El Centro) was a dilapidated old farmhouse that had been converted into medical offices back in the seventies. It sat in the middle of a parking lot, across the street from a trailer park, and behind it stretched fields that led out toward the Smithbridge mushroom farms.

As she walked up the steps, Charlotte peeked through the waiting room window. Inside the waiting room, on faded sofas with broken springs, every seat in the house was taken.

Later that afternoon, after the last patient had been seen, Charlotte was sitting at her desk. She was leafing through a pile of lab results and phone-call slips, when LeAnn popped her head in the door, her jacket on.

"See ya, Charlotte."

"Night, LeAnn." Charlotte barely looked up, but then as LeAnn started to disappear down the hall, she called out behind her, "Hey, LeAnn . . ."

She stopped. "Yeah?"

"Did I get any phone calls?"

"Phone calls . . . phone calls . . . Oh, yeah. Dr. Goodman's office called. They said to call back before four thirty."

Charlotte looked at her watch. "LeAnn, it's five minutes to five. Why didn't you tell me?"

"You were with a patient," she said. "Sorry . . ."

Charlotte felt like standing up and hollering at her, but what good would that do? LeAnn was as scatterbrained as they came. Scolding her wasn't going to change that. Charlotte punched the numbers of Dr. Goodman's office into the phone, but, as she expected, the answering machine picked up. She would have to wait until tomorrow.

No more bleeding, no more cramping either. She had been allowing herself to feel temporarily hopeful. But without the lab results, it was still hard to know. Charlotte thought about the tiny life inside her—she had already fallen into dreaming about names and imagining baby clothes. She tried to rehearse what she was going to say to Charlie: "I know the timing isn't great, but still, it's what we've been hoping for. . . ." They had been trying for how long? Three years? Four . . . ? Five . . . ? Until they had forgotten they were trying, until Charlotte wasn't sure if Charlie even wanted it anymore . . .

While Charlotte was sitting there, staring into space, Arecely came to Charlotte's office door, her movements so quiet that Charlotte didn't even notice she was there. Arecely's hair was long and styled in ringlets that were carefully held in place by a copious amount of hair gel. Even at the end of the day her pink scrubs looked freshly ironed, her sneakers were snow-white, and her makeup looked fresh.

"Charlotte?" Arecely spoke softly.

"Yes?"

"There's a patient just walked in. Says she needs to be seen right away."

"What's the problem?"

"She wouldn't say," Arecely said.

Charlotte glanced at her watch.

"Does she have an appointment?"

"No."

Charlotte looked at the stack of charts on her desk. Clinic policy was not to take walk-ins. Especially not five minutes before closing time.

"She . . . she seems upset."

Charlotte frowned, looked at her watch again, the stack of charts. It was hard for her to turn people away. "I'm sorry, Arecely, but it's too late for a walk-in."

"But I thought you said—"

"Tell her that if she wants to be seen she needs an appointment. Tomorrow."

Arecely spoke softly, but there was quiet determination in her voice. "But she's upset."

"Tomorrow."

"But you said . . ."

"I said what? That we see walk-ins now? At closing time?"

"You said we should never turn a patient away if they really have a problem, and this girl, she seems really upset, and she didn't want to give her last name. She's crying, and she says it's really important."

Arecely looked at Charlotte steadily, waiting for her answer. Arecely was twenty, and had a four-year-old son who was waiting for her at her next-door neighbor's, and yet she was willing to stay.

"Okay, bring her in," Charlotte said, then added, "And you get out of here. I don't want you staying late."

"She doesn't speak English," Arecely said.

Charlotte felt a stab of defeat. "All right, well, let's get her in and out as quick as we can."

The name on the chart, Maria Lopez, was probably not her real name. She was a slight, very young-looking girl who sat shivering on the exam table covered by a paper drape. Her hair was twined into a thick braid, and her cheeks were covered by a fine layer of coarse dark hair. Her legs, solid tree trunks with thick ankles, which hung down below the paper drape, were also covered in thick dark hair. Around her neck, she wore a gold chain with a pendant that had a shimmering image of a female face, maybe the Madonna, suspended on it. She wasn't crying, but her face was puffy and her eyes were red.

Arecely stood next to Charlotte, translating. It bothered Charlotte when she couldn't talk directly to her patients. It left her with the constant feeling that she was going to miss that one crucial and important thing. She had tried to learn, listening to Spanish tapes in her car, but she didn't seem to have any talent for it. The language barrier felt like a brick wall that obstructed the light.

"Ask her what she is here for today."

Arecely asked the young girl, and then a torrent of words came out, punctuated by a fresh stream of tears, then a hand on her belly, then more words and tears. Charlotte picked out *sangre*, blood, and *el parto*, birth, but not much else.

Charlotte had a feeling, a premonition that something wasn't quite right.

Arecely turned to Charlotte.

"She says she had a baby about a month ago. In Mexico. She didn't get the postpartum check. Now she's says there is something wrong with her boob." Charlotte noticed that on the front of the girl's T-shirt there was a small damp spot—leaking milk.

"Where's the baby?" Charlotte asked.

Arecely turned to the woman and asked her. Charlotte stared at the woman, trying to read clues to her anguish there. She strained to understand what the patient was saying—to no avail.

"She says she left it with her sister."

"In the mushroom camps?"

Arecely said something else.

"In Mexico."

"She left the baby in Mexico?" There was another long exchange in Spanish; it sounded heated to Charlotte's ears. The girl was still crying, and her hands, which gripped the paper drape, were twisting it into shreds.

"Arecely, what is she saying?"

"She says her boobs hurt, from when she stopped giving the baby the milk."

Charlotte looked at the milk spots on the girl's shirt. How long did it take to get from Mexico to Pennsylvania anyway? In spite of her constant contact with women like this one—intimate contact as she examined their bodies using her own two hands—she really didn't understand anything about them. How exactly a young woman without papers got from Mexico to Pennsylvania, or what the mushroom camps where they lived looked like.

Charlotte's brief exam was quick and businesslike, the diagnosis evident as soon as she examined the breast—it was a severe case of mastitis, a highly painful infection of the breast that needed immediate treatment. Just a few more hours without medication and she would have gotten sicker. Charlotte wrote out a prescription and handed it to the patient.

"Tell her that the medicine might be expensive. Ask her if she has the money to pay for it. Tell her that it's really important," Charlotte said.

Arecely said something that sounded reassuring, but Charlotte didn't recognize the word *dinero*.

"Arecely, does she have a way to pay for the medicine?"

Arecely shrugged. "She's going to ask her brother-in-law."

"Does she understand how important this is?"

Arecely didn't answer, and Charlotte left the question hanging there. She was doing what she could do, and she tried to repeat that to herself, but it had a hollow feel.

Those small successes, agreeing to see a patient five minutes before closing, and then finding out that she was able to do some good, those used to be the things that kept her going. She worked long hours and was underpaid, but at least, she always told herself, she was part of the solution, not part of the problem.

But somehow, lately it was getting harder and harder for Charlotte—she referred people to specialists they couldn't afford to see, prescribed medicines they couldn't afford to buy, and still the line outside the clinic never diminished.

She thought of the young woman. She very much doubted that her name was really Maria Lopez; the undocumented workers were often afraid to give their real names. Four weeks ago she had delivered a baby in Mexico. Four weeks later she was here, in a trailer outside a mushroom camp in Pennsylvania? Charlotte couldn't quite grasp how that could happen.

It was hard enough for Charlotte to imagine losing a baby when she was only two months along. What circumstances would drive a woman to leave her baby behind when the milk was still hot in her breasts? Well, that wasn't entirely true . . . but Charlotte shoved that thought aside. As she zipped up her jacket, she whispered to the fragile spark of life growing within her: "Stay alive."

Two

C harlotte drove along Birmingham Road slowly, with her high beams turned up to look for deer. There was a big farm behind her house—it had been empty for three years, and along that stretch of road, with high trees on either side, there were often deer popping out into the road unexpectedly: an amber flash, eyes, then a white flash, tail. Charlotte hadn't hit one—yet—but from the number that she saw killed on the side of the road, she felt like it was just a matter of time.

Tonight, though, what blocked the road wasn't a deer, but a large white van parked on the side of the road—its shape was so large in contrast to the two-lane highway that she was startled for a moment, and swerved, before she saw the blue writing on the side: NORTH AMERICAN VAN LINES.

Hadn't Deirdre said after Christmas? Hadn't she said that the house wouldn't be finished before then? Well, maybe they were just moving in some furniture or something.

About a month ago she had gotten a note from Deirdre, on thick vellum embossed with the Saramago family crest.

> *Charlotte, darling, we're going to be neighbors. Hard to believe, after all this time. I'm looking for a farm in Westville and bringing the horses. Can't wait to see you. It's such a help to find old friends when you are moving to a new place. Do let me know if you know of anyplace suitable.*

When Charlotte got the note, she had stared at it for a long time. She had sort of kept in touch with Deirdre—Deirdre sent notes, or called sometimes long-distance from Argentina, or London, or West Palm Beach. Charlotte didn't even think Charlie knew they had kept in touch. It wasn't exactly that she wanted to be in touch with Deirdre, but times changed and so did people, and it didn't seem right to refuse to speak to her. That wasn't in her nature.

The night she received the note, Charlotte brought the subject up with Charlie. "You remember our old friend Deirdre. . . ." As though either of them would have forgotten.

Charlie whirled around and looked at her, his face chalk white.

"She sent me a note."

Charlotte couldn't read the look on his face at all. It had been years since they had mentioned Deirdre's name, and really, when she thought about it, they had never discussed her that much.

"She's moving around here somewhere. She's buying a farm in Westville."

He stood there, lips pressed together in a thin flat line. Then when he finally spoke, his voice was constrained. "We won't see her at all. No contact. Period."

They had been married for sixteen years, and most of the time she thought she knew what he was thinking, but now he stared out into the distance with an odd look on his face—angry, but pained at the same time.

It had been such a long time; what had happened back then had faded, become less sharp around the edges. She had spent a long time atoning for it, and until this very moment, she thought she had moved past it—that it was over.

Charlie had turned his face partially away from hers, but she could still see the expression on his face.

"But, Charlie . . . couldn't we just . . . you know . . . move on?"

He turned back to face her full-on. "Charlotte. Let me make this perfectly clear. I don't ever want to hear that woman's name spoken in our home again."

Charlotte was confused. She stepped forward, laid her hand on his arm, but he batted it away and turned his back to her, leaving her in a startled silence, tears stinging her eyes.

Afterward, thinking about it, Charlotte calmed herself with the thought that she was unlikely ever to run into Deirdre by accident. Charlotte and Charlie lived in a small subdivision just on the edge of Westville, and almost all of the horse farms were out to the west. The horse people moved in their own circles, sent their children to private schools.

But there was one old farm, with an old stone farmhouse, Chester County stone, that dated back to the American Revolution. It had a rolling sweep of fields around it: the low stone walls and split-rail fences, an old bank barn with faded gray stone and weathered boards. It was surrounded by forty acres of pristine farmland—land that backed right up to Charlotte's subdivision. Until three years ago, one elderly woman had lived there, and the only people who had ever come and gone were her phalanx of visiting nurses. Now it was empty and everyone was afraid it would be sold to developers—it was the talk of the neighborhood. So Charlotte, when she wrote back to Deirdre, just happened to mention that the farm was for sale, telling herself, What are the chances . . . ? Not mentioning that the farm actually abutted her own property.

Then, one day, right around the time that Charlie lost his job, Charlotte heard the neighborhood gossip. A lady from Argentina was moving in with a string of polo ponies, and Charlotte felt it in her bones. It had to be Deirdre. Who else could it be? Charlotte felt so sick that she ran into the house, leaned over the toilet, and started spewing her guts out.

Of course, it wasn't actually the news about Deirdre that made her vomit. She was pregnant. She had dipped her own urine at the clinic and rushed home, eager to tell the news to Charlie. Sure, they hadn't really planned it, but she felt sure that Charlie would be as excited as she was.

Except that day, when she got home, Charlie was unexpectedly not at work. She found him ashen faced, sitting on the sofa in the living room, staring at a blank wall. She knew he was burned out, sick of the corporate life in graphic design, and he hadn't been getting along with his boss. She knew that deep down, somewhere inside, he was probably relieved. But still, they needed his income, especially if she was going to have a baby. . . .

So as it turned out, she didn't have the guts to tell her husband about either event—not the fact that she was pregnant by accident, not the fact that Deirdre was not just moving to the neighborhood, but moving to a farm that was just beyond the woods that bordered their own backyard.

Charlotte had long ago buried any feelings that she might have once had about Deirdre—she had thrown them down that same well where she tossed all of the other women's secrets, hiding them under the cheerful, harried do-gooder face she showed the world.

But Charlie, he was the one person who knew everything. There was nothing, no matter how black, that he didn't know. And a big reason she had fallen in love with him was that she figured that if he could love her in spite of that, he could love her in spite of anything.

But, if Charlie didn't want to talk about Deirdre, there was only one possibility—that he hadn't fully forgiven Charlotte. So that was when Charlotte clamped her mouth shut and started keeping secrets of her own.

Charlotte pulled around the big moving van, careful to wait until there were no oncoming headlights, and then slowed to turn onto Millstone Manor Drive.

Julie was sitting at the computer playing The Sims when Charlotte came in, and she was picking at a bowl of lettuce that she held balanced in her lap. She was wearing a spaghetti-strap tank that clung to her flat belly and small, firm breasts.

Charlotte threw her dirty lab coat in the laundry room, walked into the kitchen, and opened the fridge.

"Where's Dad?"

Julie jerked her head in the direction of Charlie's office. "He's working . . . I think . . ." she said, setting the salad bowl on the counter. "Hey, Ma . . . " Julie said. "Horse people are moving in."

"What?"

"The farm. They were out cleaning out the barn today, and they're putting up a new fence, and someone delivered some hay."

"Oh," Charlotte said, wondering how long it would take Charlie to notice that Deirdre had moved in next door.

Then Charlie popped his head out of his office. Charlotte could see that he had a spreadsheet open on his desktop, and she knew what that meant. . . . He had been out of work for two months, his unemployment was about to run out, and they were juggling bills.

"Honey?" He had such an odd look on his face. "Dr. Goodman's office called."

Charlotte sucked in her breath. *The baby.* She had actually managed to forget for a moment. But they wouldn't have given him the results, as that was confidential.

"They said . . . Wait a minute. I wrote it down. . . . They said beta HCG level was abnormally low. . . ."

"Abnormally low?" Charlotte said, feeling the pit of her stomach drop out from under her. It was true. She'd been feeling less nausea lately—a pleasant change, but also a sign that something might be wrong.

"Charlotte?" Charlie's brow was creased with worry.

"Mom?" Julie said, picking up on the fact that something was wrong.

"They gave you my lab results? They shouldn't have given the lab results to anyone but me."

"Charlotte." Now he looked frightened. "Is there something you don't want me to know? Is everything okay?"

Charlotte opened her mouth, certain that she was going to tell him. Sure that now she'd be able to let it all tumble out. . . . *Deirdre is moving in next door, and I'm pregnant but about to lose the baby, but if I don't lose it, I want to keep it even though you don't have a job, and I'm afraid you're going to say no. . . .*

But all the stuff she was planning to say didn't come out. Instead she just put on her keeper-of-secrets face, and she said, "Oh, it's nothing. . . . I'm just a little anemic. . . ." And she turned her back to him and headed upstairs, because she knew from experience that Charlie was skilled at reading her face. *Tonight*, she thought as she hurried up the stairs. *I'll wait until Julie is in bed and then I'll tell him.*

But that night, while she was standing in the bathroom brushing her teeth, staring at her own face, rehearsing her little speech, she felt blood trickling down her leg again, and then, as she doubled over with strong cramps, she realized it was all over.

And when she was done, she stared at the blood clots in the toilet, trying but failing to connect that to the little baby inside that she had already fallen in love with, but she couldn't make the connection, and so with a heavy heart, she flushed it down. Then she stood a while longer, and she thought about how now she really didn't have to tell Charlie about it at all, that maybe it would be the greater part of kindness not to tell him.

Except that while she was cramping in the bathroom, Charlie was Googling *beta HCG* on the laptop while sitting in bed.

So when she emerged from the bathroom, he looked up at her, with that same unintelligible look, and said, "So when is the baby due?"

Charlotte started sobbing so hard then that it took him a while to understand that "flushed it down the toilet" meant she had suffered a miscarriage, but that she was fine and didn't need any medical care, and finally, she managed to add in the part about Deirdre, and how it looked very much like she was moving in next door.

That night he held her in his strong arms and soothed her while she cried and cried and then finally fell asleep, but while he was rocking and patting and soothing her, she realized later that he didn't say much of anything.

The next morning there was a note on the breakfast table that said, *I need to go away for a while*, and Charlie was gone.

Three

When all hell breaks loose in a medical setting, before long somebody will say, "It's because of the full moon."

On Monday, at a quarter to ten A.M., Flo was standing in the middle of the reception area, one pink-painted fingernail pointed in the air like she was testing the wind. "Anybody see that full moon last night?"

Charlotte, who was scribbling notes in a chart, barely looked up when Flo spoke, but she frowned a little—it wasn't a good sign when someone mentioned the full moon before lunchtime. Of course, she hadn't shared with anyone that her husband had taken off and that she was still bleeding from Friday's miscarriage, but if she had, that would have all been dumped on the full moon with the same amount of nondiscriminatory cheer.

Charlotte closed the folder and tossed it onto the heap of unfiled charts next to LeAnn, the receptionist. But before she could leave, LeAnn, who was on the phone, put her arm on Charlotte's shoulder, cupped her hand over the telephone receiver, and said in a loud whisper, "We have a *situation*."

"A situation?"

LeAnn jabbed the HOLD button with the tip of her index finger.

"It's Milady Shreve. She wants to know if . . ."

Charlotte interrupted. "Does Milady Shreve have a chart?" When a patient called with a question, the staff was supposed to pull the chart. But just because that was what was supposed to happen didn't mean it did.

"Milady Shreve . . . Milady Shreve . . ." Flo, the office manager, said, not making any attempt to look in the chart cabinet for her files.

LeAnn covered the receiver with her hand. "She's worried about premature sperm."

"Premature *sperm?*" Every day, Charlotte thought she had heard everything. Every day, one of the patients proved her wrong.

"You know"—LeAnn arched up her eyebrows—"she said he *came early*—didn't make it *all the way in.*" LeAnn enunciated this last with the precision of a clinical diagnosis.

"Oh, I get it now," the new girl said, nodding her head as if Confucius had just spoken.

"So . . . what should I tell her, Charlotte?" LeAnn still cradled the phone between her cheek and shoulder; with her other hand, she was rubbing her belly where a fat roll flopped over the top of her jeans. "About the *prematurity issue?*" Flo was rolling her eyes, and LeAnn obviously thought the whole thing was pretty funny, but Charlotte was in no mood.

Charlotte looked past the reception desk, out into the spartan waiting room, where already every seat was filled, one person was standing, and a gaggle of toddlers roamed around the middle of the room, pushing broken trucks and leafing through torn Golden Books from the basket in the corner.

"Tell her . . . tell her . . ."

"She sounds very concerned. . . ." LeAnn's voice dripped with mock solemnity.

"Oh, for God's sake, LeAnn." Charlotte grabbed another chart from the rack. "Take a note. Put it in my desk. Tell her I'll call her back later." Then she took off down the back hallway.

"Jeez," LeAnn said, "does Charlotte have PMS or what?"

"It's the full moon," Flo said reflectively. "Gotta be."

Monday afternoon the schedule was blocked off for a staff meeting. Dorothea Wetherill, volunteer chairman of the board, stood in front of the little assembled group. She was a slight, gray-haired woman, not much more than five feet tall. She was rumored to be in her eighties, though she didn't look it, and nobody had dared ask her if it was true. In her arms she was clutching a plastic pig that was almost as big as she was. Next to her was Mark Wetzel, the clinic's volunteer accountant. Mr. Wetzel shifted uneasily on his feet and cleared his throat politely like a small punctuation mark. "I'm not going to mince words with you," he said to the assembled group. "The clinic is in serious financial difficulties." It seemed like every one of their not-too-frequent meetings started on that note.

"Yeah, so what else is new?" said LeAnn. She rolled her eyes and jammed her hand into the Chee•tos bag with a crinkly burst.

"Give the man a chance," Flo said.

They were upstairs in the health education meeting room. Flo had brought a large bag of Spicy Chee•tos and a two-liter bottle of blue Go Pop, so there were slurping and crackling and crunching sounds punctuating Mr. Wetzel's speech. He was standing, but the rest of the group was half lying on the floor, slumped on the cushions and beanbag chairs that were scattered around the room. All except for Charlotte, who was standing by the window, and Harve—Harvey Dexter, MD, the medical director—who was sitting with his belly pushed out in front of him on a straight chair in the corner of the room. He was holding his cell phone, and from the way he was fiddling with the buttons, he looked to be playing a game on it.

"Please do not underestimate the seriousness of this," Mr. Wetzel said to the group.

Charlotte stared out the window, back toward the Dumpsters and to the fields beyond, where there was a well-worn path leading across the fields to the mushroom houses. There were three men cutting across the parking lot now from the trailer park across the street, headed off toward the gray cinder-block mushroom houses in the distance. Charlotte was only half listening to Mark, his voice droning like the fly that was batting up against the dormer window.

"Make no mistake," Mark said. "There is only one more drastic step we could take, and we on the board are extremely reluctant to take it."

He paused, looking around the room again. Charlotte could hear Flo muttering under her breath, "Would you spit it out already?"

"We have an offer on the table from Communicare Corporation."

Nobody said anything at first, because nobody wanted to sound that stupid. But finally Mary Louise, who was new and didn't know any better, said, "Could you say that again? In English this time?"

Mark was a thin man, with a sparse salt-and-pepper beard that seemed designed to denote that he was a man of not just numbers but also compassion. He stroked the beard nervously, looking around the room at the women seated there.

"It means . . . that the board would sell the clinic to a private company. You would be folded into their organization, and El Centro would no longer exist."

There was a groan in the room that wasn't quite a sound . . . a collective breath whooshed out a little too loud and then sucked in again.

Everyone sat, ruminating, trying to figure out exactly what that meant. Finally LeAnn said, "Well, I mean . . . are you sure that's all bad?"

Mark and Dorothea exchanged a couple of freighted glances, as though trying to decide who should speak. But then there was a loud, phlegmy cough, and a couple of creaks from the chair in the corner, and Harve spoke up.

"This kind of clinic—this not-for-profit community thingy. It's a dying breed," he drawled. "Communicare comes in and changes everything—probably tears the whole place down, builds it from the ground up again."

"I've seen the other Communicare buildings. They're real pretty and clean," Arecely said.

Then the murmur in the room turned more positive. Maybe this was going to turn out to be good news after all.

"Ladies," Mark Wetzel said, speaking up above the buzz, his voice cracking just slightly. "Ladies, we believe that El Centro, though it has grown increasingly difficult to fund, serves an important function in the community. We are not sure that the plans that Communicare has in mind for this site would meet the needs of the community as well."

"Which means?" Charlotte said.

Mark looked around the room. It was clear that what was coming would not be good news.

"*They* are hoping to turn the place into an outpatient surgi-center—cosmetic procedures, laser hair removal, that kind of thing."

"What would happen to our patients?" Charlotte asked.

"Communicare would direct them to one of their other facilities—they have an ob/gyn clinic in Exton."

"But that's forty-five minutes away. Half of our patients walk to get here."

"That is why," Mark said, "we don't feel this offer is consistent with the goals of the organization."

"However," Dr. Dexter added, "if we can obtain reasonable guarantees from Communicare that they will use the facility to continue with our objectives, then this offer starts to look very attractive."

"We are hoping to find a large donor to increase the endowment. That's our only hope," Dorothea said.

"A large donor?" asked Mary Louise.

"We think a onetime contribution of two million dollars would put us back on an even footing."

"Two million dollars . . . ? Who has got two million dollars to give away?" Flo said.

"Oh, you'd be surprised. There is some real money around here . . . all those horse people. . . . the trick is just in getting the right person interested. We're contacting the local newspaper. Hoping that with some publicity a wealthy donor will step forward. Charlotte, Flo, you may be getting a call from a nice young newspaper reporter. His name is Paul Stone," Dorothea said.

"Right now, to try to forestall that happening," he continued, as though nobody had reacted, "we're implementing a five percent pay cut across the board."

A murmur of protest welled up.

"You wouldn't do that." That was Flo.

"No freakin' way." That was LeAnn.

This went on for a few moments, until a pronounced sniffing started. Then everybody fell silent and turned to look at Arecely.

At first Charlotte thought she must have gotten to the sad part of whatever book she was reading. When she wasn't working, that girl always had her nose buried in a book. But Arecely's book, a fat, well-worn paperback with shiny purple script on the cover, was closed on the floor next to her.

"What is it, Arecely? What is it?" everybody said.

Arecely, who was not given to dramatics, clearly was mortified by the attention. She rubbed hard across her eyes, while Flo leaned over and handed her a Kleenex.

"What is it?" Flo said. "Don't be afraid to speak up. These people here need to know what is on your mind."

"Nothing," said Arecely, who had stopped crying now, but not before she had gotten two round mascara rings under her eyes.

Mrs. Wetherill, still holding the pig, said, "My dear, we certainly want you to speak up and tell us what's on your mind." Her voice was brisk but it conveyed attentive reassurance.

Arecely stared at the floor, not looking up.

Flo reached over, patted her on the arm, said, "Go on. . . ."

"Yes," Mrs. Wetherill said. "Go on, dear."

"Well, all right." Arecely rubbed the flat of her hand against the nubs of gray carpet and sniffed again, swiping at her nose with the crumpled pink Kleenex. "It's just that . . . Lizzie told me she won't babysit Zekie anymore unless I up her pay to two-fifty an hour, and I told her okay, just this morning, I told her okay, because what else am I gonna do?"

Flo downed the last swig of her Go Pop and stood up, squaring her shoulders.

"Don't you worry, Arecely. It won't come to that."

Then she turned to Mark Wetzel.

"You've got a hell of a lot of nerve coming here and telling us that. You, who lives in one of those big houses over in the Reserve at Millstone. . . ."

He looked sheepish and stroked his beard. "We all believe in the mission of this clinic—but if the clinic isn't viable . . ."

"I could make more over at the Turkey Hill, ringing up Big Gulps at the cash register," LeAnn said, "and here I'm taking care of people's health, their life's blood." Her voice crescendoed as she realized how good *their life's blood* was going to sound.

Harve had not even glanced up during this discussion. He was still sitting in the chair in the corner, seemingly absorbed in the keypad of his tiny silver phone. Mark was making placating statements that didn't sound too convincing—*hopefully not necessary, only if there is no other way around it.*

Everyone had forgotten Mrs. Wetherill, who was standing in the corner, her arms still wrapped around the enormous plastic pig.

But now she spoke up. "Ladies, we are all very proud of the work that gets done here, but please don't shoot the messenger. I hope you are aware that Mr. Wetzel takes time off from his accounting business to do this job as a volunteer."

But that didn't appease anyone. There was an electric current of discontent crackling around the room.

"Come on, ladies," Flo said in a loud voice. "We've got patients to take care of."

Mary Louise, Arecely, and LeAnn stood up and fell into line behind her. Arecely was rubbing the tears off her face, LeAnn was licking the orange Chee•tos dust off her fingers, and Mary Louise had taken off her glasses and was rubbing them on her scrub shirt as though her life depended on it.

Only Charlotte didn't move. She was no longer looking out the window—now she was looking across the room at the mural on the wall. The early-afternoon sun was slanting through the dormer window, so that a bright beam of sunlight lit up the painting. This room was used for meetings, and for a Hispanic youth group that came to study health education. At some point the youth group had been allowed to paint some murals on the white wall, and this was a painting of a woman with long brown hair and carefully sketched features, wearing a blue robe covered with stars, a pink gown, and sandals that peeked out below her hemline.

Charlotte contemplated the painting, blocking out the noise around her. Funny, she had never really noticed it before. It was a painting of the Virgin Mary—a Mexican religious painting, not something that held any particular meaning for her. But now, with the light shining through the window onto the painting, she noticed for the first time how beautiful it was—the hands and face had been carefully sketched in pencil. Her wide eyes, flat nose, and unsmiling lips looked calm, reassuring. Her hands, drawn with great skill, were held in prayer in front of her. Charlotte gazed into the Madonna's face and again thought about her baby—about the tiny heartbeat, about how she had willed it to keep beating. About how she had lost it anyway . . .

I know you are all upset. . . . I know this has come as a shock to you all. . . . Charlotte watched the light playing against the wall, illuminating different parts of the mural, now a spot of blue on the cape, now the pink of her dress or the brown of her hair.

". . . and place it by the place where the patients check out . . ."

Mrs. Wetherill was speaking now, and Charlotte realized that she hadn't been listening. She tuned back in.

The girls were hovering around Flo now, like chicks around a hen. They had stopped short of flat-out leaving, and now they stood by the door listening as Mrs. Wetherill, pig in hand, held court.

"Just tack a little sign above it that says, 'Contributions welcome,' and leave it there by the window where the patients check out."

"Mrs. Wetherill, with all due respect"—LeAnn usually sounded cranky, but now she was bordering on rude—"our patients can barely pay their balances."

"Prices have gone up," Arecely said.

"We're already charging them twice as much as we used to."

"Girls, let's listen to what Mrs. Wetherill has to say," Flo said diplomatically, but Charlotte could tell that even Flo was not buying into the pig concept.

"We need every penny we can get. Just put the pig and the sign by the window and see what happens."

"Yeah, what happens is going to be a hungry pig," said LeAnn with a snort.

"Young lady," said Mrs. Wetherill, "you may be surprised by people's generosity."

"You may be surprised by people's generosity." That was LeAnn later, in a sarcastic voice, as she watched Flo attach the pig to the checkout window by a length of chain she had picked up at the hardware store.

"You can't be too careful," Flo said as she hammered a nail into the countertop to hold it fast.

"Yeah, it looks like it *might* have some money in it," Mary Louise said. "Even though it *doesn't*."

"And never will," LeAnn added.

"You never know," said Arecely, sounding dubious.

"Well, even if their methods are a little questionable, they are trying to help us," Flo said. "So I'm going to make the first contribution." She went to her desk, unlocked the drawer, and pulled out a little change purse, which she unclasped awkwardly so as to spare her nails.

"Just so's it doesn't look so empty," she said, and she folded up a dollar bill and slipped it through the slot, followed by a quarter, a dime, and a penny.

They all stood admiring the pig, appreciating the fact that the shadow of the dollar could be seen through its thin plastic sides.

"It needs a name," pronounced LeAnn.

"Diego?" offered Flo, apropos of nothing.

"A pig name," said LeAnn, who had obviously decided she was taking charge of the christening. "How about Babe? Like in the movie?"

"Francis Bacon?" queried Charlotte. "Oscar Meyer?"

"How about Wilbur?" Mary Louise said. "Wilbur is a good name for a pig."

"Hey, I remember Wilbur. From *Charlotte's Web*. I read that in school," said Arecely.

Charlotte looked at Arecely. She was about to give her the and-you-need-to-go-back-to-school speech but refrained, since this was hardly the right time.

"I loved that book," Arecely continued. "It was really sad."

"Very sad," said Charlotte approvingly.

"It was one of the best books we read in school. They were going to kill Wilbur. But they didn't. So he was a lucky pig."

"Nothing like school for reading good books," Charlotte said, giving a meaningful look to Arecely.

Nobody else said anything, so LeAnn said, "Sounds good. Wilbur it is."

"Some pig," Arecely said.

Four

Charlotte was bone tired when she left the clinic at a quarter past six. The sour manure smell coming from the mushroom house seemed particularly strong, not that Charlotte really noticed it anymore. Beyond the parking lot, the gray mushroom houses were floating like ghosts out in the fields in the distance.

She had been so busy all day that she hadn't had much time to think about anything, but as soon as she got into her car, all of a sudden her problems at home came crashing back down on her. Charlie was gone, and what would she say to Julie? She jerked into reverse, pushed her foot down a little too hard on the accelerator.

Bam. Her head jolted forward, then back, the seat belt locking firmly across her breastbone.

Damn. She slammed on the brake. Looked into her rearview mirror. She had banged into the blue Dumpster.

Time to survey the damage. The Dumpster was tilting precariously onto the Dumpster next to it, and some of its contents had spilled onto the parking lot. Her stomach sank like a stone in a pond. Another job to do. It crossed her mind to get back in the car and leave it like that. But Charlotte knew that if she didn't pick up the bags, someone else would have to do it. She had left the others inside the clinic still doing the close-up for the day.

You could see the Dumpster from inside the clinic on the security camera, and Flo must have been looking, because she was now walking toward Charlotte in the parking lot. It was half-dark already, but the full moon was rising.

"Lord a-mercy, look at all that shit," Flo said.

Most of the bags were light—just black bags filled with paper towels and drapes from the clinic. Charlotte and Flo worked together, tossing them back up into the Dumpster. They picked up everything until there was just one piece of trash left in the parking lot—it looked like the remains of somebody's lunch, wrapped up in a Spanish newspaper.

Charlotte stared down at the soiled mess in dismay. The thought flitted across her mind that she could just leave it there, but Charlotte was nothing if not dutiful. She bent down and grasped the edge of the bundle with the tips of her fingers.

Because it was much heavier than she had expected, about the size and weight of a five-pound bag of flour, she had to balance it on her arms. Charlotte got ready to heave it up into the Dumpster. But then something, a feeling maybe, a premonition, made her stop. There was something about the size and heft of it that made her hesitate. Something about the way it cradled in her arms that made her look more closely at the bundle, roughly wrapped in masking tape. She wondered, later, if somebody else might have just tossed it over the Dumpster's edge, whether there was something, some ghostly imprint, that made her hesitate, stop and look. As if it were something that had always been fated to happen.

"Flo . . ." Charlotte's voice came out like a squeak.

"Charlotte?" Flo must have caught something in the sound of Charlotte's voice.

Arms stiff, she held the little bundle away from her body, then bent over to set it down, then picked it up again. . . .

Flo searched Charlotte's face, then looked at the bundle. "What is it . . . ?"

Charlotte shook her head violently, trying to escape the feeling that time was collapsing upon her like the pleats of an accordion. She tried to speak, but her voice caught in the back of her throat. "I think I'm going to be sick."

Flo came closer, peered at the bundle in the twilight.

There was a foot poking out from the bottom of the package, through the thin gray plastic. One small foot, dark and stiff, curled up, tiny cracked heel, perfect little toes.

Charlotte dropped the bundle like a stone, then stood, staring at her feet for a second; then she snatched it up again. She had the nauseating feeling that she might have hurt it, even though the impression left on her arms clearly told her that the baby was already dead. It no longer looked like someone's lunch leftovers; now it was clearly a newborn baby with newspaper and rags for swaddling clothes. The face was covered, but she and Flo could see the shock of black hair and the bit of forehead peeking out from the top, as well as the telltale foot hanging out the bottom.

"Oh, my God in heaven," Flo said.

Charlotte knelt on the gritty asphalt, taking big gulps of the cool night air—choking back a strangled feeling in her throat. For a moment she paused, lifted her eyes, and looked around her, blinking hard. But still she saw the familiar open fields that surrounded the clinic.

Her hands were shaking. She pressed them together. Took another deep breath. Then, with the tips of her fingers, she pushed the paper away from the baby's face until two squinched eyes appeared and a small flat nose. Charlotte looked at the two tiny nostrils, held her cheek up to the face to see if there was any breathing, pushed the paper away to grab a thigh so she could feel for a pulse. But she knew that she was just going through the motions—this baby was cold and stiff. She set it down on the sidewalk, took a step back, felt like she wanted to wash her hands.

Going through the motions of checking the baby calmed her down a little, reminded her that she was an adult, a nurse practitioner, trained to evaluate newborns, and to provide lifesaving care, so that even now, confronted with this baby, Charlotte knew exactly what to do. She wrapped her unsteady insides around this thought like fingers grasped around a pole.

"What's going on out here?" LeAnn and Mary Louise and Arecely, who had been watching out the window of the clinic, had all come outside by now to see what was going on.

"Baby," said Flo to the newly assembled circle of people.

"Dead," said Charlotte in a voice that sounded, she thought, just like her usual voice, the one that coped with anything, no matter how unexpected.

"But where . . . ?" LeAnn said, her voice oddly thin.

"Dumpster . . ." Flo said with a jerk of her head.

It took a few moments for that to sink in.

"How long's it been dead?" LeAnn asked.

Charlotte stared down at the shriveled-up face; its skin was cracked and peely-looking, the face a dark brown. It looked like a normal-term newborn—except in its stillness it was anything but normal. She felt cold inside, coughed, pushed the feeling away.

"I really don't know," she said. "I don't think it's been dead more than a day or two."

"Maybe we should take all those dirty papers off it," Arecely said.

Flo crouched down, looked down at the little foot, prodded it with the tip of her pink-painted fingernail.

"I think we better leave it," she said. "Evidence."

"What happened to it?" Mary Louise squeaked. "Are you sure it's dead?" She looked bug-eyed, but was holding her ground, hadn't fainted or anything. This was a good sign. They had been working short-staffed until Mary Louise started. She just stood there, mouth forming a little round silent "O," but not saying a word.

There wasn't anything else to say. They stood in a ragged circle looking at the baby, the torn newspaper, the plastic and rags. Nobody seemed to know what to do.

Then Arecely stepped forward. She took off the thin white sweater she was wearing and knelt on the gravelly pavement. Charlotte wasn't sure what Arecely was going to do, but what she did was a simple act: She took her white sweater and laid it over the baby; then she made the sign of the cross. "It's not right for it to be just sitting there like that."

Then, unfrozen, they all began to shuffle and move, and mutter things, *disgusting, poor baby, how did it get in there, I wonder if it was already dead.*

Then Flo spoke up in a firm voice that said that she was speaking in her official capacity as clinic manager: "I'm going inside to call the police. Girls, you go on now; you get along home."

Charlotte didn't leave, though. She called Julie on the cell phone to let her know she'd be late. She stayed for the same reason that she always stayed, because it seemed like the right thing to do.

Five

"No, sir, it didn't come from the clinic," Flo was repeating for the fourth or fifth time. Charlotte was standing there, batting gnats away from her face, feet aching with fatigue. She wondered why police traveled in packs. There were four police cars in the parking lot by then, and all of them had their red and blue lights flashing. Every time the light flashed, it made the officer's badge wink. It was giving her a headache.

The one officer had a little notepad out, and was scratching down notes with the stub of a pencil, and a tall, dark one with a slightly scruffy-looking uniform with sweat stains under the arms was standing near him, apparently for moral support.

"Wull," he said, his voice a high-pitched tenor, "do you have any idea who might be wanting to dump a baby in the Dumpster?"

It went around like that for a while. Charlotte told the story of how she had backed into the Dumpster.

"I was running late," she said.

That seemed to interest him. He looked up at her, pencil poised over his pad, as though this was the first thing she had said that was important.

"Running late?" He was holding a big, heavy torch flashlight, and he kept flashing it at the little bundle; then, as he started to write, it would weave and bob away. Charlotte had to bite her tongue to keep from saying, *Hey, do you want me to hold the flashlight for you?*

"Why were you in a hurry?"

"Why?" she asked, wondering how that could matter at all.

"Why were you running late, ma'am?"

It was a simple question, requiring a simple answer, but Charlotte was irritated, so she snapped, "What difference does it make?"

Flo knew that Charlotte, usually the soul of patience, could start to snap when she got tired. She frowned over at Charlotte as though to say, *Don't make a fuss.*

"We were busy today, closed up late . . ." Flo said in an appeasing tone.

"Well, is there any reason why someone would be putting a dead baby in the Dumpster?"

"I'm a nurse practitioner," Charlotte said. "I don't do dead babies. Nothing to do with dead babies." Flo shot a behave-yourself look at Charlotte.

"What our doctor is trying to say—"

"Oh," said the officer, shifting on his feet. "Are you a doctor?" He looked skeptical.

"I'm a nurse practitioner."

"Well, where's the doctor?"

"There is no doctor here. . . ."

Charlotte laughed nervously. Policemen made her nervous. Flo shot her a look that clearly said, *Shut the hell up.*

"Our medical director, Dr. Harvey Dexter, is not currently on the premises. . . ."

And a good thing too, Charlotte thought. Harve was almost always drunk if you caught him past four in the afternoon.

The full moon had risen in the sky above the clinic, shining down on the parking lot like faded sunshine. It was close to seven, and Charlotte could feel the ache in her feet, the twinge she got in the small of her back after standing all day. The officers had unwrapped the baby—taken off Arecely's sweater shroud and pulled the newspaper and rags away until you could see the little shriveled-up face, the ragged length of cord, the skinny thighs.

Charlotte stared at the baby with horrified fascination. This baby was fully formed; it didn't have the translucent skin of a premature infant. Her gut told her that the baby probably hadn't been dead very long. It looked too perfect, too well preserved, as if it were just sleeping.

So as the officer asked questions and wrote, his flashlight beam bobbed up and down, sometimes just catching the baby in the face. The longer Charlotte stood there, the more she wanted to bend down and pull that white sweater, the one Arecely had left, back over the baby. The more she thought about it, the more it bothered her, until finally she stepped forward and laid the little white sweater shroud back over. But then she felt like she should do something, like the way Arecely had made the sign of the cross, but she couldn't think of quite the right gesture, so she just stood up and took a few steps back.

"Do either of you know anyone who could have left that baby in the Dumpster?"

Flo and Charlotte both shook their heads . . . but as Charlotte stood there, affirming that she had no idea, she suddenly thought of the girl on the exam table, with the Madonna pendant, the anguished tears, the milk spots on her blouse. . . .

Charlotte tried to remember exactly what the girl had said—she decided to talk to Arecely first before she said anything else.

Later on that evening, the coroner came and took the little body away, after Charlotte had left. Flo offered to stay and wait for the coroner, and Charlotte let her do it, driving away from El Centro in her station wagon with a fresh new dent in the back.

Six

When Charlotte first came in, the house was quiet, and Charlotte thought Julie might still be over at Kayla's house—the girls often did their homework together. Then she heard Julie's footsteps as she came into the kitchen, looked up and said "Hi, Mom," and opened the fridge door. She was wearing a spaghetti-strap undershirt, and a lock of hair had fallen into her face. Julie was staring at the fridge contents like she could read her fortune there.

Charlotte glanced at the clock. It was close to seven-thirty, much later than she usually got home. "Did you get some dinner, sweetie?"

"Yeah, I ate at Kayla's. Mrs. Brown invited me." Julie was still scanning the contents of the fridge in a noncommittal manner.

Normally, like a broken record, Charlotte would have said, "Julie, close the fridge door. You're wasting electricity." But this night Charlotte felt a tender lump, like a suppressed sob, catch in her throat. Julie was fresh from the shower, her hair against her head, with tender track marks of a comb. Charlotte could see her daughter's small breast mounds poking through the thin T-shirt she was wearing. Fifteen. Not exactly a baby anymore.

"Are you still hungry? There's some ice cream in there." It was a pure play for affection and she knew it.

"No, I'm not eating ice cream anymore. Too many carbs."

"Julie," Charlotte said, trying not to sound impatient, "carbohydrates are the building blocks of a healthy diet. You need carbs."

"Mom," Julie said, suppressing a sigh, using the tone she would use with a retarded four-year-old, "people don't *need* carbs."

Charlotte looked at her form, still so painfully thin, a longer, stick-legged version of the girl who loved ice cream more than anything.

Julie had selected a bagel out of the freezer, and she was now popping it in the toaster oven. Charlotte suppressed the urge to explain the carbohydrate count contained in the average bagel.

"And make sure you get to bed at a reasonable hour," Charlotte said. She was just trying to make conversation with her daughter—how was it that suddenly she didn't know what to say? She reached out and brushed her daughter's arm with her fingertips, but she could feel Julie pulling away ever so slightly.

"Whatever," Julie said, licking margarine off her fingers as she slid out of the room in her socks.

But just as she was almost out of the room, Charlotte called out, "Umm, Julie?"

"Yeah?"

"Your dad had to go away for a few days." Charlotte, the keeper of secrets. Then, hastily, without thinking, she added, "Job interview . . ."

Julie shrugged and kept walking. "I know," she said.

She knew?

"Oh yeah, I forgot. He said if you need him you can call him on the cell phone." Then Julie stepped into the carpeted hallway and disappeared toward her room.

Seven

"We're famous." LeAnn was holding the *Bayard Post*, the local newspaper, and Mary Louise was standing beside her looking over LeAnn's shoulder.

"Famous?" Charlotte asked.

"Right here." LeAnn was tapping on the paper with the eager assurance of someone who had brushed celebrity.

"Oh, my," Mary Louise said. She was starting to lose that scared-rabbit look now, her fourth day on the job.

Charlotte peered over LeAnn's shoulder and saw that she was pointing to a small item under the heading "Police Blotter." There it was, right after the DUI on State Street and the cell phone stolen from a vehicle parked on Walnut Street. Just a short paragraph.

> Found near a Dumpster belonging to the Center of La Mujer, a deceased newborn infant, apparently of Hispanic origin. Probable cause of death, asphyxiation. Found at the scene by Charlotte P. Hopper, an employee of the health center. An investigation into the origin of the infant is ongoing.

"What does that mean?" Mary Louise was still looking puzzled, although not quite as terrified as before. She was standing a couple of paces behind LeAnn, her pink teddy-bear-print scrubs oddly incongruent with her silver hair.

"It means . . ." LeAnn said, drawing the sentence out for effect, red eyebrows arched so that her hazel eyes stood out. "It means they think somebody killed it."

To say that LeAnn loved drama and emergency was an understatement. She also was the only one of the clinic assistants who had graduated from college, a fact that she constantly made everyone aware of as she lamented her forty thousand dollars in student loans.

"What did it say?" Arecely asked from across the room. "They fixed something?"

"As-phyx-iated . . ." LeAnn said, drawing out the syllables with mordant glee.

Mary Louise spoke up softly. "That means it couldn't breathe."

"That means," LeAnn whispered dramatically, "that somebody killed it."

Arecely looked down at the countertop. "I know what it means. I just couldn't hear you." Charlotte felt like wringing Arecely's neck sometimes. She was as smart as a whip, but she lacked confidence.

"But how do they know it was Spanish?" Arecely asked.

"Well, duh, it sat up and breathed 'hola' right before it took its last breath," LeAnn said.

"LeAnn." Flo's long pink fingernail tapped emphatically on the countertop. "That was uncalled for."

Charlotte didn't understand why Arecely was so credulous whenever LeAnn was concerned. LeAnn had a college degree but no common sense, and Arecely, though she only had a high school diploma, had a very good head on her shoulders.

"That's a good question, Arecely. You can't guess a baby's ethnicity just by looking at it," Charlotte said.

"Well, I guess, I mean, it did look kinda Spanish . . ." Arecely said.

"Its face was really dark," Mary Louise said.

"*Girls,*" Charlotte said. How come she always felt like the Brownie troop leader? "I think they just assumed the baby was Hispanic because of the newspaper. You can't tell what color a baby is when it's dead. And besides, you can't tell if a baby is Hispanic by looking at its skin color."

"Yeah," LeAnn said. "Look at Flo here."

Everyone turned to look at Flo, whose hair was teased up in a blond beehive, and whose light blue eyes were blinking with pleasure. She loved to be the center of attention. Of course, Flo was Italian-American, but that was beside the point. Everyone thought she was Puerto Rican—there was a steady stream of salsa on the radio in her office, she answered the phone in Spanish, and her last name was Garcia. When anyone asked her how she learned Spanish, she winked and said she used "the horizontal method."

"Well, Spanish or not Spanish, that's not the point," Flo said. "The point is the poor little baby is dead, and there's a mother out there somewhere probably not getting the care she needs."

That was what Charlotte loved about Flo: It was that in the end, she was always worried about the patients.

"Flo's right," Charlotte said. "We need to be on the lookout for any woman who comes in with unusual symptoms. Whoever delivered that baby obviously did so without proper medical care. That puts her at high risk for complications."

"I'll ask around," Flo said. "See if anyone has heard anything about someone who was pregnant and isn't anymore. I'll try to get the word out to the camps. Let them know that if anyone needs medical care . . ."

"Just keep your ears open, girls," Charlotte said.

Charlotte pulled the chart from the plastic bin outside the exam room door, opened it, and skimmed over the information. Nineteen-year-old female, Mary Smith, requesting provision of emergency contraception. Charlotte pushed the door open

Mary was a beautiful girl, slick blond hair, and a body with the even glow of the tanning salon. She was wearing a short, tight shirt; her belly button ring, with a small milky pink stone, peeked out as she shifted in her chair. She fiddled with her cell phone for a minute, then reapplied her strawberry-scented lip gloss while Charlotte wrote up the chart.

Charlotte recited the usual speech. "Emergency contraception will not affect the baby if you are already pregnant. It will not cause you to have a miscarriage. It is not as reliable as a normal method of birth control, like the pill or the shot."

Mary continued to smooth lip gloss onto her lips, nodding her head slightly, which gave Charlotte a slight hope that she was listening.

Mary looked up at her, and for the first time, Charlotte noticed the uncanny quality to her eyes—they were stunning, really, bright green, almost like they weren't real, but they glittered in an odd way, as though some spark of compassion were missing beneath them. Charlotte glanced at her chart again. Mary Smith, age nineteen—her contact info was just a cell phone number with no mailing address.

"Okay, take two pills now and two pills in twelve hours, and remember that even with emergency contraception, you may still become pregnant. Don't assume it has worked. If your period is late, you need to come back for a pregnancy test."

She stood up. Charlotte could see the goose bumps on the girl's thin arms—she was wearing a tank top and the room was cold from the air-conditioning. She tucked her purse under her arm. Charlotte noticed it was an expensive Gucci bag. The girl crossed her foot over her ankle with a flash of frosted pink toenails.

"Is that it?" she asked.

"Go right up to the window," Charlotte said, her voice brisk, the way she brought distance to an intimate encounter. But as the girl walked down the short hallway, Charlotte's eyes followed her, the narrow behind in white gym shorts, her blond ponytail flipping back and forth. There was something about her that struck Charlotte as odd, but she just couldn't quite put her finger on it.

When Charlotte came out of the room, Flo was standing in the hall waiting for her.

"Officer's here," Flo said, jerking her head toward her "office," which was actually just a little cubby cubicle, partitioned out of movable partitions.

Charlotte could just see the officer's behind; he was shifting back and forth on his feet. She knew that Flo's cubicle was plastered with posters from the department of health: THE PROPER WAY TO USE A CONDOM or HERPES, ONE IN FIVE . . .

"Officer," Charlotte said.

He turned around. "Do you have a few minutes to talk, Mrs. Hopper? I need to ask you a few questions." The cop was standing there, big and burly, jammed into his uniform. "About the homicide."

"Homicide?" Charlotte said. "What homicide?"

"Mrs. Hopper. The dead baby."

Homicide? "How long will this take? I have patients to see," Charlotte said, trying to hide her discomfort.

"Just a few minutes of your time, Mrs. Hopper."

Charlotte glanced at Flo's desk—it was scattered with confidential patient records—lab results, billing records. Charlotte made a mental note to remind Flo about the seriousness of the confidentiality of patient records. Just standing there waiting, he could have seen any number of results.

"Why don't we go upstairs to the meeting room?" Charlotte said.

They sat face-to-face in straight-backed chairs. The officer, whose name was Stolzfus, had his clipboard out, and was taking notes. Charlotte was relieved to notice that he seemed far less incompetent than the gang who had shown up the previous night. He was businesslike.

Charlotte listened to his questions.

"What time did you leave the clinic? Tell me again how the baby was found." Charlotte gave brief answers, trying hard to resist the urge to look at her watch. From where she sat, she could see the path that led over to Smithbridge Farms. There were almost always men walking down that path, rarely women, although that was the path that Arecely took to walk home. She wondered where Arecely lived—she had never even asked her. It occurred to her that she was incurious about where the women she worked with lived.

"Any of your patients who raised suspicions . . . who were pregnant, and then not pregnant anymore, or just anything . . . ?"

"I'm sorry?" Charlotte said, trying to focus back on the words of Officer Stolzfus.

"The coroner believes that the baby was alive at the time of birth. We are treating this as an investigation of a homicide. We are looking for suspects, and we feel that with the location of where the baby was found that the perpetrator may have been one of your patients. . . ."

Charlotte felt like someone had slipped on ice cube down the back of her neck.

"Officer Stolzfus, I'm not at liberty to discuss my patients with you. Medical records are confidential." But then Charlotte worried that it made her sound like she knew something she didn't want to share.

"But I'm sure you are aware that we do not do prenatal care at this clinic. We don't take care of pregnant woman. There is no reason to think that whoever left the baby there was under our care."

"But you do pregnancy tests, don't you?"

"Well, yes, but . . ." Charlotte clamped her mouth shut. For some reason she had the feeling that anything she said would be too much.

"So you do take care of women when they first get pregnant . . . ?"

"That is a matter of semantics," said Charlotte. "I wouldn't say that doing pregnancy tests qualifies as taking care of them."

She remembered the pitched battle they had fought—they used to take care of pregnant women, but it had become too logistically difficult, and so they had dropped the program several years ago. Now there was nowhere in Londondale to get prenatal care; the women had to go all the way to Kennett Square.

"Now if you'll excuse me," Charlotte said, standing up. "I've got patients to see."

"Certainly," said Officer Stolzfus. "Just take my card—if anything occurs to you, give me a call. You can imagine that we really want to get to the bottom of this. If you think back and think of someone—anyone, anything that didn't seem quite right—you can give us a call."

As Charlotte turned toward the door, there was the face of the painted mural, which reminded her immediately of the pendant around the neck of Maria Lopez. Charlotte had not done a pelvic exam on Maria Lopez—an exam that would have revealed immediately whether the girl's story were true. After a delivery, the uterus involuted at a predictable rate that told a story. One or two days after a delivery, the uterus was still enlarged, about the size of a four-month pregnancy. By the time the patient was a month postpartum—what Maria Lopez had said—the uterus would be almost back to its normal size.

Charlotte hazarded one more glance up at the patient Madonna's face, trying to read something there—some kind of sign. She hadn't said a word to anyone about her suspicions about Maria Lopez, but to her way of thinking, she hadn't needed to. Based on her exam, and what Maria had told her, there was no reason to think that her story wasn't completely true. Leaving a baby suddenly in Mexico, weaning a breast-fed baby could lead to mastitis and leaking milk—as could an infant death.

"Mrs. Hopper?" Officer Stolzfus was looking at her quizzically, waiting for her to make some kind of a move. His eyes followed hers to the painting on the wall. "What? Do they hold some kind of church service up here?"

Charlotte didn't answer; she just headed toward the staircase, the police officer following behind her.

Eight

A recely walked down the path that led toward the fields behind El Centro toward Smithbridge Farm. As she passed the Dumpster behind the clinic, she thought of the poor little baby, and crossed herself, smelling the match sulfur on her fingertips as her hand passed over her face toward her forehead. *Poor little baby*. She had been so disturbed by the sight of the little pinched-up face, its features frozen. It was a little boy, and in spite of being stiff and dead, it reminded her a little of the way Ezekiel had looked when he was born, when she used to tiptoe over to his little bed at night two or three times, staring at his face, worried that he wasn't breathing. How sometimes she had switched on the light and pulled him out of his bed, sometimes even tried to wake him, because she wasn't sure he was breathing, and she was so afraid that something would happen to him, and it would be all her fault.

When Ricky used to find her like that, he was always nice about it. He would put his arm around her and and kiss her cheek, and say, "Don't worry, Are. He's just fine."

But thinking about Ricky just made Arecely's stomach do a flip, and she hurried the pace of her steps. Maybe there would be some word from him at home . . . but then, that didn't make sense. The phone got cut off a couple of weeks ago. If he had tried to reach her, he would have called work.

Arecely turned the corner down the lane that was lined with the little white cinder-block houses with light blue trim. These little houses used to be part of the migrant workers' camp. They were the nice houses, where the supervisors lived. Only Smithbridge closed the camp a few years ago, and now they rented them out, and they weren't cheap either. Hers was the third house down on the left. They all looked the same except for different stuff out front—some had tricycles, some bicycles, and others had soccer balls. She caught sight of Ezekiel, playing in front of Lizzie's house, and he spotted her at the same moment—"*Mami, Mami, Mami,*" he called.

She jogged the last two steps toward him, catching him up, and then settling him onto the nice familiar groove of her hip bone.

Lizzie was up on the porch.

"You're late again, Arecely. What's up with that?"

"Late closing, as usual. You know Charlotte: She can't say no to nobody."

Arecely remembered, with guilt, how she hadn't told Charlotte the whole truth of why she had stayed late. It was true that she had stayed to clean the room, but she hadn't mentioned that she had gone upstairs, or what she had been doing there.

Ezekiel was squirming to get down, so she let him slide down her leg. She walked up onto the screen porch and pushed the door open, hoping that there would be a light on, but before the screen was all the way open, she could feel an emptiness, like it was cold inside. No light on, no TV turned to the soccer game. Arecely shivered a little. Her footsteps felt wrong on the floorboards, sounded wrong, like they echoed too loud.

"Ricky . . . ?" she called out, but her voice came out in a whisper. "Ricky? You here?"

It had been two weeks since he lit out for North Carolina, headed to check out the pickle industry. Two weeks since he had left before dawn when the horn of the Camacho boys' pickup truck sounded. He gave her a warm squeeze on the shoulder and a kiss on the back of her sweaty neck, up under her hair. "I'll call you when I get there, baby," he said. "I'll send money for you and the baby to come too."

"But where are you gonna be? Exactly . . ." she had said.

"North Carolina, baby; I told you, North Carolina. Great money, working in the pickle-packing plants."

Arecely flopped down on the brown sofa, then stood up again and walked over to the kitchen part of the room. *Pickle-packing plants.* It didn't even sound real. She opened the cabinet and took out some ramen noodles and a liter-size bottle of Pepsi; then she walked over to the screen door. Zekie was still playing out front with Lizzie's son, not doing much, just pushing the plastic Big Wheel back and forth on the grass.

So she walked back over, took the pot from the dish drainer and filled it up with water, and turned the stove on, watching the electric coil start to turn red. She put the water on, got out two tumblers and poured Pepsi into them, then picked one up and walked out to the front steps, waiting for the water to boil for the noodles.

She sat down on the front step and watched Zekie trying to get his leg over the next-door neighbor's bike. She looked down the lane, back toward the clinic.

Ever since yesterday, when they found the poor little dead baby in the Dumpster, Arecely had an odd prickly feeling, like the way you felt when somebody was coming up behind you but you hadn't turned around yet. She was puzzled by the way everybody had acted about it—like it was a baby, but nobody seemed to be thinking about the fact that the baby must've had a mother and daddy. She felt like the mother was wandering around and that Arecely would see her and be frightened like you were frightened by a ghost.

From where she sat, she could hear a variety of sounds: the thud of the soccer ball that Rafael and Diego were kicking against the wall, the Spanish TV from across the way floating through the window, the music from Lizzie's house. The barking of a dog in the distance, and out beyond that, the steady hum of cars whooshing past on the pike.

She strained her eyes until she blinked, looking down the lane toward the pike where the boys had driven away two weeks ago, before sunrise, when Zekie was still sound asleep.

She didn't even know which road to take to get to North Carolina. She knew it was far away, but she didn't know much else about it, except that Ricky and the Camacho boys heard there was gold there, in the form of pickle factories. It was getting too expensive to live around here—sure, the mushroom houses paid the same as ever, but their rent kept going up, and there was even talk that the farm itself would be sold to build houses on it. That was what was happening all over the place. The Camacho boys had a cousin who was out there in North Carolina, and he told them the living was cheap. So Ricky went, and waved goodbye, and . . . she didn't even remember if he had stopped to give Zekie a kiss. . . .

She did remember that when Zekie woke up in the morning and was sitting at the breakfast table, he said, "Where Daddy?" And he still said it sometimes, but really not as often as you might think.

Arecely jumped up, realizing that the ramen-noodle water must be almost boiled away. She went into the kitchenette, poured herself another glass of Pepsi, tore open the cellophane package, and broke the noodles over the steaming pot.

In one week, the rent was coming due, and she didn't get paid again until next Thursday. No matter how she sliced and diced up the money she had left, she didn't know how she was going to pay the rent. Usually they paid it part with Ricky's money and part with hers.

She looked back out toward the road. Now it seemed so obvious. She should have asked him where he was going. Not just "North Carolina"— that wasn't going to be good enough. She should've gotten the name, or a cell phone number, or just at least asked him how to get there.

"Come on, Zekie. It's time to go inside for some noodles."

"Where Daddy?" he said.

"North Carolina," Arecely said. "Pickle season."

Nine

Charlotte was standing in the driveway. She had just gotten home from work.

"Mom . . . *Mom*." Charlotte could hear Julie's voice, but she couldn't tell exactly where it was coming from.

"Julie?"

Just then Julie emerged from the woods, her silhouette illuminated by the light that was coming from behind her.

"Mom! I met the new neighbor. Come on. She wants to meet you."

"Oh, but I . . ." Charlotte tried to stall. She wasn't ready for this.

But it was too late. A dark figure was already making its way through the woods. Charlotte saw first only long legs, but even that was enough to make her heart skip a beat. "This is my mom," Julie said, as the outline of a tall woman drew near. Charlotte couldn't see her face, but the light from behind lit up masses of curly hair piled on her head—glowing golden like a crazy halo.

But it wasn't until Deirdre stepped out of the shadows of the trees onto the lawn that Charlotte could see her face—a face that she would have known instantly anytime, anywhere in the world.

"Mom, this is Deirdre—Deirdre . . . Mom."

"Charlotte?" Her voice was deep, throaty, intimately familiar.

"Deirdre?"

Charlotte felt oddly off-kilter for a moment, but before she could even identify the feeling, Deirdre's arms were thrown around her in a bear hug, and with an odd feeling of inevitability, Charlotte recognized her old friend's odor—horse barn, cigarettes, and Mystère de Rochas perfume.

Then they were holding each other at arm's length, their words tumbling over one another: *such a coincidence, who would have ever . . . what have you been doing?*

After a few minutes, Deirdre broke away and said, "Oh, but you must meet my daughter. Ariel. *Ariel!*" Deirdre called through the woods. "Oh, it's no use. Come right along with me. How handy that there is a path right through the woods. Come see my house and meet my daughter. Do you have a minute?" Again, Charlotte thought about saying no, but Julie was already trailing behind Deirdre like an eager puppy.

Charlotte fell into line behind her as though she had never stopped following her, and Deirdre took off at her brisk long-legged pace. Then she stopped for a moment and turned to Charlotte, her face shadowed in the woods.

"But what about Hopper? Is he . . . ?"

Charlotte felt a funny jolt when she heard Deirdre use her husband's old nickname, Hopper.

"Charlie, he's . . ." she remembered that she wasn't sure where he was.

"Oh, are you two not together anymore?"

"He's away," Julie said cheerfully.

Deirdre smiled, and Charlotte could see the flash of her white teeth in the shadows.

"She's adorable," Deirdre said, as though she were talking about a toddler.

Julie rolled her eyes, but Charlotte could tell she was eating it up. She felt a flutter of anxiety. What if Julie fell under her spell?

Deirdre picked up the pace again—it was a short walk. There was about an acre of woods, most of it on Deirdre's property. It was dim in the woods, and Charlotte kept hesitating, tripping over the broken branches and twigs that lined the path.

When they emerged into the clearing on the far side of the woods, the lights were so bright that it almost seemed like daylight, and Charlotte saw tall posts with bright floodlights on them surrounding the barn on all sides. The barn was so freshly painted that it looked brand-new. There was a horse peering over each half stall. One whinnied when it saw Deirdre. Beyond the barn there were paddocks, and from here, with all the floodlights everywhere, Charlotte could see a neat gravel road that curved around to the big house, and behind the house, she could see smooth sweeps of tended lawns and then gardens, and a natural-stone patio with a pool that shone aqua, lit up by underwater lights.

"Oh, Deirdre, it's lovely."

"Well, I had to find a place where I could keep the horses. I couldn't keep the entire string. I sold a few. These were the favorites."

"Juan-Luis is . . . ?"

Deirdre looked momentarily surprised, but then her face quickly righted itself.

"Oh, of course you didn't know. So silly of me. How could you?" The way Deirdre said this, it occurred to Charlotte that Deirdre was accustomed to people knowing a lot about her. Charlotte supposed that she was often written up in the society pages, but how would she know about things like that?

"Juan-Luis was—"

"Oh, there you are. I was looking all over for you. Where did you go?"

Charlotte heard the petulant tones of a teenager, and she looked up to see a figure approaching across the sward of lawn.

"Ariel, darling, come and say hello to an old friend. . . ." Charlotte noted Deirdre's tone. There was an odd coldness in it for a mother talking to her daughter.

As the girl got closer, Charlotte recognized her with a start—it was the girl from the clinic, the one she had seen just this very afternoon—Mary Smith, age nineteen. Could it just be a trick of the light?

Charlotte peered at the girl's face, trying to be sure, but then Charlotte saw in the girl's quick glance that Ariel had recognized her too. Charlotte noted again her uncanny eyes, a glittering green, hard as gemstones.

"Oh, hello, Mrs. . . ."

"Hopper," Charlotte said. "I'm Charlotte Hopper. It's a pleasure to meet you, Ariel."

The girl gave her a hard look for just a moment longer, but then seemed confident that Charlotte wasn't going to say more. Of course she wasn't going to say any more. Patient confidentiality.

It wasn't clear whether Deirdre felt the tension in the moment—it was so like Deirdre, who clearly hadn't changed that much. She seemed oblivious to the slight note of tension in the air, and started talking again in her musical voice, just gushing out all kinds of things. Wasn't it just something that she had moved in just next door? Almost as though they were fated to be together again. And wouldn't it be wonderful to see Hopper. Hopper! They had so many old reminiscences they would need to discuss. And Julie, what a lovely girl, and so good with the horses—why, she seemed like an angel of mercy when she appeared through the woods and started to pitch in with the feeding because Deirdre hadn't gotten the right help lined up yet. She had a couple of barn men, but, well, they had been just terrible and she had to let them go. And Charlotte and Julie and Hopper would just *have* to come to dinner soon, very soon, right away, never mind that the men were still working on the kitchen; they had put in the wrong granite, absolutely the wrong color, if you can imagine, and she had insisted they rip the whole thing out.

Suddenly Charlotte felt weary on her feet and she wanted to go home. She still had to make dinner, and she wasn't sure if Julie had done her homework—probably not. She got ready to cut the conversation short, remembering again with an odd rush how familiar this was—back then, at two in the morning, Deirdre would still be flush with energy, talking a mile a minute, while Charlotte would feel that she had given out long ago, stifling yawns, barely keeping her eyes propped open.

"And the house, you know, it was just dreadful—almost uninhabitable, just that one poor old lady, who had been bed-bound for God knows how long. . . ."

"Well . . ." Charlotte said, preparing to tear herself away from the conversation. "It has been so lovely seeing you. And so nice to have you next door. We'll have a lot of catching up to do. . . ." and she put her hand gently on Julie's arm and said, "Come on, hon." But Charlotte could feel just a hint of tension, a little resistance to her pull, and she looked at her daughter's face and could see that she was already under Deirdre's spell.

As Julie and Charlotte were walking away, Deirdre called out to them, "Oh, but you were asking about Juan-Luis. . . ."

Charlotte stopped walking, and turned out of politeness. "Oh, yes, is he . . . ?"

"Dead," Deirdre said, in a tone that was oddly matter-of-fact.

"He got Reeved," Ariel added.

"I beg your pardon?"

"Ariel, darling. That is such an *indelicate* way of putting it. I'm sorry, Charlotte. My husband was killed in a riding accident. Polo, actually. Just a complete fluke. Went straight over the horse's head and landed on his own. He didn't feel a thing."

"Oh, Deirdre. I'm so terribly sorry," Charlotte said, approaching her friend again, yet still feeling deep inside somewhere that she was sorry she was getting sucked back in.

"Of course, we were all terribly shocked, but you know, he was doing what he loved. . . ." She trailed off.

"Oh, I get it," Julie said, barely audible. "He got Reeved—like Christopher Reeve."

"Julie!" Charlotte said.

"No, that's quite all right," Deirdre said. "It was a mercy that he was killed and not paralyzed like that poor saint Christopher Reeve."

"And when did this happen?"

"Oh, it was a couple of years ago. I tried to stay on in Buenos Aires, but it just wasn't going to work for me, so we decided to come back to the States and live on our farm in Virginia. But Virginia wasn't quite . . ." Deirdre seemed uncertain how to finish; then, in a tone just a shade overbright, she said, "And now we're here in Westville. We're planning to start afresh."

"I hate it here," Ariel chimed in.

"Nonsense, darling. You're going to love it."

Charlotte started backing away again, drained by even this brief encounter.

"Well, Deirdre, we're delighted you're here."

Heading back through the woods, Charlotte felt a rush of different emotions crowding through her, trampling one another in a headlong rush. *Deirdre Saramago.* Dierdre Stinson. Charlotte had ceased to really think of her as real. But now here she was, and Charlotte was feeling completely unsettled. Maybe Charlie was right. But then they were all adults now. . . .

"Julie, I don't expect you to be going over there at all without my permission."

"What? Do you think I'm going to embarrass you or something? I'm not. Besides, they're really nice, and she offered me a job to help feed the horses."

Charlotte opened her mouth to protest. She laid a hand on her daughter's arm, but Julie shrugged it away.

"Don't even say it, Mom. It's like you don't trust me or something."

Charlotte wanted to say, *You're not the one I don't trust,* but then she thought about Charlie, his bizarre reaction to her mention of Deirdre—the way he had run off and left them there. Julie was right; Deirdre seemed perfectly nice, and what happened back then was so long ago.

"Of course I trust you," she said. "And if you want to work for her feeding the horses, that will be great."

Julie threw her arms around Charlotte and hugged her. "Thanks, Mom," she said, and then skipped ahead of her across the dark yard to the house.

Ten

Patients coming in to El Centro were as reliable as the tides, as reliable as the stink of the mushroom houses and the change of seasons. The next morning it was cold, the first real bone-chilling frost that promised many more similar days to come. Charlotte thought about the baby only when she parked next to the spot where the blue Dumpster used to be. By the time she got inside, there were patients filling every chair in the waiting room, and she had already moved on, from one tragedy to the next.

Once upon a time, there used to be nurses who worked in the clinic, taking blood pressure, counseling the patients, giving shots. But the nurses could command better pay elsewhere, so they had left. Then for a while there were LPNs, then trained medical assistants, but recently, the last couple of years, it had been a lot harder to recruit people, and basically they would take whatever they got.

Charlotte was standing in the back hallway, reading the note written in Mary Louise's impeccable Palmer-method penmanship. Before the patients were put into an exam room, the clinic assistant had to ask them one question—"What are you here for today?"—and write down the answer on the one line allotted for this purpose in the chart.

In that slot Mary Louise had written, *This very nice young lady thinks she has the stomach flu, but I don't think so. I think she might be pregnant, because she said she feels like an eighteen-wheeler is driving around in her stomach, and that is exactly how I felt (and you know, I've got five; even though they're grown, you don't forget something like that).* In order to fit all this on the one line provided, Mary Louise had had to squinch up her writing and then run it along the edge of the page, the way grade schoolers do when the teacher doesn't leave enough space.

It was only ten o'clock in the morning, and Charlotte was already running late, so the temptation was just to ignore it and go into the room, but Mary Louise had now lasted five whole days, which was longer than the last girl, and she was starting to look like she might be a keeper, so Charlotte felt like she should probably go ahead and try to train her a little bit.

"Mary Louise, can I talk to you for a sec?"

Mary Louise peered around the corner, her blue eyes already wide, and looking wider through the glasses she wore.

"Yes, Dr. Hopper?"

"Charlotte," Charlotte said. "Please call me Charlotte." She had discovered that there were a certain number of people who would always call her "Doctor" as a sign of respect, even though she was a nurse practitioner. With the white lab coat, stethoscope, and prescription pad in her pocket, she was surprised how many people couldn't quite choke out her first name.

"Mary Louise, about what you write here . . . under 'presenting complaint' . . . umm, you don't need to include your opinion. It should just be a statement of fact."

Mary Louise smiled at this, newly confident. "Oh, it's all true, Dr. Hopper. . . ."

"Charlotte . . ."

"Dr. Charlotte. As true as true can be. I had morning sickness something wicked. Used to have to wear them Sea-Bands on my wrists."

Charlotte looked at Mary Louise. The older woman's round face, framed with a silver bob, was surprisingly unlined, which gave her the air of a young girl. Charlotte glanced past Mary Louise to the office door, where a line of charts in a bin on the door indicated that she had a lot of patients backed up in the waiting room ready to be seen. Charlotte made a mental note to pull Mary Louise aside to talk to her later.

"I'm doing good, aren't I, Dr. Charlotte?"

Charlotte smiled, nodded; she was reviewing the chart, not really listening.

"Never woulda guessed it's my first job, huh? I mean, my first paying job, not that raising all those kids and grandbabies didn't count . . ."

Charlotte swung the exam room door open, getting ready to step inside the room. Mary Louise was coming out of her shell—but Charlotte was already starting to miss the scared rabbit.

When Charlotte came out of the room, Mary Louise was sitting in one of the chairs in the lab off the hallway, perched on the edge with her knees clasped tightly together, a clipboard balanced on her knees. Across from her was an elderly woman, hair pinned back so tightly that her hairs were broken away in the front. Charlotte felt a familiar sinking feeling when she saw her. It was Mrs. Rosalie Saxton, who lived alone just down the pike, and seemed to be able to manufacture a female complaint just about once a week, usually on Wednesday. She and Mary Louise were engaged in an animated conversation.

"Oh, I know, I know," Mary Louise said. "My auntie Ruth, she's in a nursing home. . . ."

"Bless her heart," said Mrs. Saxton.

"Well, I thought my hair was thinning"—she stroked her forehead with the assurance of a woman with a full head of hair—"but once you get into your nineties—"

Mrs. Saxton interrupted. "I'm seventy-eight."

"And that's why you have such lovely hair, dear. Once you pass eighty-five, it's a struggle to keep a single hair in your head. The last time I was down at Cedar Shores, I asked my auntie Ruth and her friends what they did, and they all said you've got to put Rogaine on it. My auntie Ruth said she wouldn't have a thread of hair on her head if it weren't for Rogaine."

"Well . . ." Mrs. Saxton sounded tentative. "I've seen the TV ads for it, but I just wasn't sure. . . ."

"Well, you can be just as sure as sure can be, dear. My auntie Ruth's got the prettiest head of hair you've ever seen on a ninety-four-year-old."

"Well," Mrs. Saxton said, standing up, "I suppose you're right. I think I'll just give it a try."

"And, of course, my secret." Mary Louise patted her bob again. "Johnson's baby shampoo. And don't go getting a generic. That's one place where the few extra pennies are worth it."

Mrs. Saxton gave an admiring look to Mary Louise's well-kept silver bob, kind of Martha Stewart-y without the yellow tinge, and then passed a hand over her own tight bun, smoothing down the broken hairs around the hairline. Mary Louise picked up her hand and patted it. She leaned in with reassuring warmth, lowered her voice, and said in a confidential whisper, "And you might want to loosen that bun a bit, dear. . . . It would soften up your pretty face." Then the two stood up together. Mrs. Saxton picked up her rectangular vinyl crocodile purse and started to walk down the hall toward the exit.

"Mrs. Saxton?" Charlotte called out, holding the thick chart in her hands.

Mrs. Saxton turned. "Oh, hello."

"You're coming with me now?" Charlotte gave a questioning look at Mary Louise, but she just continued beaming.

"Oh, no, she's all taken care of, Dr. Charlotte. She was just having a little"—she leaned forward, pursed her lips—"little problem in the female department."

"Mrs. Saxton, you are here for an appointment."

"I think I'm all set now," she said, winking at Mary Louise, and with that, she turned and pulled a couple of hairpins out of her hair. A thick gray-black tangle floated down past her shoulders. Then she lifted her purse to her shoulder and headed toward the door.

Charlotte was momentarily speechless.

"No need for her to pay all that money. All's she was having was a little bit of a beauty problem."

Charlotte opened her mouth to say something, unsure where to start.

Mary Louise sidled up next her and whispered, "I made up the bit about Auntie Ruth. You've gotta know how to talk to these ladies." She winked. "You know, you gotta hand it to me. I think I've got a bit of a feel for this job."

Charlotte was standing in the doorway to Flo's office later that afternoon.

"Flo, you know that I never complain about staff."

"A warm body is a warm body."

"And you know that I agree with you on that."

"I know you sure as hell don't like it when you're here two hours late because we are running short-staffed."

"But Mary Louise . . ." Charlotte stopped. She didn't know what to say. "She's a little, um, rough around the edges."

"Charlotte," Flo said, "she's got a good attitude. She's been here six days and she hasn't quit yet. . . ."

"Can we pair her with Arecely?"

"I can't take Arecely away from the front desk."

"LeAnn?"

"Not if we want to get out of here no more than two hours late."

"Flo, she saw Mrs. Saxton instead of me."

"Oh, well, that's nice . . ." Flo drawled. That was Flo for you; she seemed to understand what you were talking about only when it suited her.

"She came in for a consultation with a licensed medical professional, and she left with hairstyling advice."

Flo didn't say anything. They both knew that hairstyling advice might be just as useful to poor Mrs. Saxton as any medical advice. Hadn't Charlotte grumbled the last time she came in, saying they ought to just serve her tea and doughnuts in the waiting room and then send her home?

Charlotte shrugged.

"She'll learn," Flo said. "Ya hafta give her credit just for being here."

"She is being paid."

"Yeah, seven bucks an hour."

"She has a job to do."

Flo opened a manila folder on her desk. Charlotte's nose started to tickle as a waft of heavy perfume burst forth from the lavender paper that lay on top. Flo picked the paper up daintily with her long pink fingernails and passed it to Charlotte. She sneezed, then looked at the paper, a computer-printed résumé written in a fancy gothic script.

Mary Louise Redding
c/o My daughter Jennifer
15 Millstone Estates Way,
Westville, Pennsylvania

Experience
1969–2004 Married to a wonderful man. Had five beautiful babies, three daughters, two sons. Eight grandbabies.

May 14, 2004, at 10:00 A.M.
Discovered that the wonderful man was a low-down son of a whatchamacallit when he took off in my best friend Stacy's Oldsmobile Cutlass headed for Arizona, and what's worse, he took my best friend Stacy with him.

August 1, 2004
Got tired of weeping over him, since in my heart I knew he was no good anyway, packed my bags, and moved to Westville to live with my beautiful daughter Jennifer.

October 1, 2004

> *Decided that I was getting under Jennifer's feet and I don't want to be dependent on anyone, so I decided to look for a job.*

Skills

> *Over the years I have developed many skills. For example, I excel at talking on the phone and just talking in general. I am very experienced at both public and private relations. Also, my second daughter is a stylist, and I consider myself pretty good with hair.*

Flo looked at Charlotte. They'd been working together for a long time, and understood each other pretty well.

"Let's think of her as a challenge," Flo said.

Charlotte realized that she had been outmaneuvered. She walked out of the office, already looking down the hallway, where she could see that the exam rooms had filled up again. She figured that she could continue to do what she usually did—that is, to do everything herself.

Eleven

Mary Louise slipped her key into the shiny brass lock of 15 Millstone Estates Way, and pushed the door open, noticing once again the peculiar hush that always seemed to emanate from her daughter's house. These new houses—they had a different quality to them. Beautiful, yes, but not as homey, in her opinion, as the houses back home.

She had been pretty impressed when she first came out from Minnesota and saw how her daughter Jennifer was living. She knew Brian and Jennifer were doing well; they both had corporate jobs. Brian worked for a credit card company and Jennifer worked in pharmaceuticals, but the first time Jennifer drove her through the big stone gates with the sign for the development, Millstone Estates, she was surprised by how pretty and clean and shiny everything was. The houses, all of them almost brand-new, lined up along the streets, each with its own patch of verdant lawn in front, and a little curved path, neat as you please, that led up to the door.

Mary Louise pushed open the door and stepped inside, her foot barely making a sound on the thick carpet. She listened to the unfamiliar hum inside; this house buzzed. She slipped her feet out of her white nurse shoes and wriggled her toes. Jennifer and Brian didn't wear shoes in the house. It always made her feel funny to walk around fully dressed wearing nothing but her stocking feet. Of course, it made sense to keep all the white carpets clean, but Mary Louise always had this vaguely apprehensive feeling in the house. It was so clean that it looked like nobody lived there. She couldn't remember her own house ever looking like that—tumbling to the bursting as it had been with kids and dogs and toys. But this house, well, it looked just like the model home it had once been—everything just so. All the furniture clean and matching; even the art that hung on the walls looked like it had been picked to match—just like something out of a magazine.

She glanced at the clock: five-fifteen. She might as well watch the evening news. Jennifer would get home with Madison in a few moments. The hardest thing for Mary Louise to accept had been that there was nothing to do to help her daughter. When she had decided to move here, she had imagined all kinds of things she could do to help out. Why, Madison wouldn't have to go to day care, and Mary Louise could get dinner ready so that Jennifer wouldn't have to cook when she got home from work.

But Jennifer and Brian's life was so different from anything she had known. When she suggested that Madison, three, could stay home with her, Jennifer had been dead set against it. "Oh, no," she said, "she needs to get ready for kindergarten." And as for cooking, well, she did make dinner from time to time, but it seemed like most days Jennifer came home with take-out stuff from the deli at the supermarket. Mary Louise didn't like that kind of prepared food. She had seen a lot of shows about food contamination on TV, and she didn't think the food ever seemed completely fresh. And Maddy, well, she didn't seem to want any normal food; she was always eating stuff like chicken nuggets that Mary Louise didn't think was very healthy. But she didn't want to complain, so she had taken to preparing a little food for herself, nothing special, just Campbell's chicken noodle and some toast, that kind of thing.

It had been much easier since she started working at the clinic— before that, for two months, the days had dragged on and on, until the buzzing of the house seemed to buzz right inside her head.

Just then Mary Louise heard the key in the lock, and Madison came tumbling into the room, trailing a large piece of paper daubed with bright purple and blue finger paints.

"Granny, Granny," Madison called, and started to rush into the family room, but she didn't get very far. Jennifer reached over and grabbed her around the waist.

"Now, Maddy, you know better than that. Take off your shoes and put them in the cubby; then hang up your backpack and your coat."

Mary Louise had to admire her daughter's organization, but for some reason she always took it as something of a slight. She had never once stopped her children, the five of them, from tumbling into the house to hug her or the dog or their teddy bear. She had scrubbed mud marks off the linoleum floors, and picked up jackets and backpacks that always seemed to end up deposited in heaps around the doorway. Of course, maybe if they had lived in a big house like this one, with everything as neat and organized as a house in *House Beautiful* magazine . . .

Madison sat down and started tugging at her shoes, letting out a tired howl when she couldn't get one of the shoelaces unknotted.

Mary Louise was about to jump up and give her granddaughter a hand, but she stopped herself, remembering how Jennifer got touchy about things—often stopping her and saying, "No, Maddy needs to learn to do it herself."

By the time the ordeal of getting shoes, backpack, and jacket in the right spot by a tired three-year-old was over, Jennifer had whisked Madison into the kitchen and strapped her into the chair, still howling. Within seconds she could hear Jennifer's determined punches on the microwave—the chicken nuggets would be ready in thirty seconds. *I'll offer to give her the bath*, Mary Louise thought, knowing that Jennifer didn't enjoy bathtime and would often let her do it. Mary Louise couldn't help but feel that this kind of streamlined family life, with thirty-second meals, just somehow wasn't what she had expected. But it was not for her to judge. She was a guest in her daughter's house, and Jennifer was good to her and never for a moment made her feel unwelcome.

After Madison's bath, she turned her over, clean and in fresh-smelling PJs, to her mom for Jennifer's very particular bedtime routine, and she headed downstairs to her room in the basement. Jennifer had offered her a room upstairs, but she liked to escape down to her bedroom, preferably before Brian got home. She didn't want to encroach on their time. Besides, this basement wasn't like any basement she'd ever seen—not a big rec room with do-it-yourself pine paneling and green indoor-outdoor carpet on the floor. It was clean and spacious, and there were big French doors leading to the outside. A finished walkout basement—that was what Jennifer called it. It was a huge house, plenty big enough for four people—though that didn't stop her from feeling like she was in the way.

Sometimes she wondered if she should have gone to stay with her daughter Shelby, who lived in Michigan and had four kids. When she went to stay there, one of the kids had to give up his room for her and go sleep on the floor in his brother's room. And Shelby's house was much smaller. She'd been afraid she'd be a burden . . . but at least Shelby would have let her help.

Mary Louise flicked on the little TV on her dresser, sat down on the bed, and peeled her socks off so she could massage her feet. She started thinking about work—about the meeting and how the clinic might go under. Well, how often she forgot to count her blessings. There was Arecely supporting Ezekiel on her salary, and there was the poor soul, out there somewhere, who had been so desperate that she had abandoned her own baby.

Mary Louise went into the bathroom to run the bath, comforted by the sound of the voices on the TV. It was a funny thing. . . . She had eventually learned that Eddie had been fooling around with Stacy for three years—three years when she had continued to be perfectly happy, before he felt the need to "come clean," and get something off his chest. Well, he would have left anyway, she supposed, but what if he had just not told her? Ignorance is bliss, in a way, isn't it? And she'd still be home with her church and her book group and her shows, the way she was before. Happy enough.

She glanced at the gleaming bathtub—everything in this house gleamed, even the tub in the basement, about half-full. *Count your blessings*, she insisted to herself again.

That reminded her. She walked over to her top dresser drawer and slipped out the envelope in which she usually kept her money. She pulled out three twenties, then four, then, hesitating, added one more to the pile.

Money for the pig. She was fortunate, living in the lap of luxury, with an alimony check so she was only working to give herself something to do. But it would be a shame if the clinic closed.

Mary Louise could tell from the sound of the water in the bath that it was almost full. She stood in front of the mirror and slipped her shirt off, and then her bra, looking appraisingly at herself in the mirror, at her ropy neck, the moles on her chest, the slack breasts (like olive pits in socks— that was what her mother used to say). But it was a strong and healthy body. Still alive and kicking at age sixty-two—five kids later, and still going strong. She turned away from her image and walked into the bathroom, slipping into the hot water with a sigh of pleasure. *Every single day*, Mary Louise thought, *brings something good.*

Twelve

"**O**h, my God!" LeAnn paused dramatically between each word for emphasis. She was looking up at the closed-circuit TV screen, where the view that used to show the Dumpster was now filled with a UPS truck.

Charlotte glanced up at the screen and saw not just the UPS truck, but a lean man with wavy black hair and well-muscled thighs, gracefully heaving a large cardboard box over his shoulder.

"Oh, my God, water, somebody get me water." LeAnn was leaning dramatically over the front counter. "That much beauty this early in the morning . . ."

"Wull, I don't think he's that good-looking," Arecely said.

"Wull, then you are blind, girl. . . . Wait, oh, my God, he's coming to the door."

"What happened to the fat guy?" Flo had come out of her office and was looking up at the screen. The Adonis was no longer visible, because he had already come around the front of the building.

"I don't know what happened to the fat guy, but . . . oh . . . oh, my God, think Brad Pitt in bronze," LeAnn moaned. "Let this be the new guy, not just a substitute." She folded her hands in a dramatic flourish. "Please, God, I'll start believing in you if you just make this guy be the new guy."

The UPS man had come back around the back of the truck, and as he leaned over to pick up the boxes, Flo let out a little whistle, and Mary Louise came out from the back, where she had been stocking the rooms, and said, "Nice tushie."

"Jeez, you'd think nobody around here ever saw a guy before," Arecely said. "His tushie isn't—"

But she didn't have time to finish her sentence, because then the clinic door pushed open and a pair of hairy tan legs appeared, and two arms, and two large cardboard boxes.

Flo leaned over and buzzed him in, and he came into the back area, where the women stood in a semicircle waiting for the legs to put the boxes down so that a face would appear.

Which is exactly what happened, and when the legs stood up, there was a body attached, and a face, smiling broadly, with perfect white teeth, brown eyes, and a mass of curly dark hair.

The UPS man didn't appear surprised to look up to see the admiring coterie. He smiled, held up his clipboard, and said, "Hello," with a trace of an unidentifiable accent.

"Hello," said Flo, apparently the only one still in possession of her wits.

"I'm the UPS man."

Granted, he made the UPS uniform look like a Mr. Universe contestant's uniform, but still, he was stating the obvious.

"Where's the fat guy?" Mary Louise spoke up.

"I don't know where is the fat guy, but I am the new guy." His accent was sexy, like Antonio Banderas's. Only not Spanish. Italian maybe?

"Well, you're a lot better-looking than the fat guy," Mary Louise pronounced.

He smiled. "Thank you," he said as though he was used to getting compliments. He looked as if he wouldn't have been surprised if one of them had asked him for his autograph. He held up the clipboard. "Who will sign, please?"

There was a collective shuffling in the group, until, like a reluctant groupie, LeAnn stepped forward, her head hanging forward so that her hair hung in her eyes, and she tucked it back behind her ears with a kittenish flip.

She grasped the stylus and signed on the electronic sign-in board.

"Thank you," he said throatily. "So very kind."

After he left, LeAnn was completely incapacitated. She leaned over the front desk, ignoring the phone even when all four lines were ringing at once.

"It can wait," she said, holding up her hand like a queen holding the populace at bay. "Desperate situations call for desperate measures." She disappeared back to the staff room and returned a couple moments later, wrist-deep in a two-pound bag of peanut M&M's. With a tremendous rattle, she poured a pile onto the counter and started sorting them into colors, then popping them into her mouth three or four at a time.

"I mean, did you see him? Did anyone else even see him?"

"I think you'd better get a grip, girl." That was Arecely, who was making a point of the fact that she had not been swept off her feet.

"Yeah, he was a good-looking piece of horseflesh," Mary Louise said.

"Nice to know that we can count on a little testosterone infusion around ten every morning. Like a coffee break, only a man break. It'll wake us all up." Flo said.

"If I can't stop eating M&M's does that mean I'm in love?" LeAnn asked.

Charlotte peered into the back hall, frowning. "Both exam rooms are empty back there. Don't we have any patients?"

LeAnn tried to stand up, hoping to block Charlotte's view of the waiting room, but Charlotte was obviously looking over her shoulder, where plainly there were three patients waiting for one of the assistants to bring them back, take their blood pressure, and put them in a room.

"Is there a problem?" Charlotte sounded irritable. She'd been sounding irritable a lot recently.

"Man trouble," Mary Louise said.

"I think I'm in love," LeAnn said, sweeping up a grouping of six green M&M's, like she was playing playground jacks; she popped them into her mouth so it sounded like she said, "Loughmph."

Charlotte surveyed the group of women, the frown line between her eyes so pronounced that even Flo went over and started looking at the files studiously, as though she were looking for a patient's chart.

"There are three patients sitting in the waiting area, and we are booked solid today. If you guys want to get out of here at any kind of decent hour . . ."

Nobody said anything. They just stared at Charlotte like she had told them all to take off their clothes or something.

Finally Arecely said, "Jeez, Charlotte, you don't have to be so grumpy."

Mary Louise took a chart and went to call in the next patient. Flo went up to the front and tapped her fingernails on the counter and said, "Now how're we doing here?" Then LeAnn took one last handful of M&M's, not bothering to sort them by color and, jamming them into her mouth, stood up. She rubbed her palms on her scrub pants, plucked a chart from the "ready" bin, and disappeared around the back hallway, and Arecely plucked one yellow M&M delicately out of the bag and started to suck on it, muttering loud enough for Charlotte to hear her, "Jeez, it was just the UPS guy."

Thirteen

In a medical office, especially a busy one, a five-minute delay quickly mushrooms into twenty minutes, and then an hour, so Charlotte had faced a morning of grumpy patients who had been sitting out in the waiting room too long not to seem irritated when she finally got to them; plus, now she had a stack of charts on her desk that needed follow-up. Charlotte was so absorbed in trying to catch up on her paperwork before the afternoon onslaught arrived that she was surprised to see Mary Louise standing at her office door.

"There is a gentleman here to see you."

The man was standing in Flo's cubicle looking at her variety of posters, his back toward her. He was wearing Levi's and a faded black sweatshirt—from behind he looked about twenty-five, but when he turned around she was surprised to see a suntanned face that looked closer to her age—late thirties. He looked so oddly familiar that her first thought was that they had already met.

His hand was extended toward hers. "Paul Stone," he said.

"Have we . . . met?" Charlotte said, holding out her hand.

"Charlotte Hopper, I presume?"

"Yes, sorry, I thought you looked . . ." But then Charlotte trailed off, feeling stupid; she could see why she had thought she knew him—he so resembled Charlie that the two could have been brothers, except he was a lot more like Charlie used to look, a looser version of Charlie, *a happier version*. At first she couldn't place the name, but then she remembered, Mrs. Wetherill, the staff meeting.

"You're the reporter for the *Bayard Post*?" Charlotte said.

"Yup, two days on the job."

"The cub reporter?"

" 'Fraid so. My latest gig. So shall we . . . ?"

"Shall we . . . ?" Charlotte felt like her brain had departed her body. "Lunch?"

"Oh, I . . . um, no I don't usually take lunch."

"Don't worry. I cleared it with your boss." He winked. He was actually quite good-looking.

"Well, then, I guess . . ."

"Great." He put his hand on her arm. "Come on. Let's go."

Charlotte started to walk with him toward the door, but then she realized she still had her lab coat on, so she stopped, said, "Oh . . ." then turned around, then said, "My lab coat," then took a couple more steps, then turned around, took off her lab coat, and attempted to fling it onto the hook on the wall, only she missed and it fell to the floor. Quicker than she could react herself, Paul Stone reached over and picked up the lab coat, then hung it up for her. As he reached up, she could see the whorl of hair below his belly button, just over the top edge of his jeans. She felt a rush of heat between her legs and looked away, embarrassed, then back out the window, then back at Paul Stone, hoping that he hadn't noticed the little avalanche that his arrival had provoked in her—what was with her, anyway? She wasn't usually like that.

Lunch was tuna subs from Wawa out on the bench behind the shop, which gave a good view of the empty space where the clinic's Dumpster used to be, and a nice view across the fields to where the mushroom houses sat out in the distance. Paul was moving around, taking photos. Charlotte thought the mushroom smell wasn't especially noticeable, until Paul sniffed the air and said, "Whew, what a stink."

"Careful," Charlotte said. "That marks you as an outsider. Locals don't notice the smell."

"Don't know if I'm looking forward to that or not." When he smiled there were deep laugh creases around his blue eyes. See, there was a difference—Charlie's eyes were brown.

They sat on the narrow bench, facing each other. A rusty pickup truck pulled into the slot in front of them, and three short, dark men wearing trucker hats got out. They were conversing in rapid Spanish, which Charlotte, as usual, couldn't understand.

Paul had his sweatshirt sleeves pushed up to his elbows, and Charlotte was distracted by a quick thought of what it would feel like to run her finger along the well-defined groove on his forearm.

For a moment, they busied themselves unwrapping the white paper around their sandwiches. When a glob of watery, fishy-smelling mayonnaise dropped into her lap, she cursed herself for getting a tuna sub.

"Oh, no," Charlotte said. Now she would smell like fish all afternoon. She dabbed at the spot with her napkin, succeeding only in leaving a scrim of balled-up paper fragments and a slightly larger stain.

"Here, let me help you," Paul said. He opened his water bottle and poured a bit into her lap, only she started from the cold and bumped his arm, which made him spill quite a bit more than he expected to.

Charlotte's thin rayon skirt now clung to her thighs and crotch.

"Oh, I'm so sorry. I'm really sorry," he said, leaning over to rub at the wet spot with the napkin, which just added more balled-up paper to the mess.

Charlotte was so startled by the electric jolt of his touch on her legs that she jumped up, simultaneously knocking her sandwich facedown on the ground and dumping over her Diet Pepsi. She could feel her face heating up, but then Paul started laughing, a genuine laugh that started deep in his belly. It was so infectious that pretty soon Charlotte joined in.

"I don't mean to laugh," he said.

"Oh, don't worry about it. At least it's just water. I've had much worse spilled on me before."

She looked up and met his eyes, just for a second, and felt an odd jolt of recognition; she had been married to Charlie for sixteen years, but Paul was so uncannily like her husband that she felt an intimacy that wasn't merited. For a moment, he held her gaze directly. She felt the ground telescoping out from under her.

But the moment didn't last long. Paul sniffed the air again. He looked down at his sandwich uneasily. "The smell is really hard to take."

"We could go back to the clinic."

"Is there a place we could talk there?"

"Um, yeah, there's a room upstairs that we use for youth group meetings. We could sit up there."

Back in the clinic, Charlotte led Paul down the back hallway, past the patient rooms, and up the narrow back stairway that led to the upstairs room. She pushed the door open; it was a medium-size room, up under the eaves of the former farmhouse, with dormer windows that flooded the room with a pleasant light.

"Wow," Paul asked, "what is this doing here?"

Paul walked across the room toward the image of Mary. He ran the palm of his hand against the wall, running the tips of his slender fingers over it, tracing the edges of her long brown hair, the cape of blue lined with stars, and the skillfully drawn folds of her gown, down to the exposed tips of her sandaled feet. Charlotte stood back and watched him, barely breathing. His body was taut. He was caressing the painting the way he might stroke a beloved's face. Charlotte knew she was on dangerous ground here—passionate intensity was the one quality that she found irresistible. It was the quality that Charlie had—and Deirdre, of course.

For a moment, he just stood there, saying nothing. Then he turned around to face her, his face enlivened with happiness.

"That's quite amazing. Who painted it?"

"I . . . uh . . . I really don't know. I had never noticed it until the other day. It's pretty, isn't it?"

"It's *La virgen de Guadalupe*," Paul said—but Charlotte couldn't really understand the part that, unexpectedly, rolled out of his mouth in native-sounding Spanish.

"What did you say?"

"The Virgin of Guadalupe—the Mexican Madonna. You're not familiar with that?"

Charlotte shook her head. She remembered the gold medallion her patient had been wearing the other day—she felt a brief flutter of anxiety.

"She's the patron saint of Mexico. This is a beautiful rendition."

"Yes, I guess I had never noticed. . . ." But Charlotte regretted having said that, because it made her sound just like the station-wagon-driving suburban mom that she was, not the girl who had once been so entranced with the paintings of Botticelli that she had minored in Italian Renaissance studies.

But then the sound of the patient buzzer ringing downstairs reminded her of the time, and she glanced at her watch.

"Umm, Paul. The interview. I've got patients triple-booked all afternoon. If you really want to interview me . . ."

He spun around, dropped onto one of the floor pillows, and gestured for her to sit beside him, and then said, "Well, let's get going then."

"Shoot," she said.

"Well," he said, smiling, "who do you think left that baby in the Dumpster behind the clinic?"

For a moment, the question hung in the air, but then, without at all meaning to, instead of answering, she burst into sobs so violent that she ended up with her hot, wet face and snotty nose buried on Paul Stone's shoulder, as he murmured sympathy and gave her just the right kind of well-timed pats on her back.

When she finally raised her head from his shoulder, and got ready to sniff an apology, she looked up and saw the painting of the Virgin of Gaudalupe. Her gaze was steady and true, and she seemed to be telling Charlotte something, but Charlotte couldn't decipher the message.

Charlotte pushed away from Paul, and he reached his hand to tilt her chin up so he could look her in the eye.

"I'm so embarrassed," she said. "I don't have any idea why I got so emotional all of a sudden. I've been fine up until now. Absolutely fine."

"Don't worry, Charlotte. It's natural." He used his thumb to brush away a last escaping tear, in a way that felt strangely intimate.

"This better not go in the paper," she said.

"I hope you know me better than that," he said.

"I don't know you at all," Charlotte said.

"We've been through a mushroom cloud and a Virgin Mary sighting together. I think we know each other quite well by now."

He said this last with an odd confidence, a voice at once gentle and yet with as strong a pull as a riptide. She felt like she could sit there with him all day. But she couldn't. She looked at her watch.

"I've gotta go," Charlotte said.

Paul stood up and stuck out his hand, back to impersonal. "It has been a pleasure to meet you. Thank you so much for your time."

Charlotte didn't wait for him; she just beelined down the stairs toward the staff bathroom. She locked the door behind her, then slowly turned around toward the mirror to look at her tearstained face. She splashed cold water on it frantically, then dabbed it with paper towels, then remembered the wet spot on her skirt, which fortunately had dried, leaving just a grayish cast where the napkin had left some traces. She brushed at it with her hand. Then she stared back at her face again in the mirror. Her hair was chin-length, and kind of bushy. She used Clairol rinse on it now and then, because it was starting to fade and go slightly gray. Besides that, she still looked much the same as she ever had: her faded cotton T-shirt, her serviceable rayon skirt. She couldn't see her clogs in the mirror, but she knew that they rounded out the image. She looked like what she was—a do-gooder, a nurse practitioner who worked in a clinic for poor people, who believed in what she was doing, who did it out of love.

Suddenly it struck her that she was too old for this; her image was as faded and out-of-date as the clinic itself. Thirty-seven. And to think that just a few days ago she'd been thinking she was going to have another baby. Who was she trying to kid?

Charlotte looked at her watch. *Crap.* She'd been in the bathroom for five minutes. She checked herself again. Her eyes weren't noticeably red; her skirt looked wrinkled but fine. She pushed the door open, noting that there was already a chart on each of the exam room doors.

She walked around to the front to get her lab coat, stumbling slightly when she noticed that Paul was still there, leaning against the front counter next to LeAnn and Arecely, staring up at the closed-circuit TV.

"Figures they never thought to look at the closed-circuit TV," LeAnn was saying.

"Well, that nice young officer did ask me if you could see the Dumpster through the camera," Mary Louise said. "But I told him no."

"Why'd you tell 'im no?" LeAnn asked. "You know full well it points straight at the Dumpster."

"Point*ed* at the Dumpster. Not anymore. By the time he asked me, they had already dragged the Dumpster away." Mary Louise was beaming. "And how could it point at the Dumpster if the Dumpster isn't there?"

"This is pretty boring, you guys. It could take a long time. . . ."

"If you would allow me?" Paul said, and LeAnn handed him the remote. He pressed REWIND a couple of times. "What day was it that they found the baby?"

"Um, Monday," LeAnn said.

"Monday the twenty-seventh?"

"Yeah."

"What time do you close on Friday?"

"Five thirty."

"Okay, so some time after Friday at five thirty P.M." he punched the remote several times in rapid succession until the correct date and time came up; then he started pushing the fast forward and stopping it, pushing it and stopping it.

Charlotte stood there mesmerized, staring at the unchanging picture of the big blue Dumpster, and the circle of parking lot that was illuminated by the big floodlight that shone in the parking lot at night. She knew that there were patients waiting in the room, but she was seized around the middle by a feeling of dread—the Dumpster, the parking lot were clearly illuminated and in full view. Whoever had left the baby there was going to be caught on the tape. That was evident.

Just then the front door pushed open and Flo came in with a jingle of keys, swathed in a perfumed mist of hair spray and fresh nail lacquer—every Thursday morning Flo left for the "post office" at eleven A.M. and came back freshly painted and beehived. The staff was so used to it that they didn't even give it a second thought.

"What's going on here?" Flo said.

"We're looking at the tape," Arecely said. "We're going to see who left the poor little dead baby there."

"This gentleman here is a newspaper reporter," said Mary Louise, her voice puffed up with a swell of emergency-related pride.

Flo looked at Charlotte, who was standing rigid in the middle of the room, staring at the screen as though hypnotized.

She held up one hand. "Whoa, wait a minute. Hold on just one moment. Give me that right now." Flo marched over to Paul and held out her hand for the remote as though he were a recalcitrant toddler with a snatched toy truck.

"Yup, you bet. Just one minute."

"I didn't say in one minute," Flo said, continuing in strict grandma mode. "I said right this very minute."

"All right, hold your horses." Paul was hunched forward, clicking frantically on the remote like a teenager playing a video game.

Flo was not amused. She drew herself up to her full five-foot-one, raised her voice, and said in her most managerial tone, "I'm Florence Garcia, the clinic manager. That tape is clinic property, and you are not privileged to view it."

Paul looked away from the screen and beamed at Flo, sticking out his hand, but not the remote.

"*Mucho gusto, Señora Garcia,*" Paul said, the Spanish rolling right off his tongue.

"Same to you. And I'm Italian. Now give me the remote."

While everyone was staring at the showdown between the reporter and Flo, Mary Louise had apparently kept her eyes on the screen, because she let out a shrill scream and said, "Oh, my Gawd, I seen it. I seen it. Back up, back up. It's right there."

In her excitement, Flo forgot to keep up the showdown, and watched as eagerly as the rest of them while Paul pushed REWIND in short fits and starts.

Charlotte didn't see anything at all until Mary Louise shrieked again, "I seen it. I seen it."

Sure enough, you could see it; in fact, it was easier to see on slow-mo rewind. In a split second, in the blink of an eye, a white bundle appeared, as if out of nowhere, up from behind the back rim of the Dumpster, and then in a movement faster than two beats of a heart it dropped out of sight into the blackness. After he rewound it a couple of times, Charlotte, who had crept closer and closer to the screen until her face was inches from it and her shoulder brushed up against Paul's shoulder, could see the hand.

It appeared in a flash, an empty hand, five fingers outstretched, palm toward heaven like a supplicant. And then gone, so quick that you would be certain you hadn't even seen it.

They replayed it several more times after that, until LeAnn was sure that she could see a figure slinking out in the shadows and Mary Louise averred that she had seen a wedding ring. Charlotte's secret was that she was leaning on Paul now, leaning onto his rock-hard shoulder in a way that he was clearly aware of, though he wasn't letting on to the others in the room.

The videofest didn't break up until Missy Summerson, one of the regulars, came out from the back hall, pants off, with just a paper drape wrapped around her legs, and said, "Where the heck's the doctor? I been sitting back there so long I think I fell asleep." Then a moment later, "Gawd, why dincha tell me there was a man back here"—when she got a good look at him, she smiled—"and a good looker too."

They were hopelessly behind for the rest of the afternoon, for Charlotte a blur of questions and faces, then a mile-high stack of charts and paperwork that kept her there late once again.

At some point, the police had come to take the tape and left again, and Flo had gone out and posed for a stiff picture out in front of the clinic under the sign that said, EL CENTRO DE LA MUJER Y DE PLANIFICACIÓN FAMILIAR/WOMEN'S CENTER OF THE GREATER LONDONDALE AREA, and Paul had left. When Charlotte finally emerged from her office the air had finally rearranged itself to become neutral again.

Fourteen

It was the marks on her hand that Charlotte noticed first. Well, the first thing she noticed, when she walked into the exam room, was the smell. It was a fact that some of her patients had an unpleasant, albeit familiar odor: acrid cigarettes, unwashed skin, and stale clothes. This young woman was thin and pale; lank, dirty-blond hair hung around her shoulders and stuck to her face, which was dotted with a sparse collection of pimples.

She was wearing a dingy T-shirt, not quite white, with a fading pattern in glitter paint across the front, and she was undressed from the waist down, a paper drape over her lap. She didn't look up when Charlotte came into the room.

Charlotte glanced at the chart as she walked into the room. According to her birth date, she was nineteen, although she appeared much younger.

"Chaki Gibbons?" Charlotte's voice sounded overbright to herself, a compensatory mechanism when she was trying to cover up her dismay.

"Yeah . . ." The girl's voice was barely audible. Charlotte's eyes were drawn to the girl's hands. She was clasping them nervously over the paper drape. Charlotte noticed that her hands didn't look very clean and that there were black marks of some kind on her knuckles.

"What can I do for you today?" Charlotte stood with her white coat, holding a pen, stethoscope around her neck. She glanced down at the chart—where it said, *Presenting complaint*, Mary Louise had written, *She wants to get checked out to make sure nothing is wrong*. Well, at least it was only one sentence.

The girl didn't look up, didn't say anything, so Charlotte continued. "Are you here just for a checkup, or are you having a problem?"

The girl continued to study the floor, not responding.

"Okay, well, let's go over your health history, shall we? And then I'll start the exam."

Charlotte started the routine of the exam, listening intently with the stethoscope, making marks in the chart. The girl continued to keep her hands clenched, so Charlotte asked her, "Can you hold out your hands for me?"

She seemed reluctant, but she held them out flat, palms down, looking up from the floor to stare at her hands as though she were staring at them for the first time.

The girl's hands were blunt, with ragged nails that were none too clean. Across the knuckles of both hands someone had lettered, with what looked like permanent marker, F-U-C-K.

No sooner had Charlotte gotten a good look than Chaki snatched her hands away and buried them under her thighs.

"Chaki . . ." Charlotte said gently. "Did someone write on your hands?"

Still without looking up, she nodded yes.

"Who wrote that, Chaki?"

When she finally spoke, her voice sounded choked. "My boyfriend." When she opened her mouth, Charlotte saw that she was missing her two front teeth.

"And did you . . . was that okay with you?" Charlotte was trying to tread lightly, to see what exactly was going on.

"No, I didn't want him to, but I was afraid he would hurt me if I said no."

"Has he hurt you before?"

"He ain't hurt me yet, but I'm afraid he's gonna." She fell back into silence, but then she added, "He let his friend do it to me, and that's why I want to get checked out."

"He let his friend write words on your hands?"

She shook her head, staring at the floor again.

"He let his friend have sex with you?"

She looked up, and now tears were running down her cheeks, leaving little track marks.

Charlotte had been working as a nurse practitioner for fifteen years. She thought she had seen everything, but she had never seen obscenities written on someone's body.

When Chaki lay down on the exam table, she bunched her T-shirt up out of the way so Charlotte could do a breast exam. El Centro didn't use patient gowns anymore; they were too expensive to launder. Charlotte looked down with dismay at Chaki's belly. It was rounded well above the belly button—she looked to be about seven or eight months pregnant, probably closer to eight. Across the top of her pubic bone was scrawled the word *mine*.

Charlotte put her clean hands, scented with antiseptic soap, on Chaki's belly, cupping her hands around the hard stone of her uterus.

"Chaki. When did you last have a period . . . ?"

Chaki's head was turned away from Charlotte; she was staring at the wall. She didn't answer. Charlotte palpated the uterus with the palms of her hands, the cool, clean surface of the flat of her hand passing over the angry letters. She held her hand still for a moment and felt a bump, movement, rippling through the skin.

"Did you realize that you might be pregnant?" Charlotte asked. She was reaching over to a drawer under the counter, pulling out the hand-held Doppler and the conduction gel. Charlotte switched on the Doppler, which made a staticky sound, like a radio. She plopped a dab of cold jelly on Chaki's belly, and Chaki recoiled from it, like a snail when touched with the end of a finger.

"We're going to listen, to see if we can hear a heartbeat."

For a moment, more static, then the room echoed with a rhythmic swish.

Charlotte looked at Chaki's face. She was still staring at the wall, but now Charlotte could see another tear silently cutting a different pathway down her cheek, like a raindrop on a dirty car window.

Charlotte switched off the Doppler, wiped the jelly off its smooth plastic dome, and slid it back into the drawer, then turned back to face Chaki. She didn't say anything. She wanted to let Chaki speak first.

"How far along you think I am . . . ?"

"I'd say seven to eight months. But you'd need an ultrasound."

"I ain't keepin' it," she said dully.

"Chaki, why don't you sit up, get dressed, and have a seat in that chair? I'll be back with you in a few minutes."

Chaki was nineteen, not a minor. If she had been a minor, then Charlotte could have reported her situation to the police. But as it was, she could only give her information. Charlotte wrote down the phone numbers—domestic-violence shelter, the hotline. . . . She pulled out the packet of referral information for pregnant patients: where to seek pre-natal care and a brochure about adoption.

"How much does it cost?"

That was Chaki's only question.

"I'm sorry?"

"I told you, I ain't keeping it. How much does it cost?"

"Do you mean . . . the doctor's care?"

"No, I mean, to get an abortion."

"Chaki, I'm sorry. You're too far along for an abortion. This baby's going to be born soon. And the most important thing for you right now is to get safe. I'm going to give you the number for the domestic-violence shelter. I can call them right now, before you leave the office, if you want."

Later, Charlotte was talking to Flo. "I don't think she did anything. I think she went straight back home. I don't think she'll get out of there, and I don't think she's going to do anything about that baby either. She won't get prenatal care and she won't look into adoption. She'll just wait . . . show up in the hospital one of these days." Charlotte remembered the baby in the Dumpster. "Or not show up."

Flo was sitting at her desk counting up money, the crumpled ones and the fives that people paid them—five dollars toward a balance that would never be paid off. "Don't beat yourself up, Charlotte. You did what you could. What else could you do?"

"I'm afraid she's going to end up dead."

"Charlotte," Flo said. "You did what you could."

"It wasn't enough."

"Whatever *enough* is, that girl was born without it. Ain't nobody but her gonna walk out that door. You can't walk out the door for her."

Sometimes Charlotte appreciated Flo's blunt assessments, but today she didn't really want to talk about it. Ever since she had found that baby, the implications of all these loose ends, these pregnant teenagers who didn't know what to do, seemed to be eating away at her. Wasn't there a time in the past when she had felt more sure about things?

"So when are you leaving for Florida?" Charlotte asked, changing the subject.

"Day after tomorrow. Right after the in-laws leave."

"You've still got in-laws?"

"Yeah, it's driving Pedro crazy."

"He doesn't get along with his folks?"

"These aren't his folks. These are Miguel's folks." Flo was snapping rubber bands around the stacks of bills with smart precision. Miguel was Flo's ex. Charlotte could never keep track of Flo's complicated family.

But driving home that night, Charlotte couldn't get the girl out of her head, obscenities written onto the most private part of her body, no front teeth, pregnant with a baby she didn't want, and all Charlotte could do was send her somewhere else, bump her along like another link in the chain, send her to another doctor, another hospital, with no certainty she would show up.

She was still haunted by the baby in the Dumpster, and now she thought about this baby, the one who had rippled up under hand, the one whose tenacious heart had filled the little room, but it wasn't safe, and it wasn't in a safe vessel, and she had done what she could do, which, in essence, was nothing.

Fifteen

The next day, there were two pictures on the front page of the *Ba-yard Post*—and even though the *Post* was a little local paper, the pictures were still in full color. One was of Flo. She had her hands carefully locked over the fattest part of her belly, and her chin was styl-ishly tilted up and to the left to minimize her double chin. She was standing out front of the clinic—you could just see part of the sign, the part that said FAMILY PLANNING in Spanish.

The other picture caught Charlotte's attention with a punch in the stomach. It was a photo that Paul had snapped near the bench behind Wawa. Charlotte stared at the picture until the grainy picture separated into colored dots, struck by what her expression revealed. Her head was tilted slightly to the left and her hair hung down over her shoulder. She looked younger—but she recognized the expression on her face; it was an expression of longing.

Flo stood by the window with the paper folded open, reading the ar-ticle out loud with satisfaction.

" 'Flo Garcia, the manager of the clinic, was present when the uniden-tified baby was found. . . .' "

LeAnn was on the phone; she cupped her hand over the receiver. "Call for you, on two."

"Who is it?" Charlotte asked.

"She won't say," LeAnn said, studying her nails. "Sounds young."

"Is it Julie?" Charlotte glanced at her watch. Ten fifteen. Julie was in school.

"Mrs. Hopper?"

"Yes?"

"It's Ariel."

"What can I do for you, Ariel?"

"Well, it's just that . . . I think I might be pregnant."

Charlotte's heart sank. "Did you do a pregnancy test?"

"No . . ." Her voice was muffled, like she had put her hand over the phone and was conversing with someone.

"Well, you need to come in to have a pregnancy test. Let me put you on hold to make an appointment."

But when Charlotte hung up the phone, the blinking light went dark. Ariel had hung up.

"If Ar . . . uh, Mary Smith calls back, can you make her an appointment for a pregnancy test?" Charlotte said.

"Oooh!" There was a loud shriek from LeAnn, who had bolted out of her chair and shoved Charlotte out of the way as she took off down the back hall.

"Oh, my," said Mary Louise, looking up from the stack of files she was color-coding. "Maybe she felt some gas coming on."

"No, I don't think so," Flo drawled, looking up at the closed-circuit TV—the spot where the Dumpster used to be was now filled with the brown of the UPS truck.

A moment later, LeAnn emerged from the bathroom, her hair damp and scented with Rave; her complexion was almost as green as her eye shadow, and she slumped back into her chair as if on the verge of fainting.

Nobody said anything. Nobody moved. They all stood transfixed and stared at the TV screen. LeAnn was moaning softly, something unintelligible that sounded a little like *mymymy*.

"Maybe it's the fat guy," Arecely said, trying to be helpful.

"That would almost be a relief," LeAnn said, sounding like she was choking back a half-formed sob.

"Why would you want it to be the fat guy?" Mary Louise said. Her left hand was carefully splayed, with a different-colored sticker stuck lightly on the tip of each finger.

"She's got it bad," Flo said.

You couldn't see the front of the truck, just the back—anybody could have been driving that truck. But just then, a pair of copper legs flashed in front of the screen, well-muscled forearms, and a box. . . . The clinic door opened, and there were two sharp raps on the inside door.

Nobody moved. LeAnn, whose job it was to buzz people through the door, just sat there, frozen, with an uncertain expression on her face. Two more raps.

"Could you buzz him in, for the love of God?" Flo spoke up, and leaned past LeAnn, groping for the button with the hesitant jabs of a woman with expensive nails.

The box pushed through the door, and the UPS man stood in the doorway, grinning, his teeth exceptionally white in his suntanned face.

"These are heavy, and I have got two of them." His English was accented and formal. "Where do you beautiful ladies want me to put these boxes? I see you have no men here. I can put them where you want."

Nobody said anything. They stood staring like tongue-tied groupies. "You want me to put them somewhere?" he repeated, showing his Tom Cruise smile.

Again a pause, a collective shuffling. Who would show him the supply closet?

Flo, Arecely, Charlotte, Mary Louise—they all stared at LeAnn, who was seated at the counter staring at the floor.

"Well, I ain't doin' it," Mary Louise said. "That's Miss LeAnn's job." She winked and elbowed LeAnn. The women caught their breath as, for a moment, LeAnn appeared frozen to the spot.

Then LeAnn stood up. She raised her eyes as slowly and demurely as a princess—making the full effect of her green eye shadow even more noticeable. Without speaking, she made a come-hither gesture down the back hallway.

Arecely couldn't quite suppress a giggle. Mary Louise muttered a muffled, "You go, girl."

The UPS man picked up the two heavy boxes as though they were playthings and heaved one over each shoulder; he followed LeAnn down the back hall, where he obviously had a good view of LeAnn's butt, which jiggled as she walked.

It took at least ten minutes for everyone to regroup. Luckily Charlotte had gone into a room with a patient, and since she hadn't emerged yet, there was still time for some ardent speculation. . . . What was his name? When would the next UPS delivery come?

The brief encounter exhausted LeAnn; at first she could do nothing but swivel back and forth on her office chair. Everyone grouped around her as if she were a sick patient as she languidly opened a box of Tastykakes.

"Times like this call for chocolate," LeAnn said, and everyone nodded sagely. Truer words had never been spoken.

That was how it happened that when Charlotte came out of the patient room there were four charts stacked up untouched, and the waiting room was full to bursting.

"Um, girls?"

LeAnn, Arecely, Flo, and Mary Louise were all huddled around LeAnn's computer terminal, where the booking-and-appointments screen was closed and the UPS Web site was open. LeAnn was clicking fast and furious, and Arecely was saying, "His name has got to be there somewhere, don't you think?"

Right then Charlotte was certain that she was going to lose it entirely and start hollering, but she didn't get a chance, because no sooner had she appeared than LeAnn hurriedly tapped on some keys and the appointment screen came back up, and suddenly everyone was earnestly engaged in doing something that looked really important.

The phone rang, and LeAnn answered in her usual singsong voice, "The women's center/El Centro, how may I help you? *Un momento, por favor.* Flo, Spanish on line one," LeAnn called out.

Flo picked up the phone on her desk and said something in Spanish that Charlotte couldn't understand, and she headed back down the back hall to see another patient.

"Did Mary Smith ever show up?" Charlotte said.

"The girl for the PT?" Arecely said. "Nah, she got added to the schedule this morning, but she no-showed. She was supposed to be here at ten fifteen."

The patient bathroom was backing up into the staff lounge, so instead of going to the staff room for break, everybody just stayed out by the phones.

"Can't eat anyway," LeAnn said, dropping half a Tastykake with a languid flourish, then studiously sweeping chocolate crumbs off the countertop. She let out a lugubrious sigh.

"Why don't you ask him his name?" Mary Louise said.

Charlotte was sitting at her desk, looking out the window, trying to avoid being drawn into the conversation about LeAnn's lovesickness— no diagnosis or treatment during break. That was her policy.

So instead she stared out the window and worried. At any given time there were always several patients she was worried about, and right now there were three—Chaki Gibbons, Ariel, and Maria Lopez, if her name was even Maria Lopez. While she stood there, she saw a police car drive into the parking lot, with the words CHESTER COUNTY SHERIFF written on the side.

"Oh, great," LeAnn said. "Now we've got the cops on us."

Mary Louise looked out the window and said, "Flo, cop in the parking lot," confidently—as if she were really getting the hang of her duties.

The police officer lumbered up the steps, his face shaded by the brim of his cap.

"Anyone commit any crimes, before I buzz him in?" LeAnn said, leaning over to push the door button. Charlotte felt the low thrumming of anxiety in the pit of her stomach.

The sergeant was a burly man, clean-shaven, with fat cheeks that were bright red; he stood just barely inside the door, looking like a man at the threshold of a beauty salon or a bra department—sorry to be there and unwilling to go a step farther.

"Ladies," he said. "Good morning to you."

"Florence Garcia," Flo said briskly. "What can I do for you today?"

After taking a hesitant darting glance into the room, he stared carefully at his feet. From the care he took in avoiding looking up, Charlotte could guess that the condom poster, which was at eye level right behind her left shoulder, had caught the officer's eye. He had his hands clasped in front of him and he was rubbing them together. Charlotte noticed that the hair on his knuckles was dark against his skin, and that he was wearing a Kennett High School ring that was just a little too tight.

"Uh, regarding the situation . . . of the homicide."

"Yes?" Flo said. Her tone made it clear that she wasn't going to take any flak.

Charlotte saw the officer's eyes dart toward the condom poster—it was a picture of a bunch of condoms in different sizes and shapes hanging on a laundry line. At the top it said, CONDOMS COME IN MANY COLORS SHAPES AND SIZES. And then at the bottom it cheerfully announced, JUST LIKE PENISES.

Charlotte watched to see if he would glance down at his own crotch, and as his eyes darted downward, she felt victorious.

"Ahem." He cleared his throat. "On behalf of the office of the district attorney of the State of Pennsylvania . . ." He paused, looked around the room, glanced at the offending condom poster, then quickly dropped his eyes to the floor. "I am here to serve a subpoena. . . ." Past that hurdle, he seemed to gain confidence, and his voice picked up steam. "We are investigating into the matter of the homicide found on the property of the Centro de la Mujer." In Spanish, even Charlotte knew it was supposed to sound like *moo-hair*, but this guy trod through it, saying something that sounded like *dulla moo-jer*. "I need to see all of the, ahem, positive pregnancy test results for the time period of January, February, and March 2004. . . ."

Nobody said anything. For once, the women of El Centro were dumbstruck. Even Flo didn't say anything. They all cast sidelong glances at her. Normally LeAnn would have said something sarcastic; in fact, she probably would have, except that she confessed later that she was late on her car payments and didn't want to get on the wrong side of the law in case her car got repossessed. Mary Louise was blinking solemnly, big-eyed behind her glasses, and Arecely studied the countertop.

Charlotte knew that it was her job to provide the common sense, to say something when nobody knew what to say, so she said, "I'm sorry, but that is not possible, sir. Those records are confidential. We're not allowed to share them with you."

Then, as if the floodgates had opened, everybody started talking at once.

"We can't release the medical records—they're confidential."

"How do you know they even did a pregnancy test here?"

"Yeah," LeAnn said. "You can buy 'em at the drugstore. Is the drugstore gonna tell you everyone who bought a First Response in the last nine months?"

"Um, that's, um . . . I'm not at liberty to say. That's part of the investigation. And, uh, you have to give them to me. That's what the law said—because of the subpoenas. . . ." He kind of mangled the end of the word, as though he had suddenly noticed the consonance between *subpoenas* and *penises*.

"We do not have the authority to give you anything," Charlotte said, not knowing if that was an okay thing to say, but she was trying to think on her feet.

"I'm only a nurse," she said. "The doctor isn't in."

"Oh, I see," he said, temporarily stymied. "Where is the doctor?"

"Um, out," Charlotte said. Who knew where Harve was? No one ever knew where Harve was.

"So you ladies, uh, nobody's in charge?"

"That's right," Flo said.

"Nobody," Mary Louise added for emphasis.

"If you'll excuse us for just a moment, Officer, some of the girls need to get back to work. Mary Louise, LeAnn, Arecely," Flo said, "do you have the swabs ready for the male exams this afternoon . . . ?"

"The . . . ?" LeAnn said. Then she nodded her head emphatically. "Oh, you mean those extra-long swabs . . . the ones they use to do the *penile examinations?*"

Charlotte dared to look up at the officer. His face had turned a pealike shade of green.

"Well, then, uh, if no one is in charge here, I guess I'll have to come back when someone is in charge, and, uh, when do you think that will be?"

Mary Louise had ducked into the supply room, and she came out again, tapping a long-handled cotton swab across the palm of her hand as though it were a whip and she was into S and M.

"Are these the ones you were talking about, Flo?" Her voice was pure sugar, innocent as a young girl's.

The officer was edging backward, his hand extended out toward the door handle. "Well, I guess if no one is in charge here, I had better come back when someone is in charge."

"Well, yes," Mary Louise said, snapping the cotton swab smartly against her pant leg with the crisp rhythm of a drum majorette. "I guess you had better."

By then the officer was jiggling the door handle, trying to make a fast exit, but the door had to be unlocked by the buzzer.

"Officer," Flo said sweetly, "please don't jiggle that door handle. That will alert our security system."

The officer jammed his hands into his pockets and waited while LeAnn buzzed him out. Through the closed-circuit TV, they could see him jog down the steps and take off toward his squad car at a run.

He was out of sight before they let themselves dissolve in laughter. A battle won, no matter how small, was cause for celebration.

Sixteen

They had to call someone. The question was, who to call? Names were bandied about—Mark Wetzel, Dotty Wetherill, Harvey Dexter.

Finally Charlotte said, "I'm going to call Harve. He's the medical director. He's paid for being in charge."

Flo snorted so loud that a glob of spit came out of her mouth and landed on her lip. She surreptitiously wiped it away with the tip of her finger.

"I'm going to call him on his cell phone." Charlotte said.

"Well, I think we scared him away," LeAnn said. "I don't think he'll be back anytime soon."

"You know, a subpoena is a legal document. If a judge says we have to hand over the records, then we have to hand them over—or get a lawyer."

"Yeah, and how exactly is the clinic going to pay for a lawyer? With a pig?"

Charlotte was thumbing through the Rolodex, looking for Harve's number. Clearly this was going to be a problem. They couldn't just release the records—there was a privacy issue involved. She didn't know the legal ins and outs of it. She punched Harve's cell phone number into the keypad, with a sinking feeling. It was never reassuring to be dialing Harve's number.

When Charlotte got Harve on the phone, she was relieved that he sounded relatively articulate, and surprisingly he offered to come right over to "discuss the situation." Truth was, they never even knew where Harve was when he wasn't at the clinic. Arecely had put two patients in the rooms, and Charlotte headed down the hallway.

When she came out again, the girls in the front were still debating, and there was no sign of Harve. It had started to rain, a cold, pelting rain, with occasional rumblings of thunder in the distance.

"Yeah, well, I'd love it if they would release the records of the pregnancy tests. There'd be some pretty surprised people around here. Everyone would know who was cheating on everyone else—all the moms would know that their daughters were having sex between four and six p.m."

Charlotte thought of Ariel again. She hadn't come in for the pregnancy test. Well, it was probably a false alarm. Maybe she had gotten her period.

Mary Louise was staring out the window. The parking lot had emptied out, and there was no one in the waiting room—the lull no doubt caused by the rain, which always slowed down traffic in the clinic. "Hey, lookee here—the Channel Six van is here."

"Must be a flood watch," Flo said, walking over to the remote and craning her neck to see the TV in the corner of the waiting room.

She turned up the volume so that they could hear the newscast through the window—sure enough, scrolling across the bottom was a flash-flood watch for Chester County. The clinic was near the Red Clay Creek, which tended to overflow its banks every time there was a drenching rain. There had been heavy rainfall during the whole year, so now just an hour or two of heavy rain and the creek would overflow, washing up onto the roadway and snarling traffic.

You could see part of the creek from the end of their parking lot, so sometimes the news crews would come and wait there. At first the staff had been excited by the nearby presence of celebrity. But the crew never did anything besides sit in the truck for a while, so after a while the thrill had worn off.

But this time, to their surprise, two men wearing jeans—one with a big orange poncho and the other with a yellow slicker—got out and started unloading equipment from the back of the van.

"Whoa," said Mary Louise. "Look—they're getting out."

"Who is it?" asked LeAnn.

Mary Louise peered out into the parking lot. "Nobody. I guess that's the camera crew."

To their surprise, the crew carried a couple of big klieg lights across the parking lot, in the direction of the clinic, rather than down the pathway that would lead to the banks of the stream.

"Oh, my God," said LeAnn. "I wonder if this means that they think the clinic is going to flood?" The clinic had never flooded before, but there was always a first time for anything.

The rain was still pouring down in sheets. Another man, this one also clad in a poncho, had gotten out of the van, and they were lifting more equipment into the parking lot.

Just then a black Mercedes-Benz pulled into the parking lot.

"Harve's here," Flo called out. Everybody clustered around the window, watching Harve get out of his car and put up his black umbrella. They saw him go over to one of the men, who was fiddling with equipment in the parking lot. The poncho-clad man looked up from the long coil of orange extension cord and conversed with Harve for a few minutes. The ladies stood and watched, and then a few moments later, Harve came up the stairs, left his black umbrella open in the vestibule, and let himself into the clinic with his swipey card.

"Ladies . . ." he said to no one in particular, taking off his green Burberry and heaping it over the back of one of the empty chairs.

Now that Harve was here, neither he nor anybody else seemed to know what to do with him. At first nobody spoke, even Charlotte, who was looking at Harve, hoping that her dismay wasn't showing on her face. He didn't appear drunk, but he did have a splotch of something that looked a bit like secret sauce, just under one of the ducks on his dark green tie.

"So," he said, "what's everybody doing?"

"It's lunchtime," Flo said. "Do you mind if I let the girls get their lunches and then meet us upstairs in the meeting room, so's they can eat while we're going over all of this?"

"No problem," said Harve.

"In the meantime," Charlotte said, "let me fill you in."

Harve listened carefully to what Charlotte was saying, and Charlotte was heartened that he seemed interested. She felt a faint stirring of hope that he would actually understand, and help them to manage the situation.

"Of course, we can't release the pregnancy test records—those are confidential. Imagine how much trouble it would cause if all of a sudden we had to make public a list of every single person who came in here to have a pregnancy test done. We just can't let that happen."

"Well," Harve said, "you understand that they want to find the person who dumped the baby in the Dumpster."

"Yes, and I support that," Charlotte said, but even as Charlotte said it, she realized that she did not want to know who abandoned the baby in the Dumpster. "But there is no reason to think that the person who dumped the baby came here for a pregnancy test. In fact, just the opposite. It was most likely someone who wasn't in contact with the health system at all."

"What makes you think that?" Harve grunted.

Charlotte looked at him, felt hopeless. How had this man ever finished medical school? She idly wondered if he was one of those medical students whom Ronald Reagan had rescued during the battle of Grenada.

"We need a good lawyer," Flo said.

"Lawyers cost money," Harve said, "not something we've got a lot of right now."

"Well, we charge fifteen dollars a pop for pregnancy tests, and we do about fifty a week—that's cash money, revenue, flowing into the clinic, and I can promise you that if we start passing out the names of the people who have come here for them, that'll be the end of that. People'll just go over to the Wal-Mart—they can get 'em there for twelve ninety-five."

"Hmm," Harve said, rubbing his beard, where there were still a few drops of collected rainwater. "I never thought of that."

Charlotte sighed.

"Shall we go upstairs?" Flo said.

Though the rain had lulled temporarily, it was falling much harder again; it sluiced in sheets across the dormer windows and made a hollow pounding on the slanted roof.

Charlotte glanced out the upstairs window, remembering the news crew truck that had been in the parking lot. Apparently they were still there—she could see blurry orange, the poncho, moving around through the window. If it flooded, the road would be temporarily cut off—sometimes they were late leaving work because of that, though the road was rarely blocked for more than half an hour or so.

Harve sat down in the straight-backed chair he had been sitting in during the staff meeting.

The girls collapsed onto the beanbag chairs and started unpacking their lunches, and lifting plastic lids beaded with condensation from the microwave to reveal their saucy lunches.

"All right," Harve said. "I think you guys are making a catastrophe out of this, and I don't think there is a catastrophe."

"How is it not a catastrophe?" Charlotte said, incredulous. "You can't just go handing over private medical records to the police."

"I don't see that we have a lot of choice."

"We need a lawyer," Charlotte said.

"Well, I don't know," Harve said, obviously stalling. "I'd have to check with the board on that."

"That sheriff is going to come back. We need to know what to say to him."

"Tell him to call me," Harve said, his voice booming with medical authority. "I'll handle it." He stood up and walked across the room to where Arecely had a box of doughnuts open on the floor next to her.

"May I?" Harve said, plucking a powdered-sugar doughnut from the box without waiting for a response.

"Sure," Arecely said, holding up the box for him. "Have another. There are plenty." But Harve waved the box away. "No, thank you," he said. "I have to watch my cholesterol."

After he left, the rest of them sat and stared at one another.

"Umm, what just happened?" LeAnn said, her fork tines scraping against the brown plastic bottom of the Lean Cuisine container.

"I don't know," Flo said.

"I don't trust him," Mary Louise said with conviction, taking a bite of her red apple with a crunch.

"I second that," said LeAnn, pushing her Lean Cuisine away and leaning over to pluck a chocolate-covered doughnut from Arecely's box. "I think he doesn't think it's worth fighting. I think he'll just hand those records over."

There was silence for a few minutes. Charlotte took a bite out of her tuna sandwich, noticing that it had gotten soggy, and opened a bag of Sun Chips. The rain pounded down on the roof so loud that it would have been hard to sustain a conversation anyway. Charlotte looked up at the painting of Mary on the wall; nobody had bothered to turn on the lights and so the face was shadowed—it appeared darker than before. As she stared at the face, the words came to her: "She brought forth her firstborn son, and wrapped him in swaddling cloths."

How many pregnancies had there been in the environs of Londondale in the past year—how many longed for? How many unwanted? How many had resulted in healthy babies being born, and how many people had gone and gotten the slight inkling of a life scraped out of them?

None of that had anything to do with them. At El Centro, they dipped the sticks in the urine and read a result back—one line or two, a woman alone, or a mother with child . . . and then the patients left, back out in the world to do what they would.

"I want to know, ladies," Flo said, "what you all think about this. Do we let them have the pregnancy test results or not? Raise your hands if you think we should hand them over."

Flo looked around the room: Arecely, Mary Louise.

Charlotte stood up. "I'm going to call Mrs. Wetherill."

"Yeah, what good's that gonna do?" LeAnn asked. "What's she gonna use to pay the lawyer's legal fees? The pig?"

"LeAnn, that's uncalled-for. Mrs. Wetherill is a kind woman who has our best interests at heart," said Flo.

"I'm going to call her," Charlotte said. "I don't trust Harve." Lunch break had ended, so everyone gathered up their papers and lunch things and threw them in the garbage, and then they padded downstairs. Charlotte thought she could hear the thump of defeat in their footsteps, but when they got downstairs and looked out into the parking lot, still drenched with rain, everybody got excited again. The equipment from the TV van was set up in the same spot, only now a petite woman in stiletto heels and a big trench coat was jogging across the parking lot, skipping across puddles as she ducked through the rain toward the door.

She pushed the door open into the vestibule, and then peered through the glass. Arecely went up to the window.

"May I help you?" she said.

The rest of the staff had gathered around the window now; this was what they did on days when there was nothing to do. They swarmed at the window like bees around a hive.

The woman had large, dark owl glasses and one of those thin plastic granny kerchiefs that came in a little pouch. She was not tall, so when she looked over the counter and through the glass, you could only see as far as her top lip, which was carefully painted a dark brown-red.

But when she took off her glasses, Arecely's hand flew to her mouth in surprise, and LeAnn hurriedly pushed the door-unlock button, and Flo motioned her in with a regal wave of the hand.

When the door was open, she stood there with the entire group clustered around her. Charlotte, in the back of the group, was wondering who she was, as all the others seemed to already know her.

"Linda Rodriguez," she said, sticking her hand out toward LeAnn, who had jockeyed her way to the front of the assemblage. "Channel Six News."

Well, the queen of England couldn't have gotten a better reception. The ladies all buzzed into action: *Hello, welcome, what can we do for you, can I take your coat?* Only Charlotte didn't say anything. What was Channel Six News doing here? While the others seemed to take her presence as divine right, Charlotte spoke up.

"Can we help you with something today?"

"Yes," she said. "I'm looking for a Mrs. Charlotte Hopper. I'd like to ask her a few questions."

"That's her," LeAnn said, pointing toward Charlotte with obliging alacrity.

"She's the doctor," said Mary Louise.

"The *nurse*," Flo corrected, then, sucking in her belly and patting her hair, she said, "And I'm Flo Garcia, the clinic manager." Trying to press her advantage, she added,"*Soy la jefe de la clínica.*"

Linda Rodriguez smiled diplomatically. "It is a pleasure to meet all of you. We're doing a story on the baby that was found dead in the Dumpster, and maybe we can interview several of you." She looked at Arecely; then LeAnn stepped directly in front of Arecely, trying to insert herself in the reporter's line of sight, and Arecely, shy as usual, stepped back.

"I'll be happy to do it," LeAnn said.

"Mrs. Hopper?" Linda said.

Charlotte was gun-shy. Ever since her experience the previous day with the reporter Paul Stone, she felt hesitant.

"I'd need to know a little more about what questions you want to ask."

Linda Rodriguez smiled at her, but Charlotte could see the shrewd look in her eyes.

"I understand," she said. "I just thought that with this story being so 'out there' you would want to be able to tell your own version."

"What story?" Mary Louise asked.

"A terrible tragedy," Linda said with professional precision.

"Oh," Mary Louise said. "Are you talking about the poor little baby?"

"It must have come as a terrible shock," Linda continued, frowning with practiced dismay, laying a sympathetic hand on Mary Louise's arm. "About the poor little baby, I mean."

Just then Arecely let out at strangled gasp and all eyes turned to her.

But Arecely was now so engrossed in a paperback that for a moment she didn't notice they were all looking at her.

"Well," Linda Rodriguez said, "that was quite a gasp." She stepped forward, tipping up the book with her index finger so that she could see the cover. Arecely looked like she'd been caught with contraband in a school hallway. She blushed furiously, flipped the book shut, and shoved it up into the crook of her arm.

"Tess Gerritsen," Linda intoned.

Arecely nodded miserably.

"Medical thrillers . . ."

Arecely acknowledged *yes* with just the barest movement of her head.

"No wonder," Linda Rodriguez said, with a tone that said she now understood everything. "I can never put down a Tess Gerritsen myself. . . ." She grasped Arecely's hand, squeezed it, and gave her a radiant smile. Then, back to business, she said crisply, "But now about this poor little baby . . ."

"Well, I think Charlotte was more shocked, 'cause she's the one that found him," Mary Louise said.

"It would give you an opportunity to speak for yourself. To get your story out there," the reporter said, turning back to Charlotte.

Charlotte looked at her without answering, trying to think quickly on her feet. How had she not realized that this was going to attract so much attention? It was her fault, her own fault, for getting softened up by Paul Stone. Maybe if she had been more careful she could have kept a lid on it . . . but then, that was ridiculous, as they were talking about a dead baby, after all.

"I just don't think . . . I don't really have the authority." Charlotte stumbled over her words.

"What Charlotte is trying to say," said Flo, "is that it might be better for you to interview me. Since I'm the clinic manager. It might be more in my official capacity. . . ." Flo was beaming, turning on her most charming high-wattage smile, pulling surreptitiously at the hem of her floral scrub top while simultaneously sucking in her belly again.

"But," said Linda Rodriguez, her voice deepening to an authoritative TV tone, "I believe that it was Mrs. Hopper who actually found the deceased, was it not?"

Charlotte nodded, looking at Flo. Maybe it would be better if she did this herself. She would be careful about what she said.

"All right." Charlotte nodded.

"We're all set up outside."

"Outside?" Charlotte peered dubiously out the window, where the rain was still falling in gray sheets.

"We like the rain. It provides a lugubrious tone—very murderous."

"I don't think it was a murder," Charlotte said, before she clamped her mouth shut again.

Linda Rodriguez smiled, showing two rows of straight, snowy teeth. "You'll tell me all about it," she said.

Charlotte stood under the black umbrella with the Channel Six microphone stuck in her face. It wasn't actually raining that hard, just a drizzle now.

She listened with an unreal feeling as Linda Rodriguez set up the situation: a dead baby found in a Dumpster behind the family-planning clinic. An ongoing investigation into the origin of the baby who was found wrapped up in last week's edition of *Nuestra Comunidad*. For a moment, Charlotte started to tune out as Linda Rodriguez described the clinic's location in Londondale: "Just on the edge of the Smithbridge mushroom farm . . ." She stared past the bright lights, out toward the flat fields, now glinting with mud-colored puddles, and at the flat cinder-block sides of the mushroom houses, squat and gray in the rain.

Charlotte tried not to blink as she turned back toward the bright klieg lights and answered the reporter's few brief questions—how she was backing up and hit the Dumpster, how she found the baby while picking up the trash. Yes, it was wrapped in newspaper and a thin plastic bag. No, she wasn't sure how long it had been dead.

Perhaps the dramatic look on Linda Rodriguez's face looked good on camera, but in person it was comically intense. Charlotte felt the urge to giggle, but stifled it by averting her eyes from the reporter's face.

"Do you have any idea who might have dumped the baby there?"

"No," Charlotte answered. "I have no idea."

"One of your patients . . ." Linda insisted. "Or a migrant worker from the mushroom farm?"

"It could have been anyone—just anyone driving by on the pike." But Charlotte's words felt as inadequate as the sentiment behind them.

"Just anyone?"

"Absolutely," Charlotte said, hoping that her voice did not convey her hesitation. "I'm sure it was just a random event."

*   *   *

The rest of the day was mundane. The girls were distracted, talking about the TV—wondering if it would be on the six-o'clock or the eleven or both. It rained steadily, the sky dark and threatening, and Charlotte waited to see if Harve would call. She found herself glancing anxiously at the parking lot from time to time—a day that had brought Harve, a TV crew, and a process server to the clinic was not a good day. Fortunately they hadn't been busy. That would have been the last straw.

Finally, about four P.M., when the rain had slowed to a drizzle and the last patient had been seen, a beat-up white Toyota Tercel pulled into the parking lot, and Mrs. Wetherill emerged, wearing a flapping khaki duster and carrying a plate of something balanced in her hands.

It turned out that Mrs. Wetherill had brought them homemade lemon squares, their bright yellow interior the sunniest thing that Charlotte had seen that day. Mrs. Wetherill pulled up the cellophane and handed the plate around, and each of the staff picked up a square.

Charlotte bit into the lemon square with satisfaction, the tart lemon oozing between her teeth, the white dusting of powder sweet around her lips.

"Delicious," Mary Louise said. "I'll have to get the recipe."

Mumbles of assent came from around the room.

"You are all very welcome. I thought you might need cheering up, and there is nothing like a lemon square on a rainy day, if I do say so myself." Mrs. Wetherill smiled. "Now about the subpoena. Listen here: We are not going to disclose the records of those women who came to us trusting that we would protect their privacy. I'm looking into finding a lawyer. . . ."

"That's going to cost us," LeAnn said.

"Nonsense," said Mrs. Wetherill. There are plenty of good Philadelphia lawyers who will work for us pro bono."

"Pro bono?" Arecely asked.

"That means they'll work for us for free," Mrs. Wetherill said, "because we are a good cause."

"A lost cause," Charlotte muttered as she reached across to the plate. "Do you mind?"

"Help yourself, dear." Mrs. Wetherill pushed the plate toward Charlotte. "In the meantime, just don't talk to anyone. They have to give it to the medical director—that's Harve. If he's not here to take it, that'll give us some time. And don't talk to anyone. For the time being I'll do all the talking."

Everyone nodded okay. Nobody had seen this side of Mrs. Wetherill before. She seemed to know what to do. Everyone, Charlotte included, was relieved that someone seemed to be taking charge.

"Be particularly mindful of the media," Mrs. Wetherill added. She pulled out a copy of the *Bayard Post* from underneath the voluminous folds of her duster. She folded it open to the pictures of Flo standing in front of the El Centro sign, and she tapped on it with her bony forefinger. "This kind of publicity," she said, "may not be an entirely good thing."

"Well, at least now we've got Six on our side," Mary Louise piped up.

"I beg your pardon?" Mrs. Wetherill said. "Help yourself, dear," she added, picking up the now half-empty plate of lemon squares and proffering it in Arecely's direction.

"Linda Rodriguez," Arecely said, helping herself to a lemon square.

"ABC news," Flo added.

"Channel Six," LeAnn finished, with a triumphant flourish.

"Do you mean to say—" Mrs. Wetherill started to ask.

"But we're not sure if it's going to be on at six," Arecely said.

"Or eleven," LeAnn added.

"Or both," Mary Louise piped up hopefully.

"Do you mean to say," Mrs. Wetherill said, "that a reporter from the television station was here?"

"Charlotte," Arecely said proudly.

"Was interviewed," Mary Louise added.

"Right out there," said LeAnn.

"In our very own parking lot."

"Oh, dear," Mrs. Wetherill said. "Oh, well, no matter," she added. "Just remember, until that subpoena is served, we can still stall a little bit for time."

Just then the door to the vestibule pushed open and in walked Harve, an official-looking manila envelope in his hand.

"I was just out in the parking lot, and this police officer fellow approached me, and look what I got."

The five women fell into silence: Charlotte, Mrs. Wetherill, Mary Louise, LeAnn, Arecely. It was a rare occurrence when not a single one of them could think of a word to say.

"Lemon squares," Harve said, breaking the silence. "My favorites." He threw the large envelope down on the counter with a slap and grabbed the largest lemon square left on the plate. As he leaned past Charlotte, she caught the faint but unmistakable odor of vodka, mixed with the tweed of his jacket, and a faint odor of mushroom soil that always stuck to everyone when it was rainy in Londondale.

Seventeen

Charlotte actually watched the news broadcast on the sofa in her family room, with Julie sitting next to her, which seemed like the most lovely and comforting thing (other than the lemon squares) that she had experienced in a long time.

Turned out it was on the six-o'clock news, and then the eleven o'clock news, and all she had to do was yell, "Julie, I'm on TV. I'm on Channel Six," for her daughter to come running.

Talk about lugubrious. Linda Rodriguez was right. Charlotte, against the dismal backdrop of black umbrella and gray skies, looked downright cadaverous. They hadn't put any makeup on her, and so next to bright and perky Linda Rodriguez, with the carefully preserved full-power hairdo and the professional makeup job, Charlotte appeared as washed-out as an undertaker who had been swept away and then found downstream.

The interview was very brief, just a couple of questions. How did she find the baby? Did she know where it came from?

That wasn't the shocking part of the interview. The shocking part of the interview was the part that didn't involve Charlotte. It was Harold Overturf, the county district attorney, who was sitting in his brightly lit office (probably with makeup on, Charlotte thought) with a wall of imposing-looking legal books behind his head.

"We intend to find the perpetrator and prosecute this case to the full extent of the law," he said, his bony chin quivering with conviction on the screen. "This is a case of capital murder. Make no mistake. If we find the perpetrator, we will seek the death penalty in this case."

The first time she saw the clip, Charlotte sat on the sofa like a stone, snuggling down beside Julie, her battered Fannie Farmer cookbook open on her knees, her index finger marking the page for lemon squares. But the second time she saw it, she got up abruptly and excused herself, walking quickly to the bathroom and then locking the door so that Julie wouldn't see her tears.

She sat on the toilet with her pants down, staring at the gold gilt lines in the wallpaper and thinking about a girl, any girl who was desperate enough to do something like that, and about the dead baby, and about what a mess things were turning into.

Then the phone rang, and Julie called, "Mom," and Charlotte stood up and splashed water on her face and dabbed the clean guest towel in the corner of her eyes, and then looked at her face and blinked a couple of times and hoped that her face didn't show the evidence of crying.

Then she called out, "Coming, dear," in what she hoped was a chipper voice, and she emerged from the bathroom.

"Hello," Charlotte said into the phone, half wondering if someone was calling about her newfound celebrity.

"Mrs. Hopper?" The voice in the phone was hushed, sounded like it was whispering.

"Yes?" Charlotte said.

"It's . . ." The words were muffled, whispered, and Charlotte couldn't quite make it out. "It's Ariel. . . . I need to talk to you."

"Go ahead."

"I think I might be pregnant, but I couldn't get a ride to the clinic. My boyfriend broke up with me." Charlotte could hear a loud snuffle and sniff. "And my mom doesn't know. . . ."

"Ariel," Charlotte said, looking around, hoping that Julie wasn't within earshot, "I think you need to discuss this with your mother. Trust me. She'll want to know."

"Are you going to tell her?" Ariel said worriedly into the phone. "I'll die if she finds out."

"I'm not going to tell her unless you give me permission to tell her, Ariel, but I'm telling you that it would be better for you to tell her. This is your health that we are concerned about here."

"Okay," the voice said tearfully. "Oh, sorry, um, sorry, I gotta go." The phone clicked off.

Charlotte hung up the phone. But just a moment later, it rang again and she picked up.

A tentative voice at the end of the line said, "Um, hello, I . . ."

"May I help you?" Charlotte said.

"Is this, um . . ." It was a woman's voice, throaty and familiar.

"This is the Hopper residence. May I help you?"

"Charlotte?"

"Speaking."

"This is Deirdre. Sorry, I . . . Ariel just hung up the phone . . . and she told me she was talking to a friend, but frankly, just between you and me, I didn't believe her. So I pushed redial . . . because I was wondering who she was talking to. So sorry. If I'd known she was talking to Julie, I wouldn't have been concerned. We been having some . . . issues," Deirdre said into the phone. "She's getting to an age . . ." she said. "She simply won't listen." She paused but then added, "Oh, you know how girls are—Ariel has still got her nose out of joint from the move. She wanted to stay in Virginia. Listen," Deirdre said, her voice brightening up, "I want you to come for coffee. Sunday, can you? Around ten?"

Charlotte felt the oddest combination of emotions. Part of her was eager to go, but part of her hung back. "Well, I'm—"

"Just come on over around ten. We have so much catching up to do."

Charlotte didn't ever actually say yes or no; then Deirdre was making kissing sounds into the phone and Charlotte rested it in the cradle. *Sunday at ten.* She didn't get a chance to sit down, though, because the phone rang for a third time. It was Flo.

"Whadja think?"

"I think I looked terrible."

"No, no," Flo said. "You looked fine. But whatdja think of the Overtoff, Overtopp . . . whatever his name was?"

"They'll probably never know who did it."

"Yeah, they ought to just forget about it and move on."

Eighteen

Arecely carefully stuck the lab strip back into the cellophane patch and folded it into a tiny square. She wrapped it twice in a paper towel, then rolled another paper towel around it for good measure. She crushed the little Dixie cup that still had a couple of drops of pale urine clinging to the insides, and dropped that into the trash. Would anyone wonder why there was a Dixie cup in the trash? No, that was silly; besides, hardly anyone used the bathroom upstairs off the meeting room. Arecely looked at her face in the mirror. It looked chalky in the early-morning light filtering through the small window. Her stomach churned; she felt the temptation to heave and tried to push it down, but she could feel the bile pressing upward in her throat. She turned on the tap and splashed cold water on her face, bringing her cold, wet fingers up underneath her hair. This calmed the nausea a little bit; then she held her wrists under the water until the desire to vomit started to fade.

She emerged into the silent room. The clinic was completely quiet except for the faint buzz of the heat. Arecely was there early, and the clinic wouldn't open for another hour.

She stopped in the middle of the room, feeling unsure what to do with herself. She hadn't wanted to wait until the clinic was open, when LeAnn would be all into her business, so she had dropped off Zekie at Lizzie's, groggy over his orange juice, telling her that she had to get to work early.

Lizzie had looked at her with suspicion. "What's wrong with you? You don't look good, girl."

"Just a little tired, I guess," Arecely said, turning her back slightly as she buckled a groggy Zekie, clad in a diaper and a Bob the Builder

T-shirt, into Lizzie's speckled Fisher-Price high chair. His little belly was warm, and she ran her fingertip over the firm whorl of his belly button.

"You heard anything from Ricky?" Lizzie asked kindly.

Arecely stood up and looked at her friend. Lizzie was still wearing the big T-shirt and shorts that she had slept in, her bleached golden hair was pulled back in a ponytail, and she didn't have any makeup on, which made her look young. Her boyfriend, Martin, was working the night shift at the Tastykake factory. He hadn't come in yet, so it was just Lizzie and her, and Zekie, and Lizzie's little girl, Jessica, who sat on the floor holding a bottle of juice and watching *Blue's Clues* on TV.

Arecely hadn't told Lizzie that she was worried about where Ricky was, but Lizzie probably knew that something was up. This was the first she had mentioned it, though. She certainly hadn't told Lizzie why she needed to go in to work early. She was afraid that Lizzie would guess just by looking at her. She didn't know how people could always figure out when somebody was pregnant, but it never seemed like there was much point in hiding it for long.

Arecely stood in the middle of the upstairs room unmoving, and let the reality of her situation sink in, sink down to the tips of her hair and the ends of her toes, and to the pit of her stomach, which was squirreling around again, making itself known.

There was something about seeing those two pink lines lined up right next to each other. It reminded her, for some reason, of the backs of Ricky and the Camacho boys, the way they had looked through the back window of the pickup truck driving away.

Arecely walked over the painting of Mary and made the sign of the cross.

Hail Mary, mother of grace . . .

She stood up and went to the little broom closet, where she had left a stub of a candle in a small glass holder, with a pack of matches. She lit the candle and set it in front of the painting.

Arecely started thinking about the little baby, the one in the Dumpster, about the hand. . . . She got chills all the way down her arms just thinking about it.

Arecely struck one match, which fizzled out, then a second one, which caught. She lit the small white candle and placed it on the floor in front of the painting, and she watched as the small flame cast golden flickers against the blue hem of the painting.

Dios te salve, Maria. . . .

Arecely stayed there, kneeling on the floor until she could see from her watch that it was time to go downstairs to open up the rooms.

She looked at the small steady candle flame, and thought for a moment about leaving it lit, but then, with a small puff of air, she blew it out and stood up, and then trod silently, alone, down the stairs.

Nineteen

The girl was back, but Charlotte didn't realize it right away. Arecely just said, "Spanish in room two," and handed her the chart, and she glanced at the chart while opening the door.

She looked at her note from the previous visit, written in her familiar cramped, semilegible black ballpoint.

24 yo female status/post normal vaginal delivery appx one month ago, weaned recently. Complaining of breast pain steadily worsening over the past twenty-four hours.

Glancing at the perfectly routine note, she did not immediately register which patient she was dealing with. She looked at the exam table where the patient was sitting with the front of her blouse unbuttoned. At first, Charlotte did not recognize her, but then she scanned the chart again and she realized—this was Maria Lopez.

Today her face looked impassive, her cheeks ruddy. Thick black eyebrows traversed her face like roadways, and her long coil of hair was hanging over her left shoulder. She held her hands clasped tightly in front of her.

When Charlotte realized that she was face-to-face with Maria Lopez, she was taken aback—as though seeing someone she thought was already dead.

"Arecely?"

Arecely said something to the patient that Charlotte knew meant, "What brings you here today?"

Arecely turned and looked at Charlotte. "You told her to come in for a recheck."

Of course. A recheck. Charlotte had completely forgotten that she had told the patient to come back in a few days.

"How is she feeling?"

As Arecely turned and spoke to the woman in Spanish, Charlotte noted again the contrast from the previous visit. The woman's voice was flat, her face as impassive as a stone. Gone were the traces of milk on her blouse, the anguished twisting of her hands. Now she appeared completely normal. Except . . .

Charlotte stood and watched the girl as she conversed in Spanish. There was still something that seemed unusual to Charlotte, something that raised the hair along the back of her neck. Her impassivity seemed heavy, ominous.

But Charlotte had a job to do, and so she began to recite the questions: Any pain? Any fever? Did she complete the antibiotic?

Arecely translated the questions, and the woman responded in monosyllables—*sí, no, no, sí* . . . Charlotte wondered what, if anything, Arecely was thinking about; she wondered what Arecely knew but wasn't telling her. Watching them converse in Spanish was like observing people through a translucent curtain, where you could see them moving, but not quite clearly.

Charlotte commenced the exam. The woman pulled back her shirt and pulled her thin black bra out of the way. Charlotte looked at her left breast, where the infection had been, cupping the patient's warm skin in the palm of her hand. The area of infection was greatly diminished. Though she could still see some redness, the infection was almost resolved. When she finished the exam, she stood for a moment, staring at the patient, seeing the image of the hand, the hand that was caught on the videotape replaying through her mind as it had replayed on the screen.

"Tell her that it looks better. She can come back for a recheck if she has any further problems."

Charlotte started to write in the chart, all businesslike, then picked up the chart and prepared to leave the room. But as she reached the doorway, she turned and looked at Maria Lopez's flat, affectless face, and she hesitated. She had done her job: a breast recheck. The patient had come in for a specific purpose, and Charlotte had fulfilled that purpose and her duty was done. But still she could feel curiosity pushing up in the back of her throat like bile.

Instead of leaving the room she looked at the young woman, doubly veiled behind her impenetrable language and her impassive expression.

If only she could speak Spanish, Charlotte was sure that she could get closer to the patient, could talk around the issue of the abandoned baby at least enough to get a sense of the thing.

For some reason Charlotte thought about the nineteenth-century male doctors who had examined women from behind a drape in order to protect their modesty. What it would have been like to grope blindly like that.

She stared at the woman, unable to leave the room, her heart pounding uncomfortably with something that felt quite close to anger.

"Arecely, ask her how her baby is doing."

Arecely looked slightly surprised. "Charlotte, don't you remember? She said she left her baby in Mexico."

"I know, I know. I just want to know how the baby is doing."

"But she might not know. . . ."

"Ask her anyway."

Arecely shrugged, then muttered something in a low voice. The woman reached up and fingered the flat gold medallion that hung around her neck. She answered in a monosyllable.

"She said the baby is fine."

"That's all she said? That the baby is fine?"

"Charlotte?" Arecely's eyebrows were drawn down; she had flexed one arm up in front of her and was rubbing her finger along the bone of her forearm.

Charlotte realized that her voice was shrill, her professional demeanor cracking, but still she needed to know.

"Ask her how she knows the baby is fine."

Arecely hesitated, opening her mouth as though she were thinking of asking a question, but then she didn't ask; she shrugged again and turned to the patient, saying a couple of long sentences.

Charlotte's heart was pounding, and she felt like her head was being squeezed.

"Arecely?" she said sharply. "What is she saying?"

"She didn't say anything. She said the baby is fine. . . ."

The memory of the small, pinched face of the dead baby came back to Charlotte. She looked at the woman seated on the exam table— waited to see if she would show shame, or remorse, or anything.

Arecely patted Maria on the arm, saying something that sounded re-assuring.

"What was her baby's name again? Ask her her baby's name."

Arecely looked at her a bit oddly.

Maria looked up, unsure whether she was supposed to stand up or not.

"The name," Charlotte said. "Ask her the baby's name."

Arecely said something, and then the patient answered.

"Maria," Arecely said. "The baby's name is Maria."

And what did that prove? Nothing, absolutely less than nothing. Charlotte walked out of the room.

She walked down the blind end of the hallway, feeling her heart pounding, her palms sweating, a constricted feeling in her chest. Charlotte looked at Arecely, who was already walking down the back hallway.

"Arecely?" Charlotte called out.

"Yes?"

"Did she say anything else about the baby?" Charlotte asked.

Arecely looked at her quizzically. "Like what?"

"Just, you know, anything."

"No, she didn't say anything about the baby."

Charlotte stood looking at her for a moment longer. Arecely's face was inscrutable.

Warring in her mind were two sentiments—an intense desire to know if Maria Lopez was the woman who had left her baby in the Dumpster, and a fear that felt like concrete lodged somewhere in her bowels. She wanted to know, but she didn't want the responsibility of knowing. As she looked at Arecely, it started to make her feel angry. For seven years she had come here, to the edge of this mushroom farm, to this run-down clinic, and touched people, and talked to them in the most intimate ways, and yet she remained a stranger. She didn't know what Arecely knew, didn't know what was discussed right in front of her.

Maria Lopez was the last patient of the morning, and Charlotte didn't have to decide whether to confide her doubts in anyone else, because everyone was clustered around the window, staring at the parking lot.

Today was as bright and sunny as the previous day had been stormy. The sun was shining, and even the parking lot looked fresh-scrubbed and clean.

Charlotte walked up to the group. "UPS man?" she asked, expecting to see the familiar brown truck.

"I wish." LeAnn groaned.

Charlotte peered over Flo's shoulder, and to her surprise, she saw two people in the parking lot: a white-haired man and a stoop-shouldered, sandy-haired younger man. Both were holding what appeared to be placards, but the signs were turned so that Charlotte couldn't read what they said.

"What on earth?" she asked.

"I haven't got the faintest idea," Flo said. "I thought I had seen everything . . . but this . . ."

"Looks like a picket line," Mary Louise said. "I think they must be on strike."

"On strike for what?" Flo snorted in a tone that said that she wasn't born yesterday.

"Conditions," Mary Louise said confidently. "They must be on strike for conditions."

That seemed to satisfy everyone, because nobody said anything else. They just stood watching the two men, who were pacing in a small circle out at the far end of the parking lot, close to the entrance from the pike.

While they were standing there, a small, mud-speckled car peeled around the corner into parking lot, causing the two men to split to the sides and scurry like chickens parted by a broom. The car pulled into a parking slot not quite straight, and Mrs. Wetherill got out. They watched from the window, but when Flo realized that Mrs. Wetherill was walking back toward the picketers, she said, more to herself than anyone, "Well, I better go check this situation out."

Mary Louise looked like she was going to follow, but Flo shook her head, and so Mary Louise fell back a step. The group stood for a moment longer, watching Flo stride briskly across the parking lot, but then they lost track of Flo when the big brown UPS truck pulled into the lot and in front of the door.

This time the door was ajar, and so the UPS man burst through it before LeAnn had even had a chance to disappear to freshen up.

"Good day, ladies," he said.

"Hello, there," Mary Louise said in a friendly manner. "We're not on strike," she said. "In case you were wondering. And by the way, young man, I'm Mary Louise. And what is your name?"

Charlotte saw that LeAnn was turning a furious red. "I'm Charlotte," she added, and then Mary Louise added, "And this is LeAnn."

"Osama," he said, smiling even broader, so that his teeth glowed like an Ultra Brite commercial.

"Beg pardon?" Mary Louise said.

The smile faded just slightly, a worried crease flickering across his smooth brown forehead just for a moment.

"Sam," he said. "My name is Sam."

"Well, I could have flat-out swored that you said Osama," Mary Louise said. "Like Osama bin Laden," she added, sticking her finger in her ear and shaking it a little bit. "Never mind, and it sure is a pleasure to meet you, Sam," she said. "Now, LeAnn, why don't you show Sam where to put that box?"

"Yes," he said. "My name is Osama, but you can call me Sam."

"Well, then," Mary Louise said, smiling brightly. "It's a pleasure to meet you, Osama, and Sam it is."

After he had left, LeAnn sat reflectively licking the icing off of a chocolate Tastykake.

"Osama," LeAnn said mournfully. "Osama. Who would've thought? I thought he was Italian, you know, or maybe Greek, but Osama . . . You wouldn't think they would let him drive a UPS truck."

"Now, now," Mary Louise clucked. "You can't judge a book by its cover, and you can't judge a young man by his name . . . although I'll admit it is a most unfortunate name—so I think we should call him Sam, as he wishes."

"Osama . . ." said LeAnn mournfully. "Osama . . ."

But before she got to ruminate much further, Flo burst in through the door, followed close on the heels by Mrs. Wetherill.

"Protesters," Mrs. Wetherill said.

"Nut jobs," Flo added.

"What do you mean, protesters?" Charlotte asked. "They don't like the UPS man?" The UPS man, Sam, was backing his truck out from in front of the window, so Charlotte looked out and saw the stoop-shouldered man and the sandy-haired man pacing out by the road, their placards, still inscrutable, hanging over their shoulders.

Just then the older man's sign tipped at an angle so that she could see the writing on it. There were bold black letters that said DEAD BABIES, with a red circle with a slash through it, and underneath it were the words, BUT THE MIDWIVES DID NOT AS THE KING OF EGYPT TOLD THEM, BUT SAVED THE CHILDREN ALIVE.

Charlotte could feel the blood draining out of her face, and her mouth dropped open in big round O.

Mrs. Wetherill laid a papery hand on her forearm and whispered, "Not to worry, dear. They're just a little confused. Lovely men, really, just not quite"—she tapped on her head—"well, you know."

"Nut jobs," Flo added, punching the number of the state police. "But as far as I can tell, they seem harmless."

LeAnn, who was seated at the desk, let out a sigh so long and mournful that it sounded like a vacuum that had just been switched off.

"I'm in love with a terrorist," she said.

"Nonsense," Mary Louise said. "He seems like a perfectly nice young man."

"Well, I'm calling the police anyway—they've got me on hold," Flo said, tapping her fingernails on the Formica.

LeAnn sat up straighter. "You're calling the police?" And with that she burst into loud sobs.

Flo, who apparently was still on hold, said, "I just think it would be better."

LeAnn started to wail even louder; she grabbed a fistful of Kleenex from the box, and started scrubbing her red nose.

Flo put the phone down. "Well, I'll admit, they do look pretty harmless. If you feel that strongly about it, I guess I don't have to call."

"They . . . they?" LeAnn squealed. "You mean he has an accomplice?"

As though on cue, the younger, sandy-haired placard bearer turned so that Charlotte, who had remained immobile through all this, could see the writing on his sign. On it there was a picture of a blue box with a circle and a line drawn through it, and no writing whatsoever. Charlotte didn't have to wonder what the box represented for long, though, because on the other side of the placard, in angry red letters, it said: DUMPSTER=DEATH.

Charlotte wasn't quite sure if she was going to laugh or cry; she didn't realize she was laughing until a big chortle escaped from her mouth. But the mirth was cut short when Arecely called over from the checkout window, "Um, Charlotte, the chart . . . ?" Charlotte looked down and realized that she was still holding Maria Lopez's chart, and that Maria was standing at the checkout window, waiting for Charlotte to circle a diagnosis code so that she could pay for her visit and leave.

"Oh, sorry, um, I . . ." Charlotte was flustered, annoyed with herself for so thoroughly forgetting what she was doing; she hurriedly found the correct diagnosis—*mastitis, resolving*—and handed the chart to Arecely.

She caught one final glimpse of Maria Lopez on the security camera as she walked through the back parking lot. She held her hands clasped in awkward fists, not quite meeting in front of her belly, and her eyes were cast downward, her thick coiled braid hanging over her shoulder. As she disappeared off the screen, Charlotte found herself hoping that she would completely disappear, go away, never to come back, never to tease her with the intimation of proximity to something terrible, but hidden just out of her sight. Let the police handle it. It wasn't her responsibility.

Apparently Flo had gotten hold of her friend Giselle down at the state troopers' office.

"Mmm-hmm, mmm-hmm, two men carrying signs right out by the street there, on the sidewalk. Okay, okay, sounds good." Flo punched the receiver off with her knuckle, then placed the phone in its cradle.

"They're sending someone right over."

Mary Louise held up her arm, balancing it so that the Timex on its narrow golden band hung over the blue veins on her wrist where she could see it. "Girls, it is twelve twenty, and nobody has gotten a bite to eat so far. I'm going to KFC for a bucket, and I'm not taking no for an answer. LeAnn, you go freshen up. It'll help you develop an appetite."

Ten minutes later they were all sitting around upstairs in the youth room, eating wings and drumsticks, and using up wads of napkins. There wasn't much talking. It seemed that with the morning's excitement they had all worked up an appetite. Over the group, the painting looked benignly at all of them. Charlotte stared at the painting for a long moment; then, licking the last of the salty grease from her fingers, and brushing the crumbs from her lab coat, she stood up and looked out the window. The two protesters were sitting on the grass, a red-and-white-striped box between them, their placards lying on the lawn beside them.

Mary Louise had come and stood next to Charlotte. "Yup, got 'em a box. Just didn't feel right driving past with a twenty-piece box and not giving them anything. I just got them the fingers with mashed and slaw. Figured anyone would like that."

Mary Louise turned and stood face-to-face with the painting of the Virgin, then to Charlotte's surprise, she pulled one of the big blue cushions over and got down on her knees.

In a flash, she said, "Mary, please bless my beautiful daughter Jennifer and help her to make the right decision, and help me to do the right thing by her too. Amen." Then she added, as an afterthought, "And God bless that pig and all that he represents." Then Mary Louise winked at Charlotte, who was standing there looking at her, dumbfounded. And Mrs. Wetherill, who had just come up the stairs, said, "Hear, hear."

"Would you like a piece of chicken, Mrs. Wetherill?" Flo said.

"Oh, no, but thank you, dear. I don't digest that kind of thing very well. I think I'll just stick to my vegetable-and-protein juice."

Not being religious herself, Charlotte wasn't sure what the protocol was on commenting on the contents of a prayer, but just as she was mulling over whether she should ask Mary Louise what was the matter with Jennifer, Flo, who was Catholic, and probably understood this stuff better, spoke up.

"Now what is going on with your daughter Linda, Mary Louise?"

To Charlotte's surprise, Mary Louise, who was normally the soul of self-possession, started wringing her hands and blinking in a way that definitely looked like blinking back tears.

"Well, now that you ask . . . Well, then, I don't want to burden you all with my own little worries."

"Come on, Mary Louise. Tell, tell." the girls clustered around Mary Louise, kneeling down on the cushions next to her. Flo put her arms around Mary Louise, and Arecely surreptitiously handed her a Kleenex, then, glancing up at the Mary in front of her, quickly made the sign of the cross, and Flo, also realizing where she found herself, followed suit.

Mary Louise got off her knees and swung around, settling her bottom into the cushion, took off her glasses and mopped her eyes, and then blew her nose with an emphatic honking sound.

"Oh, just me and my little problems, and with all that's going on here, I just don't feel right going on about myself."

Flo put her hands on Mary Louise's shoulders and said, "Now, Mary Louise, your concerns are no less important than anyone else's concerns, so don't you go talking like that. Why, you're a valuable part of the team here. Isn't she, girls?" And the group started nodding and patting and murmuring *yes, of course* so emphatically that Mary Louise burst into tears all over again, which restarted the routine—Arecely with the Kleenex, the mopped eyes, and the honking nose. Then Mary Louise sniffed a few times and took a few sobby intakes of breath. Flo patted her on the arm a couple more times, and said, in her gentlest voice, "Now, Mary Louise, what could possibly be wrong with that beautiful daughter of yours? She's not sick, is she? Or having a problem with Brian?" Mary Louise sniffed and shook her head no.

"Well, you all are going to think I'm so silly."

Again, a swell of shaken heads and reassuring nos.

"Well," Mary Louise said, putting her glasses back on and squaring her shoulders, "it's just that Brian—that's Jennifer's husband . . ." The girls all nodded their heads. They already knew. "Well, he's getting transferred to Mobile, Alabama, and they talked it all over, and, well, they've decided they're going to go." Mary Louise's eyes were red, but fortunately dry behind her big glasses.

There was a collective pause while the group sorted out what to say, and who should say it. Then Flo, in her capacity as clinic manager, spoke up. "Now, Mary Louise, dear. Of course, we're all going to miss you very much. But you know that your daughter Jennifer would never leave you behind." The group agreed with this, and everyone else chimed in—*of course not, you'll go with her, not the end of the world.*

But Mary Louise stood up, brushing off their pats and reassurances. She turned and glanced at the Virgin behind her, as though for reassurance, and said, "I'm sixty-two years old, thirty years married to a traveling salesman, and I'm tired of following. The thing is"—her voice crescendoed with emotion—"I just don't think I want to go!" And with that, she stamped her foot, and the whole group stood up and clustered around her, bubbling excitedly, *that's right, you don't have to, why should you, why, you can stay right here with us!*

Just then the buzzer sounded, which meant that there was a patient at the door—which had been locked for lunch—trying to get in for an afternoon appointment.

Charlotte glanced at her watch and then hurried down the stairs when she noticed that they were already five minutes late to open the door.

When she got to the window that opened onto the vestibule, she saw Rosalie Saxton, her hair loose around her shoulders and curled in giant waves, her face half-obscured by the pig that was on the counter there.

"You have an appointment, Mrs. Saxton?" Charlotte asked.

"Oh, yes, dear. I'm here to see that darling Mary Louise. And I've brought some fresh zucchini bread for the rest of you."

For a half second, Charlotte opened her mouth to protest, but then she closed it again.

"How lovely of you, Mrs. Saxton. Mary Louise will be right with you."

Charlotte glanced out the front window to see what the protesters were doing. They had obviously finished their lunch and were back at their posts. But her stomach did a somersault when she noticed who was standing next to them, notepad in hands, clad in nicely cut Levi's that showed off his firm, muscled butt. She found herself momentarily hoping that he would stop by the clinic to say hello, but she didn't have to hope for long, because a moment later, Paul Stone turned, and, catching sight of her by the window, he waved and walked purposefully toward the clinic door.

Twenty

Charlotte wasn't at all sure how she ended up driving down Creek Road in Paul Stone's weathered VW Bug a little faster than she was used to, and maintaining a stunned silence.

She remembered Paul's invitation to "go somewhere to talk after work to discuss new information." She remembered that Julie and Kayla Brown were at the Browns' working on a history project—and then by an odd fluke how the last three patients had canceled, and Flo had said, "Go on, get out of here. We'll manage just fine."

But now, as she leaned against the car door, trying to create distance between her body and the body of this stranger, she couldn't remember how she thought it would be okay to go with him, or why she had agreed when he had suggested a coffee place he knew—not too far, with a great view along the Brandywine.

Of course, he *would* drive a VW, a *vintage* VW. Charlie had had one just like this—the same color, a faded navy with a tan interior. How many times had she and Deirdre squeezed together in the passenger seats, with Charlie driving—*Hopper* driving. He used to drive too fast in those days too.

Paul wasn't saying anything. He had the window rolled down, his right hand draped over the steering wheel, his left arm resting on the car door. Pleasant, crisp October air was blasting through the windows. Charlotte felt like a fugitive on the lam. She had left the clinic early—something she never did—and now she was speeding along with a virtual stranger, someone she wasn't sure she knew well enough to trust.

Paul reached over and fiddled with the radio. A song came into focus—it was Tracy Chapman. . . . *you've got a fast car.* . . . Of course. It would be an old song; it would be a song about a car. Charlotte reached up and loosed her hair from the clip that was holding it, and shook it out into the wind. She lifted her chin and tilted her face, and as she felt the full affront of the wind rushing over her, she started to close her eyes. She stayed like that, face tilted up, eyes closed, letting the music and the wind wash through her. She told herself that the driver hadn't noticed, but as the song ended, the car halted at a stop sign; she opened her eyes to find that Paul was looking straight at her, his gaze both frank and appraising.

Charlotte sat up immediately, flustered, feeling that she had been caught out somehow, exposed.

"That . . . song . . ." she stammered.

But Paul seemed to take no notice of her embarrassment. "This is the place," he said, flicking on the directional, which ticked with the old familiar VW sound.

He turned off the road into a parking lot that led up behind a faded frame barn. From the outside, it looked dilapidated, but as he led her around to the back, which was actually the front, she could see that it had been renovated—large panes of glass covered the back of the building, making spacious rooms evident inside. The ground was uneven, old cobblestones with grass growing up among them. Charlotte wobbled, almost twisting her ankle, but Paul's hand shot out to steady her, lingering, it seemed, for just a moment, and then letting go. Just beyond the barn were the banks of the Brandywine, the brown water gurgling along at a brisk pace.

"It's a gallery," Paul said, "but we can have coffee out here on the terrace."

"It's lovely," Charlotte said. "I can't believe I never knew it was here."

"A well-kept secret," Paul said, smiling at her, as though he too had intimate secrets that were kept well.

Again he put his hand lightly on her upper arm, to guide her around the pathway to where there was a lovely terrace overlooking the creek— surrounded by planters filled with bright flowers, and charming little wrought-iron tables and chairs. Again she was uncomfortably aware of the light pressure of his fingertips on her arm, and this time she shrugged, and, tactful, aware of her every gesture, he pulled his fingers away and gestured with his arm toward the table.

After they had been served coffee, in mismatched thin porcelain antique cups, Paul's demeanor changed, and he was all business. Or perhaps his demeanor hadn't changed, and it was only Charlotte, relieved to have facts to focus on, who felt more at ease. She loved the way her little coffee spoon pinged against the fragile cup, garlanded round with sprigs of violets; she loved the way the cream, richer than she was used to, swirled in the little cup.

"This is a lovely place," she said.

Paul grinned as though he were personally responsible for its loveliness. "Glad you like it," he said.

For a moment they sat in pleasant silence, enjoying the beauty of the surroundings. Charlotte could feel some of the day's tension draining out of her. She was glad she had come.

"I've been doing some research," Paul said. His tone was now brisk and businesslike. "Asking around down around the camps, trying to see what, if anything, people know."

"And where do I come into all this?" Charlotte asked.

"Well, I thought you might be able to shed some light on the information that I found—maybe help me put it in perspective. I was talking to some people, sources down around the camps, just asking if anyone suspected anything, if anyone knew somebody who had been pregnant—and then, you know, run off, or whatever."

"How do you know Spanish?" Charlotte interrupted.

"Peace Corps," he said. "Honduras. I was down there helping on road-building projects for two years."

"How interesting," Charlotte said.

"Well, it seems that there is a story going around. Hard to tell whether it's true or not."

Charlotte leaned forward, picked up her cup, took a sip.

"There's a lady who lives in the Smithbridge camp, name of Norma Vasquez. She's American—born and raised here, of Puerto Rican descent. Anyway, her husband works in mushrooms. He's got a good job— what they call a loader."

"A loader?"

"They're the ones who shovel the new loads of humus into the mushroom houses. It's hard work, backbreaking really, but the pay is decent.

"So this Norma . . . Anyway, people are saying that she is going around telling everybody that somebody showed up there, maybe a few weeks ago, saying that she was Rogelio's wife from Mexico. Came into the camps, looking so pregnant she was about to pop, and asked somebody where did Rogelio Vasquez live. Well, the somebody—and I haven't been able to find out who that person was—points out the trailer where he lives, and she heads off in that direction."

Paul paused here, took a ruminative sip of his coffee, stared out at the creek for a moment, then looked back toward Charlotte, that same genial crinkle, a part of a smile, dancing around the corners of his eyes.

"And so . . . ?" Charlotte said.

"And so," Paul continued, "apparently, she heads off there—and it's late, about ten o'clock at night. But you know, the loaders work late, after all the mushroom workers are gone. And supposedly this person sees this pregnant lady head down toward the trailer, and then knock on the door, and supposedly Norma opened the door, and the girl went inside."

"So . . . ?"

"Well, hang on, I'm getting there. So this part is according to Norma. Apparently this girl arrives at the trailer at ten o'clock at night, and tells Norma that she is Rogelio's wife, and that she has come from Mexico— just arrived, come looking for him. So Norma says that the girl got confused, that she must be looking for a different Rogelio Vasquez, that she must have come to the wrong place, and so the girl took off, and Norma hasn't seen her since. Norma didn't mention that the girl was pregnant. When I asked her, she just clamped down her lips and said she didn't know this girl and wasn't going to get into anybody's private business."

"I'm sorry, Paul. I don't—"

"Well, the buzz around the camp is that the girl was pregnant, and some say that everybody knew that Rogelio was married back in his village, and some say people even know the girl, although nobody will admit to knowing her personally. But in any case, people are saying that what really happened is that the two, Norma and the girl, got in a catfight, and that there was so much screaming and bumping around that the neighbors came around to see what was up."

"They were fighting?" Charlotte said. Somehow there was something about this story that was lost on her.

"Well, in any case, several people—you know, a reliable group—told me that an unknown Mexican girl came out of that trailer crying, wailing loud enough to wake the whole neighborhood, and that she took off running, and just ran out of there, disappearing into the night—maybe off into the fields, or down along the railroad tracks."

"And was she pregnant?"

"Well, nobody seems to agree on that. Some people say that they saw clear as day that she was with child, and far along too, but others, just as many, say no, she wasn't pregnant at all. But the thing is, two different people said they saw the same girl standing at the SCOOT bus stop in broad daylight about two weeks later, and both of them agreed without a doubt that she wasn't pregnant then. And one of them said they asked her where the baby was, and she just stared past them and muttered, '*Así lo ha querido dios.*' "

"Which means?"

"You know, it was the will of God, something like that."

"I'm sorry, but you're losing me here."

"Well, they interpreted it to mean that she was telling them the baby was dead."

Charlotte stared out at the bubbling brown water that was coursing along in front of her, a little faster than usual because of the recent heavy rains.

"Did anyone say what she looked like?"

"Just a few things. She had a long dark braid, and was wearing a gold medallion . . ."

Charlotte could feel her fingernails digging into the tablecloth.

"A picture of the Virgin Mary?"

"Yeah, I know," Paul said, smiling ruefully. "That's like saying a white male with medium-brown hair. . . . doesn't give you much to go on."

Paul looked straight at Charlotte. She noticed the way he looked at her, so intent upon her, as if he were going to read her like a book. He slipped his hand over hers for just a moment—his bare hand, hers graced by a gold wedding band.

"This is really getting to you, isn't it?" he said. "Why? Why does it matter so much to you?"

Charlotte moved her hand out of the way and pushed it into her lap. "You know, I found the baby, and that makes me feel responsible, like"— she hesitated, struggling for words—"like maybe I . . . This is going to sound crazy."

"No, really, go ahead."

She looked at him. He was looking at her warmly, really focused, not like Charlie, who it seemed had been half distracted for as long as she could remember.

"Well, I mean, the baby . . . the poor little baby was down in the Dumpster, you know, covered by trash, not . . . not anything dignified at all."

He nodded, his blue eyes looking straight at her, intent, burning her with their intensity. He looked like he just might understand.

"But when I bumped into the Dumpster the baby rolled out, and it was as if, you know, I was meant to find it . . . and I thought, maybe the baby's little soul . . . This is crazy—" She broke off, looked at him searchingly, but he didn't seem to be laughing.

"Like maybe it needed to get out of the Dumpster to let its soul slip free." She stopped talking abruptly and stared past him, out toward the creek again, surprised at herself, surprised that she had articulated this sentiment that right up until this very moment she hadn't even known she felt.

She hazarded a glance back at Paul's face, but he was still looking at her respectfully. Obviously he was a good listener.

"But I don't . . ." she said, forcing the words out. "I don't . . . want to have to be responsible for . . . whoever put the baby there . . . you know, left it for dead, or . . . or . . . killed it . . . or whatever. That's not my job. My job is to take care of people, and just because I found it, or because I found it at the clinic, doesn't mean that I should have to have anything to do with finding the person who did it. I really . . . I really don't want to know."

Again she stared past Paul, afraid to look at his face, afraid that she was rambling on like an idiot, no idea why it was that she felt this sudden need to articulate her innermost feelings to a total stranger. But then, she did know why, in a way, because Charlie, the man who slept beside her every night, would never have understood this, and so, even if he hadn't taken off, she knew she still would have kept it bottled up inside. But she stopped short of telling Paul the whole story either. That it even occurred to her to tell him left her feeling profoundly shaken.

Then to her utmost chagrin, she started sobbing again, and quick as a flash, Paul was squatting at her side, handing her a tissue, draping his arm in a way that was almost, but not quite, brotherly around her shoulders, and she was leaning into him, and mopping her eyes, and sniffling, and he was making gentle soothing sounds.

"I'm sorry," he was saying. "I'm so insensitive. I already knew how much this was bothering you. . . . I just . . . thought . . . you might find it helpful to know anything I know."

Charlotte sniffed and, coming back to her senses, tried to shrug his arm off her shoulder, but he kept it planted there, so she acquiesced and let it stay, and then, giving in just a little further, she let herself lean into him—his firm weight against her like an appealing ballast.

Then, as she conquered her tears, he took his arm off her shoulder and swung around to the other side of the table, sat back down in front of his yellow pad, and started tapping his pencil against the pad as though he hadn't just had his arm around her, as though this moment of intimacy had never happened.

"I just figured that you'd rather hear it from me than hear it for the first time from law enforcement. It's all going to come out anyway."

Then, just as suddenly, he jumped up, waved away her offer to chip in, and disappeared inside. When he came out, he dug around in his pocket for some crumpled dollars that he laid on the table, anchoring them down with a saltshaker so they wouldn't blow away in the cool afternoon breeze.

"Shall we head out?" he asked. And soon they were whizzing back up Creek Road, still a little too fast, and this time, Charlotte was careful to sit straight up in her seat and keep her eyes wide open.

He dropped her in front of the clinic without so much as a "see you later," and Charlotte was relieved to see that the protesters had wrapped up for the day and that everyone else had gone home. She climbed into her car and backed out of the driveway, glad to be heading toward home.

Twenty-one

Sunday morning, coffee at Deirdre's. Charlotte decided to walk along the road instead of cutting through the woods so that she would arrive at the front door. In the distance, she could see the house—tall and imposing, set back from the road behind an immensity of lawn. Out beyond the house, on the other side, she could just see the tennis courts, surrounded by high hedges of arborvitae. Though she had driven by this house at least twice a day every day for years, she had never really realized how big it was. Standing in front, just shy of the tall stone pillars that led to the long driveway, she felt momentarily small. For a moment, she was struck by the old feeling, long forgotten, of the way she often used to feel around Deirdre, a combination of awe and fear, admixed with equal measures of both envy and delight.

That was how it had always been with Deirdre; it was just that after all these years Charlotte had forgotten.

But her reflections were cut short. Deirdre, in a whirl of flying hair and gesturing arms, flew out the big double front doors of the house and rushed out, running down the driveway.

"Charlotte, darling. There you are. Come in, come in."

Then, holding her at arm's length, she said, "Oh," and, "Look how lovely it is to see you. Charlotte—don't you ever change? You haven't changed at all."

This led Charlotte to a burst of self-conciousness, and she reached down and tugged at the waist of her jeans, pulled on the hem of her T-shirt.

"And you too . . . you . . ."

"Nonsense, I've aged terribly. Altogether too much sun."

And it was true that Deirdre had changed quite a bit. She was thinner now—bony and angular, and her face was latticed with the fine lines of someone who had spent a lot of time out in the sun. She was dressed simply—blue jeans and some kind of barn boots, but Charlotte could guess that everything, from the sterling-silver clasp in her hair to her leather boots, muddy, was probably exquisite and one-of-a-kind. Deirdre had been beautiful, stop-turn-around-and-stare beautiful, and now almost twenty years older she was still arresting, a head-turner, the kind of person you'd turn to look at twice because she looked like she must be "someone."

When Deirdre pushed the double doors open, Charlotte was surprised—the Colonial house was just a shell; inside, the house was modern, and architecturally stunning. There were uneven random-width floors, a few beams and artfully exposed brick walls, but the entire back of the house had been pushed out and was covered with floor-to-ceiling windows. Deirdre walked briskly toward the back of the house, soon surrounded by a couple of golden retrievers and a Jack Russell terrier, who came up to Charlotte and bumped her hands with their wet noses. Deirdre led her to a glass-walled sunroom overlooking the back gardens and the pools. From here it looked like all of Chester County belonged to Deirdre. In the foreground was her carefully landscaped pool, the water glittering aqua in the sunlight, surrounded by wide expanses of lawn. Then out in the distance, there were peaceful green fields, dotted with green trees, an old bank barn, and way off in the distance, the light glinting off the water of the Brandywine Creek. It was as though everything in the world belonged to her—there was no trace of Charlotte's neighborhood, Millstone Manor. It was completely hidden behind the band of woods.

Deirdre showed Charlotte to a chair next to a pretty wrought-iron table in the sun-drenched room, and walked across the terra-cotta tiles into the adjoining kitchen.

"Don't mind the granite," Deirdre said, as she got out a French press coffeemaker and started preparing to make coffee. "I know. It's perfectly dreadful. What can I say?"

Charlotte was not sure she had ever seen such a beautiful kitchen; the "dreadful" granite that Deirdre was referring to was a lovely stippled rose—there were wide expanses of it that shone with perfection. Everything gleamed—the stainless-steel appliances, the buffed-wood cabinets.

"Now, Charlotte," Deirdre said, "start at the beginning, and tell me everything."

Charlotte felt the hair on the back of her neck stand on end.

How many times, after Deirdre had missed a few days of Charlotte's life, a few weeks during vacation, sometimes even a few hours, "Start at the beginning, and tell me everything."

But this time Charlotte wasn't sure where to start. Her brief bio sounded so uninteresting. Married Charlie. Had Julie. Went to nursing school, became a nurse practitioner. Worked at El Centro . . .

Deirdre brought over a little tray and set it on the table, as usual effortlessly elegant. She poured out two cups of coffee, the scent pungent and aromatic—no doubt some special brew that cost lots of extra money.

"Okay, so . . ." Deirdre leaned forward, looking at her. It was true her face was thinner now, and she looked older, of course, but Deirdre was still a stunner—that thick curly hair, those fantastic almond-shaped wedges for eyes. Charlotte had always found it immensely flattering just to have her friend look at her so intensely, and right away she started slipping into that old feeling.

It wasn't long before Charlotte and Deirdre were exchanging confidences.

"Juan-Luis drank. It was terrible. He was dead drunk when he fell off that horse. Never would have landed like that if he hadn't been. Just fell smack on his head like a stone. Thank God, I didn't see it. But I've always been able to imagine it. . . ." Deirdre was leaning forward, her long fingers clasped, eyebrows arched up. "Apparently he just fell, and people heard a snap, and then . . . that was it. He never moved again."

"Oh, Deirdre, how perfectly dreadful," Charlotte murmured. It came easily to her, slipping back into the role of the cherished confidante. Deirdre, whose stories were always dramatic, outrageous, and Charlotte, the loyal friend, the listener.

"So now, tell me about all of your good works."

Charlotte told Deirdre about El Centro—about the money problems, about the dead baby in the Dumpster.

"Oh, yes, sounds dreadful," Deirdre said, in a polite way that indicated that she found the entire topic sort of dull. "You'll have to let me know when you have a charity drive," Deirdre said, as though to close down the subject.

"Well, you see," Charlotte said, "we have this pig. . . ." But then she trailed off, because a young woman had come into the kitchen. Deirdre turned and said something to the woman in rapid Spanish, and the woman—clearly a housekeeper of some kind, as she was wearing an apron with a pair of rubber gloves hooked over the waist tie—turned with a startled look and then nodded, mumbled an answer, and hurried out of the room.

Deirdre turned back toward Charlotte and smiled graciously.

"New help." She shook her head conspiratorially, including Charlotte, with her gesture, into the world of people who understood problems with help.

But Charlotte was staring past her, toward where the young woman had disappeared, startled at the sudden recognition.

"Isn't that . . . Maria Lopez?" Charlotte blurted out, and then immediately regretted it; she had no right to betray her patient's confidentiality.

"Maria Lopez? Oh, do you know her? Has she worked for you? No, I don't believe that's her name. Let me call her in. Just a minute. Maria. *Venga* . . ."

A moment later, the same young woman stood before them. Charlotte thought she looked terrified, but Deirdre didn't seem to notice anything.

"*Dime. ¿Cómo te llamas?* Is this the person you were talking about?"

Charlotte looked up at the square face—she had seen it once looking anxious, and once looking impassive. Now the features were flattened out with fear. She felt ashamed to have the woman called before her to be stared at like that.

"Maria," the woman whispered. "Maria Sanchez."

"Oh, I'm sorry," Charlotte said. "She looks a lot like another . . . girl . . . I know."

"They do all look a bit alike, these Mexicans, don't you think? So Mayan," Deirdre said.

"No, I really don't think so," Charlotte muttered, offended. "No, it's just . . ." she trailed off, uncertain what to say.

Deirdre said something else that Charlotte couldn't understand, and the girl whom she knew as Maria Lopez disappeared again, across the wide floorboards and into the shadows of the house, taking her secrets with her.

Charlotte had a sour taste in her mouth from this exchange. She was trying to remember if Deirdre had always been like this. She didn't recall Deirdre denigrating other people. Had she changed from living for fifteen years on an Argentinian plantation, married to one of Argentina's wealthiest men, or had she always been like that, and Charlotte just hadn't seen it? It seemed so long ago.

But she didn't get too much time to think about it, because a moment later Deirdre's daughter, Ariel, appeared from another direction.

"Ariel, come and say hello to Charlotte."

Charlotte noted again the tone that Deirdre used to address her daughter, conspicuously lacking in warmth.

"Hello, Ariel," Charlotte said.

"Talking about me?" Ariel said bluntly.

"Indeed, we were not. We hardly think you're that interesting," Deirdre said.

Ariel rolled her eyes. Charlotte took in the full extent of what she was wearing—jeans that looked almost shredded with age, except for the small Prada label on the back pocket, and a too-tight, too-short T-shirt with the words BITCH SLUT embroidered across her chest.

Had Julie come out dressed like that, she would have promptly gotten the march-back-to-your-room-and-take-off-that-dreadful-shirt-this-instant speech, but Deirdre didn't particularly seem to notice what she was wearing.

"Coffee, dear?"

"No," Ariel said. Then, fixing her eyes on Charlotte with a look of challenge, she added, "Just looking at it makes me feel like puking."

Charlotte noted again the young woman's unusual expression. Her eyes were a pretty shade of green, but there was something just a bit odd about them—something hard. For a half second a flash of Deirdre as she had been at that age came to her. Deirdre had always been beautiful, stunning, but with something unusual about her eyes.

Charlotte looked at Ariel, her eyebrows rising almost imperceptibly. Was Ariel trying to tell her something?

"Oh, Ariel, what a disgusting way of putting it," Deirdre drawled. "You can simply say, 'No, thank you.' "

Charlotte noted again the lack of warmth between the mother and daughter. Not the typical teenage thing—more like a distance, a coldness. It was odd.

"Well, I do feel like puking," she said. "Not that, you know, it's any of your business." Ariel picked up a biscotti from the edge of the counter, nibbled it inquisitively, then put it down—right back on the plate that Deirdre had been serving from. Then she headed off into the bowels of the house again, leaving them for a moment in silence.

"Oh, aren't they impossible at this age? Frankly impossible." Deirdre leaned forward, eyebrows slanted up like airplane wings, ready to unleash another confidence.

"She's the reason I sold the farm in Virginia." Deirdre had a stage whisper she used to great effect. "She was seeing someone much older—Bruce O'Hanlon—do you know him? Oh, of course, you don't know him. The horse trainer—he rode in the . . . oh, when was it . . . maybe the 'eighty-four Olympics. Trains out of Middleburg. Older. *Much* older. Fifty-something. Had a history of going after rich women of a certain age, and then there he was, mixed up with Ariel, who is really just a baby. A disaster. She wouldn't listen to a word I said, so I up and sold the farm, just like that. I'm not sure she'll ever forgive me."

Charlotte didn't need to ask, because she knew how old Ariel was—seventeen, to Julie's fifteen. She remembered exactly when Deirdre had run off with Juan-Luis, three months shy of their college graduation—and the birth six months later.

"Oh, Deirdre, you did the right thing. Absolutely. Girls that young don't belong with much older guys. Believe me. I see the consequences of that kind of relationship all the time—"

Then she cut herself off and blushed, because obviously they both knew that Juan-Luis, the Argentinian playboy, must have been at least twice Deirdre's age. Charlotte didn't know exactly how old he'd been, but he was probably in his thirties back then at least—if not in his forties.

Deirdre, always quick to pick up on nuance, spoke up quickly. "Don't worry—of course, Charlotte, I know you're right. Juan-Luis was much, much too old for me." Again the whisper. "We were never happy. . . ." She leaned back in her chair and sighed passionately. "But it was . . . how can you say it . . . a crazy love."

"It must have been terrible to lose him so suddenly," Charlotte said, then turned her head as she heard a sound at the end of the room. She saw that the girl, Maria, had come back into the room, and was quietly dusting bookshelves in the shadowy far recesses of the room.

"Ah, yes . . ." Deirdre said. *"Así lo ha querido Dios."*

But Charlotte didn't have time to ask for a translation—both women turned their heads suddenly and half rose from their seats as a tremendous crash emanated from the end of the room.

Charlotte was momentarily confused, not sure what had caused the noise, but Deirdre rose quickly from the table and strode across the room, her muddy boots thumping hollowly on the wooden floor.

Now Charlotte could see that it was the girl, Maria, who had knocked something over—a big porcelain vase of some kind, and it lay shattered on the floor.

Deirdre was shouting at Maria in rapid, incomprehensible Spanish, and the girl started sobbing loudly and pulled her apron up over her face, bending her head down but staying immobile in the downpour of Deirdre's tirade.

Then suddenly the tirade ended, and Deirdre was putting her arm around the young woman and handing her a Kleenex, talking to her in soft, murmuring tones. Then Deirdre got the broom and dustpan from the kitchen and started sweeping up the shards, smiling at the young girl in her most charming and heartwarming manner. When all was done, Deirdre poured the young woman a cup of coffee, which Maria took outside onto the terrace, and Deirdre came back to join Charlotte, smiling calmly, as though nothing had just happened.

"Household help," Deirdre said for the second time that morning. "Poor dear, she's as green as they get, and jumpy, but I'm sure she'll do just fine."

"I hope that vase wasn't something special to you."

"Absolutely not," Deirdre said. "Just something the decorator picked out. I didn't particularly care for it at all."

"I was just wondering, Deirdre, what you said," Charlotte said.

"What did I say about . . . ?"

"Um, you know, you said something in Spanish, um, just before she knocked over the vase."

"I did?"

"Yes, I said, 'I'm sorry that you lost Juan-Luis so suddenly,' and you said something . . ."

"I don't even remember what I said. I must have said, '*Así lo ha querido Dios.*'"

"Which means?"

"Oh, it's what the Spanish say—you know, God's will. 'It was as God willed it,' something like that."

Charlotte looked at Deirdre, and almost—*almost*—felt like she could see an odd flash of yellow light in her eyes, but then Deirdre pulled herself together and gave Charlotte her most illuminated smile. "I don't really believe that, of course. The man was stone drunk." She sighed. "But you know, he was a good man."

"Do you think it upset Maria when you said that?"

"My dear Charlotte, whatever are you talking about? We weren't even speaking to her. She's just clumsy. They all are, when they start. It's purely nerves."

"But perhaps, if she had lost someone . . . ?"

Deirdre looked at Charlotte a moment too long—appraisingly.

"My dear Charlotte, you always have had the most original ideas." Then she hastened to add, "Always Charlotte. I'm so glad to have found you ever so much the same."

Somehow, when Deirdre said this, it occurred to Charlotte that it had been so long since they had seen each other, and that in fact she was scarcely the same person at all. Fifteen years of working in health care, of being married, of raising a daughter. While on the outside, she might look like a photograph faded by going through the wash a few times, on the inside, she was different. Totally different . . . wasn't she?

"But you . . . you ended up with Hopper—now, that . . . that was the prize."

Charlotte peered at the dregs of coffee in her mug.

"More coffee," Deirdre said. "Let me."

"No really, I . . ." She stood up. "It's been lovely. So lovely catching up. And we'll have to do this again soon."

"What luck," Deirdre said. "What divine luck we've had, finding each other again. Now the only thing left is to see Hopper."

Hopper. Why was it so hard for Charlotte to remember back to when Charlie had been Hopper?

"It will be the three of us together again."

"The five of us," Charlotte said.

"Five?" Deirdre looked puzzled.

"The children," Charlotte said.

Deirdre threw her head back, laughing. "Oh, of course, silly me, the children."

"Well, it certainly is odd that we've ended up neighbors again," Charlotte said, afraid that her voice was betraying her newfound misgivings about letting Deirdre back into her life. "Quite a coincidence that you ended up moving to Westville."

Deirdre was standing next to her, holding out her jacket for her. She tipped her head back and laughed again in her musical way.

"Oh, but it wasn't a coincidence. I just found myself so alone in Virginia, with Juan-Luis gone and all of the troubles with Ariel, and I thought to myself, If I only I could see Charlotte, my ballast. Then, when

I remembered that you lived in Westville, horse country, it seemed like the perfect invitation of fate.

"Of course, I didn't know"—Deirdre smiled beguilingly—"that you'd find me a farm right next door. . . . So that just proves it."

Charlotte was so stunned by this unexpected revelation that she almost didn't know what to say. "Proves what?"

"Why, that I did the right thing in coming here. We'll be the best of friends again. Just like old times."

Deirdre attempted to link her arm through Charlotte's, just the way they used to do, but Charlotte instinctively pulled away.

"I . . . thanks for the coffee, Deirdre. Lovely house." Charlotte found herself rushing toward the door as though she wouldn't be able to breathe until she got out of the house.

Twenty-two

On Monday morning, Julie needed a ride to school because she had to be there early for a club meeting, so Charlotte was the first one to get to the clinic. She was relieved to see nobody in the parking lot, no cars, no protesters. She sat in her office, methodically working her way through the stack of papers. It was soothing, predictable—sign, date, sign, date. Then she paused for a moment, listening, when she thought she heard footsteps coming from the upstairs room. . . .

Her office had no windows, but she knew it was windy outside, probably just something scudding against the roof. She sat like that for a moment longer, but hearing nothing further, she focused back on her work.

But a few moments later, she thought she heard a toilet flushing. Now she felt slightly frightened.

Charlotte stood up, irresolute for a moment, trying to decide whether she should pursue the source of the noise, or do nothing. Now she heard footsteps again, more clearly. Perhaps one of the girls had come in early? But the security lock had been on when she got there. She had had to punch in the code to unlock the door. Charlotte could feel the hair standing up on the back of her neck. She walked out of her office and glanced out into the parking lot. Now the Channel Six news van was there. She stood still, listened carefully, heard nothing.

Just to appease her curiosity, she decided to head upstairs.

Charlotte paused at the top of the stairwell, forgetting for a moment why she had come. The hazy morning light filtered through the dormer windows, softening the edges of the room so that it seemed bathed in a benign glow. In the morning light, the painting of the Virgin was particularly illuminated, seeming to glow from within, and more than ever she was reminded of the Botticelli of her youth, the way the painting had glowed for her from within, as though a beacon on a dark night. Charlotte stared at the painting, feeling a chill seep into her bones. She hadn't realized it, but her world had darkened and closed in on her again, taking her by surprise, happening all of a sudden. The miscarriage, Charlie's disappearance, Deirdre's reemergence. Pushing around the edges of her consciousness, she realized too, was the fact that her hands had held a dead baby, a baby that came up from the depths of the trash can like a ghost that you'd been waiting for, for many years.

The room was still and silent. Mary was smiling modestly, eyes downcast. Along the wall, like offerings, were a few things—an empty cup stained faintly blue from soda pop, an empty Wawa bag with a bagel/sausage wrapper half stuffed into it. Charlotte noted, with surprise, that there were a couple of candle stubs, mostly burned all the way down, in cheap glass holders, the kind you got at the dollar store.

Funny. But she didn't have time to think about it, because just then she heard a distinct rustling sound coming from behind the closed bathroom door—she whirled around, startled by the close proximity of the sound, but then just as suddenly she heard a half-stifled scream coming from behind her in the stairwell.

Charlotte, who had, without realizing it, knelt in front of the painting, jumped up, startled, and whirled around in the direction of the scream.

At first, in the dim light of stairwell, Charlotte couldn't see anything, and so she started backing away, contemplating an escape route—should she open a window and scream, or barricade herself in the bathroom?

But a split second later, amid more screams, Arecely came into view—hot coffee spilled all the way down the front of her scrub top, which she was rapidly pulling over her head while screaming, "Ow, ow, ow," in pain. Charlotte quickly took in the situation and reacted by grabbing Arecely's arm.

"Come on. Let's get some cold water on that." She could see the spatter of burn marks across Arecely's chest, and pulled her toward the bathroom door.

But Arecely tugged away and wrenched her arm loose, dropping her scrub top on the floor in a heap, along with a Burger King bag that she had held clutched in her hand. She took off down the stairs, and Charlotte ran after her, following her to the bathroom at the foot of the stairs and following her inside, where Arecely was splashing water on her reddened chest.

"Okay, it feels a little better now," she said after a moment, and plucked a couple of paper towels from the rack and started patting it dry. "That coffee was hot—it was burning me something awful."

"Arecely, I am so sorry. I didn't mean to startle you. I didn't hear you on the stairs." Charlotte remembered for a moment that she had thought that the sounds were coming from the bathroom behind her, but then she shoved past the thought.

"No, I'm sorry. I didn't mean to startle you. I didn't know you were here."

"Let me take a look at that," Charlotte said, now that Arecely was finished patting herself dry.

Charlotte reached out to Arecely's chest and touched carefully with the tips of her fingers—the splashes of red were already fading. It wasn't much of a burn. She was going to be fine.

Arecely suddenly seemed to notice that she was half-naked. She looked down at her bra, which had a couple of splashes of pale brown on it, then down across her belly.

Charlotte noticed that Arecely blanched and then shot a hand out to the white porcelain sink to steady herself.

"Are you okay?" Charlotte said.

"I'm okay," Arecely said, turning her head and ducking into the toilet stall.

"I'm going to go look for another shirt for you," Charlotte said, walking out the door without waiting for a reply.

She walked over to the laundry area, where there were always a few extra scrub tops in case anyone got dirty. She grabbed one off a hanger, then carried it back to the bathroom.

"I'm leaving it right here on the sink," Charlotte said, then left without waiting for a reply. She glanced at her watch. Only ten minutes until the time when staff would be arriving. Her pile of labwork still sat on her desk, mostly untouched.

She turned back toward the stairs, deciding to go pick up Arecely's dirty scrub shirt and her breakfast from where she had dropped it.

Charlotte walked up the stairs. When she got back up into the room, the transcendent quality of the early morning light had been replaced by the more prosaic and utilitarian light of the workday. She stooped to pick up Arecely's dirty shirt, her eyes turned toward the painting, which now looked flat and ordinary, no longer glowing from within.

Now where was that Burger King bag? Charlotte looked on the floor, but there was no sign of it. Hadn't Arecely dropped a bag on the floor, right next to her scrub top—a bag that smelled of hash browns and a sausage buscuit?

Twenty-three

Arecely tugged at the hem of the scrub top, trying to pull it down a little lower. It didn't fit her very well. She wished Charlotte had chosen one of the bigger ones, but she didn't want to call attention to herself by changing one clean scrub shirt for another. Her stomach had had that raw feeling inside ever since she had vomited after spilling the coffee all over herself. She had tried nibbling on some saltines, but nothing seemed to work. The sour churning was still creeping up the back of her throat every minute. It was all she could do to keep it down.

Arecely was in the exam room tidying up. Trying to keep busy, to stay off Charlotte's radar. Charlotte had been oversolicitous all morning, hovering around. *How's your chest? Do you want me to look at it?* She didn't think Charlotte had heard her vomiting, but still . . . And so what if Charlotte did know she was pregnant? It wasn't really any of the nurse's business anyway. Plus, she knew Charlotte. *Oh, isn't that wonderful? Isn't that great? Congratulations,* she would say. Charlotte treated everyone the same—any slut or cokehead, any fourteen-year-old anybody could see shouldn't be having a baby, Charlotte would smile and say something nice. But she wouldn't really notice. She wouldn't clue in if something was really wrong, if somebody needed to do something in a hurry—if the baby's father was fixing to beat the crap out of her, or if somebody didn't have any place to go. . . .

That was Charlotte. She knew, but she didn't know. She could figure out what was wrong with you—yeast, or trich, or chlamydia—but even so, Arecely didn't think that Charlotte could always see what was right smack in front of her. It was like she saw what she wanted to see, and what she wanted to see was a world where everybody was nice, and did the right thing . . . Only the world wasn't like that. You could try to be that way yourself, but you shouldn't go around waiting for others to be that way too.

That was how she felt when she had to tell Charlotte what the patients were saying in Spanish. It was right there, clear as day, but Charlotte couldn't hear it. Couldn't hear it unless Arecely translated it. It was just a weird thing to be standing right in front of someone, looking at them, but blocked off so that you couldn't see them at all.

It had been really slow at the clinic all day, lots of no-shows, lots of cancellations. The protesters were still out there, circling like vultures with their signs. What exactly were they protesting, anyway? Arecely didn't get it. Everybody already knew that you didn't put a dead baby in a Dumpster unless you were crazy, or desperate, or something. So what was the point of protesting? It didn't make any sense.

Arecely stood next to the clean countertop, carefully folding paper drapes into squares and stacking them neatly next to her. Her actions were precise and steady, but inside she felt shaky and odd. She had always been the first one into the clinic, and this morning, when the alarm was switched off when she got there, she should have noticed that something was amiss. But she had been so impressed by all the newspeople hanging around that she hadn't even thought about it. Linda Rodriguez had smiled at her and said, "Hi, Arecely," just like that. "Hi, Arecely, I brought something for you." And Linda had popped right out of the van and handed her a paperback book, pressed it into her hand, and said, "I thought you might like it."

And so that was what she was doing when she went inside. When she should have been paying attention to the alarm system, she was thinking, *Hi, Arecely*, just like she really was somebody, and reading the description on the back of the book. It was called *The House on Mango Street*. A book from Linda Rodriguez, who had been paying attention to her, and remembered that she liked to read. *Hi, Arecely* . . . So that was what happened when you let your head get in the way of things.

Or she could have noticed Charlotte's sweater and purse on her chair in the clinician's office. And since she came in the front parking lot this morning, instead of walking through the fields, she didn't even notice Charlotte's car, which must've been parked around back, away from all the TV vans.

So she had walked in and headed up those stairs, eager to get rid of the coffee and sausage biscuit, since the smell had been making her a little queasy, not realizing at all that Charlotte was already there.

If only she hadn't jumped and spilled her coffee . . . But then again, it could have been worse, because even while her chest was burning, she had still had the presence of mind to run down the stairs to the bathroom.

But now, thinking about this, she just felt stupid again. She had Zekie counting on her, and now this new baby, announcing its intention to stay by making her sick all the time. Arecely put the clean folded drapes away in the drawer and then pulled latex gloves on and popped open the lid of the trash to empty the red biohazard bag. She did it quickly, as this was accompanied by the familiar wave of nausea.

So what was she doing? Arecely picked up the red bag and looked around the room, everything clean now and smelling of antibacterial spray. She felt a small sense of satisfaction at the clean and organized space she was leaving behind, but the satisfaction was muted by the worry that she wore over her shoulders like a cloak.

But then again, what could she do? If it weren't for the fact that she was pregnant, for the fact that the smell of stale cigarette smoke made her nauseous, then she might not have known either, she might have gone happily along the way behind the wall of not knowing, just like Charlotte. But once you did know, then what? What were you going to do? Were you going to turn your back and walk away? Arecely felt a few mild cramps in her lower belly—just another way that the baby reminded her it was there. Well, you did what you could, Arecely thought. You did what you could, one woman to another, and hoped for the best.

Arecely leaned over to pick up the red bag, which she was going to carry out to the trash, but she must have stood up too quickly, because she felt light-headed and started seeing swirling lights around her eyes.

The next thing she knew, she was lying on the sofa out near the clinician's office, with an ice pack held to a bump on her forehead. She opened her eyes, blinked for a moment, and saw Mary Louise, looking at her intently through her glasses, and Charlotte was waving a small white tube that smelled horrible in front of her nose, and as the odor really hit her, she started to sit up again, positive that she was going to barf. Mary Louise reached up and smoothed her hair away from her brow, just the way her own mother used to do it. Arecely leaned a little closer to Mary Louise, away from Charlotte, because Mary Louise's smell was comforting—a little baby powder, a little hand cream, a combination of smells that seemed to soothe her stomach.

"Now there, there, dear," Mary Louise said soothingly, and Arecely closed her eyes for just a moment, letting go in Mary Louise's comforting presence. "You're all right, dear. You just passed out. I bet you didn't eat any breakfast this morning—isn't that it?"

Arecely noticed that through the nausea and the slight throbbing of her head, she could now feel the unmistakable signs of hunger. Arecely could hear Charlotte, kind of in the background, saying, "But she had a sausage biscuit . . ."

But Mary Louise was ignoring her. "The girl is hungry," she said. "It's as plain as the nose on my face."

Later, after she had eaten half of Mary Louise's ham-salad sandwich, and drunk all of her fresh iced tea, and eaten two-thirds of her apple while Mary Louise had clucked and protested, "Go ahead and finish. A growing girl needs to eat," she sat against the cool wall upstairs and listened, without paying too close attention, while Mary Louise said a little prayer to Mary about her daughter Jennifer, which made Arecely feel a little less embarrassed while she said a prayer of her own. For a moment, as she sat there, looking at Mary's kind eyes, she wondered if she should tell Mary Louise what was going on, but in the end she didn't. Then she and Mary Louise went back downstairs, and Mary Louise gave her a nice pat on the forearm and said, "Now there. Now you've got some pink in your cheeks," and Arecely started to feel better for the first time that day.

Twenty-four

There were people in the parking lot, people like mad—the news crews; the protesters, who somehow during the day had gone from two to nine or ten; and then there were the gawkers—people who had just come to look at the spectacle. It was pretty warm outside, so most of the people were in shirtsleeves—some wearing old rock-concert T-shirts, a few moms with babies in strollers. They primarily seemed interested in waving at the TV people and trying to get on camera. Somebody, an older woman barely five feet tall, with her hair in a graying bun, was selling tamales; and another person, a man, had a flat cardboard tray hung around his neck, and on it were steaming cups of *champurrado*, and a basket of hard-boiled eggs. The troopers had roped off the edges of the parking lot, so that the people would stay back, but every once in a while a group of two or three teenage boys would push forward, waving their arms—"Over here, over here"—at the cameramen.

There were two state trooper cars guarding the entrance to the parking lot, making sure that cars could pass through, but aside from the TV factotums going in and out on coffee runs from time to time, there were no patients.

LeAnn, Flo, and Mary Louise spent much of the morning watching out the window—there was nothing else to do. Arecely had scrubbed the exam rooms to a fare-thee-well before she had passed out. All of their papers were filed; all of their charts were in order—nobody was coming in.

"Well, would you want to walk past that circus to get your birth-control pills?" Flo said, to no one in particular after an especially long lull. The women didn't know how to be not-busy together. They had long since run out of things to say.

"Right. Teenager comes in to get pills. Her dad sees it on the evening news," LeAnn said.

Now, while they were watching, a green Porsche convertible with the top down pulled into the parking lot. From the passenger side, Dorothea Wetherill got out, a kerchief that made her look sporty tied around her head. From the other side emerged a tall woman wearing a green business suit. She plucked a briefcase from the backseat.

"Now who is the heck is that?" Mary Louise said.

"Briefcase, Porsche. The lawyer . . ." Flo breathed. "Who else could it be?"

They walked across the parking lot, seemingly oblivious to the crowd of people who were watching, and came in the front door.

"Good morning, everybody," Dorothea said. "This is Barbara Volpone."

"The attorney," Flo said, confident now.

"Hello, everyone." Her voice was deep and throaty, her manner commanding. She was very tall and skinny as a stick, with jet-black hair that hung to just above her shoulders, then turned up with an insouciant flip. She was commanding rather than pretty, with a long, angular face and eyebrows that formed a V so confident that they seemed to shout victory.

"Quite a circus out there, but not to worry," she said, taking her green suit jacket off and throwing it over a chair. "Now first order of business— have they been blocking access to the clinic?"

"They who?" Flo asked.

"The protesters," Barbara said.

"We haven't seen anyone all day. Not a single patient," LeAnn said.

"Well, when we came through, the driveway was clear. Has it just recently been cleared?"

"Well, to be fair," Mary Louise said, "I don't think those nice men with their silly placards were exactly blocking the way. It's just that . . ."

"It's just that . . . what?" Barbara made it clear that she would brook no unfinished sentences.

"Well, people are coming here for Pap tests," Mary Louise said.

"And to get birth control," LeAnn said.

"And for pregnancy tests," Flo added.

"And?" Barbara said, clearly not doing the math.

"And . . . well . . ." Mary Louise said, pausing as though trying to think of exactly what to say.

"Can somebody get to the point here? I have exactly twenty minutes before I have to hit the road again."

"It's embarrassing to come to El Centro for an appointment when there are news crews standing outside. And whole crowds of people standing watching the news crews. And if you came for an appointment, all of those people would be watching you."

"Embarrassing?" Barbara said, tapping her finger against the countertop as though this were a complication that she hadn't planned for. "Why on earth would it be embarrassing? You're losing me here. . . . I mean, they're just getting Paps and birth control and stuff, right?"

"People from this part of the county are very shy," Flo said diplomatically.

Barbara's V deepened until it looked less like victory and more like a bird in flight. She peered suspiciously at Flo.

"It's a cultural thing," Flo said. *"Es una problema cultural,"* she added for a touch of authenticity.

Barbara's eyebrows relaxed. "Oh, a cultural thing. I see. Well, we have to be sensitive to that."

Just then, though, a lime green Mazda Miata came into the parking lot and pulled into a slot so fast that even from inside the clinic, they could hear the sound of squealing rubber. And a girl got out, so nonchalant, so seemingly oblivious to the crowds who were watching her, that she could have been completely alone. She was tall, and wearing a cropped T-shirt that showed off her Britney Spears–type body, and she walked slowly across the parking lot, her blond ponytail flipping back and forth as though she believed being watched by paparazzi were her due.

"Well, here you go. Here comes someone, and as you can see, she got right through," Flo said.

"Good, then I won't be needed in here. I'm going out to talk to the press."

"I'll come," Flo said.

"From now on," Barbara said, looking at Flo from beehive to nurse's shoes, "media is my domain."

Flo looked like she was going to be hurt, and then changed her mind. "Fine," she said. "And welcome to it."

Barbara snapped her briefcase shut and pulled on her jacket with a one-handed tug that somehow restored her to her previous state of perfection; then she buzzed out the door so that she crossed paths with Ariel Saramago, who brushed through the door just as Barbara was leaving.

Twenty-five

A riel was chatting on her cell phone while Charlotte was dipping her urine for a pregnancy test. Normally, while she was waiting for the dipstick to show one line or two, she asked the patient a series of questions—last menstrual period, any bleeding or spotting, any cramping or pain. But there was something oddly assertive about Ariel, and Charlotte decided to wait her out. It wasn't as though she were in a hurry anyway—Ariel was the first patient she had seen all day, if you didn't count Arecely, who had inexplicably passed out.

Charlotte stared at the dipstick—the negative line always showed up first, and sometimes, when she stared at the strip, the positive line would seem to blink in and out in front of her eyes, as though it hadn't yet decided what it wanted to say. So now Charlotte stared at Ariel's pregnancy test and tried to will it to stay negative—as though she had some control over that, or some control over anything. But she couldn't shake the feeling that she wanted to send Ariel out of the clinic with a negative pregnancy test, and so send her out of her own domain.

Ariel finally stopped talking, flipped her little silver phone shut, and dropped it into her Kate Spade bag. Charlotte turned to her, and not quite looking at Ariel's unusual eyes, she started through her litany of questions, marking down the answers in the slots on the chart.

She turned her back on the dipstick in order to write, willing one last time that when she turned around there would still be only one line.

"First day of your last menstrual period?" Charlotte said, and wrote the answer on the paper.

"Any bleeding since your last period?"

"Well, actually, I have been spotting a little bit."

Charlotte looked up from her paper the eye.

"How much spotting?"

"Um, I kept thinking my period was coming on, but it never really did."

"Any pain?"

Ariel reached up her hand and pointed toward her lower belly, down and to the right from her opal belly-button ring.

"Just there?" Charlotte said, now fully focused. "Just on one side, or do you feel the pain all over?"

"It's mostly just there."

Charlotte turned around, looking over her shoulder, knowing what she was going to see—two thin pink lines.

She turned back around again. "Do you feel the pain all the time? Or just sometimes?"

"Well, pretty much all of the time."

"How bad is it? On a scale of one to ten, ten being the worst pain you've ever felt, how would you rate this pain?"

"Oh, it's not bad. I guess it's a two or something."

"Do you feel pain anywhere else? Your shoulder? Your jaw?"

"No, I just feel it down where I showed you. It isn't very bad—I mean, right now I can hardly feel it at all."

Ariel seemed very calm about the whole thing.

Charlotte looked directly at her. "The result of your pregnancy test is positive."

Ariel shrugged. "Oh, I know. I did four of them at home."

Charlotte pulled up her roller stool and turned directly to face her. "Okay, I need you to listen to me very carefully."

Ariel shrugged, and Charlotte noted again the gemstone quality to her eyes, and how eerily familiar it was to her. She resisted a momentary feeling of tunneling backward through time, drawn in by those eyes, but quickly her surroundings brought her back to herself—the antiseptic exam room, the white lab coat she was wearing. This was her domain, and she was in charge.

"This is the situation, Ariel. You are pregnant, you are spotting, and you are having some pain. Those can be symptoms of a potentially dangerous complication called an ectopic pregnancy, or a tubal pregnancy. Have you ever heard of that? Do you know what that is?"

Ariel shrugged, looked past her. Now Ariel was acting like a teenager, and so Charlotte felt on more comfortable turf.

Charlotte pulled out her teaching tool—a picture of the female reproductive tract; the ram's face of the uterus, the two horns of the fallopian tubes. She showed Ariel. "Here's where the egg implants in a normal pregnancy." She pointed to the space inside the uterus. "And here's where the egg implants in a tubal pregnancy." She pointed to the picture of the slender, fimbrillated fallopian tube. "If the egg implants up in here— Are you following me?" Ariel nodded, although her expression continued to be totally blank. "Look at the tube. See how slender it is? In real life it's narrower than a drinking straw. There is no room in there for an embryo to grow. If it implants there it is not a viable pregnancy, but also it could do you a lot of harm."

"I'm keeping the baby," Ariel said hastily.

"That is your choice, Ariel, but first we need to make sure that this is a normal pregnancy, and if it's not a normal pregnancy, then you will need treatment right away."

For the first time Ariel seemed to understand that she was going to have to do something. "So what am I supposed to do?"

"Does your mother know you are here?"

"I'm eighteen," she said, jutting out her chin.

"No, you're . . ." Charlotte looked at the chart. This time she had used her real name—no more Mary Smith, age nineteen, but the birth date indicated that she was a few days past her eighteenth birthday.

"But I thought you were—"

"Oh, for chrissakes, I turned eighteen over the weekend. Do I have to show you my driver's license?"

Charlotte nodded her head. She needed to know if Ariel was a minor.

Ariel groped in her bag for her wallet and then flipped it open—sure enough, she had turned eighteen two days earlier.

"Okay, I can see that you are eighteen, but I still want to know: Does your mother know you're here?"

Ariel shook her head vehemently. "No, and she's not gonna. She was mad enough last time I got pregnant."

Charlotte let that comment slide without notice. "What about the baby's father? Does he know you're here?"

"He's in Virginia," she said. "I could call him. . . ."

"Well, listen to me carefully. Do you understand what I told you about the tubal pregnancy?"

Charlotte listened while Ariel said it back.

"And you understand that there are serious complications associated with this condition, including death?"

Ariel nodded her head.

"The only way to be certain is to have an ultrasound. You need to go to the emergency room right now and have an ultrasound to make sure that it isn't a tubal pregnancy."

"Why don't you do that here?" Ariel asked.

"Because we don't have an ultrasound machine or anyone trained to use it. You have to go to the ER—not tomorrow, not next week. You need to go today. Right now. Do you understand?"

"Are you going to tell Deirdre?"

"Federal law prohibits me from discussing your health care with anyone, including your mother, without your prior written consent."

"Which means?"

"Which means, no, I'm not going to tell your mother unless you ask me to, but I'd feel a lot more comfortable if we brought her into the picture."

"I'm not going to tell Deirdre," Ariel said emphatically.

"Your choice. Now do you know where the hospital is?" Charlotte wrote down the directions for Ariel, and repeated them three times. "I'm calling over there and telling them to expect you in about twenty minutes."

"I'm really hungry. Can't I have lunch first?"

"No, don't eat. Just in case. Wait for them to tell you it's okay. Go straight there. Do you understand me?"

Ariel still hadn't betrayed any real emotion. She seemed strangely noncommittal about the whole thing—but that was probably just her age.

What Charlotte really felt like doing was putting her in the car and driving her to the hospital herself, but where was that coming from? This was Deirdre's daughter, and she was overreacting. She sent patients to the hospital to rule out ectopic at least two or three times a week. It was a common situation; anyone in early pregnancy with pain or spotting got an automatic ultrasound. She always impressed upon them the seriousness of the potential problem, but she also knew that most of those with symptoms would turn out to be fine. And ectopic pregnancies were dangerous only if they went undiagnosed.

Charlotte switched herself into businesslike mode. She wrote up the referral and finished filling out the chart. She then emerged from the exam room and sent Ariel to check out. She had done her job, Charlotte thought. Same way she would have with anyone.

Then she stood with the rest of the girls, who hadn't budged from the spectacle at the window, and watched Ariel walk back through the parking lot, still looking for all the world as though she thought the people were all gathered there to look at her.

Only after Ariel had roared away in her little lime green car did Charlotte pick up the phone and call over to the registrar at the hospital. She gave the particulars over the phone and asked them to fax over the results.

After that, it seemed that patients decided to brave it, and they started at first to trickle in, and then to come in with a more regular rhythm. Charlotte got busy, and the rest of the afternoon passed at a more normal pace. She didn't think about Ariel again until the end of the session. Long waits were typical at the ER, and Ariel's symptoms would have put her low on the totem pole to be seen. But after Charlotte finished her last exams and finished up her paperwork, she realized that she'd had no phone call from the hospital, so she called over.

The unit secretary put her on hold for a long time, but finally came back and said that they had seen no one by the name of Ariel Saramago that day, and that she wasn't even registered and in the waiting room or she would have shown up in the system.

Charlotte felt the pit of her stomach seize up. "What about Mary Smith? Did you have a Mary Smith there?"

"Honey? Did you say you was looking for Ariel Saramago or Mary Smith?"

"I'll remind you that I'm Charlotte Hopper, the nurse practitioner from El Centro, not 'honey.' I referred my patient there, and it is extremely important that I find out the outcome of her case. I'm aware that this patient has used the alias Mary Smith in the past."

Charlotte heard a grunt on the end of the line, then, "Honey, I'm putting you on hold." She hung on, irritation swelling inside her until she could feel tears forming in her eyes.

Finally a friendly young voice got on the line.

"This is Dr. Elliot, one of the residents. How can I help you today?"

"Hi, this is Charlotte Hopper. I'm the nurse practitioner from El Centro." And she went through her spiel again—the referral for rule-out ectopic, the patient who sometimes used an alias.

"Well, we don't have her registered, but maybe she gave us a fake name. I've been here all day. What did she look like?"

"Oh, you wouldn't have missed her—a pretty blonde in a skintight cropped T-shirt. She has a kind of a Britney Spears vibe going."

Dr. Elliot chuckled. "She wasn't here, I don't think—and I would remember. But listen, since you're worried about ectopic, I'll go through the files and see if we saw anyone for a rule-out ectopic. When would she have gotten here?"

Charlotte remembered that she had looked at her watch.

"She left here at two—it's a fifteen-minute drive. She did say something about stopping to get something to eat, although I told her not to." But even so . . . Charlotte glanced at her watch. It was already six thirty.

"You know, for whatever reason, we were dead slow all afternoon, and I was here all day. Didn't leave the floor that I can recall—but listen, I'll check it out, see if I might have missed her."

"She's eighteen and seems responsible, but I don't know. I was just worried that she wouldn't follow up."

"You know, ultimately it's up to them, not us," the young doctor said kindly.

"I don't really believe that," Charlotte said.

"Neither do I," the voice said. "But what are you going to do?"

So Charlotte gave the resident her cell phone number and her home number, and she took off her lab coat and straightened up her desktop, preparing to leave. She was last again, having shooed everyone else out the door.

The office was darkening, and quiet inside, although there was an odd glow in the main reception area. She couldn't see, but she guessed it was probably klieg lights in the parking lot that were shining through the window.

She picked up her purse, then paused for a moment, remembering that she had left her cell phone in her lab coat pocket. Then, turning around to walk out of her office, she screamed, startled as she realized that someone was standing in the doorway.

"Oh, jeez, Arecely, don't startle me like that!"

It had taken half a second for Charlotte to recognize Arecely in the dark, with the glow behind her.

"I'm sorry, Charlotte. I didn't mean to startle you."

"Why are you still here? I told everyone to go ahead. . . ." Arecely had been acting so out of character lately. Usually she rushed out as early as possible to be with Zekie. "Is everything okay at home?"

Arecely paused for a moment as if she weren't sure what to say, but then she spoke up: "Oh, Lizzie was taking him 'n' Jessica out to get Happy Meals—you know they have those new *Shrek* toys, and the kids really wanted them. . . ."

"You know, it doesn't matter. I was just surprised. Do you want to walk out together?"

Arecely and Charlotte walked out of the clinic together in the glare of the lights, and as they walked down the steps, Charlotte realized that there was a cameraman shooting right toward them. It was chilly out tonight, and windy, with a strong fall nip in the air. She pulled her thin jacket closed and shivered, noticing that the crowd that had been there earlier had disbursed, and she was grateful for the obscurity of the shadows past the perimeter of the spotlight. She fumbled with her keys in the darkness, and happy for the quiet isolation of her own car, she drove out of the parking lot.

Twenty-six

At eleven, when the local news came on, Charlotte was in the kitchen washing up.

Julie shrieked from the other room, "Mom. Oh, my God, Mom! It's you. You're on TV again."

Charlotte hustled back into the room and plopped down on the sofa next to Julie, wiping her hands on her jeans.

There was Barbara Volpone, standing with Linda Rodriguez, the El Centro sign clearly visible in the background. Charlotte came in just on the end of the bit of conversation and didn't hear what Barbara said. Then the report cut to the district attorney, Harold Overturf, just like the last time, sitting in his office behind a massive desk, lots of impressive, heavy-looking legal tomes behind him.

"A capital offense," he was saying. "We will find the killer and we will prosecute her to the full extent of the law."

Charlotte shuddered; then it cut back to the clinic, and Julie shrieked, "Mom, oh, my God, Mom, that's you!" And there were Charlotte and Arecely, walking down the steps of the clinic side by side.

"Oh, I hope Dad is watching. . . . Do you think he's watching? Can we call him?"

For a moment, Charlotte was stymied, unsure what to say. She was unused to lying to her daughter, but she was desperate to buy a little time. She wanted to talk to Charlie. She didn't want to say anything at all to Julie.

"Sweetie, this is the local news. It won't be on . . . in . . . the place where he is. . . ."

"Oh," Julie said. "Well, then we should ask someone to TiVo it. Too bad we don't have TiVo. I could ask Ariel. . . ." But by now the segment was finished, and the announcer was saying, "Stay tuned for sports and weather."

Julie shrugged. "Well, it'll probably be on tomorrow night too. Mom!" she said, jumping up. "I have to go check on the horses again. I'm supposed to look in on them once before I go to bed."

"Julie, it's ten o'clock at night. It's pitch-black outside. Deirdre will have to check them herself."

"But she's not there, and I promised."

"What do you mean, she's not there?"

"She told me she was going out of town, and I'm going to feed the horses."

"But she didn't even mention it to me. I'm going to call over there right now."

"Jeez, Mom, you treat me like a baby. I'm fifteen. She doesn't have to ask your permission." Julie had her hands on her hips and was rolling her eyes.

Charlotte walked over and picked up the phone, dialing Deirdre's number, which she had scribbled on a pad next to the phone.

But as she stood there, the phone rang and rang, until she felt like she could hear it echoing through the massive empty house.

"Mom, I have to go. I promised."

"Okay, then I'm going with you,"

"That is *so* not necessary."

But Charlotte ignored her, and they pulled on jackets, grabbed flashlights, and headed out through the dark woods.

Julie took a quick look at all of the horses. Charlotte couldn't even imagine exactly what she was looking for. They seemed to be standing quietly, their heads hanging over the half doors, blowing puffs of mist into the night air. Charlotte was trying to tamp down her sense of profound irritation at Deirdre. Wasn't it just like her to impose? She gazed at the dark house, semilit in the distance like a ship off a darkened coast at night.

The light in the pool was turned on, and it shimmered like an aquamarine jewel in the dark landscape. Charlotte was weary, and Julie was taking a tremendous amount of time with her task, so Charlotte wandered off a little from the lit-up stable yard, heading toward one of the teak benches that lined the path connecting the stable to the backyard and pool. But as she walked up the rise toward the bench, she noticed something odd about the pool—a dark shadow against one of the walls.

Though the air was still, the surface of the water was fractured, rippling, so that the object in the pool appeared to be moving in an odd jerky way—it looked like a giant spider or an octopus.

Curiosity drew her closer. She had an odd fear that one of the horses had fallen into the pool, that perhaps somehow Julie was responsible.

When she got to the edge of the pool, she stood there, staring down into the jewellike depths, trying to decipher what she was looking at. A moderate breeze had kicked up; it was cold, and she pulled her jacket tighter around her, tugging at her zipper. It was almost November—surprising that the pool was still open, and from the faint mist of steam rising from it, obviously Deirdre kept it very well heated.

Charlotte lifted her eyes, scanning the distance she had come from, wondering whether she should call out because Julie might be looking for her. She walked around to the other side of the pool, her back turned momentarily to the barn, staring down into the depths at the odd black bobbing form—

Charlotte screamed, and at the same moment, instinct kicked in. She kicked off her shoes, jerked off her jacket, and dove into the pool, the water as warm as blood.

Pressure pounded against her ears; air crushed her lungs as she tugged, the arm, the hair, the back of her neck—anything she could get a purchase on.

Under the water, though her vision was blurred, she could see the face— eyes open, mouth open in a silent scream. She floundered, tugged, tried to push up against the raspy surface of the bottom of the pool.

Finally, air exploding, lungs collapsing, she was forced to let go and surface for air.

Julie was already standing at the side of the pool, her voice shrill with fright.

"Mom? Mom? What's going on?"

"Julie, peel off your jacket, shoes, and pants, and jump in and try to help me. We've got to pull her up."

Julie was already stripping down before Charlotte finished talking. They dove down, and together they tried again, pulling on the body, which simply wouldn't budge. The body swayed, hair waving to and fro like it was alive and dancing. But they couldn't, either one of them, stay down for long—Charlotte made one final desperate grab at the collar, but when she broke to the surface—lungs bursting, sucking in cold night air—she came up empty-handed, except that clasped in her hand she had a broken bit of gold chain, and in her palm a flat gold medallion emblazoned with an image of the Virgin Mary.

Julie was preparing to dive down again, but Charlotte stopped her.

"We . . . can't," she said, still breathless from the effort. "She's . . . too . . . heavy. . . . We need to call nine-one-one."

"There's a phone down at the barn. I'll go," Julie said, pulling herself out of the pool soaking wet, steam rising from her body like an aura. Charlotte ran after her, barefoot, clutching their two jackets, and by the time she got down there Julie, who had pulled a horse blanket around her, was talking calmly on the phone to the emergency dispatcher, while rubbing the water out of her hair with the thick woolen horse blanket.

It seemed like it took forever for the police to come, and Charlotte and Julie sat on the Brown Jordan patio furniture, huddled together, wrapped in horse blankets for warmth. Julie hid her head against her mom's shoulder, like she used to do when she was a child, keeping her eyes averted, but Charlotte kept her eyes fixed on the bobbing image in the pool, frustrated beyond all else by her own impotence—the water like a wall through which she couldn't penetrate.

When the police and EMTs finally arrived, they pulled the body out of the pool with a hook, and once up on the surface of the patio, it was clear how bloated and dead the body obviously was. Though they went through the motions of trying to resuscitate her, they pronounced her dead on the scene.

Then Charlotte found herself answering the same questions over and over again.

The homeowner was away. No, she didn't know where. No, she didn't know how to reach her. Her daughter was caring for the horses; she came with her because it was late. She saw something in the pool; they tried to pull her out, but she was heavy.

"Yo, Brad, her pockets were stuffed with rocks," one of the EMTs had called over at one point.

Yes, she did recognize her; she was the Saramagos' housekeeper. She wasn't sure what her name was, but thought it might be Maria Sanchez.

At three o'clock in the morning, Charlotte lay in bed, trembling. Julie, who after all was said and done had been far too spooked to sleep alone, was lying in Charlie's spot, finally fallen into the solid slumber of a healthy teenager.

But Charlotte, who had drunk hot tea, and taken a hot bath, and wrapped herself in blankets, couldn't stop trembling. Finally she got up and dialed the number of the emergency room at the hospital, and asked for Dr. Elliot. Obviously he was working a typical long resident's shift, because he got on the phone sounding wide-awake.

"Dr. Elliot, Charlotte Hopper here, the nurse practitioner."

"Ah, yes, the one who gave me hope all day, certain that Britney Spears would walk through the door at any moment."

"Have you seen her?"

"No Britney, no pregnancies, no rule-out ectopics all day . . . sorry."

It was only after she hung up that she realized she was glad that Dr. Elliot, in his eternal dawn of a long resident's shift, had never thought to wonder why she was calling in the middle of the night.

Twenty-seven

If Charlotte had any sense, she would have called in sick to work, and she would have kept Julie home from school. But Julie was up and dressed by six, heading out the back door wearing mucker boots to check the horses.

Charlotte turned over in bed, staring at the red lights on the dial, rubbing her eyes, trying to will them to stay open. It took her a few moments before the events of the night before came back to her, one by one—Ariel going missing, then the horrific night by the pool, finding Maria.

But she didn't want to let Julie go over to the barn alone, so she kicked off the covers, pulled on a pair of jeans and a sweatshirt, and headed out into the cold morning. There was a light frost on the ground, leaving a whitish sheen on the leaves that had fallen; they crunched underfoot as she walked. In the bright morning light, the whole scene of the previous evening in the swimming pool seemed so improbable, as though she had awoken from a dream that still seemed real. As she emerged from the woods, she heard Julie's voice. At first she thought she was talking to someone, but then, as she drew closer, she realized that Julie was talking to the horses as she fed them. Charlotte looked across the yard toward the pool area, expecting to see something—pehaps yellow caution tape, which would indicate what had happened the night before, but there was nothing. Just the still surface of the pool, softened by the white mist that rose above it.

"Julie?" Charlotte called out, so as not to startle her daughter.

"Oh, hi, Mom." Julie said. Charlotte studied her daughter: jeans, a barn jacket, and a messy ponytail. Her face was untroubled—she didn't even look tired, in spite of the fact that she had been up so late.

"I just came to check on you. Do you need any help?"

"You don't need to check on me, and I don't need help."

"Well, I just . . ." Charlotte trailed off, unsure what to say. She watched for a moment as Julie unhitched the gate and shoved the large animal aside with her shoulder so that she could carry the rubber bucket of grain into the stall. Charlotte was so impressed with her confidence. Julie, at fifteen, seemed so able to handle anything—she remembered how Julie had dived in to try to help her, how she had run down to the barn and been able to talk calmly to 911. Julie didn't know anything about horses, and here she was competently taking charge of six of them.

It gave Charlotte a measure of satisfaction. She had tried to teach her daughter a confidence she felt she herself had lacked. At twenty, Charlotte had not done well when faced with an emergency situation. Seeing Julie cope in a crisis showed her how self-confident her daughter was.

"Sure you don't need any help?"

"*Mom!*"

"Well, keep your eye on the clock. You can't miss the bus today. Dad's not here." She heard how natural it sounded—*Dad's not here.* "And I have to go to work."

"Mom," Julie said with a toss of her ponytail. "I *know.*"

Charlotte trudged back through the woods alone. On top of everything else, she felt like a bad mother. Julie didn't seem too traumatized about the drowning, but was she? And more important, Charlotte hadn't told her anything about Charlie. She needed to get in touch with him. To talk to him.

When she got back inside the house, the phone was ringing.

"Hello?"

"Mrs. Hopper, Detective Flynn."

Her first thought was Charlie. Had he been in an accident?

"Is something wrong?"

"I just wanted to bring you up to speed about the Sanchez case."

Okay. Not Charlie. Charlotte took a deep breath. "Um, I think it might be better if you talk to our clinic manager. She's referring all phone calls to our lawyer."

"I . . . Beg pardon, Mrs. Hopper . . . I'm not sure . . ."

It was only then that Charlotte realized her mistake. The Sanchez case. Last night.

"Oh, I'm sorry. I thought you were someone else."

"No problem. I know you were up late, and now it's early in the morning."

"What can I do for you?" Charlotte walked into the kitchen and pulled out one of the chairs. She felt too exhausted to stand up.

"On behalf of the department, we just wanted to thank you and your daughter for attempting to rescue the victim. We are filing this case as a suicide. She had rocks in her pockets, and it turns out she had left a note—something in Spanish, but our translator said it made it sound like she was planning to do herself in."

For a moment, Charlotte didn't say anything, just sat heavily in the chair and sucked her breath in slowly. Then she asked, "Were you able to get hold of my neighbor?"

"Yes, we reached her on the number your daughter gave us. She's away on family business. Out of the country."

"In Argentina?"

"I believe I couldn't say, ma'am. Not at liberty. Just out of the country—that's all I heard."

"Oh, I see . . ." said Charlotte. "So Ariel . . ." She trailed off.

"Beg pardon?"

"Oh, I was just wondering where her daughter was. She must be with her."

"One would presume," Detective Flynn said. Charlotte thought she could detect a hint of exasperation in his voice. Charlotte looked out the window and saw Julie hurrying across the yard.

"Anyway, just wanted to let you know that you did the best you could. Homeowner said that she was going to let her go for mental instability. Seems like she was an undocumented from Mexico, hadn't been here long, and was upset about something. Homeowner thought it was the death of a child."

"Well, I appreciate your letting me know," Charlotte said, hurrying to end the conversation, since Julie was coming in the door.

"We find it helps if you know you did all you could. Pleasure talking to you, Mrs. Hopper, and just remember that we're here if we can be of any further assistance."

"I appreciate that," Charlotte said, hanging up the phone.

Julie kicked off her muddy boots and ran past her up the stairs, calling behind her, "Hey, Mom, I thought you said you were going to work."

Charlotte looked down at herself and realized that she was wearing the same grubby jeans she had put on this morning, her hair pulled back in a rough ponytail. She glanced at the clock. It was already almost eight.

She passed Julie in the hall upstairs. Julie was now carrying her backpack and getting ready to go.

"Julie." Charlotte placed her hand on her daughter's arm.

"Mom, I gotta go. I'm gonna miss the bus."

"The police called."

Her daughter stopped.

"Yeah?"

"That lady. The one in the pool."

Julie shrugged, refused to meet her mother's eyes. "Mom, I know which one."

"That was the police. They were just calling to say we did all we could. There wasn't anything anyone could do."

Charlotte saw the tears fill up her daughter's eyes. She slipped her arm around her shoulders.

"Are you sure you're okay?"

Julie rubbed her eyes, sniffed, nodded. "Mom, I'm going to miss the bus."

"If you feel . . . like it's getting to you, you're going to call me, right?"

"Look, Ma, don't make a big deal of it? Okay? I gotta go."

Charlotte reached over to give her daughter a kiss on the cheek, but she was already heading down the hallway, and so her lips ended up brushing the warm air left in the space where her cheek had been.

Twenty-eight

Arecely felt the crunch of frost under her feet as she walked across the field toward El Centro. She had slipped the landlord's money under her door on the way out. Two weeks of rent, all she could manage right now, and the last twenty came from her *tío*—she had to tell him that Ricky was gone, but he was coming back, and her *tío* had shook his finger as he peeled off the twenty, saying, "Arecely, you gotta use your head. Don't be thinking you can come back to me again."

She walked across the field in the early-morning light, down the lane, then across from the mushroom houses, carrying her plastic bag, the box of crackers, a quart of milk, and a tin of chili that banged against her thigh as she walked.

Nausea roiled around in her stomach like an uninvited guest that didn't know when to leave. She quickened her steps a little. Now, with the news crews setting up shop in the parking lot, she was afraid not to arrive really early.

Obviously she had gotten herself into a predicament so complicated that she couldn't see the way out anymore. Last night Lizzie had yelled at her, complaining that she didn't want to take Zekie so early, even though she was just dumping him on her couch still asleep. She couldn't manage the rent without Ricky, and now here she was, pregnant again.

When she arrived at the edge of the clinic parking lot, she was relieved to see that the lot was still empty. She hurried across the asphalt and quickly swiped her security card, then disabled the alarm. Once inside she threw her coat down and hurried up the back stairs, her plastic bag clutched in her hand. With dismay she smelled the odor of cigarettes in the hallway, reminded herself that she would have to come back with the Lysol spray. She sneezed twice, then gasped for a moment as a wave of nausea rose up the back of her throat and burned the inside of her nose. She swallowed hard—no time to lose. . . .

But this time, it was too close—no sooner had she opened the door and said in an urgent whisper, "Run," than she saw the ABC News van swinging around the corner into the parking lot.

Arecely clicked the clinic door shut and reactivated the lock. A quick glance up at the clock told her that she still had a half hour before the rest of the staff would be arriving. No time to lose. She headed for the cleaning supply closet to get the Lysol spray, but as she passed the check-out window, her eyes lingered on the pig for a moment, and without meaning to she stopped.

Arecely picked up the pig, still chained to the countertop, and rubbed its cool plastic surface against her cheek.

"Some pig . . ." she whispered, then, feeling foolish, clamped her mouth shut. Realizing she shouldn't have stopped there, she tried to make herself put the pig down. But instead she held it up to the light, where surprisingly she could see that there were other bills, more than she could easily count, shoved into the pig's belly along with the money that Flo had first put there.

Now the pig felt hot in her hands, and Arecely told herself to put it back on the countertop and walk away. But then she thought about her situation, and how the pig was for charity, and about how she might, just might, be able to use money to get herself out of the predicament she found herself in.

In spite of the warning bells that Arecely heard going off in her ears, she decided to turn the pig over just once and shake it—she would shake it just once.

Arecely made the sign of the cross, then mumbled a prayer. "*En el nombre de la Virgen Maria, que se haga tu voluntad.*"

As she said the prayer she held the pig upside down, one hand on its plastic snout, the other on its tail. The sound that the chain made, rattling, seemed louder than the trains that ran out on the tracks behind her house, and as she shook, first one folded bill fell out of the pig, and then another, falling with a whispered smack onto the countertop. For just a moment, Arecely trembled when she saw the bills lying there, afraid even to touch them, knowing that she could just shove the bills back through the slot and nobody would ever know what she had done.

Hand trembling, she reached over and picked up one of the bills, holding it away from her as if it might burn. Still shaking, she unfolded it and saw, to her astonishment, that it was a one-hundred-dollar bill. She froze for a second, and then reached out like lightning, grabbing the other bill.

She kissed the bills, once each, the bitter money smell bringing bile up to her throat and gagging her; then she shoved them deep into her pocket while she whispered to herself, *"Gracias, Mariacito."*

She glanced at the clock—just a few more minutes—then rushed to the supply closet, grabbing the Lysol, which she sprayed all the way up the stairs. Then she ran around the upstairs room, gathering wrappers and candle stubs, shaking out the pillows, giving them a quick spray of Lysol, and rescattering them about the room.

As she finished, she looked up and, without meaning to, realized that the Santa Maria was looking at her, and suddenly the money in her pocket felt as though it were hot—on fire. Holding the burning bills in one hand and the Lysol in other, she ran down the stairs by twos, eager to shove the money back into the pig—feeling like it was scorching the palm of her hand, but as she reached the bottom of the stairs and rounded the corner, she saw the office door push open, and in walked Flo. Without thinking, Arecely shoved the two bills deep into her pocket, said good morning to Flo, and walked past her to the supply closet, where she put down the Lysol on the shelf and turned around, now empty-handed, to face the workday.

Twenty-nine

It was a three-ring circus all day. The news crew was already out in the parking lot when Charlotte got to work. They didn't seem to be doing anything, but the van was there, parked across three places as though they had taken up ownership.

The patients had come back—the sky was dark and menacing, but it hadn't started to rain, and after all, women could only go so long without their birth-control pills, or putting up with a vaginal itch, so today the flow of patients was relentless, the waiting room full to overflowing.

By ten A.M., somebody had tried to flush a dirty Pampers down the waiting room toilet; by ten forty-five, a three-year-old had vomited up his Froot Loops in the middle of the carpet; and by twelve forty-five, it was evident to all of them that none of them was going to get lunch.

What was more, Charlotte had a splitting headache from being awake most of the night, and Arecely seemed inexplicably slow—not herself at all. She was forgetting to do things—putting patients in the rooms without taking their blood pressure, mixing up lab slips. Things that really weren't like her at all.

After several such episodes, Charlotte stopped Arecely in the hall and said, "Is everything okay, Arecely? Everything okay at home? You just don't seem like yourself today."

Arecely quickly averted her eyes in a way that made Charlotte think she didn't want her to see tears, but Charlotte, now that she was getting a good look at her, could see that she was pale and tired-looking, and that her face was thinner than usual.

"Arecely, you need to take lunch."

Arecely shook her head, still not looking up at Charlotte.

"You really need to eat something. Why don't you grab a break? Mary Louise can take over."

"We've got five Spanish speakers in the waiting room. . . ."

"I'm running late anyway. Just go ahead and take a break."

Arecely shook her head and turned a shoulder to Charlotte, who didn't have much time to think about it as her charts were stacked up, and so she headed into the next room.

Being busy wasn't all bad, though, because the day passed quickly. She had stopped for only a few minutes to try to make phone calls—two calls to Charlie's cell phone, but he had it switched off, and one attempt to reach Deirdre in Argentina, using the number that Julie had given her. No luck.

The days were getting short now, and it was starting to get dark already—just a few more days, past Halloween, and it would already be pitch-black when she left. She pulled on her coat and walked toward the door, ready to get out of there, to get home. She would take a shower and make it an early night.

But as she headed out toward the vestibule her heart thunked twice hard, then missed a beat—there was Charlie, waiting for her, just in front of the clinic. Suddenly she realized that Charlie wouldn't just show up like that unless something was wrong.

Julie—

She rushed toward the door, but then the person outside turned and she caught a glimpse of a profile that caught her up short. It wasn't Charlie at all. It was Paul Stone. How could she have thought it was Charlie . . . ? For a moment, Charlotte just stood there, one arm in her jacket, heart thudding as though it were trying to send her a message in Morse code that she couldn't understand.

She didn't want to talk to him, considered waiting him out for a while, but no sooner had she ducked back into her office than she heard Flo saying, "Why, Mr. Stone, of course, come right in."

And Charlotte didn't manage to do anything; she just slipped her other arm into her jacket in a hurry, as Paul Stone already had his hand stuck out to shake hers, and a warm smile was rippling across his face. Charlotte put her hand into his, aware how smooth it felt, and felt the warmth of his hand close around her.

"Charlotte," he said.

Without quite meaning to, she took a step forward, closer to him; then she could feel her knees going weak. She blinked a couple of times, rubbed her nose to try to break the feeling.

He was still smiling at her, still clasping her hand. His eyes didn't waver from her face, and he didn't say anything for a moment.

But then Charlotte took control of herself and wrested her hand from his, taking a hurried step back.

"Hello, nice to see you. What can I do for you today?" She averted her eyes, settling them on the condom poster, which she studied like a book for a test.

"Just had a few more questions—if you don't mind, that is. Thought I could take us for coffee again."

Suddenly she thought of Charlie's note lying on the kitchen table, the tinny computer sound of the recorded voice saying, "The customer is not available at this time" when she tried to call his cell phone. She took her eyes off the condom poster—looked back at Paul. The crow's-feet crinkling around his eyes made her want to reach out and touch him.

"Can you . . . Do you want to do coffee or dinner or something?" he said, then added, as if for a good measure, "So I can ask you a few more questions . . ."

Charlotte could feel that she was just about to nod yes, and to follow him, but then with a rush of relief she remembered—Julie. With Charlie gone she didn't want to stay late and leave Julie home alone.

"No . . . I'm sorry. . . . I'd love to but right now I can't. . . ." The office phone was ringing, and so she spoke up a little in order to be heard. "My daughter is home and I need to be getting home."

"Charlotte," Flo said, coming out of the office. "That was Julie. She wanted me to tell you that she's going to her friend Kayla's house to do homework, so she told you not to worry if you were going to be late."

Paul Stone didn't even say anything—he just smiled and put his hand ever so lightly on Charlotte's arm to guide her toward the door.

"He's going to interview me again," she called over her shoulder to Flo, to no one in particular, as she let Paul's warm hand guide her out the door.

Out in the parking lot, it was dark and cold. Charlotte was surprised to see that a little knot of protesters was still there. They were holding candles in mittened hands and stomping against the cold, their breath coming out in mingling clouds.

Charlotte vaguely remembered that she had promised herself not to get back in Paul Stone's car, but soon she was settling into the bucket seat and buckling herself in.

As they pulled out of the parking lot, neither spoke, but when they got to the edge of the driveway, where the small knot of people with candles had gathered, Paul slowed down the car and rolled down the window.

The same two men who had been there all along were there, plus another man with a long beard, so disheveled looking that he might have been homeless, then a small, lumpy woman with black glasses and gray-dyed-blond short hair. The last woman, with long dark hair, looked familiar, though at first, in the glow of the candle, she couldn't connect the themselves to the face. But then in the half dark, her features reassembled herself and Charlotte recognized Mrs. Rosalie Saxton. Charlotte glanced at her placard and could just make out the lettering on it—it said, VISUALIZE WORLD PEACE.

As they drove down the Maryland Pike, Paul talked and Charlotte listened. She was shivering, and he had noticed without being told and turned up the heat, which was now blasting hot, dry air that was making her eyes water and smart.

"I looked into the 'protesters' a bit," he was saying. "The two old guys . . . they're parishioners at Willowglen Chapel, but it seems that they took it upon themselves to come down and protest. When you ask what they're protesting, they're not quite sure. They said they were against dead babies."

Charlotte shivered again and muttered, "Aren't we all?"

"The lady with the glasses—she's the older guy's landlord, and the guy with the beard . . . he usually sleeps out in front of Wawa and I think he just saw the candles and thought it might help him get warm."

"So they're nuts . . . ?" she asked, embarrassed that her voice came out in a nervous whisper.

"Oh, and the other lady . . ."

"Rosalie Saxton."

"She said, 'I just like to join in when I see a good cause.' "

"That sounds like Rosalie," Charlotte muttered, not loud enough to be heard over the Volkswagen's chug.

Charlotte pushed herself down in her seat and looked out the window at the dark trees and fields she was driving by.

Before long, Paul had pulled off the road onto a gravel driveway, but it wasn't until she got out of the car and heard the fast gurgle of the Brandywine that she realized he had brought her to the same place where they had come for coffee before.

Tonight the creek smell was dark and redolent with mysteries of fallen trees and muck and mold. Charlotte was surprised that it was so loud, but Paul spoke up above the sound. "The creek is very high—any rain in the next few days and they're saying it's going to flood."

The terrace where they had sat before was closed up, the flagstones slick with damp; the wire tables and chairs looked forlorn, chairs tipped haphazardly against tables, their metal frames faintly greenish in the dim light.

The back of the building was painted barn red. When Paul pushed the door open to let Charlotte in, she was surprised to see a charming café and restaurant built into the old mill, its stone and red-plank walls adorned with artwork.

"Oh, Paul," Charlotte said, her hand flying to her mouth, "this is lovely. I had no idea."

A young man with a pierced eyebrow and the telltale paint of an artist under his fingernails came up with two menus and led them to a secluded table nestled up against the stone wall.

He thought they were a couple, Charlotte realized with a start.

"Oh, uh, we're not here to eat . . ." Charlotte said, then trailed off, feeling like a fool.

"Oh, come now, my treat. Your daughter's not home. Let me buy you dinner while we talk. It would be my pleasure—unless your husband . . . ?" He trailed off without finishing the question, one eyebrow slightly cocked over his smiling eyes.

"No, it's . . . I . . ."

"The food is delicious. . . ."

More to get her eyes off Paul's compelling face than anything else, Charlotte looked down and started to study the menu. She was hungry, and the food did look good.

There was something about this place that reminded her of her old life with Charlie. Charlie used to always drag her off to these hidden gallery places. He always wanted to be surrounded by paintings—was happiest in a place like this, where there was paint on the walls and paint under everybody's fingernails. It was amazing, when she thought about it, that she had never been here before. In the old days, Charlie would have found it and dragged her here—gotten to know the owner, talked about getting some of his own stuff up on the walls. But now Charlotte tried to remember how long it had even been since they had looked at art together, how long it had been since he had shown her something new.

Paul had ordered each of them a glass of white wine, and Charlotte hadn't objected. She was running her fingers up and down along the glass stem, then taking gulps of the wine. The glass had been refilled before she quite realized she had finished a first one, and the edges of the room began to soften, and she started to be able to look directly at Paul's face again.

Paul started to fill her in on some of the details of the case that he had been following.

"The DA is getting aggravated because he chose to make this a high-profile case, not realizing that it was going to be difficult to solve."

"But why did he want it to be high-profile?"

"Oh, nothing, just politics. He's jockeying to be elected to state attorney general. Who isn't against dead babies? It's a gimme. Great publicity that makes him look tough on crime."

"But they don't know who did it?"

"Best I can tell, he thought it wouldn't be too hard to figure out. He made the assumption, probably wrong, that the baby was put there by one of the clinic patients and that everyone would figure it out right away. Now he's kinda stuck. I think he's wishing the whole thing would just go away."

"What about the Mexican girl?" Charlotte said. She took another big sip of her wine to steady herself.

"Oh, that . . . Well, she turned out to be something of a chimera."

"A chimera?"

"You know, more a product of the collective wisdom over in the camps than anything else."

"I'm not sure I understand."

"Now nobody can recall really seeing her, and some people are saying that the woman who came to fight with Norma Vasquez that night was actually her sister-in-law, Irene, who lives in Kennett."

"So . . . do you think it'll just blow over . . . ?" Charlotte asked, draining her wineglass without really meaning to, and then seeing the waiter fill it up to the brim again. She looked at Paul's glass—he had scarcely touched it. Okay, at least there was a designated driver. She picked up the glass and took another greedy sip. Then she turned and stared out the window, afraid to look at Paul's face, because when she did, she felt like drawing toward him.

"Well, I can see why you are hoping it will," he said, with a note in his voice that Charlotte first thought oddly insinuating, before she realized that already she had had too much to drink.

"Excuse me for a moment, please," Charlotte said, rising from her seat, and shooting her hand out, just for a moment, to steady herself on the wall.

"Of course," Paul said with a smile. "I've got a couple of pieces up," he called behind her. "See if you can guess which ones are mine."

"You're an artist?" Charlotte said, although now she wasn't surprised. He would be an artist—he had all the signs; she had just missed them.

The bathroom was around the corner and down a long corridor. She wasn't paying much attention to her surroundings, but when she got partway down the hallway she stopped in her tracks, arrested by three small portraits, almost miniatures, that were hanging on the wall, illuminated by a single light.

Each painting portrayed a young mother holding a baby. The center one was slightly larger, which gave the effect of a triptych, although each painting was separate.

The first was an anemic white teenager, maybe fifteen, wearing a black Nine Inch Nails T-shirt. The baby in her arms was wearing nothing but a faded Elmo T-shirt and sagging Pampers that looked like they needed to be changed. One of the mother's hands, with black-painted fingernails, held the baby, and with the other hand she tugged at the edge of the diaper.

The second image was of another woman, darker skinned, perhaps Hispanic. The mother was wearing a McDonald's uniform, snug over her breasts and splattered with grease. But the baby in her lap was immaculate, dressed in a fancy baseball outfit, perfect, right down to the little striped socks and tiny cap. The mother was gazing down at her baby, but something about her eyes made it look like she was thinking about something else.

The third picture, the largest one, was the most disturbing. The face looked so familiar that Charlotte felt that she knew her, but she couldn't put a finger on quite who it was. Unlike the other two, the mother looked not at the baby, but straight out, as though looking at the camera in a photograph. The baby she held in her arms, slightly at arm's distance, was as pale as marble, the skin vaguely translucent. But the baby was still as a stone.

Most disturbing of all, on each baby's right hand, there was a bloody wound, a hole, with blood dripping down the mother's thigh. Charlotte remembered from endless gallery walks with Charlie the holes in the hands—they were called stigmata, the stigmata of Christ. Looking at gruesome medieval paintings Charlie had explained that to viewers in the Middle Ages the stigmata indicated not pain, but something glorious yet to come. Still, the sight of a baby with a hole in its hand . . . Charlotte leaned on the wall to steady herself, then she turned and ran down the hallway toward the bathroom, feeling as though the room were spinning.

Too much wine. Charlotte drank very little, and almost never on an empty stomach. She washed her face, rinsed out her mouth, patted her hair, and tried to make herself presentable again. She realized how plain she looked, how middle-aged and drab without any makeup. Finally she pulled herself together enough to walk back down the corridor. As she passed the paintings again, the eyes of the mother who stared defiantly out at the world instead of at her baby seemed to bore into her back as she walked down the hall.

The food was already served, and Paul smiled at her when she came back—the kind of smile that makes you feel pretty.

"Did you guess which work is mine?"

She looked into his eyes for a moment. They were the part of his face that was most different from Charlie's face. Charlie's eyes were a warm brown that always put her in mind of a golden retriever. But Paul's eyes were blue and glittered with an intensity that tickled down the backs of her thighs.

"I . . . I didn't really look around. I didn't realize you were a painter."

"Yeah, reporting is just my day gig, but I must say I'm sort of getting into it—it's kind of like painting in a weird way."

"Like painting?"

"Yeah, daubs of different colors of paint that eventually tell a story—first you just have colors and a blank piece of canvas, but after a while something you can recognize seems to emerge."

She and Charlie used to talk about painting, before all they talked about was the mortgage, and cutting the grass, and how Julie was doing in school, and the clinic, and all the other details that somehow seemed to come to make up a life, even if at first you didn't think that was what you had in mind.

Then she felt the stab of white-hot heat, of anger, of betrayal.

Charlie was gone. He had left her. Left her and Julie, and she didn't know where he was. It was as though she hadn't realized the extent of his betrayal until that very moment. She leaned forward, looked directly into Paul Stone's face, and let herself swim right in, let his gaze engulf her fully, crossing the threshold of betrayal. But with Charlie gone, and Paul right here, smiling at her, she wasn't even sure if it was a betrayal.

Charlotte put her spoon into the butternut-squash soup she had ordered, but couldn't bring herself to raise it to her lips. She put the spoon back down, embarrassed that her hand was trembling and that the spoon clattered, then picked up the thin, cool stem of the glass.

Paul reached out across the table, put his hand out, stopped for a moment halfway, then took a lock of hair and tucked it behind her ear, and Charlotte let him, leaning in closer to allow his palm to cup the back of her head. Then he slipped his hand down along her arm, leaving a track of electrical sparks, until he rested it over her hand, rubbing the base of her palm with the broad, flat pad of his thumb.

Charlotte leaned in even more; the table was narrow. She tilted her face up. She closed her eyes.

Paul's hand grasped her chin and tilted her face upward.

"Charlotte."

She opened her eyes and looked at him, his eyes more purple than blue at this distance, his lips wet and slightly parted.

"Just like you, Charlotte. A picture starts to emerge . . ." he said. He leaned in closer so that she could see the saliva clinging to his teeth, smell the faint fruity odor of wine of his breath.

A *picture starts to emerge.* . . . And then Charlotte sucked in her breath and drew back. The face—the face in the painting. She knew who it was.

Deirdre.

"Charlotte . . ." he said, moving closer.

"Paul." She sighed, lifted her lips up toward him, felt herself abandoning control.

"Charlotte, I . . . know about the baby," he said.

Charlotte drew back, confused. She looked at his face, which now seemed closed up tight, like a puzzle put away in a box.

"The baby . . . ?" How could he know about her miscarriage? Did Dr. Goodman tell him? But medical records were private.

"But how could you possibly . . . ?"

"It's part of the public record."

"What are you talking about?"

"Deirdre Stinson. Baby boy. New Haven, Connecticut, 1988."

"I . . . I, uh . . ." Charlotte was grabbing her jacket, the butternut soup untouched; then in her haste she knocked over the half-full wineglass that clattered off the table and shattered, loudly, on the stone floor.

"I . . ." She was backing away from the table. Backing as if she were being pursued, until she turned and ran out of the restaurant into the cold, dark night.

But of course she was trapped there, as she had come in his car. It was cold. Her thin jacket wasn't enough, and the branches of the trees were whipping furiously above her, the creek so loud that it sounded like cannon fire in her head. She twirled around in the parking lot one time, then looked at the door to the restaurant.

Then for an odd second everything went black. At first she thought she had passed out, but then the lights flashed back on and she realized that the wind had just made the electricity go out for a moment. As soon as the light turned back on, she could see Paul standing in the doorway, and she realized that she had no choice. She had to go back inside.

When Charlotte came back in, the waiter was just finishing cleaning up the glass shards from the floor. She slid back into the chair across from Paul, muttering, "Sorry, I . . ."

"Don't worry about it." He reached across the table and put his hand on the table. "I'm so sorry. I didn't mean to upset you like that. I didn't know it was a secret," he said. "About the Stinson baby . . ."

Charlotte gazed out the windows; she could see tree branches whipping in the wind. "It's not," she whispered.

"Well, I guess I shouldn't have sprung it on you like that. I thought you would want to know that I knew—that I understand where all of your . . . mixed feelings . . . are coming from."

Neither one of them spoke. She didn't know what to say. Now it was apparent that she had overreacted. Behaved badly. Given herself an appearance of guilt when there was none.

"Hey, I think I know which paintings are yours," Charlotte said, trying to change the subject.

"You do?" Now Charlotte could hear it in his voice. The artist's pride. It was a note that she would recognize anywhere.

"Yes, the three paintings of the girls with infants. The Madonna motifs . . ."

Paul frowned, then said in a constrained voice, "No. Those aren't the ones."

"Oh," she said. Now she was the one who felt like a fool. Why had she been so sure those paintings were his? Well, of course. It was his interest in the painting of Mary at El Centro.

"Oh, sorry . . ." She trailed off. "I thought there was something . . ."

"Familiar about them?" he asked.

"Yes, I guess that's it," Charlotte said. "But obviously I was wrong."

Then nothing. Silence for a moment. But as she sat there, Charlotte started to get mad all over again.

"Why do you know so much about me anyway? Who the hell are you?"

Paul looked at her, smiled a slow half smile, so that just one corner of his mouth drifted upward. So Charlie-like.

Then the smile left his face and his eyebrows creased in sympathy. He reached across the table, patted the top of her hand.

"I am who I say I am. I'm a painter—somewhat—and a reporter—a new gig, to earn money. And I'm finding I like reporting because I'm interested in stories." He paused for a moment, took a sip of his wine, looked out the window, where the trees were still crashing around. "I'm interested in your story, Charlotte."

The way he said it, it sounded like a compliment. Charlotte looked up from the table, looked at Paul's face, and with a pang, she realized how lonely she was, how hollow down at the core because Charlie was gone.

"Well, there's nothing interesting about my story."

"Do you want to . . . tell me a little bit about the drowning?"

Charlotte felt her stomach lurch.

"It was Deirdre Stinson's housekeeper?"

"Saramago."

"I beg your pardon?"

"Deirdre Saramago."

"Right, her married name. And you just . . . happened to be over near the pool?"

Charlotte took a sip of water. "Why exactly are you asking me this stuff? What's it to you anyway?"

He reached out, cupped his hand around her elbow. "Has it occurred to you that you might be in trouble?"

Charlotte jerked her arm away from him. "In trouble? Why? Why on earth would I be in trouble?"

Paul shrugged, then smiled again, that slow smile that spread across his face like a sunrise. "Let's hope I'm wrong," he said. "I just thought . . . I just thought you should know that . . . well, two dead bodies in two weeks . . . I've heard . . ."

"What have you heard?" Charlotte's voice got shrill. "What have you heard? What are you talking about? How could I possibly be in trouble?"

"It's just that given . . . your history . . . there's bound to be some talk. And I just thought . . . I just thought you should be aware of it."

Charlotte didn't know what to say; she was stunned. Her feet felt frozen to the floor, and she looked at his face, studied it hard, wishing that somehow she could will him to unsay what he had just said.

She had nothing to feel guilty about. This was a crazy situation, and she felt like the room was imploding in on her, starting to spin.

"I think we'd better go," she said.

"Charlotte, you really don't understand. I came here to try to help you. I thought you needed to be aware that people are talking. I'm on your side. Believe me, I am."

"I really would like to leave now."

"Of course," he said. His smile was disarming, his eyes kind. "I'm terribly sorry. I've upset you, and that wasn't my goal."

When they stepped outside, the wind was so strong that a gust of the icy air pushed the door too far open, so that it banged against the front of the restaurant. Charlotte leaped forward to grab the door, stepping in front of Paul, who was zipping up his coat against the wind.

"Just use common sense," Paul said to her, although she could barely hear him above the racket that the wind was making.

The light outside on the terrace was dim, and Paul was much taller than she was. She tilted her chin upward to look at him, trying to hear him over the wind. But she waited just a half a second too long, and then, almost before she knew it, she felt his warm lips close against hers, their contours white-hot, and she felt herself giving in toward the center, where she would start to drop away.

She pushed back, but not until a moment or two later than she should have. "Paul, no," she said, "that's not what I—"

"Of course," he said stiffly. "Terribly sorry." She could see that the tips of his ears were red, though from the cold or from embarrassment, she couldn't say. They walked back to the car and rode in silence all the way home.

Julie came stomping in the side door, bringing a breath of cold air and the fresh smell of straw on her jacket, just as Charlotte was saying goodbye to Paul at the front door.

"Who was that?"

"Who was who?"

"I thought I heard you talking to someone."

"I was on the phone."

"With who?"

"Dad," Charlotte said, without realizing she was planning to lie.

Julie leaned over, and to Charlotte's surprise she lined up her boots upright and placed them neatly along the mudroom wall. Her amber hair was hanging loose over her shoulder, but she tucked it behind her ear with a graceful movement before she stood up and looked at Charlotte.

"That's odd," Julie said.

"Odd? Why?"

"Because when I talked to him, he said that he wouldn't be able to call back later."

"But . . ." Charlotte was furious at herself. Caught in her own lie. "But what did he say?"

"Oh, nothing," Julie said. "You know. Just what he told you, probably . . ."

Julie was already standing in front of the fridge with the door open, scrutinizing the contents.

"No, really, Julie, what did he say?"

"Mom, jeez, I told you—nothing. I don't really remember. I'm beat, Mom. I gotta get up at six for the horses again. I'm going to bed." And she headed toward the stairs.

"When is Deirdre coming back, anyway?" Charlotte called after her.

"Day after tomorrow. She's going to pay me for all the feeding. I'm going to collect big."

Thirty

After it was all over and Deirdre was gone, back to her family's estate in Tuxedo Park to recuperate, Charlotte felt like she dwelled in silence. She wasn't going to any of her classes, doing any of her homework. On the rare occasions when hunger pushed up into her consciousness, she would buy something in a cellophane package and then eat it as if it were sawdust, shoving it into her mouth and then dropping the wrapper onto the street, as though the world were worth so little that it didn't matter if she sullied it more.

All Charlotte really recalled from those days was her spot in the art gallery, a cool, smooth bench upstairs in the medieval and renaissance room, where she sat in silence for hours on end, hours when she should have been outside, attending to things, attending to her classes. But those few weeks were shut off in time. As Charlotte remembered it, the room was cloaked in darkness, and there was no light except for that which illuminated the painting—the painting that she was able to stare at for hours on end, the image that made her feel like somewhere, down at the long tunnel of her despair, there might be hope. Charlotte had not been raised with religion, and she didn't know how to pray, but meditating on the Madonna's face seemed to be as close as she could get to some intimation that following despair there might be something else.

The art gallery itself was constructed of cement, the walls harsh gray blocks, rough to the touch, profoundly inhospitable and cold. Each day, as Charlotte trudged up the stairs, running her knuckles against the bare walls until they almost started to bleed, she felt engulfed by the sheer inhumanity of the place, and in that inhumanity felt respite.

It turned out she was not a depressive by nature, and she snapped out of it, but not before her grades had slipped—a onetime occurrence that nonetheless had ruined her GPA.

By the time the early jonquils were pushing up along the sidewalks, warming up the sides of the gray gothic buildings, by the time that the grass had grown thick and green, and the students had shed sweaters, and the professors had pushed open the heavy windows with their stubborn casements to let in a few breaths of fresh air, it seemed that Charlotte was healed again. Only her academic transcript bore the traces, once orderly with a procession of As, now scarred and ragged, ripped apart by Ds. Charlotte felt the breezes caress her bare arms and felt her blood start to stir again; the hard, frozen silence of February and March started to thaw, enlivened by her very own young and vital being.

Hopper and Charlotte met most evenings at Yorkside for a slice of pizza around ten o'clock. Charlotte had gone months scarcely eating at all, until her clothes hung off of her bones, but now, with the spring, her appetite returned with vigor.

They barely spoke when they were together. Charlotte, once she woke up and realized that she was flunking all of her classes, now did nothing but study; even during meals, her stacks of spiral notebooks were always pushed in front of her.

Hopper was working on his senior installation in art, and he was always paint-splattered and half-exhausted, but he looked happy.

Before, they had been like sunflowers, their faces turned toward Deirdre, the sun; but now Deirdre was gone, and the spring sunshine seemed to cut a broader swath, to shine down all around, not just on Hopper and Charlotte, but also on the new grass, and the budding trees, and the newly bare legs of the students.

It was on one such evening, Charlotte remembered, that she was wearing shorts and that the evening was warm. She and Hopper finished their slices and gathered up their greasy paper plates and empty wax paper cups and jammed their books into their backpacks, and then, as they were leaving the pizza place, joining the throng out on the sidewalk on York Street, she turned her head and looked at Charlie, and he looked back at her, she felt the space closing between them as surely as when you shut a book with a confident thunk. He bent over and nuzzled her ear for a moment, and she slipped her arm through his, and that was it. After that, Charlotte and Charlie stayed close together, as close as the spellings of their two names. Charlotte never called him Hopper, and Deirdre and the winter that had passed were never spoken of between them again.

By fall of the following year, Charlotte noticed that most of her friends seemed to have forgotten that she and Charlie hadn't always been a couple. In fact, there were times that she herself forgot it, and maybe she would have forgotten the whole episode altogether if it weren't for that one semester on her report card, studded with Ds, and the somber notation at the bottom: *academic probation*. That, and the image of Mary that for ever so long seemed to be etched against the back of her eyelids, there to confront her, to taunt her, and ultimately to re-assure her.

But even that too over time had faded. The wound had healed over and the scars were hidden.

Thirty-one

T he next morning, when Charlotte arrived at the clinic, she was amazed to see that everything looked like it had gone back to normal. The news van wasn't there, just a few scattered cars in the parking lot—Charlotte recognized Flo's car, and Mary Louise's car.

Charlotte turned into the parking lot, feeling a big weight drop off her shoulders. Maybe, just maybe, things were going to start to get back to routine.

Inside the clinic, the girls looked businesslike. There were a few people in the waiting room. LeAnn was on the phone, Mary Louise was color-coding charts, and Arecely—Charlotte noted again how thin and peaked she was looking—was in the back taking a patient's blood pressure and asking questions in Spanish.

Flo was sitting in her cubicle, but when she saw Charlotte, she stood up and came out into the main chart area.

"No Channel Six," Charlotte said.

"Heavens, no," Flo said. "Didn'tcha watch the news this morning? They're all over to Cochranville. They're trying to evict that man, and he's holed up in his house with a twenty-gauge shotgun. . . ."

"They say he's got enough ammo to last him three days," Mary Louise chimed in.

"Yup," LeAnn said. "I saw it too. They're calling it PA-co."

"What's PA-co?" Charlotte asked.

"You know," Flo said. Sometimes she treated Charlotte like she was retarded about things that happened in the news. "P-A, like Pennsylvania, you know, instead of Waco."

"Well," Charlotte said. "It sounds like a mess, but I'm glad they've got something else to think about besides us for a change."

"Harve called. He's bringing the lawyer over. Said we're supposed to be ready."

"Ready for what?" Charlotte asked.

Flo looked at Charlotte, ruminating for a moment; then she patted her beehive and smiled. "He didn't say. Ready for anything, I guess."

The rest of the morning passed quickly, lots of patients seen in a blur. Arecely was quiet and still looked preoccupied, but she wasn't as distracted as she had been the day before, and Charlotte forgot about it. They managed to stay on track, timewise, and so they were just finishing up the morning schedule when two loud *kerthunks* and a moan sounded from the reception area. Arecely and Charlotte, who had just finished seeing a patient, rushed out to see what the problem was and saw LeAnn sprawled on the floor holding her knee, the UPS man standing just inside the doorway, and Mary Louise smiling.

"I'm sorry, terribly sorry. Oh, so very sorry," said Sam, kneeling down next to LeAnn. "I startled you. I did not realize that the door was going to push open. Usually it is locked."

Mary Louise stepped forward and took the packing box from Sam. "Oh, now, don't you worry. Maybe it was just ajar a little bit. It happens all the time," she said.

It does? Flo mouthed—she had emerged from her office. Mary Louise turned her head toward the ladies and gave a broad wink.

"LeAnn, are you okay?" Charlotte said. "Flo, why don't you run get her some ice?"

But LeAnn was already starting to get up. "I just . . . banged my knee . . . is all."

Sam was already there, with arms outstretched, and LeAnn leaned on his arm as she hopped up, balancing on one foot. Then, like a queen with her handmaidens in attendance, she accepted ice from Flo, and a vanilla Tastykake from Arecely.

"What happened?" Charlotte said.

"The door opened up."

"Sorry, so very sorry."

"And I was startled."

"Very, very sorry."

"She fell right off her chair," Mary Louise said. "I thought she plumb fainted or something."

"Are you feeling dizzy or light-headed or anything now?" Charlotte said, poking experimentally at LeAnn's knee, which seemed to have made a full recovery.

"Here, let me see if you can walk," Sam said, grasping LeAnn gently and gallantly by the arm.

LeAnn stood up, tentatively; then, after brushing some Tastykake crumbs from the front of her scrub top, she leaned, perhaps more than was strictly necessary, against Sam's well-muscled arm, and took a limping victory lap around the reception area, her red hair hanging over her face just enough to indicate what a close call it had been.

It was lunchtime anyway. Mary Louise took orders for *tortas*, "Beef, pork, or chorizo?" she said, and counted heads.

"Of course, Sam, you'll join us for lunch." Flo said.

"Well, I . . . I'm not sure," Sam said. "Company policy . . ."

"Nonsense. We're inviting you. You get a lunch break, don't you?"

Sam nodded gravely.

"Well, you're here, and we've all got to eat."

In the excitement of LeAnn's fall and their new guest, they had forgotten that they were expecting Harve and the lawyer. As it happened, Mary Louise was just coming in the door with a cutoff cardboard box filled with the fragrant *tortas* from the Mexican store next to Wawa when Harve arrived as well, looking unusually slicked back and wide-awake, and with him was the skinny lawyer in six-inch high heels— Barbara Volpone. There was a third woman with them, a fifty-something woman with short dyed-brunette hair, and a gray no-nonsense suit. She was carrying a clipboard, and she did not look amused.

Charlotte, who was finishing the last couple of charts while waiting for Mary Louise, came out to say hello.

"Charlotte Hopper," she said, sticking her hand out toward the woman she hadn't yet met. "The nurse practitioner."

The gray-suited woman looked her up and down appraisingly, making Charlotte self-conscious about her workmanlike khaki skirt and worn-down clogs. This was the kind of woman who had everything lacquered into place—perfect hair, perfect nails. She was wearing nylons. Charlotte, under her khaki skirt, was wearing knee socks.

"Patricia Lynch," she said, her voice as curt as her appearance indicated it would be. "You are the one who found the . . . demise . . . on clinic property, are you not?"

Charlotte nodded. Who was this woman? Another lawyer? She didn't seem quite like a lawyer. But before she could wonder further, Barbara Volpone introduced her. "Charlotte, Ms. Lynch is director of patient services."

"And vice president of nursing,"

"And vice president of nursing," Barbara added, "at the Communicare Health Corporation Services."

"CHICKS," Patricia said briskly.

"I beg your pardon?"

"CHICKS. Communicare Health Corporation Services. Otherwise known as CHICKS."

"Oh, right, of course, but what can we do for you today?"

"Ms. Lynch is here to do a preliminary site evaluation," Barbara Volpone said.

"Are you a member of the board?" Charlotte asked. There was something about this that was making her very uncomfortable. She wished Dorothea Wetherill were here. The first chance she got, she was going to slip away and dial her up.

"A member of the board?" Patricia laughed this away with obvious merriment. "Oh, dear, no. I'm a member of the CHICKS acquisition and crisis-management team."

"I smell them *tortas*. What's taking you . . ." Flo trailed off as she came in and saw the cluster of people.

"Dr. Dexter, Miz Volpone," Flo said, nodding in her most managerial style. She looked directly at Patricia Lynch, sucking in her belly. "May I help you with something?"

"Flo, this is Patricia Lynch," Harve said.

You could almost see Flo unsheathing her claws. Charlotte could tell she didn't like the looks of this Ms. Lynch right from the get-go. Maybe it was the suit, or the clipboard, but Charlotte could sense that Flo wasn't sure whose side the woman was on. "Florence Garcia, clinic manager. And you are . . . ?"

"Here to conduct a preliminary evaluation. And I have limited time," she said, turning to give a meaningful look to both Harve and Barbara in turn. "So shall we?"

"Got extra *tortas*. If you are wanting any," said Mary Louise, who hadn't spoken up until now.

Patricia and Barbara both gave dubious sniffs. Harve shot his hand out toward the foil-wrapped sandwiches, but under the reproving glance of the two ladies, he withdrew it again, sticking it in the pocket of his overcoat.

"I'll just be showing them around the clinical setting," said Harve. "Why don't you ladies just run along and enjoy your lunch break?"

So Flo, Charlotte, and Mary Louise headed up the stairs to the meeting room, where Sam was seated on the floor on a pillow, with LeAnn a comfortable distance away, giggling and hanging on his every word, and Arecely was standing near the dormer window, looking out toward the fields.

"*Tortas!*" Mary Louise called out merrily, and everyone gathered around, grabbing foil-wrapped sandwiches. Flo passed out the cups and started pouring out orange soda, and everybody sat on the floor.

It wasn't a sunny day; in fact, the sky was clouding over and it was dark outside. Charlotte glanced up at the painting of Mary on the wall, the calm smile, the outstretched hands, and she felt a moment of peace come over her. Today had seemed almost close to an ordinary day. Maybe just a few more ordinary days and then Charlie would come home, or at least call her, and things could go back to the way they were before.

She looked up at the painting, and said to herself, *Please, Mary. Let things just be the way they are supposed to be.* Then she folded back the foil on her sandwich and took a bite.

Sam had finished his sandwich quickly and now stood up, preparing to leave. Charlotte noticed again how exceptionally handsome he was. No wonder LeAnn was so smitten with him. And he seemed, if you could really tell, to be nice enough.

"So kind of you ladies to invite me to have lunch with you. Now I really must to go."

"Anytime," Mary Louise said. "Sam, you are more than welcome. Now, LeAnn, if that leg is feeling well enough, why don't you show Mr. Sam downstairs?"

LeAnn's leg wasn't feeling quite well enough, so she needed to lean on Sam's arm. They had just made it to the top of the stairwell when the heads of the three visitors, Harve, Barbara Volpone, and Patricia Lynch, appeared, like Cerberus at the stairwell door.

"This room is used for meetings. There is a youth group that meets here, and, ahem . . . as you can see . . . sometimes the ladies come up here to have lunch," Harve was saying.

Patricia Lynch sniffed once; then Barbara Volpone sniffed twice. Both had the kind of stick-thin figures that indicated that they rarely ate.

"Do you use a cleaning service?" Patricia asked. She walked over to the bathroom door, opened it, sniffed again, then closed it.

Then she stood looking around the room. When she caught sight of the mural of Mary on the wall, she stopped cold, picked up her pen as though it were a rapier, and said, "Oh, no, this won't do. This won't do at all. A religious image in a medical clinic? How on earth did that ever get there anyway?"

"I know," Harve said, shaking his head. "I never got it either. Some Mexican religious thing, I guess."

"I don't see to how it's doing any harm there," Mary Louise said.

"It's the girls, you know, the girls from the youth group who painted it," Flo added.

Charlotte had yet to figure out exactly what was going on. She decided that she needed to slip down the stairs to her cubicle to get Dorothea Wetherill on the phone.

The three visitors were more or less blocking the stairwell door, so Charlotte had to edge past them, saying, "Excuse me," and brushing up against the wall. As she passed Patricia Lynch, she saw that on the other woman's clipboard there was a list of notations, and at the bottom of the list she had written in all caps and twice underlined: WHITE PAINT.

Charlotte practically sprinted down the stairs, found Dorothea Wetherill's number, and hurriedly punched the keys.

"Hello?" Charlotte was surprised, as Dorothea's voice sounded older over the phone than she thought of her in person.

"Dorothea. Charlotte Hopper, from El Centro. I think you should come over here right away. Harve is here with a couple of people . . . the lawyer and . . . some other lady."

"What lawyer? What other lady?"

"I don't know who the other lady is. She keeps calling herself CHICKS."

"CHICKS? You mean she is from Communicare?"

"Yes, that's what she said."

"You just hang on, dear. I'll be right over."

"Thanks," Charlotte said.

She emerged from her cubicle and saw that the patients for the afternoon had already grouped around the front door in the vestibule, waiting for someone to buzz them in. Charlotte went over to the door to push the buzzer, and the women poured over the threshold like ants on the trail of spilled sugar.

Bringing up the rear was Officer Stolzfus. Charlotte leaned over and pressed the buzzer to let him into the back office.

"Miz Hopper," he said, "I'm going to need you to come down to the station to answer a few questions."

Thirty-two

O ne thing that Charlotte remembered was how Charlie had always been there for her—then. She had felt completely alone, unexpectedly abandoned, because Deirdre had been whisked off to Yale–New Haven Hospital. And so suddenly, after an event that had so dramatically concerned the two of them, Charlotte was left completely alone, healthy in body, just hollow, like one of those Dutch Easter eggs that are blown out and then decorated. She was all painted up like Charlotte on the outside, so that nobody could see that she was just a fragile shell with her insides completely empty.

But then, somehow, Charlie was there when she went down to the police station, down in a part of New Haven that she had never seen before, a part of the city that she would have considered off-limits—too far off campus, too dangerous.

He was there, sitting in a metal chair. She remembered its peculiar color, a dark grayish green or greenish gray, like dull gunmetal. . . . Charlie had a sketchbook in his hands, and some charcoal pencils, and he was just sitting there in the hard metal chair, and he was waiting for her. Charlie didn't talk much to her then, as if he understood that she was hollow inside, that even something as soft and malleable as words might be strong enough to break her. He just waited in silence, and sat with her in silence, and walked with her in silence.

Charlie was there too when she walked along Grove Street, surrounded this time by burly men in uniforms. Charlie, wearing only softened jeans and an old flannel shirt, untucked, walked beside her, softening the space that was otherwise harsh—nothing but sharp edges: overpolished motorcycle boots, gold badges, holsters with guns. Then too, harsh edges of metal trash cans, everything cold, everything dead, everything hard enough to give you bruises on your shins should you stumble across one in the middle of the night. As she walked, fragile, cold inside, blown out, raw, she allowed herself, just sometimes, to bump up against the flannel-soft warmth of Charlie's shoulder, and feel his heat there, and from knowing that he was alive she could feel that she was alive too.

Thirty-three

Charlie still wasn't answering his cell phone, but she got hold of Julie.

"I may be a little late getting home from work today," Charlotte said, trying to keep her voice steady. "Just wanted to see what you're up to."

"Is it okay if I go over to Kayla's again? We're working on that history project."

Charlotte was relieved. She didn't want to have to explain anything to Julie.

"Yes, go ahead. But I want you home by ten."

"Okay, Mom."

"I love you."

Next she went to Flo; she debated, briefly, telling a fib, inventing a toothache or something, but then, with Officer Stolzfus standing in the vestibule, a version of the truth seemed like an easier answer.

"Flo, you're gonna have to cancel the rest of my afternoon. They need me to come down to the station for a little additional questioning."

Flo was seated at her desk, listening to salsa on her radio. She quickly minimized the solitaire game that had been up on her computer screen, and then turned around.

"More questions?" Flo was no dummy. She could probably hear the note of self-doubt in Charlotte's voice. "They have to do it now? During clinic time?"

"He's out there waiting for me," Charlotte said.

"You know, I bet by now they just want to mop this thing up," Flo whispered conspiratorially.

"I think the DA's getting embarrassed that he doesn't have any suspects."

Flo narrowed her eyes, looked quizzically at Charlotte. "You really think so?"

"I do," Charlotte said. "That's what Paul Stone was telling me, the reporter. . . ." But then she clamped her mouth shut again. She needed to be careful about how much she said.

"You . . . you sure everything is okay?" Flo said. "It's not . . . you know, starting to get to you or anything?"

"I'm fine," Charlotte said. "Why wouldn't I be?" But she could hear the false note as she spoke. She looked at Flo for a moment, wondering if Flo could hear it; then she turned away, out toward the vestibule where Officer Stolzfus was standing, one hand resting on his holster, shifting on his feet.

Charlotte followed the squad car down the Maryland Pike toward the state troopers' office. She was trying to control a feeling of panic that seemed to be overtaking her. Several times, when she stopped at a red light, she pushed the auto redial button on her phone—trying to reach Charlie—and each time she got the repeated message, "The customer you are trying to reach is not available at this time," she felt her level of panic rise. It was as if somebody had given her a shot of novocaine when Charlie left; all she had felt was the tingling, but now the novocaine was wearing off, and she was starting to feel the massive, jarring black hole of pain.

The state troopers' barracks was not far away—just down the road. It was a low, square building, constructed of yellow bricks with aqua trim around the windows. Nothing like the ornate, heavy gothic architecture of the police station in New Haven—but why was she even thinking about that? Charlotte was gripping the steering wheel so hard that when she turned off the ignition and let go, she left two damp traces where her hands had been.

As she stepped out of the car, she felt her knees tremble, then pulled her coat tighter, convincing herself that she was shaking from the cold.

Inside, there was a staticky sound of a police radio, and a barren waiting area with a glassed-off partition, behind which sat a heavyset blond officer in a crisp uniform and too much makeup. For a moment, Charlotte hoped she would be asked to wait, but Officer Stolzfus waved his security badge at the door, and then ushered her through.

The room he brought her into had a lone fluorescent bar hanging from the ceiling, and the single casement window was set up high and faced north, so that only a cold light trickled through. The walls were cinder block, painted a shiny pale green. The room was unfurnished except for a rectangular table surrounded by metal folding chairs. Though the room had a cold look to it, it was actually stuffy and overheated. Charlotte could feel herself sweating under her thick jacket; she took it off and settled into the chair that Officer Stolzfus was pointing to.

A couple of other people came into the room, a young-looking woman with brown hair who looked familiar and gave her a sympathetic smile—Charlotte thought she might be one of her patients. The other was a thin man whose face was traced with old acne scars.

Suddenly, with the three people there, one with a pad and pencil out in front of her, Charlotte felt how alone she was. Shouldn't she have someone with her? A lawyer or something? But wouldn't a lawyer imply that she had done something wrong? Charlotte rubbed her hands together under the table. She would answer their questions; then, when they let her go, she would call Dorothea Wetherill. She thought again of Charlie. Now it was urgent. Somehow she needed to find out where he was.

"Okay, Ms. Hopper. Thank you very much for coming down here today. We just want to ask you a few questions, and we hope that you will answer them to the best of your ability," Officer Stolzfus said.

Charlotte nodded.

The questions started simply enough. She went back over the story of how she had found the baby in the Dumpster. She was backing up her car, she tipped over the Dumpster, the baby was among the things knocked out. Flo was there when she found it. She checked it and the baby was already dead.

Then the thin officer started asking her questions about finding Maria Lopez dead in the pool. She was with her daughter who was feeding the horses; she wandered toward the pool, then saw a body in there. She attempted to bring the body to the surface, and then her daughter helped her, but the body was heavy and they couldn't lift her. Her daughter called an ambulance.

Yes, she knew that she was Deirdre Saramago's housekeepker. No, she didn't know anything else about her.

The thin officer leaned forward, rolling the pencil between his thumb and forefinger, and fixed her with a stare.

"Had you ever met her before?"

"Yes," Charlotte said, trying not to sound hesitant. Now she wished she did have a lawyer. She wasn't sure how much she was allowed to tell. "I had coffee with Deirdre on Sunday, and the housekeeper was there.

I remember that she was dusting and broke a vase, and she got very upset."

"Is it possible," the thin man said, "that you might have seen her at the clinic?"

Charlotte pondered how to answer. She knew she had better tell the truth, but she wasn't allowed to talk about her patients. She hedged.

"You know, I don't remember everyone I see in the clinic. Usually, if I see a patient in another context, I don't even remember them, or they look vaguely familiar, but I'm not sure why. Any of you could have been my patient, and I probably wouldn't remember. . . ." Charlotte tried not to look particularly at the female officer, but a quick glance sideways and she thought the officer looked like she was blushing a little bit.

"So you are saying it is possible?"

"I'm saying that if a person has been at the clinic and then I see them elsewhere, it is likely that I might not recognize them. Besides, whatever happens in the clinic is protected by patient confidentiality." Charlotte thought her answer sounded reasonable, although she wasn't quite sure. If they pushed it much further, she was going to have to refuse to answer, and consult an attorney. The patient was dead, so perhaps she didn't have rights anymore. The problem was, Charlotte wasn't sure.

"Are you aware that the housekeeper left a suicide note?"

"I was told." Charlotte's head snapped up, and she looked at Officer Stolzfus, who had spoken.

"Yes, I think you were told that the deceased had rocks in her pockets— big chunks of cement—weighing a total of more than twenty pounds."

"So that's why . . ." Charlotte said, remembering with a rush what it felt like, thrashing and holding her breath underwater, trying to tug on the arm, the hair, anything, and feeling like Maria was anchored to the bottom of the pool.

"Did she give a reason?" Charlotte asked.

"The note was in Spanish, and it was pretty cryptic, but it said something like, 'God killed my baby, and God is killing me.' Then a bunch of stuff about 'Mercy unto me, Virgin Mary, and forgive me for what I have done.' "

"God killed my baby?" Charlotte asked.

"That's what the note said," said Officer Stolzfus.

"And so you think . . ." Charlotte said.

"We don't think anything," said Officer Stolzfus.

"Necessarily," said the other man.

Then the young woman started speaking. "There is something else we'd like to ask you about, Mrs. Hopper."

"Sure," Charlotte said. Oddly enough, she was starting to feel a little bit better. If Maria Lopez did put the baby there . . . if the case was solved . . . somehow it would be easier for Charlotte to be able to shut it all up and call it a closed case. . . .

"We just want to ask you a few questions about the events of January 1988. . . ."

It was so hot in the room. She needed a breath of fresh air; the smell of carpet disinfectant and blasted, overheated air was overwhelming. She looked up at the casement window, but it had bars on it and was sealed up tight. It didn't even look like it opened.

"Uh . . ." Charlotte looked around at the three faces. What had looked a moment ago like benign interest, or something close to boredom, now looked hostile, malicious. "Um, it's very hot in here. Do you think I could . . . ?"

"Could I get you a glass of water?" the female cop asked.

"Sure," Charlotte said, wiping her hair off her forehead, feeling where the sweat was making it stick.

A moment later, Officer Goodwin, the young female officer, had returned with two Dixie cups of cold water from a cooler. Charlotte downed the first one and then took a couple of sips of the second one. While she was drinking, she tried to remind herself that she had done nothing wrong, that she had no blemish on her record.

"I'm sorry, but do you mind if I ask how you know about that? It was . . . I wasn't . . . I wasn't accused of doing anything wrong."

"We just need to look into it—same two players, you and Deirdre Stinson. She moved into the neighborhood about a week ago, and now we've found two dead bodies since."

"But you said yourself that Maria Lopez killed herself."

"Maria Lopez?" The officer jotted something down on his yellow legal paper.

"Um, the housekeeper. I thought that was her name."

"So can you tell us about the events of January 1988?"

"What do you want to know?" Charlotte said, her voice low, her heart feeling like lead.

Thirty-four

When she was finished she could have gone home, but instead she went back to the clinic, hoping that Dorothea Wetherill would still be there.

When she pulled into the parking lot, she was relieved to see Dorothea's little Toyota parked slantwise in the parking lot, and Harve's black Mercedes was gone.

She parked the car and got out, realizing that her knees felt as shaky as she did. But she was going to put it behind her. She wasn't accused of anything, and how could she be? She hadn't done anything wrong.

It wasn't even five o'clock yet, but there was dense cloud cover, and so it seemed almost dark. The front door of the clinic burst open and two women came out, laughing and talking in excited voices. At first Charlotte didn't recognize them—the taller one was wearing a black leather jacket and black pants. Big gold triangles dangled from her ears, and she was carrying an enormous pink-and-black purse. The other one was shorter, and her raven black hair was swinging around her shoulders. She was wearing a trench coat with the belt tied smartly around her waist, nylon stockings, and stylish black pumps.

"Charlotte? You're back. How'd it go?"

"Mary Louise?" As she got closer, Charlotte started to recognize her, glasses off, lots of makeup, and hair beehived up in a way that looked worthy of Flo.

"Mary Louise. I didn't recognize you. Your hair . . ."

"Mario," she said. "Flo sent me over there."

"It's . . ." Charlotte was speechless.

"Mario did mine too," came the girlish voice beside Mary Louise. "Gives me a whole new look, don't you think?"

"Well, I . . ."

"We're going out on the town," Mary Louise said.

"Girls' night out," the other woman added.

"Three Little Bakers," Mary Louise said. "Dinner theater."

"To see *Pillow Talk*." The other giggled. Then she added in a sultry voice, "I never cared that Rock Hudson was gay. Did you?"

It was nice to see that Mary Louise was making friends, although Charlotte couldn't figure out for the life of her who this woman was.

"Okay, Charlotte, we'll see you later."

"Good-bye Dr. Hopper," the other woman added.

Dr. Hopper? One of the patients? Charlotte took a good look—hot pink nails, lots of eye makeup, big, fake ruby clusters at her ear. At least, Charlotte assumed they must be fake. She couldn't believe it, but . . .

"Rosalie?"

"Yes?"

"Well, um . . . I hope you have fun."

The two women giggled as they sashayed across the parking lot. Rosalie Saxton. Obviously she had a side that none of them had ever seen before.

Charlotte skipped up the steps, feeling, somehow, just a little more lighthearted.

Thirty-five

Jennifer took a fit when Mary Louise told her she wasn't going. *Daughters.* It was funny, because you could never quite tell how they were going to react. When she told them that their father had run off, Shelby and Denise started to cry, but Jennifer, who had always been her hard-nosed one, told her, "Good riddance."

Mary Louise was down in her basement room, taking things from the boxes in her bureau and packing them up. She opened the small white cardboard boxes where she kept her costume jewelry, some of it old and falling apart. There was a heart-shaped pin with a broken clasp that Denise had gotten for her one year, for her birthday, saved up out of her allowance money. She'd had to wear that pin every time she went out, prominently displayed on the front of whatever party dress she was wearing, even if it didn't match.

What Denise never knew, Mary Louise remembered, was that that son of a bitch Eddie had made her take it off and shove it in her pocket in the car on the way to some party that he was always dragging her off to. She remembered one night—they were going to a Christmas party at his boss's house—Eddie Junior wasn't even a year old yet, and she'd had a devil of a time getting the kids ready for the sitter. He had been wailing the whole time, while she was trying to take her shower, while she was doing her hair. Suddenly, standing there, she could remember the exact combination of smells—the Aqua Net, the diaper pail full of borax and bleach in the corner, her own Cacharel perfume. . . .

When they finally got in the car, she was bone tired and wishing to everything that they didn't have to go, and then Eddie started in on her. . . . How come she hadn't lost all her baby weight yet? He liked it better when she used to wear that little red dress (the one that didn't fit her anymore), and didn't she know better than to wear that goddamn fake-diamond heart pin? It made him look like a cheapskate for buying fake jewelry for his wife. Never mind that she didn't have a real diamond heart pin; never mind that she'd cried her eyes out when Denise gave her the pin, saved up with her own money and bought it at Newberry's because it was so beautiful.

Mary Louise stared at the little brooch in the palm of her hand. Sometimes it was dangerous keeping things because of the memories that they held. It wasn't the thing anyway that held the memory, was it? Sure, the little pin brought back the good memories, but the bad stuff came along unbidden. Mary Louise rubbed the tip of her middle finger as she remembered how angry she was when she jerked the pin off her dress—that was how the clasp got broken—and how she pricked her finger as she jammed it into her pocket, how she put her finger into her mouth and sucked on it, the bitter iron taste of the blood in her mouth as she reminded herself *not* to cry, as it might ruin her mascara, how she didn't realize right away that she had spilled three small bright red drops of blood onto the front of her white party dress, and how she had stood in the corner the whole evening with her one hand held just so, so that nobody could see the spots, and hadn't really talked to anyone, or eaten any of the canapés that were circulating around on Bakelite trays.

And she remembered how Eddie had yelled at her in the car on the way home. He was driving, and he'd had too much to drink, of course, because everyone did in those days, but she didn't have the good sense to tell him that she should drive, because in those days she still had some kind of an idea about what a good wife should be.

Mary Louise looked at the pin for another long moment. It brought the face of Denise right up, exactly as she had been at the age of ten, her eyes shining, holding up the small velveteen box with her little trembling hands. . . .

Mary Louise blinked a couple of times. Well, she could still cry over that one—sentimental mama tears that would be with her, no matter what, until the day she died. She didn't need the object to remember that.

She sniffed, grabbed a perfumed Kleenex from the box on her bureau, dabbed at her eyes. Then she stood up and threw the little pin in the trash. She waited for a moment, looking at it, hesitating. It wasn't too late to pick it up and put it back in the small white box, where it usually nestled on a bed of cotton, its presence in her top drawer unquestioned for all these years.

But Mary Louise noted that she felt a little better now, just slightly lighter, as though she'd lost a pound or two. She went back to the top drawer, and she started pulling out other stuff—kindergarten art projects, faded pictures that had never quite made it into albums, broken bead necklaces that she'd always thought she might be able to repair—in it all went. Into the trash with a tinkle and a rattle of protest, but now Mary Louise was beyond the point of being sorry. She kept thinking about the smooth countertops and clean walls of her new apartment—she stopped a couple of times to finger the two fresh-cut silver keys with their rough edges that were attached to a paper clip with a paper tag on which was written the number 309.

She speeded up her pace now, working steadily, fast enough that she started to break out in a bit of a sweat. She was ruthless in her closet— she pushed her scrubs, her work clothes, off to one side, but one after another, she took her old outfits, staid mother-of-five party dresses and just-run-to-the-grocery-store pantsuits, and she laid them on the bed, ready for her to take them to Goodwill.

Very few things actually went into the suitcases—so few things that when she was done, two of the three suitcases were still empty. She thought about all of the rest of the stuff that was packed into a storage unit back in Minnesota.

She would make five copies of the little keys and send one to each of her children. "If you want it, go and get it," she was planning to say. Then, whatever was left, she would tell them to dump it. A clean start.

As she folded her scrubs and put them into the suitcase, she thought about how she would decorate her little apartment—a new sofa, white leather, because she wouldn't have to worry about scuffing feet, and a glass table—yes, glass; she had always loved the light and airy way that glass looked.

Mary Louise had to run up the stairs and out back four times to empty her wastebasket, then another three times to load up the trunk of her car with the Goodwill stuff, and when she was done, there was nothing but her three suitcases, one full and two empty, sitting on the clean mattress of her bed. Jennifer was letting her take the bed, because she wasn't planning to have a guest room in her new house in Mobile (and Mary Louise decided not to dwell on what she meant by that).

When she came upstairs Jennifer came over to her, all solicitous, and put her arm around her shoulder.

"Doing okay, Mom?"

"I'm all done."

"You can still change your mind, you know."

"Sweetie pie, I'm not planning on changing my mind. I've already done paid my deposit. I've got my key."

"But, Mama," Jennifer said, "to think of you all alone like that. And with family so far away." Jennifer blinked a couple of times, and Mary Louise was astonished to see something that looked suspiciously like tears.

"Honey child, we're all of us alone anyway. Besides, I've got my work and my friends. A lady got five kids, believe me, she's happy to be alone sometimes."

"All the time," Jennifer said. "You're going to be alone all the time."

Mary Louise was going to say something like, *Yup, and I'm planning to enjoy myself thoroughly,* but she could still see baby Jennifer, the youngest of her three daughters, the tough-as-nails one who learned not to cry when her big sisters pushed her around, and who loved them anyway, so she decided to go easy on her.

"Don't worry, honey. I'll be all right. And I can still come visit for the holidays."

"Oh," Jennifer said, sniffing just a little. "Well, you know, this holiday Brian and I were thinking of taking Madison to Telluride. Once you're three you can take skiing lessons, and . . . you know, being as we're going to be in the South and all, we'll probably miss the snow."

Mary Louise patted her daughter's arm. "Well, isn't that wonderful? And don't you worry, because I wasn't talking about *this* Christmas. Me 'n' Rosalie already looked into getting tickets for a cruise. You know how much I hate the cold weather."

Jennifer stared at her mother, and Mary Louise couldn't quite read the expression, whether it was astonishment or just a tiny little bit of pique.

"Well," said Mary Louise, "if you don't mind, I'm going to make myself a cup of tea, because *Oprah's* going to be on soon. Then I have a nice young man coming over to load up my stuff with his pickup truck at about five P.M."

"But . . ." Jennifer said. "You mean you're leaving today?"

"Oh, yes. Oh, I'm sorry, dear. Didn't I tell you? The moving companies are so danged expensive, so I've got this lovely young man with a pickup truck. He called me earlier today and told me it was supposed to rain tomorrow, so wouldn't it be better if we did it today?"

"But Madison is on a playdate right now. If you're gone when she comes back, she won't know where you went. Besides, Brian and I were thinking about going out tonight—Brian wanted to catch a movie."

"You know, I bet if you asked LeAnn from my office she would babysit for you. Nice young girl. Always seems desperate for money. Why don't you give her a try?"

Jennifer just stood and stared at her mother. Didn't say a word. Mary Louise went over and wrote down LeAnn's phone number on a piece of paper, handed it to her daughter, and then proceeded to fill the kettle with water.

"Tea, dear?"

But Jennifer was already punching the phone number into the keypad.

"Around five P.M.," she heard Jennifer say. "Perfect."

Mary Louise smiled, put an Earl Grey tea bag into her cup, and poured hot water over it, releasing the delicate scent of bergamot.

Normally she would have gone back downstairs, but she had already unplugged her TV set, so she carried the mug into the family room, flicked on the TV, and settled back into the sofa, sipping her tea and feeling, if the truth be known, 100 percent satisfied as she pulled an afghan over her knees and settled in to watch her favorite show.

The program was just ending when the doorbell rang—Mary Louise could never get over the rich, millionaire's-house sound that her daughter's doorbell made. She jumped up from the couch, bringing her empty cup with her, which she slid onto the kitchen counter, then went to open the door.

"I am here."

"Osama, hello. Wonderful. And right on time, I see. Come on in."

But before she had even shut the door, she saw a little green Neon slowing down in front of the house, so she stepped outside and waved.

LeAnn caught sight of her and pulled into the driveway, parking next to Sam's white pickup truck.

She came to the door, looking rushed, a worried frown on her forehead. She was wearing an old gray sweatshirt, and her hair was pulled back into a frazzled bun.

"Hi, LeAnn. Come right on in. Jennifer is expecting you, but she had to go pick up Maddy from a playdate. You remember Sam, don't you? He's here to help me move."

When LeAnn looked up and saw Sam, one hand grabbed the hem of her sweatshirt to pull it down, and the other flew to her hair to pat it smooth, but her hazel eyes lit up with sparkles. Sam gave a diffident smile—like the one Tom Cruise does just as a teaser, to let you know the big one is to follow. LeAnn turned her head just a little, just enough to be able to see the flash of white teeth. She blushed a furious red, then made a grunting sound that was probably supposed to be "hello" but sounded a lot more like "humgumphpbh."

"LeAnn, dear, Sam's here to help me move. Such a nice fellow."

But LeAnn didn't look up again, and so Mary Louise showed her to a sofa, handed her the remote, and told her to wait for Jennifer.

Then, humming "Some Enchanted Evening" under her breath, she ushered Sam over to the basement stairs, and the song stuck in her head all the while that she and Sam were loading the pickup truck, all the while that LeAnn was sitting on the sofa, making friends with Maddy, who had come back from her playdate.

By the time they got ready to leave, Maddy was sitting content as could be on LeAnn's lap, while LeAnn read to her *Are You My Mother?*

LeAnn was busy trying to pretend that she wasn't looking up each time that Sam passed, carrying a heavy object that showed off his muscled physique to better advantage.

Finally, when they were all ready to go, Jennifer stood at the doorway and whispered to her mother, "She's wonderful." Sam smiled, and seeming to have gotten up his courage, he called across to her, "Maybe I will see you at the office, Miss LeAnn?"

Jennifer threw her arms around her mother and squeezed her tight, and Mary Louise squeezed back, but gripped in her hand she had the keys to her new apartment, and she was eager to get going so that she would be set up in time for bedtime.

"I'll lead the way, Sam," Mary Louise said.

"Okay," he said, "I follow."

And Mary Louise left her daughter's house behind and drove away into the night, toward the spanking-new active-adult-over-fifty-five community where her new apartment was waiting for her, with fresh paint and carpet so new that it still smelled of the factory.

Thirty-six

It poured steadily through the weekend, that hard, drenching kind of rain that made November seem like November. All weekend Charlotte had been waiting for Charlie to call. By Sunday afternoon she went upstairs to her room, locked the door, and started pushing redial over and over again—hoping that somehow she could get his cell phone to pick up. Then, in tears, she had started rooting around in his bureau, something she had resisted doing until now, and she felt dirty as she rummaged around in his sock drawer, shoved her hands among his sweaters. Charlie's heady aroma emerged from the sweaters, which made her cry, and she picked one up and held it against her face, breathing in the scent in big warm sobs, then shoving it down again in disgust—he had taken off and left her, left his own daughter, no contact, his cell phone turned off. Then, more angry than sad, she rubbed her tears away with her fist and continued with her mission more methodically, searching his drawers for something—but she didn't know what she was looking for. What was she hoping for?

Right now what she wanted more than anything was to find an instruction manual that said, *Charlotte's Book of Instructions for Life.*

She flopped back on her bed and must've fallen asleep, because when the phone rang, she didn't quite wake up, just thought, *Let Julie get it,* and rolled over. Then a few minutes later the phone rang again, and suddenly she thought, *What if it's Charlie?* She jumped up off her bed and ran to her bureau to get the phone, but by the time she picked it up all she heard was Julie's voice saying, "Okay," and the voice of Deirdre Saramago, tinny from a long-distance call, saying, "Right, then. Good-bye."

Charlotte got up off her bed, unlocked her door, and then splashed water on her face before going to look for her daughter.

"Julie. *Julie?*"

"Yeah, Mom?"

"What did Deirdre want?"

"How did you know it was Deirdre?"

"Oh, I picked up the phone, but you were already saying good-bye."

Charlotte had come downstairs, to where Julie was sitting at the kitchen table leafing through a magazine.

"Nothing." Julie shrugged.

"Well, she must have said something."

"She just said she was coming back Tuesday afternoon. She wants me to keep feeding the horses through tomorrow."

"That's it?"

"Oh, and Dad called."

"Dad?" Charlotte felt the panic catch in her throat. She attempted to make her voice sound casual. "What did he say?"

"Oh, nothing. Just, you know, hi. He wanted to talk to you, but I told him you were asleep."

"Asleep? Julie! Why didn't you come get me? I wasn't asleep."

"Oh, come on, Mom. I could hear you snoring. It was only Dad. I didn't want to bother you."

"Well, next time wake me up."

"Jeez, Mom, chill," Julie said, shrugging her bony shoulder.

Charlotte paused, stood there at the threshold to the kitchen, trying to figure out how to proceed. She thought about how to make her voice sound casual. "So what did he say?"

"Who? Dad?"

"Yes, Dad."

"He said, you know, that he's still coming home when he said he would, and—"

Just then the phone rang, and Julie swiveled around on her chair to grab the phone.

Julie said, "Hi," and hunched over the phone a little, the universal sign of a teenager who wanted privacy. But instead of stepping back a pace, as she usually would have, Charlotte crowded in—maybe this was Charlie calling back. . . .

Mom! Julie mouthed. *It's for me.*

Charlotte took a step back and then turned away, heading to the laundry room to pull warm clothes out of the dryer.

She could hear Julie's voice in the other room, lilting up and down. It sounded like she was talking to Kayla. She hung up the phone a few moments later and came into the laundry room to shove her muddy boots on, no doubt going to check Deirdre's horses.

"Julie . . ."

"Yeah, Mom?"

But then the words stuck in her throat. She just didn't want Julie to know that anything was wrong between her and Charlie.

"Where's your slicker? It's pouring."

Julie rolled her eyes. *"Really?"* Then she pushed out the back door, leaving Charlotte standing there holding one of Charlie's T-shirts, warm from the dryer. After the door was closed, Charlotte buried her face in its softness and closed her eyes; then she pulled it away from her face and threw it down without folding it.

Coming back when he said he was going to . . . What kind of nonsense was that? She needed him, and he had left. Charlotte wasn't sure how she was going to feel when he came back.

Then she thought about Paul Stone again—how she had melted when his hot lips pressed against hers, and she felt a tremor that she recognized as desire. She wanted to see him again.

When Charlie had walked out that door, he had set the world spinning in a new direction. So he was "coming back," but you could never come back to exactly the same place. The world spins just a little bit on its axis every time you walk out your front door, and when you come home, you always find it in a slightly different place.

Charlotte could still feel the traces of the interview at the police station clinging to her, like the sour aftertaste of milk. Charlie had pulled her up once out of the muck, but this time she was going to need to pull herself out.

She picked up his T-shirt that was lying in a crumpled heap on top of the dryer, and she folded it and smoothed it.

That evening Julie was sitting on the sofa watching one of the TV makeover shows, and Charlotte said, trying to sound casual, "Mind if we switch over to the news?"

"Oh, why? Do you think there's going to be something about the clinic again?" Julie asked. "Are you going to be on TV?"

"I sincerely hope not," Charlotte said, too softly for her daughter to hear her.

She didn't have to watch long—it was the lead story. "Possible link between drowned housekeeper and baby found in Dumpster," said the voice-over. "More after the break."

First the camera panned across the front of Deirdre's estate. On camera it looked somehow even more palatial and imposing.

"New DNA evidence regarding a possible connection between the housekeeper at the estate of Deirdre Saramago, the widow of billionaire Argentinian financier Juan-Luis Saramago, and the baby found in a Dumpster at El Centro de la Mujer. Ms. Saramago was out of the country on family business when her housekeeper was found dead in the swimming pool, an apparent suicide. The case is seen as a possible link to the infanticide because of a note: *'God killed my baby.'* "

"Mom! Why didn't you tell me?"

"I didn't know," Charlotte said, a half truth.

"But—"

"Shush! Here it comes."

Charlotte waited through the commercial; then there was Linda Rodriguez, standing in front of the same state troopers' office Charlotte had been in.

"A preliminary DNA typing by pathologist Dr. Edgar Munt finds that there is no match between the housekeeper found drowned who left a suicide note saying that God had killed her baby and the baby abandoned in the Dumpster."

The scene cut to a laboratory. "So the probability that she was the perpetrator, Dr. Munt?" Linda Rodriguez was asking.

"Low," said the pathologist. "I'd say on the order of less than one percent. Not a match at all."

"And so the hunt for the unknown woman who ruthlessly left her baby in a Dumpster continues. Linda Rodriguez, ABC News, Channel Six."

"Jeez, Mom. So can you believe that? She left a suicide note saying that God killed her baby? What do you think? What do you think made her do it?"

For some reason, all of a sudden, Charlotte thought of Ariel . . . Ariel with her positive pregnancy test. Charlotte hoped that Deirdre had had the good sense to help her take care of it.

"Julie?"

"Yes, Mom."

"When you talked to Deirdre, did she say anything about Ariel?"

"About Ariel? Like what?"

"Oh, I don't know. Like is Ariel coming back with her?"

"Oh, Ariel didn't go to Argentina with Deirdre."

Charlotte felt her stomach lurch.

"Are you sure? How do you know? If she didn't go with Deirdre, then where is she?"

"Oh, she's . . . You know, I'm not sure where she is, exactly."

"Well, wait. . . . How do you know that she didn't go with Deirdre?"

"Because Deirdre asked me if I had seen her. She wanted to know if Ariel was staying at the house."

"And what did you say?"

"Well, duh, what do you think I said? I said I hadn't seen her, and I didn't think she was staying at the house, but I wasn't really sure."

"*Have* you seen her?"

"Ma, jeez. I just finished saying I hadn't seen her. But I mean, I'm not exactly hanging around there. I just go check on the horses."

"Well, if you see her, you've got to tell me," Charlotte said.

"Okay, Mom. Chill. I will. If I see her, I will tell you." Julie was using the tone that she used when she thought Charlotte was being particularly stupid.

"It's time for bed now," Charlotte said.

"Okay, Mom. You know, did anyone tell you *you* are acting weird? I'm not a four-year-old, you know. I have a little homework. Then I'm going to bed."

"It's this hour and you haven't done your homework yet?" Charlotte said, grumpy. She was crabbing at Julie for no reason, and she knew it.

She knew what Charlie would tell her if he were here. He would knead her tense shoulders and say, "You can't carry the weight of the world on these, you know."

And Charlotte would say, "Yes, I can. It just gets heavy sometimes."

So he was coming home. Only now she just wasn't sure how she felt about that.

Thirty-seven

The protesters were back. Or had they ever left? Charlotte wasn't sure. She didn't remember seeing them on Friday. The rain was cold and stingy, battered on a chilly wind, and the protesters were huddled under black umbrellas, their signs nowhere in sight. But there was something about the small knot of people that seemed agitated. Charlotte peered at the group, trying to see if Rosalie Saxton was among them, but she couldn't distinguish anyone, just a gaggle of black umbrellas and dark-colored parkas. But she noticed that they had moved. The group used to stay out by the parking lot entrance, but today they had moved down, so that they were on the grass directly across from the clinic entrance.

She parked her car and hurried across the parking lot, ducking her head against the rain.

Inside, Flo and Mary Louise, LeAnn and Arecely were clustered around the window, looking out at the group of people outside.

"Good morning, everybody," Charlotte said.

"Well, we've got a call in to Mrs. Wetherill, but if this doesn't beat all get-out."

"What's that?"

"Well . . ." Flo said, drawing it out in a way to get maximum attention. "You know Our Lady of El Centro?"

"I beg your pardon?"

"The Virgin of Londondale . . . ?" Flo was enjoying this. "Somebody spotted the painting of Mary through the window last night," Flo said.

"And they think that they had a vision," Mary Louise added.

Charlotte peered out the window to the cluster in the parking lot, and as if on cue, one of them dropped to her knees, as though she didn't even notice the rain and the puddles.

"But . . ." Charlotte wasn't sure what to say.

"And it is kinda weird," LeAnn added, "when you think about it, since it's dark up there at night. How're they gonna see the painting through the window?"

"Can you see it now?" Charlotte asked. "Have you looked?"

"I'll go look," Mary Louise said.

"Well, then, I'm going too," Flo said, as though she thought going outside to look through the window required her official imprimatur.

Then everybody starting pulling on their raincoats. There weren't any patients yet, and with this kind of pouring rain, it was likely to be slow all day.

Outside they stood in a little knot in the rain, peering up at the window, squinting.

"Glory be to God!" called out a thin man from behind their little group, followed by a cluster of excited choruses.

Flo looked around at the group and rolled her eyes.

"A miracle has been visited upon us," said a sandy-haired man.

"I'll take care of this," Flo said to the girls.

She straightened her shoulders and readjusted the position of her purple umbrella on her shoulder.

Charlotte felt cold rain trickling down the back of her neck. She wanted to go inside, but she couldn't help but want to watch this little encounter.

Flo had a loud voice, and she spoke up in her most authoritative tone. "Now who exactly saw what? And when exactly did they see?"

The sandy-haired man seemed to be the spokesman for the group, but his voice was low and trembly, so Charlotte couldn't pick up the words. After a few moments of this, she decided it was foolish to stand out in the parking lot getting wet.

"Shall we?" Charlotte said. Mary Louise and LeAnn didn't look like they were going to budge, but Arecely, who was dressed only in pink scrubs and a light sweater, turned to follow Charlotte inside. Charlotte had noticed that Arecely had been looking poorly lately. . . . She wondered what was going on with her. This morning she was pale, and had dark circles under her eyes. She would try to get her aside at some point today, and ask her if everything was okay.

They were almost back inside when the Channel Six news van pulled into the parking lot.

"Oh, no," Charlotte said aloud to no one in particular. "Not what we needed at all."

And then, just a second later, there was the UPS van. Charlotte walked up the steps and pushed the door open, leaving her unfurled umbrella in the vestibule, and shivering as more cold water trickled down the back of her neck as she took off her coat. Arecely swiped her security badge, and they went inside. Then Arecely sank down in a chair near the window.

"Arecely, are you sure everything is okay? You seem kind of . . ." Charlotte hesitated; she wasn't sure what to say.

"I'm fine," Arecely said, but her tone was dejected, and Charlotte didn't hear much conviction in her voice.

"Are you sure you're feeling okay?"

"Well, I'm just . . . I guess I might be a little tired. I haven't been sleeping that well."

"Oh," Charlotte said. She didn't add anything. She felt tapped out on sympathy.

Just then the door pushed open, and LeAnn came in with a bunch of beautiful yellow roses in her hands, so big that they covered her face.

Arecely let out a low moan and then fainted, right on the spot, just slid right down out of her chair and almost conked her head on the floor.

At the same moment, Flo pushed through the door, followed by Mary Louise, and right after her, Linda Rodriguez.

"Smelling salts," Charlotte called out, kneeling down next to Arecely, clasping her hand around her cool wrist, feeling her pulse.

"I don't know what's going on with this girl," Charlotte said, taking the little spirit-of-ammonia tube from Flo and tearing it open, her eyes smarting at the sharp fumes.

"She's gotta be pregnant," Mary Louise said. "My Denise passed out like that every single time. She could never keep it from us, 'cause of the passing out."

"Or it could be the roses." Charlotte turned her head to see that this was Linda Rodriguez speaking.

"The roses?" Mary Louise said.

"Right," said Flo. "Could've been the roses."

"Under the circumstances, I mean," said Linda Rodriguez.

"Right," said Flo again.

Charlotte could see that Arecely was blinking, starting to come around, and as she did she started to wave away the smelling salts.

"Roses . . ." she muttered. "I can smell the roses. . . ."

Flo and Linda Rodriguez gave each other a look. Then Linda dropped to her knees and said something in Spanish to Arecely that Charlotte couldn't understand, and Arecely opened her eyes all the way, and blinked a couple more times.

"Oh, sorry, sorry," she said, trying to get up, but Charlotte put her hand on her shoulder and said, "Give it a minute, Arecely. If you're going to sit up, you need to sit up slowly."

"I'm just so sorry," Arecely said. "It was just, when I saw the roses . . ."

"You don't need to explain," Linda Rodriguez said. "I'll have to admit, they gave me a bit of a start myself."

"The roses!" LeAnn said as she came back into the room, holding the splendid bouquet, which she had put in a large empty peanut-butter jar.

LeAnn sighed. "They're beautiful, aren't they?"

"They must be a sign," Arecely said.

"Oh, I'm sure they're a sign," Mary Louise said to LeAnn, giving her a wink and a pat on the arm. "And as for you, young missy," Mary Louise said to Arecely, "I'd wager you didn't have breakfast. I bet you were feeling queasy and didn't want to eat." Arecely had been white as a sheet, but when Mary Louise said this, she blushed.

"Of course, dear, five children, three daughters, eight grandbabies . . . you can't fool me for a sec. Now, Flo, if you don't mind, I'm going to pop straight over to Wawa for doughnuts and milk for this child."

Then Charlotte, who felt like she'd been trailing paces behind during this entire conversation, suddenly looked down at Arecely with comprehension, and said to no one in particular, "Is she . . . ? Arecely, are you . . . ?" And with that, Arecely burst into tears and started sobbing out loud.

"I wasn't telling anyone," she said.

"I'll be back in a jiffy with those doughnuts," Mary Louise said. "Any special requests?"

"I'll take the chocolate kind with sprinkles on them," Linda Rodriguez said.

Then Arecely added, "Um, do you think you could make it chocolate milk?"

So by the time Harvey Dexter showed up with Patricia Lynch in tow, the women of El Centro, plus Linda Rodriguez, were doing what they usually did on slow mornings: They were eating—licking sugar glaze off their fingers, and globs of cream filling from their shirtfronts, and powdered sugar from their lips and chins.

Arecely was sitting in state, taking delicate sips from her chocolate milk while Linda Rodriguez asked her questions about her life story—about baby Zekie, and how she had wanted to go to college but hadn't quite gotten a chance. And did she like *The House on Mango Street?* Because if she did, Linda had lots more books like that. And pretty soon the part about Ricky being away in North Carolina just kind of leaked out.

"Ricky's gone?" Flo said. "Why didn't you tell us? How long's he been gone? Does he know about the new baby?"

"Ricky . . . Ricky . . ." LeAnn said. "Oh, yeah, I forgot to tell you. . . . Ricky called asking for you, Arecely, about three or four days ago. Said he was trying to reach you on the phone but couldn't get through."

At that, Arecely looked like she was about to faint again, and Linda Rodriguez, who had a surprisingly good mothering instinct for a TV reporter, quickly picked up the chocolate milk and told Arecely to take a sip. Charlotte, speaking quite softly, almost whispering, said, "Did . . . uh . . . LeAnn. I don't suppose Charlie called?" And LeAnn said, "Oh, Charlotte, yeah, Charlie did call, a couple of times. . . . Don't tell me I forgot to give you the message."

Just then the phone rang, and Mary Louise picked up.

"El Centro de la Mujer, can I help you?" She pushed the hold button, gestured at LeAnn. "For you, dear." She winked. "And don't forget to thank him for those lovely roses."

LeAnn was so excited that she tripped, managing to knock over Arecely's chocolate milk as she righted herself, which spilled half on the computer keyboard and then started dripping down onto the vinyl chair and onto the floor.

It was just at that moment that the door pushed open and there was Harvey Dexter, accompanied by Patricia Lynch. She was wearing a damp black trench coat and spike heels that were totally unsuitable for the weather. In order to unbutton her trench coat, she had to lean over to place on the floor the can of white paint she was holding.

"None too soon, I see," Patricia Lynch said. "This should have been done a long time ago. A vision of the Virgin Mary indeed!"

"Oh, no, you don't," Flo said. "I don't know what you think you are doing. But you may not touch anything in this clinic without permission from the board. Harve?" Flo said, turning to Harve, who was looking in a halfhearted manner at the rain out the window.

"Excuse me," Patricia Lynch said haughtily, "but I *am* the board."

"I beg your pardon?"

"I believe you heard what I said. There have been some changes in management. We're planning a meeting to discuss them with staff, but right now we've got an emergency management situation."

"The Mary sighting," Linda Rodriguez said.

"The *purported* Mary sighting," Patricia said.

"Haaarve?" Flo and Charlotte and Mary Louise all spoke in unison, as they closed ranks around him, shoulder-to-shoulder. Harve took a step back, closer to the window, and leaned against the table where the chocolate milk was spilled. He jerked his hand up, then wiped it absentmindedly on the outside of his coat. "Well, uh . . . we were going to have a staff meeting this afternoon, but er . . . PL here thinks that—"

"PL?" Flo snorted. "Who exactly is PL?"

"Yoo-hoo." Patricia Lynch waved.

"Harve, what in the name of Jesus and Mary is going on here?" Flo did not sound amused.

"Er, ahem, I think you ladies were aware that there were some pending changes coming down the pike, and, uh, we were planning to let you all know in a more *formal* manner . . . with a staff meeting . . . but, uh . . ."

"This 'Mary' thing is a potential public-relations disaster, and there is a news crew van out in the parking lot even as we are wasting time here, Dr. Dexter. We'll have to address the staff concerns at another time," Patricia said.

But the ladies had Harve pretty much pinned against the wall, and he clearly wasn't going anywhere. Meanwhile, Mary Louise slipped out of the formation and strategically placed herself so that Ms. Lynch would not be able to get past her to go up the stairs.

"Harve?" Flo said. Her tone made it clear she would brook no nonsense.

He shook his head, leaned on the table again, which only caused more chocolate milk to start dripping off the table and onto his shoe. He looked longingly out the window, where it was still raining hard and the sky was somber.

"Come on, Harve," Flo said.

"Dr. Dexter," Ms. Lynch said, in a tone that somehow managed to sound both commanding and obsequious. "Staff concerns can wait."

"I'm sorry, ladies. . . ." Whatever he was going to say, Harve obviously didn't want to say it right then and there, with all of the ladies of El Centro grouped around him, within arm's reach.

"You are sorry . . . about . . . *what?* Flo said. "In the name of holy Jesus, spit it out, Harve."

"The clinic has been sold," Harve said. "Patricia Lynch is now the acting manager."

"And my first act as manager is going to be to apply some white paint to that religious painting upstairs. Any fool could have guessed this might happen."

Patricia lifted her chin and raised her eyebrows, then bent over to pick up the paint can; she tottered on her high heels just slightly, like an ungainly crane. "There is no time to waste. If media gets hold of this, it could be very ugly."

That was the exact moment that Linda Rodriguez chose to step forward with her hand outstretched. "Linda Rodriguez," she said to Ms. Lynch.

"ABC News," Flo added.

"Channel Six," Charlotte said.

Patricia Lynch dropped the paint can. It landed on her toe with a crunch so loud that there was little doubt she had done herself harm.

"Owowowowowow," she wailed, hopping precariously on the other spike heel.

"Here, a chair," LeAnn said, shoving over the rolling office chair, into which Ms. Lynch sank, apparently not noticing how much chocolate milk was still on the seat.

"I'm getting ice," Flo said, sprinting toward the staff room.

"Let the doctor take a look at it . . ." Mary Louise said.

"Why don't we try to slip that shoe off?" Charlotte said gently, dropping to her knees.

Flo came back with a blue ice pack.

Ms. Lynch's face was screwed up in a most unattractive manner, and she was whimpering, very loud, not quite in tears, but almost. "It hurts, it hurts, it hurts. . . . Call an ambulance. I command you. Call an ambulance right now."

"First let me see if I can get that shoe off for you, and let me get some ice on it. That'll help with the pain and keep it from swelling up so much. Plus, I want to make sure it's not bleeding."

Patricia Lynch shifted around in her chair; then her eyes narrowed into a frown, probably as she started to feel the chocolate milk seeping through her skirt. She tried to jump up, but lost her balance as the chair started to roll away from her, and so she plopped back down with a damp squish.

"Don't be afraid," Charlotte said, her voice still calm and patient. "I'm not going to hurt you. I just want to get that shoe off and take a look."

"All right. If you insist. But I want the doctor to do it."

"Charlotte is the doctor," Mary Louise said. "She's our nurse practitioner."

"That's precisely what I mean. If anyone is going to look at it, it's going to be Dr. Dexter."

Harve backed up a step or two and shook his head. "No, I, uh, no . . . I'm . . . uh, that's a foot, and I'm a gynecologist. I don't think . . . I really don't think . . . the liability . . . Um, let's see, did anyone call nine-one-one?"

Arecely walked over to Ms. Lynch and put her hand on her shoulder. "I know it hurts," she said. Ms. Lynch sniffed and rubbed a tear from the corner of her eye. "But let Charlotte here take a look at it. She's a real good doctor. I swear."

"Well." She sniffed. "All right. I suppose. . . ."

So Charlotte gently wriggled the spiked pump off Patricia Lynch's foot while Ms. Lynch let out a lot of very undignified howls. "Stop, wait, don't. It hurts, it hurts, ow. Stop. You're hurting me." She wailed while Charlotte wriggled the pump in micromotions, trying to slip it off. Flo, who was standing behind Patricia Lynch, was giggling from time to time, but tactfully, she timed her giggles to the moments when the nurse-manager was howling the loudest so Ms. Lynch was none the wiser.

Finally Charlotte pried the shoe free and inspected the big toe, which, though encased in a nude-colored stocking, still was obviously discolored and starting to swell.

"I'm just going to put this ice pack on it," Charlotte said.

"Ow, be careful, ow," she said.

Charlotte brought over another chair and carefully placed Ms. Lynch's foot and the ice pack on the chair.

"You're definitely going to need an X-ray," she said. "One of us can drive you to the hospital. I'm not sure an ambulance is necessary."

Just then the buzzer in the vestibule sounded, and LeAnn, who had just hung up the phone and had a starry look on her face, called over. "Guys, hate to break up the party here, but we have three patients waiting outside."

So Flo said sweetly, "Dr. Dexter, we've got patients to see, so why don't you run Ms. Lynch over to the hospital, would you?"

And Mary Louise said, "And let me just get that paint can out of the way before somebody trips over it."

And Charlotte said, "Yes, Harve. That makes the most sense if you run her over to the ER." But then she sniffed the air tentatively, to make sure she didn't smell vodka. Then, reassuring herself that he seemed to be only an afternoon drinker, she repeated, "Would you mind?"

And Harve, who seemed to know that he was outnumbered, shrugged and said okay.

And then Linda Rodriguez, who hadn't said anything up until this point, said, "Well, it was lovely to meet you, Ms. Lynch, and I must be getting back out to the van. We're here to cover the rising creek." And she turned around and slipped out the door.

Then Patricia Lynch said to Arecely, "Help me up. Don't just stand there. I need some help getting up." Arecely reached out her hand and helped Ms. Lynch stand up from the chair.

"I think you're going to need these," LeAnn said, bringing over a wad of tissues. "You've got chocolate milk all over your butt."

Somehow, though, Harve managed to get her out of there, hopping like a stork on her one spike heel, with little bits of Kleenex clinging to the big wet stain on the back of her skirt.

"Good-bye, Ms. Lynch. It was a pleasure to see you this morning," Flo said.

"Paint over the Virgin," Patricia Lynch called out as she was hopping out the door. "That's an order," she added with as much dignity as a person with a smashed toe and a chocolate-milk stain could muster.

"I will," Flo said pleasantly, and then, after the door shut, she said, "Just as soon as I see a virgin, which, seeing as this is a family-planning clinic, I'm guessing won't be for a good long while."

And so, in spite of everything else, they started the day kind of cheerfully, putting patients in the rooms and getting on with business as usual, because this was, after all, just like any other day.

Thirty-eight

G iven the torrential rains, there was a surprisingly good flow of patients through the morning, but as it got closer to lunchtime, and the rain was coming down even harder, there were no cars left in the parking lot except for the news van, and the little huddled knot of protesters, even with their umbrellas, looked extremely bedraggled.

When Charlotte came out from seeing the last patient, she said, "Flo, have you heard back from Mrs. Wetherill?"

"I've left at least ten messages for her. She just isn't calling back."

"Did you try her cell phone?"

"Her cell phone and her home phone. I can't imagine why she isn't calling. She always calls back right away."

"Do you think it's possible that they really sold the clinic?" Mary Louise asked. "Without telling us? Or anything?"

"No, I don't think so," Charlotte said. "Mrs. Wetherill would never let something like that happen."

"Well, I hope there was a huge, long line at the ER and that horrid Patricia Lynch is stuck there," LeAnn said.

"Paint the Virgin." Flo sniffed.

"Still, we need some kind of plan."

"I don't think . . ." Arecely said. "I don't think it's right to paint over the painting."

"Well, I'm with you on that one," Flo said. "It's not like it's doing any harm."

"Besides, look what happened to Patricia Lynch when she was going to do something about it."

"Yeah," said LeAnn.

"Yeah," said Flo.

"But you know," Charlotte said, "it probably isn't a good idea to have those fanatics out there thinking that they've seen a vision."

"That's true," Flo said. "Remember when they thought they saw a vision of Mary up in the window of St. Mary's Hospital down in Delaware? It started out kinda slow, but within a couple of days, they had people driving in from all over the place—as far away as Canada—turned into a real nightmare. First she was in the window. Then when they covered up the window, people started seeing her up on the roof. I mean, I believe in Mary as much as the next guy, but in our case, I don't think seeing a painting through the window counts as a miracle, if you know what I mean."

"So let's invite them in," Mary Louise said.

"What?"

"Let's let the protesters in and see for themselves that it's only a painting. Besides, I'm sure they're getting hungry. I can run over to Domino's and pick up enough pizza for all of us."

"But that still doesn't explain how they saw the painting in the first place," LeAnn said. "You can't see it through the window. So how did they know?"

Trust LeAnn, Charlotte thought, to want to draw out the drama, but still it was true. She wondered what trick of the light had allowed them to see the painting through the window at night.

"Um . . ." Arecely said. "I . . . um . . . I think I might know."

She looked sufficiently pale and stricken when she said this that Mary Louise shoved a chair in her direction—the chair that was now wiped free of chocolate milk.

"Yes?" Flo said.

"Um . . ." Arecely said. "If you light a candle in front of the painting, then I think you can see it out the window at night."

"But nobody would light a candle up there," Charlotte said. "It's against the fire code."

"Somebody might," Flo said.

"If they were praying," Mary Louise added.

"If they found themselves pregnant, and their man was gone to North Carolina," Flo said.

"And you know, it's not for nothing that I passed out, and then smelled roses when I was coming to, and then right after that, LeAnn told me that Ricky had called."

"Is that what happened?" Charlotte asked. "Did you light a candle because you were praying, and maybe that's how the painting was lit up, because you left the candle burning?"

"Oh, no, I wouldn't leave the candle burning," Arecely said.

"Well, then how . . . ?"

Arecely looked really stricken. She looked around at the group of faces, then down at the floor, then out the window. She made the sign of the cross and muttered something softly to herself in Spanish; then she looked up.

"I guess, I must have . . . left it burning," Arecely said.

Charlotte bent over and put her arm around Arecely's shoulder. "Well, then, don't worry, Arecely. Obviously the clinic is still standing— and it's always better to tell the truth."

Arecely started sobbing, and Mary Louise spoke up above her sobs. "I'm going to get pizza. Does everybody like pepperoni?"

Charlotte went into her office, determined to catch up with some of the infernal paperwork, and LeAnn busied herself getting Arecely some water from the water cooler.

"I'm calling Dorothea Wetherill again," Flo said.

And for a few moments, silence descended upon the clinic for the first time that morning. It was quiet enough that they could hear the rain's relentless pounding on the roof.

But Charlotte hadn't been at her desk for more than a minute when Flo called out, "Charlotte, phone for you on line one."

Charlotte picked up the phone, and at first all she could hear was the tinny static of long distance.

"Hello." Charlotte could feel her heart pounding with certainty. This was Charlie. It had to be.

"Charlotte, darling." With a sinking heart, Charlotte recognized the voice of Deirdre Saramago. "I don't suppose you've seen my Ariel, have you?"

"Deirdre, where are you?"

"I'm in Buenos Aires, at the airport, actually. My flight has been delayed, but I'll be back by tomorrow morning. Julie has been such a *jewel* to look after the horses. I've been trying to reach Ariel—I even broke down and called that *asshole* Bruce . . . but he says he hasn't seen her. So I just wondered if . . . ?"

"Do you mean to tell me that you left her alone, and *you don't know where she is?* Deirdre, she's seventeen."

"She's eighteen, and . . . well, I didn't think she'd be so hard to keep in contact with—she's difficult, but usually she's better than this."

"Deirdre, she's . . ." Charlotte sat there, gripping the phone, grappling with trying to figure out the right thing to do. There was a possibility, albeit slim, that Ariel's life could be in danger. Charlotte could break confidentiality to save a life—but Deirdre was in Buenos Aires. . . . What would she be able to do?

"Deirdre, listen. I'm concerned that she may be in some kind of trouble. Do you have any idea where she could be?"

"Oh, Charlotte, always the dramatist. If I knew, would I be calling you?"

Charlotte sensed a chill, a chill so profound that it felt like it settled somewhere deep in her bones, like ice seeping into her marrow. She could feel her hand shaking as she gripped the phone receiver.

"Deirdre. Think! You need to think about where she could be. I'll try to find her, but I need some help here. Are you sure she's not at the boyfriend's? Can you give me his number?"

"Charlotte . . . if I'd known you were going to overreact like this—"

"Just give me the names or numbers of anywhere she could be. . . ."

"I'm sorry. You're fading out on me. . . . I can't quite . . . I'm calling from a pay phone at the airport. . . . I can't quite . . ."

"Deirdre, she's pregnant and . . ."

Charlotte heard the connection go dead. She stared at the phone receiver in her hand in disbelief. She held on to the phone. Pressed it up to her ear. Jiggled the toggle switch a little bit, but all she got back was silence, and then a dial tone.

Charlotte sat in her cubicle and weighed her options. Should she report her as a missing person? That was hard to do. She wasn't a relative, and Ariel could be almost anywhere. . . . She could be staying with a friend, a boyfriend. Deirdre didn't even seem concerned, and she was the girl's mother. Charlotte shivered, felt that chill again. She thought about the positive pregnancy test—the spotting. The chances that Ariel really had a severe complication, a tubal pregnancy, were low, but still, it was a real possibility. As far as Charlotte knew, Ariel had not been to the emergency room. . . . She sat there, rubbing her hands together, thinking, trying to figure out the best thing to do, until she heard Mary Louise's voice calling like the pied piper. "Everyone, pizza."

Charlotte went out into the reception area, and there was Mary Louise, with three boxes of Domino's stacked up on top of one another, and behind her in a line were five bedraggled, wet protesters, their umbrellas unfurled and dripping on the floor.

"Upstairs, everybody . . ." Mary Louise called out. And she led the way, enticing the motley crew with the scent of hot cheese and pepperoni, and they all climbed up the stairs under the deafening roar of the rain, which continued, without ceasing, to pour down.

Thirty-nine

I t took three trips up and down the stairs and back outside and then inside again to convince the doubting-Thomas protesters that the vision of Mary was less than supernatural.

Flo made an official announcement that in spite of concerns regarding the fire code, it was okay to light the candle—"in the interest of scientific inquiry."

And, in fact, it was true. When the candle was lit, you could see the face of Mary through the upstairs dormer window, bathed in a rosy glow of light.

Charlotte stood in the parking lot, not far from the spot where the blue Dumpster used to be, and saw the face of Mary. It floated ethereally in the window, as if she were spirit made flesh. It was a moving sight, even though they all knew that there was nothing particularly mystical about it.

The first time, the most histrionic of the group—the woman with the short blond hair, the landlady—fell onto her knees and starting chanting the Hail Mary.

But by the third trip, everything had pretty much calmed down, and that time, Flo stayed behind. She had shoved the dormer window open, and she yelled out the window, "Okay, I'm going to blow it out now." Then she blew out the candle—which made Mary's face disappear into the shadows. After repeating this exercise several times, even the short-haired lady got up off her knees, grumbling about her sciatica, and started brushing the gravel off the big damp spots on her pants.

So by the time they settled around the pizza, everybody was wet and a little chilly. Flo broke into the first-aid box and pulled out the army green wool blankets, and she distributed them, along with the pizza, to the protesters—the sandy-haired man, whose name, it turned out, was Kenneth, and the stoop-shouldered man, Bill, and the landlady with the short blond hair, whose name, not surprisingly, was Mary. Plus the homeless man from Wawa and one other fellow, a skinny teenager wearing a suit and tie who looked like a probable Jehovah's Witness, but nobody seemed to know where he had come from.

The pizza had gotten a little cold, but it was nice and warm in the upstairs room, and something about the visitors and the pizza and the rain gave the room an unexpected air of festivity.

The landlady, Mary, must've been really hungry from all that rapture, because she fell right to it and ate three pieces of pepperoni pizza in rapid succession, but when she was done, she started to get a little chatty.

"So what is it that you ladies do here?" she asked.

The ladies all looked at one another. Nobody was quite sure who should start.

"We take care of women," Mary Louise said. "You know, just the usual female stuff."

"We screen people for cancer," Flo said.

"And do pregnancy tests," Arecely said.

"You screen people for cancer?" Mary said, shifting her weight on the floor pillow and making a minor adjustment to her broad bosom. "My daughter has been pestering me to get a mammogram. Do you do anything like that?"

"Yes," Charlotte said. "We can refer you for a mammogram. No problem at all. You just need to schedule an appointment."

Mary looked cautious. "But I don't have any health insurance," she said.

"We work on a sliding-fee scale. People pay only what they can afford to pay."

"Really?" said Mary. "I had no idea you did all that. I guess I didn't really know what you do. . . ."

By the time the protesters were ready to leave, they had all gotten friendly with one another, and Mary Louise encouraged them all to stop by the pig on the way out. "If you want to help us with our mission."

Just as they were ready to go, Charlotte said, "Do you mind if I just ask you guys one question?"

"Not at all," said Kenneth, the stoop-shouldered one.

"It's just that . . . what made you want to come out here with those picket signs?"

"Well," said Kenneth. "It just didn't seem right somehow, that baby being in that Dumpster. And I just felt like I wanted to do something. And this was the one thing I could think of to do."

"But," Charlotte said, "don't you have to be protesting *against* something?"

"Well, gosh," said Kenneth, "I guess I never thought about it that way. I'm against dead babies. Aren't you?"

"Oh, most definitely," Charlotte said. "Terribly opposed to them."

"Me too," said Mary Louise.

"Me also," said Flo.

"Anyone not against dead babies?" Charlotte asked.

The group just stood and looked at one another, shaking their heads.

"Good," Flo said. "So we all agree. Now you good people won't have to stand out in the rain, because you know that we are keeping an eye out on our end."

"Well, that is darn good to know," said Bill, the younger man. " 'Cause if the truth be known, I am getting a little tired of standing out in the rain."

"You're in good hands with us," Mary Louise said.

So Mary stayed to make an appointment for an annual exam, and Kenneth and Bill and the others headed back out into the rain, but by then the sky had lightened, and the rain had slowed to barely a drizzle.

The afternoon was busy. Since the rain had let up, the patients started coming out. The girls passed one another in the hall with a wink and an elbow. "I'm against dead babies," one said, and, "Me too," another would reply. It was windy now, and a little bit of blue started peeking through the clouds. So the mood in El Centro lifted a little bit, even though they were obviously all still worried deep down. No word yet from Mrs. Wetherill, and though they kept watching cautiously out the window for the return of Patricia Lynch, there was no sign of her. Then, at about three thirty, the phone rang.

"Phone for you, Flo. It's a Benjamin Wetherill," LeAnn said.

"Benjamin?" she mouthed, her eyebrows creasing. They all knew Mrs. Wetherill was a widow.

Everybody stopped what they were doing to listen, clustering around Flo until she made an aggravated back-off motion with her hands.

But they could all tell something was wrong. Flo was fidgeting with her fingers and frowning, shaking her head.

"Yes, I see. Oh, yes, I see. Terribly sorry to hear that. Of course."

"What? What is it?" Charlotte whispered.

But Flo just kept shaking her head and nodding, murmuring, "Yes, terribly sorry. Yes, we'll keep her in our prayers."

"Flo?"

"What happened?"

"What's going on?"

Everybody was standing in a semicircle around Flo, who had depressed the phone button but hadn't put the handset back in the cradle. She looked around the group, catastrophe written all over her face.

"Come on, Flo. You gotta spit it out," LeAnn said.

"That was Dorothea Wetherill's son, Benjamin. He was explaining why she hadn't been returning our calls."

"What—what is it? Is something wrong?" Charlotte said.

"She had a stroke. She's in intensive care. They're not sure she's going to come around."

The group stayed in stunned silence for a moment, and then one by one they started sniffing and wiping away tears.

Then finally LeAnn asked what they were all dying to ask: "What is the story with the clinic? Did he say anything? Did he know anything?"

Flo was just shaking her head, and from the way that she was staring at the floor, not wanting to look up at them, Charlotte knew. . . .

"He said . . . 'Look, I'm really sorry, guys.' " Flo sniffed a little, and Mary Louise silently handed her a box of Kleenex.

She cleared her throat and blinked a couple of times, trying to hold steady. "He said that they had called an emergency meeting the day Dorothea went into the hospital, and that he has power of attorney, so he agreed to waive her participation."

"What?"

"Oh, my God."

"Then you mean . . . ?"

"Girls. Listen up. He didn't really have any information to give us."

But clearly it didn't sound good, and one by one they fell into silence.

That was when it really hit Charlotte. She looked around at the shabby reception area, and through the window at the broken-down couches in the waiting room. The whole place could use a coat of paint. The roof leaked. The gray carpet was worn to bits, and was wearing clean through under the rolling office chairs. Sure, there were pictures on the wall, of Zekie, and Mary Louise's grandbabies, and Julie a few years back in a school picture. And the usual collection of signs: IN GOD WE TRUST—ALL OTHERS PAY CASH. I'M OUT OF MY MIND BUT FEEL FREE TO LEAVE A MESSAGE.

Shabby, yes. Dysfunctional, frequently. She looked around at the girls: LeAnn, Mary Louise, Flo, Arecely. Next to Arecely's desk there was a pile of books: *Of Mice and Men*, *How the Garcia Girls Lost Their Accents*, *Shopaholic Takes Manhattan*, *The Dirty Girls Social Club*. At LeAnn's desk there was a half-eaten box of Oreo Double Stuf, a *People* magazine, and a picture of Antonio Banderas stuck to the wall, next to a UPS logo sticker. And her roses were arranged in a Skippy jar. Mary Louise's desk had a *Country Homes* magazine, and a Boscov's furniture clearance circular, and a bottle of vitamins, and some lilac-scented hand lotion.

And up on the window ledge, chained in place, was the plastic pig, which even Charlotte could see was fuller than it had been that first day, when Flo had put a couple of dollars in so that it wouldn't get hungry.

Nobody was saying anything. They were all just standing there in stunned silence.

"Remember when she brought us lemon squares?" Arecely said.

"Remember when she brought the pig?" Flo said.

"Okay, we need to find out when visiting hours are."

"No, her son said no visitors," Flo said.

"Okay, then, let's collect some money for a gift," Mary Louise said.

Everybody went and got their pocketbooks and folded some bills and handed them to Mary Louise—and Mary Louise made a big show of not looking at how much each person was giving her, just tucking the money into an envelope discreetly.

Then the clinic door swung open and a patient came into the vestibule, and everyone resumed her place.

Charlotte glanced out the window. Across the fields, there was a bright slanted light filtering through the clouds in distinct rays. When she was a small child, she used to believe that those rays came through the clouds when someone important was being born. Maybe it was true. Maybe somewhere, someone important was being born, someone who would have the ability to save the world, or do some good in it. Right now she had one more patient to see, and then she wanted to go home and ask Julie what Charlie had really said about when he was coming home.

Forty

Maybe if they hadn't all been so upset about Dorothea Wetherill, somebody would have noticed when it started to rain again in earnest. Charlotte certainly didn't notice. She was back in exam room three with her last patient of the day, Darla Beckwith.

Today Darla was wearing loose leggings and a flowing pink maternity top. Her blond hair was poofed out in big, loose curls, and the thick blue glaze of her eye shadow did nothing to diminish the startling baby doll blue of her eyes.

"Well, I had a blood test, and I was right," Darla said. "I'm pregnant. I just need a paper that confirms it so I can sign up with WIC."

Charlotte stared at the note in front of her in the patient chart, blinking, thinking that maybe she was looking at it wrong. Next to the spot in the chart marked, *pregnancy test result*, there was a big fat minus sign. Could it be a mistake?

"Could you . . . uh . . . could you excuse me for a minute?" Charlotte needed to go out and double-check with Mary Louise—could she possibly have recorded the result wrong? That didn't seem likely, but . . .

Darla Beckwith stared at Charlotte. Her eyes reminded Charlotte of those of a kitten in a Disney movie.

"You know, I hope you don't mind my saying this, but you have terrible customer service here. Do you know you did the exact same thing the last time I was here? You can't just run out of the room. This is an important issue. My pregnancy is very important to me. . . ."

Charlotte didn't hear the end of her sentence. She walked out of the room, her ears burning. She remembered the last time this particular patient had been here, what it had felt like to have blood trickling down her leg. It was as though all of her dreams had trickled away with it.

Mary Louise was cleaning up in the lab. Out in the hall, Charlotte could hear a deafening roar—apparently it was raining again, hard.

Charlotte shoved the chart under her nose and showed her the pregnancy test result. "Are you one hundred percent certain that was negative."

"Oh, yes," Mary Louise said. "Look, it's right here." She pointed to the countertop, where there was a Dixie cup full of urine with a pregnancy test strip lying across it. One thin pink line. Negative.

"Thanks," Charlotte said.

"No problem," Mary Louise said.

Charlotte rapped twice on the exam room door and went back in.

"Well," Darla said in a petulant tone. "I thought you were never coming back. You know, being pregnant, I have to eat on a regular schedule or I get *faint* from *low blood sugar*. I was feeling dizzy just now and I thought I might faint and fall right off the exam table."

"Darla," Charlotte said, breaking in on Darla's monologue.

"Fortunately, I always keep a protein bar in my purse," Darla continued. "It's just the thing for low blood sugar . . . for someone *in my condition*."

"Darla!"

"What?"

"You're not pregnant, Darla."

Darla barely looked up. She was unpeeling the wrapper from a chocolate-covered protein bar with her pink fingernails.

"Darla." Charlotte felt like screaming in frustration. "You're not pregnant! Do you hear me? Your pregnancy test was negative."

Darla shrugged and took a bite of the protein bar, chewing thoughtfully. "You know, it was the same for my girlfriend. . . . Her tests never showed up either."

"Darla," Charlotte said, "I thought you said that you had a positive blood test."

"Well, I went to the hospital and they took a blood test, and they said they would call me but they never did, so I knew it came out positive."

Charlotte knew she was at the end of her rope, because she had no sympathy left for this patient, no kind words, no desire to try to figure out what was driving her. She glanced at the patient's chart.

"Look, it's too early this cycle for a test to come out positive. If you don't get your next period on time, then come back in and we'll repeat the test."

"I knew it. Just like my girlfriend."

"But, Darla, right now you're not pregnant."

Darla gave her a playful slap on the arm. "Well, what am I going to believe, a bunch of chemicals, or what my body is telling me?"

Charlotte didn't even answer. She wrote down *pseudocyesis* in the chart, and came back out of the room, relieved that Darla was the last patient of the day.

Now it was pouring and the sky was pitch-black. On any other day, Flo would have been shooing them out the door. That much rain, the creek had to be high by now, and the roads might flood, but this day they were all so stunned by the news about Dorothea Wetherill that it seemed like they should talk about it for a moment before they all left.

Charlotte trudged up the dark stairwell, feeling completely defeated. With the mournful sound of the rain pounding on the roof, she started to realize that she was going to have to admit defeat. Arecely was pregnant again, and her boyfriend had run off on her—all those books she read didn't seem like they were going to get her into college after all. Ariel . . . Charlotte didn't like to think about Ariel, not knowing where she was on such a cold and rainy night. And Deirdre! Charlie had been right all along about Deirdre. Maria Lopez was drowned, and the baby . . . nobody knew whom the baby belonged to.

It seemed like everything she had done didn't amount to a hill of beans, and all the hours, all the days she had stayed late, with aching feet, trying her best—nothing had worked. With Dorothea Wetherill in the hospital, it seemed like their last hope was gone. Then Charlotte was stricken again—what if the stress from the clinic's crises had contributed to Dorothea Wetherill's health problems?

As she got close to the top of the stairs, she blinked a moment. For just a second, she caught sight of the visage of Mary, her face beaming out toward Charlotte. She stepped forward, eager to come into the presence of the image and be calmed, but then the face disappeared, and Charlotte was surprised by what seemed like sudden darkness. Hadn't there been a light on as she was walking up the stairs? Had the electricity gone out? She turned to look at the stairwell, where the light was still burning. *Odd.* With all the rain, it was as dark as nighttime upstairs. But Charlotte had seen Mary's face. She was sure she had seen it—bathed in a glow of amber light.

Trembling, with slow steps, she entered the room. She fell to her knees in front of the painting and felt tears coursing down her cheeks.

Kneeling there, she thought about all of the people she was sorry about: Dorothea and Charlie, Ariel and Maria Lopez, the dead baby in the Dumpster. She thought about Darla Beckwith, who wanted a baby so badly she was able to imagine it, and about Chaki Gibbons, the girl with no front teeth, who swore she didn't want to be pregnant, even with a baby kicking her in the ribs.

While she knelt there, the others came and joined her. Arecely came in quietly and knelt beside her, then Mary Louise, then LeAnn and Flo. Nobody said anything—nobody appeared to notice her tears. Charlotte could feel a kind of a bond taking shape among them, a silent elastic connection as they knelt there.

Just then she heard a sound behind her, coming from the bathroom, and she spun around. The quiet moment was broken.

"Did you hear that?" Charlotte said. "It sounds like someone is in the bathroom."

Flo stood up. "I thought I heard someone cough."

"Me too," said Mary Louise.

"I didn't hear anything," said Arecely, but Charlotte noticed that her hands were shaking.

"Arecely, are you okay? You're not feeling faint again, are you? When's the last time you had something to eat?"

"Well, I'm going to take a look," Flo said. They stood for a moment longer, ears straining in the silence, but nobody could hear anything except the pounding of the rain. Just then the quiet rumble of the rain was pierced by a siren—a fire truck or an ambulance.

Flo walked over to the window to look out. "Jesus, God in heaven!" she said.

Forgetting the sound they all thought they had heard, they rushed over to the window—there in the lit-up parking lot, they could see too clearly.

"Okay," Flo said. "Enough lollygagging. The creek is up—look at the parking lot. If we don't get out of here, we'll never make it home."

Everybody trumped down the stairs and grabbed jackets, and they all lined up in the vestibule while Flo got the security lock ready. But just as they were getting ready to go, Flo said. "Oh, no, we left the light on upstairs. I've gotta go turn it off."

"I'll go," Arecely said, and without waiting for an answer, she disappeared into the dark.

"You go on," Flo said to LeAnn. "Don't wait for us. You've got to get across the creek as quick as you can. Otherwise you'll have to take the long way around."

"Drive safely," they called after her as she skipped through the giant puddle the parking lot had turned into, got into her car, and drove away into the night.

Looking through the window, Charlotte noticed that there was no traffic on the pike now. They should have closed the clinic early. . . . Normally when there were heavy rains they were more cautious.

"We need to head out," Charlotte said, her voice tense.

"Arecely?" Flo called back into the clinic. "Arecely . . . come on. We've got to get out of here."

Suddenly Charlotte got an odd, creepy feeling. She remembered hearing the cough upstairs, how she had thought there was somebody in the bathroom. What if . . . ?

"Arecely?" she called out, rushing back into the dark clinic. "Arecely, are you okay?"

She ran toward the stairway. It was as dark as midnight, and she groped her way along, feeling her way up the stairwell with her hands—this time she couldn't see Mary's face. She couldn't see anything except blackness, and the rain seemed to be hammering inside her head, drowning out even the sound of her own breathing.

She heard something. A low moan. Charlotte took the last few stairs by twos. "Arecely, are you okay?" She bounded into the room, flipped the light switch.

Arecely was leaning against the bathroom door. "Now, come on. You've got to unlock it. Just unlock the door so we can help you." She whirled around, looked at Charlotte, stricken.

"I'm . . . she's . . . Charlotte. You've got to help me."

"Explain to me what is going on."

All of a sudden, the lights dimmed, then flashed back on. There was another sound, a keening, from behind the bathroom door.

"Arecely?"

The lights dimmed again, then went off entirely, plunging them into total darkness. Neither spoke. They waited a beat, two; then the lights came back on again.

Charlotte stared Arecely in the face. "Arecely, explain now what is happening and I'll try to help you."

Just then the lights flickered again and then went off. Again the women waited for a moment, but this time nothing.

From behind the bathroom door came a louder groan, followed by sobs, and Arecely started pounding on the door, saying, "Come on, open the door. Let me in. We can help you. The doctor is here."

Now Charlotte could hear Flo's voice calling, "Charlotte, Arecely, you need to get down here. . . ."

And then, "Jesus, God in heaven," and then, "Oh, my God, I'll try to get the state troopers on the phone," and then there was Mary Louise at the top of the stairs.

"Water's sloshing around the clinic steps now. Girls, where on earth . . . ?"

Another yell, this one really loud, came from behind the dark bathroom door.

Mary Louise's voice said, in the dark, "Hoo, boy, looks like we got more than one problem here."

Forty-one

J ust then Flo appeared at the top of the stairs, carrying a flashlight.
"I've got bad news," Flo said.

"Well, I guess I do too," Arecely said.

"You can say that again," Charlotte said.

"Okay, who goes first?" Mary Louise said.

But since there wasn't any moaning going on right then, Flo just
started talking.

"Look, girls. I hate to tell you this, but we are stuck here right now.
We can't get out. Giselle down at the troopers' office told me that the
creek rose ten feet in the last half hour."

"That's why the water's sloshing around the clinic stairs," Mary Louise
said.

"She said, 'Whatever you do, don't try to drive out. There's cars
stranded everywhere . . . and the troopers are focusing on trying to help
people who are stuck out in this.' We have to stay put."

"But what about LeAnn?" Mary Louise asked.

But no one got a chance to answer, because just then there was a loud
howl, louder than any of the previous ones, and before anyone got a
chance to say anything, the door to the bathroom burst open. Flo shined
the flashlight, and there, like a deer caught in headlights, stood Chaki
Gibbons, who let out another godforsaken yell. Mary Louise screamed.

Arecely said, "I can . . . uh . . . I can . . . explain."

"What on earth?" Flo said.

And Charlotte was so stunned she felt like she was going to topple
over. "Chaki Gibbons?"

Forty-two

There wasn't much doubt what was going on with Chaki Gibbons. Charlotte got Mary Louise to start timing her contractions, and she sent Arecely and Flo downstairs with the flashlight.

"Arecely, I need the Doppler, the heartbeat monitor, out of the drawer in room two. Flo, go call the state troopers. Tell them to send out an ambulance, a fire truck, whatever they've got. Tell 'em we've got a woman in labor here and she needs to get out to the hospital."

A moment later Arecely came back with the Doppler, holding a lit candle in her other hand. It took Flo a few more minutes to come back.

"Charlotte." Clearly something was wrong from her tone of voice. "I'm sorry. The phone is dead. I couldn't get through to nine-one-one or to anyone."

"Anyone have a cell phone?" Flo asked.

But nobody said yes. Nobody had a cell phone. Charlotte had lent hers to Julie this morning.

"Well, then I guess we're on our own."

Just then Chaki started howling again, slumping down against the wall, yelling, "I can't, I can't, I can't."

"Five minutes apart," Mary Louise said. "And, dear, you most certainly can. In fact, you don't have a lot of choice in the matter. Now you're going to find this thing a whole lot easier if you just get up and walk around a little bit." Chaki stopped howling and took Mary Louise's arm.

Arecely had knelt down and lit a variety of candle stubs—apparently there were quite a few tucked around odd corners of the room. The face of Mary flickered benignly in the soft light. Mary Louise had Chaki by the arm, and was leading her in a slow circle.

For a while the room settled into a kind of silence. Every five minutes Chaki would squat against the wall and start moaning, but now her moans didn't sound quite so anguished, and Mary Louise was breathing with her, rubbing her back, and saying soft and soothing things.

Then there was the loud sound of a horn—hoo-hoo-hoo—that sounded like it was coming out from the parking lot.

"Oh, thank God," said Charlotte. "That must be the ambulance."

"Not unless there was divine intervention," Flo said. "Remember, I couldn't get in touch with the troopers?"

"Then it's probably a fire truck come to evacuate us."

Arecely was looking through the window. "I can't see it very well, but I can tell it's a big truck."

Chaki had started another contraction, and she managed to huff out, "I'm not going anywhere!"

"I'll go see what's going on," Flo said.

Charlotte went over and crouched next to Chaki, placing the round dome of the heartbeat monitor on her bare distended belly, and she listened carefully as the steady *whoosh, whoosh, whoosh* filled the room. Charlotte hadn't taken care of a woman in labor in a long time, but it was coming back to her. She had worked as a labor-and-delivery nurse, and there were plenty of times in the middle of the night when Charlotte had delivered a baby when the doc hadn't made it to the hospital on time, but still . . . Now she felt an overwhelming sense of relief. They were going to be rescued, and Chaki could go to a hospital, which was where she belonged.

But no sooner had she finished this thought than she heard a loud thumping sound on the stairs, and turned to see the up-and-down bob of the flashlight beam.

"Well," said Flo, "I've got good news and bad news." And right behind her, there was LeAnn, sopping wet with a T-shirt bundled around her ankle, leaning on the arm of Sam, the UPS man.

It took a few moments for LeAnn to get settled on a pillow with her ankle propped up and for the story to tumble out, in pieces—Sam's piece, LeAnn's piece.

She had run out across the parking lot, ready to leave, gotten in her car, and started to drive, but she hadn't gotten much past the Brown Derby when the water had suddenly risen to the level of her car door. She was able to get out and walk through the floodwaters, toward the side of the road, but as she got to the side of the road, her foot had caught on a downed branch and she had fallen. She managed to get up, but she could barely walk, her ankle too painful.

"I was sitting up on top of a mailbox," LeAnn said. "Just wondering what the heck I was going to do if nobody came by."

"I was driving really slow, thinking that I might get stuck, and feeling bad for all the cars I saw by the side of the road," Sam put in.

"When I looked up and saw him," LeAnn said, wrapping one of the green army blankets tight around her shoulders.

"And there was a girl, alone, sitting on top of a mailbox."

"So he walked through the water and he picked me up."

"I was just so grateful that I found her."

"But we were afraid to go forward, because the water was obviously only going to get higher out closer to the creek."

"We came back as far as the clinic."

"And I could see the Mary face through the window, so I knew you were up there."

"Look," Flo said, "without further ado—let's get Chaki out of here. Charlotte, you go along with them. Sam, you're going to have to use that truck to drive out of here."

"I'm sorry, madam," Sam said. "But I do not think that is advisable."

"Sam, this woman is going to have a baby. It's an emergency. We need to get her out of here."

He nodded, then bowed his head slightly. "I understand, but I think it is not wise. The water is too high for my truck now."

"We stalled three times before we got here," LeAnn said.

"It is better for her to be inside where it is warm than to take a chance that we will be stuck out there."

Charlotte felt resignation settle into the pit of her stomach. He was right. Chaki wasn't in any danger right now. In fact, since this was her first baby, she might not deliver until morning . . . and by then, certainly the floodwaters would have gone back down.

"She has to go," Flo insisted.

"No, he's right," Charlotte said. "It's safer for her if we stay."

"Hey," said Mary Louise. "You must have a cell phone."

"Yes," he said. "I do."

"Okay, call nine-one-one and tell them we have a woman in labor here. Actually, if you don't mind, I'll do it," Flo said.

After Sam unhooked the cell phone from his belt and handed it to Flo, she dialed 911 and then they heard her saying, "Yes, in labor . . . Yes, 1532 Maryland Pike . . . Yes, we're on the second floor. We're dry. No, no electricity . . . Mmm-hmm . . . mmm-hmm. Okay, all right. Then we'll sit tight and wait."

Flo held her hand over the phone. "They want to know how long it's going to be."

"How long it's going to be?"

"Until she has the baby."

Charlotte let out a long sigh. "You know, it's hard to tell. Probably not at least for a few more hours—it could be two to three hours, or it could take until morning. These things are unpredictable."

Flo relayed the information, then said, "Roger. Okay. We're not going anywhere."

"What'd they say?" Chaki said. She was between contractions right then.

"They said that the road is blocked both ways—from the north by the creek, and in the south there was apparently a flash flood and there are a lot of cars stranded in the roads. They're calling around to get a rescue helicopter, but she warned me that may take a while."

"I don't want to go nowhere anyway," Chaki said, the last word trailing off into a groan as another contraction started. Mary Louise, who was right next to Chaki, crouched down and softly talked her through it, her hand resting on Chaki's shoulder.

Just then the buzzer downstairs rang.

"Somebody's here?" Charlotte said. "Maybe a rescue truck got through . . . or the helicopter?" She peered out the window, but the parking lot was dark and silent—she couldn't see much. She could just barely distinguish the outline of the UPS truck, but that was all.

"I'm going to go see," Flo said, but before she had even headed down the stairs they heard a male voice calling, "*Hola?* Hello? Is anybody there?"

Arecely let out an ear-piercing shriek that at first didn't sound like a word, but then slowly formed itself into an utterance that sounded like "Ricky."

Arecely took off down the stairs, so they didn't get to see the joyful reunion, but a moment later, she came back up, dragging a skinny young man who was wearing shorts and rubber boots that were sloshing with water.

"Everybody, this is Ricky," Arecely said.

Chaki chose that moment to start another contraction, this time with a loud howl that got Mary Louise going, whispering whatever her secret incantations were while she kneaded Chaki's back and shoulders.

"Oh, I'm sorry . . ." Ricky said. "I didn't realize—" His words were cut off by a loud yelp, and they waited in silence for a few moments for Chaki's fury and Mary Louise's soothing words to wane. When it was quiet again, Ricky took off his trucker hat and wiped his brow; then, looking slightly intimidated but still up to the task, he said, "How're ya'll doing? ¿Cómo estan ustedes?"

"But how'd you get here?" Flo asked.

"I just walked," Ricky said. "That flood don't go much farther than the edge of your all's parking lot. That field over there, it's dry."

"Are your phones working?" Flo asked.

"Nope, and the lights are out too."

"Do you think a truck could get across the field?"

"Yeah, if was all-wheel-drive it could."

Charlotte could see Flo's point—if they could get a truck across the path in the fields, maybe they could take Chaki out that way.

"But the problem is, you can't get outta the camp on the other side either. We're flooded on both sides. Even if you get her out, we can't get out the front way. . . . Maryland Pike is completely blocked off. You'll never make it out."

"But I can go, can't I?" Arecely said. "I want to get home to Zekie," she said.

"Yeah, and I think you guys probably have a lot to talk about," Flo added.

"Long as you don't mind getting wet . . ." Ricky said, then added, "Actually, baby, you don't even have to get wet, because I'm planning on carrying you."

"Just go on," Flo said. "You go on ahead."

Then Chaki, who was sitting on the floor, leaning against some pillows with her eyes closed, resting between contractions, said, "Arecely? I know I probably got you in trouble and what all. But I'm going to tell everybody thank you for saving my life."

Arecely got a panicky look on her face. Obviously they had all been so busy worrying about the flood and about Chaki's being in labor that nobody had really stopped to think about what she had been doing hiding in the bathroom in the first place.

Arecely stood, shifting from one foot to the other, looking tortured.

But Flo slipped her arm over Arecely's shoulder and said, "Now, isn't that just plain nice? And now you get along home to Zekie."

"Have a good baby, and, uh, I'm glad I could help, and um . . . actually, I gotta go. . . ."

She grabbed Ricky's hand and started tugging him toward the door, and everybody called out, "Now be careful" and "Just come back if you get stuck out there." But they didn't make it quite out the doorway, because Ricky swept her up into a long embrace, just like something out of the movies, and the girls all started clapping and whooping, until they were interrupted by a loud moan, followed by a popping sound that sounded like a snapping rubber band. Charlotte swung around—she would know that sound anywhere—and sure enough, Chaki was standing in a gathering pool of fluid.

"I think my water done broke," Chaki said in a tone that was surprisingly matter-of-fact; then she sank down into another contraction that from the sound of it was even more intense than the one that came before.

They shooed Ricky and Arecely out the door, and then Charlotte said, "I think I'd better check her. Look, maybe some of you could give us a little privacy."

Charlotte glanced over at LeAnn and realized that she had fallen asleep. Her ankle, still propped up on the floor pillows, was swollen, so it was probably just as well.

Sam, who obviously had good instincts, said, "I'll carry her downstairs. She can sleep on the sofa down there." And he carefully scooped her up in his arms and carried her from the room without awakening her.

When they were gone, Charlotte knelt on the floor next to Chaki. She slipped off Chaki's underwear, which was saturated with clear, sweet-smelling amniotic fluid. She put a glove on, wondering if she'd be able to remember how to do a cervical exam—it had been at least ten years since she'd done one.

But as she slipped her gloved hand inside, it came back to her, and she could read the exam like she was reading text on a page. She felt the firm, rounded form of the baby's head. She felt the lip of the cervix, surrounding the head. Chaki was about seven centimeters dilated. Another contraction started, and she could feel the head bearing down against the lip of the cervix.

"Contractions getting closer now," Mary Louise said. "They're about three minutes apart."

"Is everything . . . okay?" Chaki whimpered; then she started crying.

"Everything is fine, Chaki. Don't you worry about a thing," Charlotte said.

But in spite of the calm sound of her voice, Charlotte could feel that she was drenched with sweat under her clothes. The dark, enclosed room, the feeling of being trapped—she sensed that doom was impending and the world was closing down around her. She strained her ears, wondering if she might hear the distant rumble of helicopter rotors, but the sound of the rain was deafening, and she could hear nothing else. She peeled off her glove and dropped it into the wastepaper basket in the corner.

The fact that Chaki's labor seemed to be progressing normally did nothing to change the fact that Chaki had been hiding in the bathroom in the clinic. And who knew how long she'd been there, as now Charlotte started to remember all the times that Arecely had acted funny in the last couple weeks. It didn't change the fact that Chaki hadn't taken care of herself, and hadn't gone to the hospital. Nor did it change the fact that when she finally did get there, she would have Child Protective Services coming after her, trying to find out if she was an unfit mother.

Sam popped his head back in the room, politely averting his eyes. "Can I be of some other assistance?" he said.

"Actually," Charlotte said, "can I use your phone? I want to try to reach my daughter."

"Sure," he said, stepping into the room.

Charlotte punched in the numbers of her cell phone, but she kept getting a message that said, "All circuits are busy. Please try your call again later." She pressed redial several times. Finally she heard the phone start to ring. It rang only once; then Charlotte heard Julie's voice.

"Mom, is that you? Mom, I don't know what to do!" Julie's voice was shrill, panicked. Charlotte's heart started to hammer. What was wrong?

"Julie, is that you? Julie, what's the matter? Are you flooded there? What's wrong?"

"Flooded? No. What do you mean? No, I mean, it's raining hard, but, listen. It's Ariel. . . ." There was static on the line, and Charlotte couldn't hear.

"What? What did you say?"

"It's Ariel."

"What about Ariel?"

"I found her on the floor in the barn—she's passed out. Something's wrong with her. . . . It's like she's asleep."

"Julie. Call nine-one-one."

"I tried, Mom. I tried. There's something wrong with the cell phone. It's not working right. And our house phone doesn't work either, and all the electricity is out. What should I do? I don't know what to do."

"Julie, calm down. Are you with Ariel now?"

"She's here in the barn. That's where I am."

"Julie, you know how to do CPR. Check her. Is she breathing?"

"Yeah, she's breathing, and I could feel her heartbeat, but it's like she's passed out or something. Mom, what should I do?"

"Julie. Listen. Put a blanket over her. If you can't get through to nine-one-one, then you have to leave her there and run to the neighbors'. They can drive her to the hospital. . . ."

"Are you sure? Mom, are you sure? Because I'm really scared. It'll take me fifteen minutes to get to the neighbors'. I'm scared to leave her alone. Are you sure you're stuck?"

"Listen, Julie, you're doing fine. Whatever you do, don't panic. Just keep calling nine-one-one. And run to the neighbors' at the same time. Go to the Browns'. Explain what's going on. Get them to help you. Okay?"

"Mom, I'm—" But the connection went dead. After that, though Charlotte tried and tried, she couldn't connect again. All circuits were busy.

Charlotte felt a cold, dead feeling inside, but she tried to redirect her thoughts to inside the room, where Chaki's labor was obviously now progressing rapidly, and the lights still flickered across Mary's face.

Flo and Mary Louise each put a hand on her arm. "Charlotte, what's going on? What's wrong? Is everything okay?"

Charlotte felt her knees shaking and a hard ball of anguish form in her throat. She swallowed and peered across at Mary's face. Bathed in the soft candlelight, she looked almost alive, like a friend might look—sort of like the face of Mary Louise as she helped Chaki through each contraction. Charlotte took a breath.

"It's . . . Julie," Charlotte whispered. "She's stuck at home alone, and she found one of the neighbor girls passed out, and she can't get through to nine-one-one."

Flo took hold of her arm. "Now I know that Julie, and she is one smart girl. There's a lot of people stuck in bad situations right now, but she's going to do the best she can. You can count on it. And as for you, Mama, we're as stuck as we can be, with our own problem to deal with, so you're going to have to just let it go and trust in God for now."

Charlotte nodded. She was trying to hold it together, because it was looking more and more like Chaki's baby was going to be born here, in the flickering candlelight. She walked over to the image of Mary and pressed her forehead against the cool plaster, taking in the faint scent of oil paint and the gritty texture of the wall itself. She closed her eyes, and for a moment, she was alone, plunged into silence and darkness. "Please," she whispered. "Help Julie, help Ariel, help Chaki. Let Charlie come home. Let an ambulance come. . . ." As she stood there, she tried for just a moment to pretend that the whole room had fallen away, and that she was alone. But the next sound she heard was unmistakable—a loud moan that turned into a grunt. Chaki was pushing. The baby was on its way.

Forty-three

"Okay, listen up," Charlotte said. "I'm going to need a bunch of things, and I need you all to help me. Bring me a bunch of blue chux pads from the exam room downstairs. I need a basin of clean water. In exam room three, there is a kit that I use to put in IUDs—it has sterile scissors and hemostats—they look like clamps. I'm going to need those." Mary Louise stood up, but Charlotte said, "No, I need you here," so Flo and Sam headed down the stairs.

Sam was the first to come back up, carrying a basin of fresh water, a stack of chux, and another first-aid-kit army blanket in his hands.

Charlotte noted out of the corner of her eye how amazingly helpful he was—he folded the supplies neatly where she could easily reach them. His movements were deft and confident, and he seemed totally nonplussed by the fact that Chaki was now lying propped on pillows with her legs wide apart. It was typical for women in labor to lose all sense of modesty, but wasn't Sam from the Middle East somewhere? Shouldn't he be feeling awkward somehow?

But it was Mary Louise who actually asked him. "Well, Mr. Osama, if I didn't know any better, I'd say you'd done this before."

Sam smiled bashfully, his teeth glowing in the candlelight. "In my country, I am a doctor," he said.

"In your country?" Flo asked.

"Iraq."

Charlotte felt just a tiny bit better then. She looked at his hands—he had long and slender tapered fingers with incredibly clean nails. Another pair of hands. Chaki's baby was going to be fine. All of the indicators told her so, from the normal course of labor, to the clear amniotic fluid, to the measured descent of the head down the birth canal.

She and Chaki were not alone here in this room. She looked around at the circle of faces—the warm confidence of Sam's smile, the motherly sound of Mary Louise's susurrations, Flo's brisk helping hand, and around all of them, like a warm embrace, was something that felt like it closed the circle—the spirit of Mary, maybe, a presence of something gentle and kind and pure and good.

Chaki pushed with all her heart and soul. She pushed and pushed and pushed, letting out a grunt now and then, but besides that, bless her heart, she barely made a sound. Between contractions she closed her eyes and fell back on the pillows and looked as though she were sleeping. Her face was tired and sweaty, but remarkably peaceful, and Mary Louise tenderly wiped her forehead with a washcloth, gently wicking the sweat of her labor from her brow.

Charlotte held the Doppler up to her belly before and after each contraction, and each time the determined thump of the baby's heartbeat filled the room, strong, steady, and even.

Then, all of a sudden, the baby turned the corner and there sat the round, wrinkled expanse of scalp. The circle closed in, and there was nothing left except for the baby, which just a few moments later slipped its way, silent, pink, and welcomed, into the small circle of friendship and light.

Forty-four

It was a boy, and Chaki promptly christened him Sam. If Charlotte had to guess, he weighed about six and a half pounds, and he pinked right up and let out a cry so lusty that a moment later LeAnn was thumping up the stairs on her sound leg, coming to see the good news.

Charlotte delivered the placenta, and Sam had the basin to catch it at the ready, and Chaki went from looking spent to looking like the happiest person in the world, smiling all the way, instead of keeping her lips shut to hide her missing teeth like she usually did.

They were all so high on the moment that at first nobody noticed the kaliedoscope of flashing lights—it all seemed like part of the beauty of the moment. But then Charlotte heard loud thumping on the downstairs door, and Flo went over to the window and cried out, "Fire truck! In the parking lot!" She ran down the stairs and a few moments later there were six fully suited-up firemen with big rubber boots and reflective slickers filling up the room. That was when Charlotte noticed that the kaleidoscope was coming from the flashing lights on the engine outside.

"Floodwaters receding," one of them said. Though he was probably speaking in a normal tone, his voice sounded oddly loud.

"Chopper was still busy over toward Harrisburg, but we can get the trucks in and out now. Heard you've got a pregnant woman here. . . ."

The baby chose just that moment to squeal, and the six burly firemen spun around in unison, noticing for the first time Chaki and her baby, who were nestled on a plump pile of pillows and blankets on the floor.

"Hi," Chaki said.

"All right, we've got a baby situation here. Somebody get the stretcher," one fireman boomed.

"Mom and baby are fine," Charlotte said. "But it would still be a good idea to get them to the hospital."

"How are the roads out there?" Mary Louise asked.

"You guys are warm and dry here. Floodwaters are back down, but the roads are a mess. No going anywhere until morning."

"But I need to get out of here—my daughter . . ." Charlotte started to say.

"Well, we can get you as far as the hospital," the captain said, "but after that, you're on your own."

She followed the firemen down the stairs, and she had to hold on to the side of the truck as it cleared the floodwaters. Then, once they got to a clear part of the road, there was an ambulance waiting, and Chaki, baby Sam, and Charlotte were whisked away to the hospital.

Charlotte got out, stunned to see lights on and a normal hustle and bustle of activity; this area was completely unaffected by the flood.

She leaned down and gave Chaki a hug, and whispered into her ear, "Just remember, you're a good mama. Nobody can take that away from you." Then Chaki and the baby were wheeled away through the big double emergency room doors, and Charlotte was left standing in the parking lot, not quite sure what she was going to do next. But she knew what she needed to do. She needed to go inside and find out if Ariel Saramago was on the patient list. This was the closest hospital, and so Charlotte thought this was where the neighbor would have brought them. Still, she hesitated outside the swinging emergency room doors, afraid to go in. She had last spoken to Julie two hours ago; whatever was going to happen had happened. The image of the face of Mary flashed across her mind's eye, and Charlotte took a deep breath, preparing to go inside.

But then the parking lot filled with sirens wailing and lights flashing as another ambulance pulled up.

It screeched to a stop, and the crew got out, moving with the rapid movements of people who knew the situation was urgent—the big ER doors whooshed open, and several people rushed through. They pulled the first stretcher out so quickly that Charlotte didn't see much, just a blur of a body being carried through the door with the kind of haste that said that something was terribly wrong.

But there was a second stretcher in the ambulance, and when it came out, the orderly paused just long enough for a loud cry to escape from Charlotte's lips. She saw only a flash of amber hair, but it was enough for her to know.

"Julie . . . ! Julie . . . ?" Charlotte didn't even realize she was screaming, but by the time she made it through the doors, there was no sign of the stretcher, and her path was blocked by a stout nurse wearing pink scrubs who was blocking her way and saying, "May I help you?"

Forty-five

J ulie had a fractured ankle and two bruised ribs. Charlotte sat in
stunned silence when the doctor made her sign papers to release her
daughter for a tox screen to check for drugs and alcohol in her blood.
The ER doc was handsome, like a doctor on a TV drama, which just
made the situation seem more unreal. He spoke seriously, but Charlotte,
who kept thinking about George Clooney, had to get her mind to focus
back on the task at hand.

"Your daughter is an underage driver. Her car went off the road in
flood conditions. Apparently she was swerving to avoid a deer. She
wasn't the only car on that road to have an accident, but the passenger
in the car was unconscious at the time she was found. Because of these
circumstances, we believe that a tox screen is warranted." Charlotte absorbed that information as though through a wool blanket. She took the
paper and signed the consent form. "How is the passenger . . . ?"

"I'm sorry. I can share that information only with next of kin," he
said. Charlotte could see a mix of pity and disapproval in his eyes—the
way he would look at any mother of a screwup who had run off the road,
who shouldn't have been driving, whom he suspected of using illegal
substances. . . .

"I'm sorry, Mom. I'm sorry, Mom . . ." Julie kept repeating. "I shouldn't
have taken the car. I just didn't know what to do. . . ."

Julie was lying on a hospital bed in a partition with the curtains pulled
shut.

"Oh, Julie, it's okay, but why didn't you go to the Browns', like I told
you . . . ?"

"I did, Mom. I did. I ran to the Browns' but they weren't home, and
then I ran down the street to the Shiffmans' but they weren't there

either. . . . I just got scared. I thought I should run back to check her and when I got there, she felt really cold when I touched her and her lips looked blue . . . and the way she was breathing was all funny. I tried to call you, Mom, but the phone wasn't working. I was afraid she was going to die."

Charlotte stroked her daughter's forehead, smoothing the hair up off her face. "It's okay, sweetie. You did the right thing. You were brave to even try."

Julie's ankle was swollen and bruised. While they were waiting for the doctor to come in, Julie closed her eyes and appeared to doze off a little, and so Charlotte was left with her own thoughts. Two girls, forced to make decisions about the best way to help someone . . . Arecely had clearly understood that Chaki was in danger, and so she had helped her to hide in the clinic—the wrong decision, and yet the outcome was okay, and maybe better than it would have been if Chaki hadn't found a place to hide.

It hurt to think of it, but she could imagine Julie, alone in the barn watching while Ariel's lips turned blue, and trying to come up with a plan. Julie was a brave girl; Charlotte knew that already from the time she had jumped into Deirdre's pool and tried to help Charlotte rescue Maria Lopez.

Nobody would tell her anything about what was going on with Ariel. Charlotte knew that she wasn't in the ER, that she had been taken straight up to the ICU. She had no idea what the problem was, but she knew of a possible worst-case scenario: the positive pregnancy test, the spotting. Still, Ariel knew the risks; she must have already gotten checked out, mustn't she have? It was hard to know what else could make a healthy teenager pass out like that.

She had been sitting there for several hours when she saw a young resident walk through—Dr. Elliot, the one she had spoken to on the phone the previous week. He looked like a typical resident, a lab coat stained by ink marks and sagging from the weight of all of the cheat sheets and instruments he kept in his pockets. He looked so young, hardly looked old enough to be a doctor, although he had to be at least in his late twenties.

He went to the nurses' station, and as Charlotte strained her ears, she realized that they were talking about Ariel. . . . Though the doctors were supposed to protect patient confidentiality, sometimes they apparently thought that nobody could really understand them when they were talking in medical lingo. Charlotte got up and walked over toward the magazine rack, hoping to hear what he was saying. She couldn't catch much of it, but she heard him say, "Positive tox screen—cocaine . . ." and also, "Condition extremely guarded." *Cocaine. That would explain a lot.*

When Charlotte saw a police officer come into the ER, she was afraid. Julie already had her cast on her leg, and the doctor had informed her that Julie tested negative for any illegal substances, but still, Charlotte wasn't sure what was going to happen. The police officer asked her to leave the room, but didn't actually stay too long. On the way out, she tipped her hat to Charlotte, and said to her, "Just a formality, ma'am, underage driving . . . but it looks like she had a good reason." With a start, Charlotte recognized the blond woman from the state troopers—her former patient.

By midnight Julie was discharged, but they had no way of getting home. But it didn't matter, because Julie refused to leave anyway.

"We need to go wait for Ariel. If we leave, she'll be completely alone."

"Julie," her mom said, "she's still unconscious."

"She's still alive, isn't she?" Julie's voice betrayed her worry.

"Julie, they won't share much with me . . . but I don't think she is doing very well."

"It doesn't matter. There should be somebody here who knows her." Julie was adamant. Charlotte had given the nurses the scant bit she knew about Deirdre's whereabouts—that she was coming back from Buenos Aires . . . which was all she knew. She hoped that they would be able to track her down.

The chairs in the waiting room of the intensive care unit were narrow and hard, designed to make it impossible to lie down no matter how tired you were. Julie pressed on the armrests to hold herself awkwardly upright, the only sign she gave that her ribs were hurting, her metal crutches propped on the chair next to her. Charlotte thought she was holding up okay until she noticed that there were tears running down her daughter's face, silent and wet, like rain.

Charlotte grasped her daughter's bony elbow and whispered, "You did what you could, Jule-Jule. There was nothing else you could do." But even as she pressed her lips up against the gentle whorl of her daughter's ear, she knew that her words weren't good enough. She knew that trying hard wasn't enough, and that Julie, her daughter, had stepped into a black place that she as her mother had never wanted her to go.

The nurses in the ICU wouldn't let them past the heavy pneumatic swinging doors, wouldn't give them much information at all—just to say that her condition was serious and that she was unconscious.

They were stuck there anyway, no way to get home, and so they sat, not quite touching in the hard metal chairs. Finally Charlotte decided to see if the cell phones were working again. She dialed her home number. The phone rang, and she expected the answering machine to pick up. With a start, she heard Charlie's voice. "Hello?"

She must have dozed off, because she awoke to a tap on her shoulder, and in front of her stood Charlie. Julie had fallen asleep too, slumped down on her chair in an awkward position.

He knelt down beside his daughter, and Charlotte saw the look on his face—fear.

"She's okay," Charlotte whispered. "Broken ankle, but it's not serious, thank God."

She thought he might say something, but he didn't. He just scooped up the sleeping Julie in his arms without waking her, as if she were a toddler in PJs, and started walking so quickly toward the elevators that Charlotte had to scurry to keep up. She watched his broad back in front of her, and tried, but couldn't read what he was feeling. She had known him so well, for so long, and in the set of his shoulders, she thought she could read anger or blame for letting Julie get hurt on her watch. That made Charlotte realize that she was still angry at him. He had left, and if Julie was hurt, it wasn't only her fault. . . .

They rode down in the elevator silently. Julie still had not woken up. Charlie said nothing, just stood holding his daughter in his arms, looking down into her face with his brows creased, and Charlotte, grappling for words, could think of nothing to say.

As they were leaving through the main doors, she saw a black limousine pull up in front of the big doors. There was Deirdre, wearing black glasses and looking as elegant as a movie star. She gave no sign of seeing them. Charlotte opened her mouth to call out to her, but then she turned and looked at Charlie, who was already heading out to the parking lot with Julie in his arms.

Charlotte hesitated just a moment longer; then she stepped off the curb and jogged to catch up with Charlie.

The odd thing about flooding is how some areas can be completely underwater while others stay dry, and how as quickly as the waters rise, they recede again.

Charlie took them the long away around, and up on the highway bypass, the roads were dry and traffic was proceeding normally. In fact, if you didn't know, you would have no way to guess about all the flooding that had gone on. Tersely, Charlotte filled Charlie in about the events of the evening—about how she was stuck in the flood, how Julie had found Ariel unconscious. About what she had overheard about Ariel and cocaine, and how it was that Julie had chosen to try to drive her to the hospital in the car. Charlie didn't say much—didn't say anything really—and Charlotte was so tired that she just wanted to close her eyes and shut out everything. She didn't even want to ask him where he had been.

Julie didn't wake up in the car, and when they pulled into the driveway, she stayed asleep, even when Charlie picked her up, carried her up the stairs, and tucked her into her bed, arranging her heavy leg cast under the blankets, and then pulling the covers up to her chin.

Charlotte slept a deep, blank sleep, but before the sun was fully up, she was awakened by what sounded at first like a fire alarm, but was actually somebody pushing the doorbell over and over again in rapid succession.

She was halfway down the stairs, pulling on her robe, heart at her throat, before she really remembered the events of the night before. She was rubbing sleep out of her eyes when she caught sight of Deirdre's Range Rover through the window, and at that moment, she was jolted awake as the memory came back to her.

Deirdre didn't ask to come in; she just bolted straight past Charlotte. The composure that Charlotte had seen on her face when she had passed her in the hospital parking lot was now gone. She was openly weeping, her face distorted, her eyes wild. Her hair was pulling out of her bun.

Deirdre was howling, sort of chanting, really; "Ariel's dead, Ariel's dead, Ariel's dead. . . ."

Charlotte stepped back as though stunned by a physical blow, and stood staring at Deirdre, unable to speak.

Thank God, Charlie came down the stairs then and helped her half lead, half drag Deirdre to the back of the house.

"Don't let her wake Julie," Charlie whispered tersely. Julie had woken up once during the night, and Charlotte had given her daughter pain medicine that was likely to keep her in a deep sleep—at least she hoped. But Deirdre's howls echoed through the room like an ambulance siren.

Her story poured out in jumbled fits and starts—awkward pieces that could hardly be put together, and as she listened, Charlotte felt as though the present were being fractured through a mirror so that past and present were jutted together at oblique angles.

Charlie brewed up some tea, and Charlotte saw him slip a generous slosh of bourbon into it, then some lemon and sugar, and he brought it to Deirdre, setting the cup and saucer in front of her on the table.

Charlotte watched her cautiously, the way a child watches a mother who has just finished a temper fit.

Deirdre picked up the cup and started to take greedy sips. She rubbed her nose with her hand as the steam from the tea made her nose run, until Charlie quietly brought her a box of tissues. He then poured more bourbon into her tea, which she didn't seem to notice. She was rocking back and forth on the chair, keening, "My baby is dead, my baby is dead, my baby is dead. . . ."

The sun was up now, and after the rains of the night before, the sky was clear, and the early-morning sun shone through the windows. Charlotte looked around her kitchen, saw the familiar homey environment—the pictures stuck to the fridge with magnets, the neat row of blue-and-white canisters on the clean countertop. It was probably just exhaustion, but it felt like the room was spinning. Charlotte sat right next to Deirdre, almost pushed up against her, and she kept trying to do things for her—handing her a tissue, urging her to take a sip of tea.

Deirdre wasn't making a lot of sense, but Charlotte tried to coax the story out of her.

"Deirdre, honey," she said, stroking her hair. "You have to tell us what happened."

"They said she bled to death." Deirdre's voice had an eerie, high-pitched sound that was almost inhuman.

"She . . . bled . . . ?" Charlotte's own voice seemed disembodied too.

"By the time she got to the hospital"—now her voice was a monotone—"she had lost so much blood that . . ." Deirdre didn't say anything more. Just sat at the table taking more sips of her tea, staring at the wall.

"That . . . "

"That it was too late," she said. Deirdre looked out the window as though she had just noticed it was there for the first time.

When she started talking again, her tone was completely different. She sounded oddly matter-of-fact. "I've asked for an autopsy. I'm going to get to the bottom of this. I just don't believe it. I don't believe what they are saying. . . ."

"What they are saying?"

"That she was pregnant . . . Not my Ariel . . ." Now Deirdre's voice sounded odd, cold, not so much sad as angry or bitter. She stood up and went over to the counter, where Charlie had placed her Gucci bag.

"I've got sleeping pills," she said, rummaging around in her bag, from which she pulled an astonishing assortment of plastic vials. "And don't think that bastard Bruce is going to get away with this. . . . I'm going to get him for statutory rape."

"Statutory rape . . . ?" Charlotte was confused. "But Ariel was—"

Deirdre cut her off. "I'm personal friends with the minister of the interior in Buenos Aires. He's one of Juan-Luis's cousins. He'll issue a doctored birth certificate as soon as I ask. Poor Bruce—he's going to find out that Ariel was only sixteen. Won't that be an unpleasant surprise?" A harsh sound escaped from her lips, a laugh that sounded more like a caw. By now Deirdre had found a mirror in her purse, and pulled out a small makeup bag—she was eyeing herself critically as she touched up her makeup. There was something so practiced about her mannerisms that they belied her grief of a moment before.

When she turned around, her face was composed, but beneath the facade, Charlotte could see that it looked strangely wooden, and fear stirred in her, deep fear, crawling up from her belly like a snake from a pit.

"I've got to sleep," Deirdre said. "Hopper, here's my address book. Call the first three names listed under Saramago. Tell them what has happened. Then call the ambassador. He's listed under A. He can help with the funeral arrangements."

She opened an amber-colored vial and shook what looked like several pills into her hand, then tossed them into her mouth and swallowed them without water. "I'm going to lie down," she said. "I'm going to need to sleep."

Charlotte was getting ready to go pull out the sofa bed for her, but Charlie held her back. "Give me your keys. I'll drive you home."

"But . . . I . . . ." Then she was sobbing again. "No, I can't. I can't be alone. I need someone to take care of me."

"Charlie . . . ?" Charlotte said, hesitating, wondering if they should let her stay. Deep down she knew she wanted Deirdre to leave, but casting her out seemed cruel. She scanned Charlie's face, looking for a sign that he would soften, but didn't see it.

"Give me your keys," he said sternly.

Deirdre rummaged around a bit more in her purse, then handed the keys to him. Charlie grasped her elbow firmly and led her toward the door.

When Charlie came back, Charlotte was just sitting there, slumped at the kitchen table, staring out the window at the path that led to Deirdre's house. Now, in retrospect, it seemed so obvious. She couldn't keep Deirdre from moving to Westville, but she should have listened to Charlie and kept that door between them shut.

Charlie slipped into the room, put his arm around her, kissed her cheek.

"Was she okay?"

"Charlotte." From his tone of voice, she could tell that he had something important to say. "I'm going to make the phone calls for her, but that is it. Besides that, no further contact. Do you understand?"

"But, Charlie—"

"Charlotte, I mean it. I mean it more than I've meant anything in my life."

"But, Charlie . . . Ariel is—" Her voice was cut off by a sob; she couldn't finish the sentence. "No matter what we may think of her actions . . ."

Charlie took hold of her chin and pointed her face toward him. "Charlotte."

She tried to look away, but he held her firm, so that she had to look in his eyes. "Charlie, Julie is upstairs in her room doped out on Vicodin with a broken ankle and two cracked ribs because she was trying to save the girl. Even if you don't like Deirdre, it's disrespectful to Julie to act like the girl's death doesn't even matter."

"Charlotte." Charlie's voice was controlled, but she could hear in it the low undertones of anger. "Since when do you think that a child's death doesn't matter to me? Are you trying to accuse me of being callous? Like I don't care? How many casualties does this family have to have before you see what she has done to you?"

Charlotte was angry now too. So angry that she could feel her hands shaking, and she felt like hollering and pointing toward the door. He had left. He had already left once, and now he was back, while she was trying to pick up the pieces from the second most dreadful night of her life—only now he wanted to pass judgment.

She thought about Ariel—or she tried to think about Ariel, but all she could feel was a kind of generic sadness at the loss. She didn't know the girl well, and that odd glassy quality she had, that quality that was so like Deirdre in a way . . . Charlotte shook her head, trying to clear her mind. Charlie was the one who was callous. She was tired, exhausted, worried about Julie, worried about Deirdre, grief-stricken, needing sleep. . . .

Charlie was standing, shifting from foot to foot. He looked like he might be just about to walk out the door again, and she realized that she felt oddly neutral about that, as if she weren't really certain she cared.

But he didn't turn his back and leave. Instead, he dropped down on his knees beside her and slipped her hands between his.

Charlotte looked at his face—he looked tired and careworn too. She looked deep into the recesses of his familiar brown eyes.

"I know what you think of Deirdre, Charlie, but this is her baby. . . ."

Charlie held up his hand as though to physically stop her from talking. She looked into the reflecting pools of his eyes and was stunned to see tears—he rarely cried. She could hardly ever think of seeing him cry. "Charlotte," he said, but his voice was all choked off low in his throat. He averted his eyes, rubbed her fingers between his palms, swallowed a couple of times.

"Charlie? What is it?"

She could see the tears threatening to spill over, the earnest way he was blinking them back.

"Charlie?"

He walked away from her, over to the window, but as though the view out the back toward Deirdre's woods offended him, he turned abruptly and walked across to the other window, the one that faced out to the laundry lines in the side yard.

"Charlotte, there's something you don't know."

"What is it?"

"Something I didn't tell you, but . . . well, I think I should have. I guess . . . I guess I thought all this time that you knew. Or I was telling myself that you knew. . . ."

Then Charlotte felt it dripping into her insides—the old fear, that long-ago, long-submerged fear. . . . Whatever it was, she was sure she didn't want to hear it. She stood up.

"Charlie," she said, trying to make her voice sound bright, "maybe you should make those phone calls now. Isn't it late or something in Argentina? People will need to make travel plans."

But Charlie ignored her as though she hadn't spoken, and plunged on. "Deirdre's baby—"

"Oh, I know, Charlie, I know. Poor Ariel. I wish I could've . . . somehow I should've . . ." She was babbling, trying to keep him from talking.

Charlie walked back across the room. He put one hand on each of her shoulders. He said, "Charlotte. Please. Listen. You just have to listen."

Charlotte was afraid, but she kept her mouth shut. She looked at him.

"Charlotte," he said slowly, patiently. "I'm talking about Deirdre's *other* baby."

Oddly enough, though it was the thing that had brought them together, they never, ever talked about it.

"Oh," Charlotte said, looking away from him, looking anywhere but at him.

"That *other* baby," Charlie said, and then abruptly he turned and walked out of the room, just calling over his shoulder as he left: "The other baby was mine."

Forty-six

Looking back, the thing that Charlotte always found difficult to remember was how the entire situation had been pervaded by fear. A fear so thick and palpable that it seemed to hang from the ceiling, coat the walls, muffle sound, and make the air hard to breathe.

As she had sat at her desk in the quiet dormitory working on a paper, it had seemed peaceful, but the moment that Deirdre popped her head in the door, from that moment on, the quiet, the isolation, the muffled quality that the snow had created took on a sinister cast. As if fear were a giant hand that could hold you in its grip. That was how it was.

"Charlotte," Deirdre said, "something's wrong." It wasn't the words. It was something about the way she said them. And Charlotte hesitated a moment before she turned around because she knew, without quite knowing it, that she didn't want to know what was wrong.

Slowly Charlotte scraped her chair back, away from her desk.

Then Deirdre screamed. At least, it sounded like a scream, but the sound was as muffled as the night itself, and Charlotte was convinced that nobody outside the room could hear it.

Their rooms, though small and cramped, were called a suite. Two tiny bedrooms, a short hallway, and a bathroom—institutional in its simplicity—a black-and-white-tiled floor, a stall shower with gray marble slabs for walls, and a toilet.

Deirdre whirled around and disappeared into the bathroom. She locked the door behind her with a click, and Charlotte jumped up. She tried the brass handle of the door, but it was locked.

She leaned in, tapped tentatively on the door. "Deirdre? Deirdre. Is everything okay?"

For a minute or two she heard nothing; then she heard an odd, almost inhuman sound—like a howl of pain that turned into a groan at the end.

"Deirdre? Deirdre. Are you okay? Unlock the door. Let me in. Do you want me to call a doctor?"

There was no answer from inside the bathroom. Charlotte stood outside the door, forehead pressed against the wood, uncertain.

"Deirdre?"

She stood there but didn't hear anything, until she started wondering if Deirdre had passed out, but no, she could hear faint sounds—movements and the occasional cough or clearing her throat. Finally Charlotte decided to go sit down again. Deirdre obviously wasn't feeling well, but if she didn't need help, Charlotte might as well go back to work.

Charlotte sat back in her desk chair, and tried to focus on the notes and papers in front of her, but now her concentration was shot. She was keeping one ear cocked, listening for sounds from the bathroom, but she heard nothing. She looked out the windows, where snow was piling up on the sills; then she pressed her forehead against the cold glass and peered out into the dark courtyard. The snow was piled up in drifts, and the walkways were snowed over and hadn't been cleared yet. School was closed for Martin Luther King Day, and a lot of the other students had gone away. There wasn't a soul outside, and as she looked across the courtyard at the facing dormitory, she noticed that almost all of the lights were out. She felt again that feeling of being in a muffled cocoon, and as she stood there, she could feel the anxiety start to lessen; it was probably nothing. But only for a moment, because the next moment Deirdre was screaming again—this one was piercing, bloodcurdling, and the cold from the window suddenly seemed to envelop Charlotte in a veil of ice.

"Deirdre? Deirdre, what's the matter?" she yelled as she headed back toward the hallway.

The bathroom door burst open, and Deirdre plunged out, running down to the end of the hall toward the little nook where their minifridge and kitchen supplies were located.

"Deirdre?" Charlotte said, starting to follow her. But as she passed the bathroom, the door now ajar, she screamed. Streaking across the black and white tiles was a trail of blood, so red that for a moment Charlotte thought she might faint.

"Deirdre, what . . . ?"

Deirdre had her back to Charlotte, but she spun around, and Charlotte saw that she was holding a long curved knife with a rusty blade—it was the old knife that they kept for cutting cheese and bread.

Charlotte froze. She could feel her knees trembling. It seemed that they were both trapped in one endless moment. Deirdre was at one end of the hall, hair flying out at crazy angles from her head. She was wearing a shapeless plaid bathrobe so much too big that it had probably belonged to her father. She could almost have looked like her normal self, except for the knife.

Charlotte was desperately trying to put the pieces together, but a coherent image wouldn't form—it was just jagged, sharp edges of things stuck together, a pool of blood, a knife. But the pool of blood came before Deirdre grabbed the knife. Then Charlotte realized that Deirdre was brandishing the knife at her, and she got scared, took a step back, held out her hand. . . .

Right then Deirdre let out that earth-shattering howl again. *Didn't anyone hear? Wouldn't someone, anyone, hear her frenzy and come through the door?* Charlotte took another step back, then another. Deirdre blocked her pathway to the door. Charlotte stepped back. But right now Deirdre's eyes were rolled back in her head, and she was crouching low over the floor, and she was moaning . . . and grunting. She was no longer holding the knife up. Now it hung limply in her hand.

Then whatever had gripped her seemed to come to a sudden end. She held up the knife again, this time in a way that was clearly threatening.

"Get out of my way." Deirdre's voice was as cold as the steel blade of the knife she was holding, and Charlotte took one step back, and then another. Deirdre's face looked at once the same but totally different—as if it were a mask carved from wood.

Charlotte stepped back slowly, her eyes trained on Deirdre's eyes; they were glassy, like marbles.

"I said move. Get out of my way. For God's sake, Charlotte, what is wrong with you? I'm not going to hurt you."

That last bit sounded almost like herself, and Charlotte let her defenses down and shuffled out of the way. "Oh, sorry, sorry, Deirdre. It's just that . . . what's wrong? I saw the blood and . . ."

But as soon as she got out of the way, Deirdre pushed past her into the bathroom, closed the door with a solid thud, and Charlotte heard the door latch.

This was the part where Charlotte always looked back and wondered how it was that she had made the decisions that she had made. Was it the snow? The muffled silence of the snow? Deirdre was locked in the bathroom, and Charlotte could easily pick up the phone, or walk out the door and try to find help, and when she thought back, this had constantly

disturbed her. What had kept her there, head pressed against the bathroom door, saying, "Deirdre, open the door. Deirdre, open the door"?
Tears were streaming down her face, and she did think about leaving,
didn't she? But she could still remember thinking that the phone was too
far away—she was crooning through the wood, "Dee-Dee, open the door.
Come on now. Don't . . . don't do anything terrible." Sobbing, then stopping her sobs to listen, and shaking all over because she couldn't inter-
pret the sounds she was hearing—movement, and grunting, and
swishing, and more grunting.

As she stood there, Charlotte was now forced to think over the past
few weeks. Maybe she had known something was wrong. Deirdre had
been acting strange for a while, sleeping late, cutting her classes, wearing loose, sloppy clothes, letting her laundry pile up undone on floor.
Charlotte had been on the verge of saying something—how many times?
Is anything wrong? But she hadn't dared. Instead she had gone along, pretending that she had noticed nothing, that nothing was wrong.

"Dee-Dee. Come on now. You can open the door now. Just open it."

Like a person who was talking someone down from a twentieth-story
window, Charlotte remembered thinking that they were attached as if by
a cord, that as long as Deirdre could hear her voice she couldn't possibly . . . But still, it was all unfolding in front of her eyes like an amalgamation of every bad movie she had ever seen—Deirdre slashing her
wrists . . . Deirdre hacking her own throat . . . and so she stayed there,
and she pleaded, then listened, then tried to jimmy the door, then listened again.

When she thought about it later, Charlotte realized that what had
seemed like hours was really only a few minutes—five or ten minutes at
the most. It all happened so quickly. But she was in a suspended state of
time then, and it could have been hours or days. She wasn't aware of
time passing . . . only the cold sweat of fear that drenched her under her
clothes, and her heightened sense of hearing that must be akin to what
blind people's hearing was like.

But looking back, thinking back, and remembering back, the one
thing she did not remember ever hearing was anything that sounded
like—

The door opened suddenly—so suddenly that Charlotte stumbled
forward into the bathroom. She saw blood everywhere, smeared all
over the floor, dripping across the toilet, and streaked across the sink,
where the knife was resting on top of a bloody clump. There was so

much blood that for a moment her head spun and she closed her eyes, grabbing out and gripping the cold edge of the shower stall to steady herself, and then she kept her eyes closed for a moment, afraid to open them, because she thought she had seen Deirdre standing in front of her, looking intact—but that couldn't be, because of all the blood.

Charlotte cracked her eyes open. Deirdre was standing in front her. She looked normal—except like a wax museum copy of herself.

"Everything is okay now," she said. Her voice was metallic, monotone.

Again Charlotte tried to take in the scene. There was so much blood that for a second that was all she could see.

Until—

"No! No!" Charlotte screamed. "You can't leave it on the floor like that—it's cold." Instinct kicked in hard, like a toe in the ribs, when she saw it.

There was a scrawny newborn baby splayed out on the tile floor in a puddle of murky fluid.

Without thinking Charlotte picked it up and brought it close in to her chest, now not noticing the blood and slimy, cheesy white substance that seemed to be coating it.

"Deirdre, what . . . ? What happened?" Charlotte hadn't yet understood what the baby was doing there, but she knew that it needed to be wrapped up, to be warmed. She grabbed towels from the towel rack, and wrapped them around the baby.

She carried it, held close to her, into her room, where she laid the awkward bundle on her bed.

"It's okay now," Deirdre repeated in that same eerily calm monotone. But Charlotte wasn't listening. She was looking at the baby; now she could see that something was clearly wrong with it.

Its head seemed too small, and its tiny eyes appeared to be glued shut. She pulled the blankets of her bed up around it, then pulled the towel down a little bit. There was something wrong with its skin too—it was too thin, almost see-through. And the color. She didn't think it was the color a baby was supposed to be—a dark purpley blue. *It was because it hadn't started breathing yet. . . . Didn't the doctor do something, in the delivery room, to make it start breathing?*

"Deirdre, quick, we need to do something." She looked up, but Deirdre wasn't even there.

Slap it! Wasn't that it? Didn't she need to slap it? Now it was clear to her what was wrong. The baby was as still and silent as a stone. It wasn't breathing.

She picked it up, held it in one arm. It was so light. Shouldn't a baby be heavier than that? It was so tiny. The baby's skull was almost translucent, and so small that it fit in the palm of her hand. Her hand was trembling, but she held it up, trembling, and tried to slap the baby's back. But she was afraid. It was so tiny that she might crush it. But it wasn't breathing. She tapped once, gently, once again, a little harder with the palm of her hand. Terrified, she laid it back down on the bed again. But now it was becoming clear to her: Something was wrong with this baby. It was too small. It was the wrong color. It wasn't breathing. . . .

She pulled the sleeve of her sweatshirt down over her palm and rubbed some of the cheesy stuff off the baby's chest—it was white and had the consistency of Crisco. Then she leaned over and pressed her ear against the tiny rib cage, which felt cool to the touch. She closed her eyes and listened hard. But she heard nothing. Nothing but deep, muffled silence, like the silence of the snow outside.

She waited for a few moments longer; she stroked her finger along the thin cheek; she stroked the inside of the baby's hand. But the baby was still, cold, silent, gone off to another place. Gone before it even got there.

Charlotte didn't cry. Because now normal thoughts were starting to break through her panic.

She left the still baby in the mass of towels on her bed and went to look for Deirdre.

Deirdre was sitting on the toilet, rocking back and forth. Her eyes had a terrible otherworldly cast. Charlotte took it all in again, the blood, the strange look on Deirdre's face, and she noticed something else—that Deirdre was a shade paler than before, and she thought there was something off about her lips, like they were turning a purplish color.

Again, when she looked back on it, she used to imagine that she walked into the other room and called 911 without saying anything, and that she left Deirdre there, rocking on the toilet, until she heard the comfort of sirens in the distance.

But that wasn't what actually happened. What really happened was that she stood at the doorway, pleading with Deirdre, just as she pleaded before when the door was closed.

"Come on, Dee. I'm going to call student health. You look really sick. . . . I'm going to call them. You need to get over there." But Deirdre just kept shaking her head, and rocking, and saying, "No, no, no—everything is fine now. Everything is okay."

She left Deirdre and went back in her room to look again at the tiny infant. There was a long length of umbilical cord. It was tied into a square knot at the end, and with revulsion Charlotte realized that Deirdre must have tied that knot. Past the knot, it bore the unmistakable sign of being hacked with a dull knife. She touched the cord tentatively with her fingertip, and shuddered when she felt how cold it was.

Charlotte couldn't stand it. She went into Deirdre's room, barely noticing the piles of clothes, the unmade bed, the untidy stacks of books. After rummaging around in her closet for a moment, she found Deirdre's snow boots; then she went into the bathroom and started shoving them onto Deirdre's feet. Deirdre was trembling, shaking like a leaf, which scared Charlotte, but she didn't put up a protest. Then Charlotte grabbed her own boots and both of their jackets. She shoved Deirdre's arms into the jacket sleeves. Deirdre felt oddly limp, and she didn't say anything, but she allowed Charlotte to put the jacket on her. Charlotte grabbed one of her own wool hats and pulled it over Deirdre's head. Then she grasped her arm and pulled her off the toilet. Her heart started beating faster when she saw the crimson blood that filled the toilet bowl.

Charlotte knelt down and tugged Deirdre's underwear and jeans up into place, and leaving the button front unsnapped because it didn't fit around her middle. Then she led her out of the bathroom, and down the hall. Still Deirdre put up no protest. Then, almost as an afterthought, Charlotte ran back down the hall, wrapped up the silent and still body in the towels, and grasped her arms around it.

Outside there were at least two feet of snow, and it was still coming down hard. Nobody was about. Mercifully, it was a short walk to the student health center, but it was tough going because none of the paths or sidewalks had been cleared.

All they had to do was make it half a block and then around one corner, and though the drifts of snow made it hard to walk, with each step Charlotte thought, *We're almost there, we're almost there*, and she could imagine the incredible relief she would feel when she entered the lighted place and handed over her two charges, one dead, one alive.

It was so close, except that what happened was that they made it only quarter of the way down the block. As they passed the big green Dumpsters out behind the dining hall, Deirdre stumbled, and then sat down in the snow.

"Come on, Dee," Charlotte said. "Come on, get up. We're almost there. Just a little farther." The cold, the snow—there was nobody about. Charlotte started thinking that Deirdre might just die there, right there in the snow, next to the Dumpsters.

But Deirdre didn't die. She staggered to her feet and stood there swaying.

"Are you holding it?"

"What?"

"Is that what you've got in your arms. Is it . . . it?"

Charlotte nodded; she wanted to appease her, to get her going, to drag her the last few steps through the snow so she could give her away.

"Don't worry, Deirdre. I've got the baby." Maybe Deirdre didn't know that the baby was dead. Maybe she could string her along a little, just enough to appease her. "Come on, Dee-Dee. Everything is okay. I've got her. Everything is going to be okay."

"No!" she shouted. Her voice was so loud that Charlotte looked around to see if anyone else had heard, but the street was still deserted.

"Nothing is going to be fine. Nothing." Then her voice got really low, and she started the odd crooning she had been doing before. "You know what you're going to do? You're going to throw it. Take it and toss it right now, right there, right into that trash can, and then I'll go."

"Deirdre. Are you crazy? I can't do that. I can't throw it in the trash. . . ."

"It's *dead*," she said. She sank back down on her bottom in the snow, and now, Charlotte felt true fear seize her, because, though the light was dim, she could see that there was a dark stain spreading out in the snow around Deirdre. She was bleeding, and her blood was soaking into the snow.

Charlotte started sobbing. "No, Deirdre, no. Just get up." She tugged on her arm, but Deirdre wouldn't budge. She peered down at the bundle in her arms, and suddenly realized that it had come half-unwrapped and that there was an arm sticking out—like a drumstick on a raw chicken, only not so plump. Now it was stiff as a stick, and its weird translucent skin was making it appear to glow in the half-light.

"Throw it," Deirdre said.

"No," Charlotte said, tugging on Deirdre's arm again.

"I said throw it," Deirdre said, only now her voice was high and shrill, and Charlotte could hear it echoing down the empty street, bouncing off of the empty buildings.

"No," Charlotte said. "I won't, and you have to get up right now. Or I'm going to leave you here."

Then Deirdre, as though totally oblivious to the cold, lay back on the snow and said, "Okay, fine, just go ahead and leave me. . . . I'm not going anywhere. I'll be fine in the morning. I don't need any help."

Charlotte took one step back, two steps, but as she readjusted the bundle in her arms she uncovered the baby's face by accident—the sightless eyes, the sunken cheekbones, the blackish lips, the sucked-in skull.

"Deirdre, get up." She tugged again on Deirdre's arm, but there was no use; she was a deadweight.

"No, just leave me here. I'm not going anywhere with . . . that thing." Her voice was breathy and thin, and her eyes were closed.

Charlotte tugged hard on her arm again, but she wasn't strong enough to get her up.

"Just throw it . . . and then I'll come."

Charlotte backed up a few paces, preparing to sprint to the clinic and get help, but the dark stain on the snow, and Deirdre's stonelike face . . .

Charlotte reached down, and in a motion too rapid to be thought about, she swept out a little hollow in the clean snow; then she laid the baby there, pulling the towel up so that it covered the little shrunken face.

"Sorry," she whispered, her words disappearing in a puff of mist. "Come on," she said, hooking Deirdre under both arms as she started to half drag her along. "I did it. Now let's go."

It wasn't far at all, and in just a few moments, they were stumbling through the glass doors of the student health building, where one sleepy-looking nurse was sitting at the check-in desk.

"Name, please," she said, bored, not impressed by their obviously disheveled appearance.

"She's sick. She's really sick. You need to take care of her," Charlotte said, her words coming out in little breathless bursts.

"Name, please," the nurse repeated.

"Deirdre. Deirdre Stinson. She's—"

"Date of birth," the nurse said.

"November eighteenth," Deirdre said. "Nineteen sixty-seven."

"Class?"

"Junior," Charlotte said. "But listen. You've got to listen, see—"

"Sign here," the nurse said. "Have a seat."

"But she's—"

"I'm bleeding," Deirdre said, swaying so that she almost fell to her knees.

"Oh, I see," the nurse said, grabbing a wheelchair with a single deft movement, and almost shoving Deirdre into it. "Let's head straight to the back."

That was it. Deirdre disappeared behind the swinging doors with the nurse, and Charlotte was left alone, standing in the empty waiting room with the lime-green-and-orange color scheme.

Afterward, she liked to tell herself that if only the nurse had asked, if only someone had asked, she would have told them everything—about what had happened, and the knife, and how Deirdre had collapsed in the snow, and about where the baby was. But after standing for a few more minutes in the waiting room of the infirmary, she turned around and went back outside. Then she traced the path that had been made by her and Deirdre's footsteps, not even bothering to look at the snowdrift near the Dumpsters as she passed. . . . In fact, she could no longer remember exactly which one it was. When she got back to the dorm room, she took out her Comet and a sponge and she scrubbed down the bathroom, scrubbed up every trace of blood and slimy gunk until it was clean again, and threw the knife, wrapped in a bloody towel, into the trash for good measure. Then, just as the sky was starting to lighten through the windows, she climbed into bed and fell into a heavy, dreamless sleep.

Later it was hard to explain all this, though she tried, patiently and carefully, to explain it to the police, to Deirdre's parents, to her own parents, to the dean of the university, to Charlie. They kept asking her, "Why did you leave the baby in the snow, and why didn't you tell anyone it was there?" And she kept repeating, hoping they would understand, "But the baby was already dead. . . ." But the hard thing was that it never made a lot of sense to her either. The only thing that made sense to her was her own fear, which seemed to have piled up in drifts around her until it had completely muffled her judgment.

Forty-seven

A riel Saramago's funeral was as elaborate as an affair of state. Outside St. Patrick's Cathedral, there were lines of Mercedes and limousines. Apparently the whole Argentinian community had turned out. The ambassador was there, and a couple of famous Argentinian movie stars.

Deirdre sat in front, flanked on both sides by people who Charlotte thought were probably members of the Saramago clan. Deirdre was dressed in the kind of black clothes that it seemed you would see only in movies—a fine black linen suit, a small black cloche with a little black veil, and giant owl-eyed dark glasses that implied that they were hiding her tears.

She held a white linen handkerchief, which she dabbed on occasion against her pale cheek.

The Cathedral was gothic, with towering vaulted ceilings and flying buttresses across the top. The mass was in Latin. It was vaguely chilly in the nave, and the pews were crowded. They sat about two-thirds of the way back, on the left—at a remove that made Charlotte feel somewhat detached as the service droned on in a language she couldn't understand. On one side of her sat Julie, who was oddly quiet and resolute in the surroundings. On the other side Charlotte leaned against the firm warmth of Charlie's shoulder. She blinked a few times, testing her eyes to see if there were tears, but mercifully her eyes were staying dry. She didn't want to lose her composure, for Julie's sake.

Charlotte rubbed her forehead. A headache bored between her eyes; she had lain awake in bed, going back over the moments when she had crossed paths with Ariel, trying to think of a point at which she could have intervened to change the course for the girl who now lay in the casket at the front of the cathedral, as still as the stone pillars in the nave.

The sadness settled like a weight around her shoulders, and she sat and grieved silently, grieved at her own impotence, at her realization that she had done what she could, and it wasn't enough. It wasn't enough to undo the rest of the factors that had plagued Ariel—a crazy mother, a dead father, a fifty-year-old boyfriend, a dangerous drug habit. Too little, too late. Charlotte's part of the puzzle was too small, in the end, to change the outcome. But that didn't stop Charlotte from feeling the full weight of her own failure to make a difference.

By the time they got to the cemetery, it was raining, the slow, steady drizzle of November. The grounds were still sodden from the heavy rains of the week before, and the heels of Charlotte's seldom-used black pumps kept sinking into the turf, so that when she pulled her foot up the shoe came up off her heels and the cold damp soaked in through her nylon stockings.

At the graveside, the Mass of burial continued in Latin. Charlotte, Julie, and Charlie were toward the rear, and so Charlotte's impression was more of the backs and shoulders of men and women in overcoats, and not so much of the grave in the open plot of land. There was a cold wind that kicked up from time to time. Charlotte pulled her coat tighter around her shoulders, stared at the dark trees without leaves against the gray sky, and cast sidelong glances at Julie. Each of her daughter's cheeks had a mottled red patch up on the cheekbone. She was not crying.

Charlotte couldn't see very well, but when it was Deirdre's turn to throw a clod of earth onto the casket, she apparently swooned— Charlotte caught a glimpse of her pallid face, as beautiful as that of a porcelain doll, as two large men in expensively tailored overcoats (Ariel's uncles?) caught her between their arms and lowered her into a chair.

When the service was over, they trod back through the sodden grass to their car. Charlotte slumped back in her seat, kicked off her damp pumps with bits of grass stuck to them, and closed her eyes.

Charlie turned up the heat, and she slept all the way back down I-95 until they pulled into their driveway.

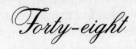

Forty-eight

The headline said, *Flood Baby*, and it was right on the front page of the *Bayard Post*. There was Chaki in the middle, holding baby Sam, her mouth closed carefully to hide the gap in her teeth, and flanked around them, like a bunch of proud parents, was the whole crew: LeAnn and Sam, Flo, Charlotte, Arecely, and Mary Louise.

They passed it around at Chaki's baby shower, which was also, semi-officially, Mary Louise's housewarming party.

"Jeez, ML, the place looks swank," Flo said. "I love the white couches."

Mary Louise beamed, and took everybody on a full house tour—kitchenette, living/dining, bedroom (with deck!), and a sparkling bathroom, where they all admired the extra-large spa-style tub.

"I'm the luckiest lady in the world," she said. "I don't know why I didn't think of this living-alone stuff before."

Arecely was kind of quiet—she had brought her book with her. Charlotte noted that it was *Anna Karenina*, the Oprah's Book Club edition. Arecely was scrunched down in the corner of the couch, with a teal pillow tucked under her arm. Charlotte whispered, "Is it good?" and when Arecely just grunted, she knew not to press her further.

Everybody had brought food and gifts for baby Sam. Mary Louise had brought the cutest bassinet with a nice blue ruffly bed set to go with it. Chaki was so happy that she put baby Sam in it and he promptly fell asleep. Mary Louise put a finger up to her lips and rolled the bassinet across the carpet and into the bedroom; then Chaki set to opening the rest of the presents. There were cute little baby outfits, and baby bath stuff, a plug-in bottle warmer, and three nice receiving blankets that Rosalie Saxton had sewn herself. Of course, the nicest present of all was probably from Sam. He had brought a box of Pampers so big that he didn't even get it out of his truck.

"Now why didn't I think of that?" said Flo.

"It's a complete two-month supply," Sam said, smiling shyly.

Chaki told them about the shelter where she was staying, and she said it wasn't too bad at all. There was another girl there named Crystal, and she had a baby too. They were thinking about going in for a place together.

When the doorbell rang, Charlotte looked around, wondering who wasn't there, but she was taken by surprise when Flo came back with Linda Rodriguez.

She was carrying a box so big that she couldn't quite see over it, and Sam, gallant as always, jumped up and placed it on the glass coffee table.

Linda looked elegant. "I can only stay a moment," she said. "I just wanted to bring over a gift."

She scanned the people seated, picked out Chaki, and went around to give her a quick hug, then took a step back, and said, "Oh, I'm sorry. You probably don't even know me."

Chaki blushed a deep beet red. "Sure, I do," she said. "You're the TV lady. I seen you over there lots of times."

Linda stuck out her hand and said, "Linda Rodriguez."

Chaki looked at the hand for a moment, as though she wasn't quite sure it was okay to offer her own; then she held out her hand, which was scrubbed clean now, no signs of the marks that used to be there, and said, "Me, I'm Chaki, Chaki Gibbons. And my baby—but he's sleeping now—his name is Sam."

"Do you think he'd mind if I took just a peek?" she whispered.

Chaki flushed even redder with pleasure and jumped up from the sofa. "As long as we're real quiet," she said, then added, "He's got a brand-new, pretty bassinet."

This whole time, Arecely had barely looked up from *Anna Karenina*, except to say hello to Linda, but pretty soon she was flipping pages again. Charlotte could see that she was getting close to the end, and even a visiting TV celebrity couldn't compete with Vronksy and Anna at that point.

When Linda came out from admiring baby Sam, though, she dropped onto the sofa next to Arecely and whispered something in her ear. Then she pulled a sheaf of papers out of her briefcase, and handed them to Arecely, and said, "I'll be calling you in about a week to see if you have any questions." Then she looked at the book in Arecely's lap and she added, "Ooh, *Anna Karenina*. Lucky you," and she jumped up from the couch and blew kisses all around.

But just as she got to the door again, she stopped. "Oh, and I just wanted to tell you that I'm sorry about your clinic, ladies. You were doing a good thing there. But I also want you to know that I believe things have a way of working out in the end." Then she blew more kisses and hurried out the door, leaving a cloud of Eternity perfume in her wake.

Arecely was too consumed in her book to stop and explain what the papers were about. Chaki opened up the big box, and inside was a brand-new car seat. She cried out in pleasure—the one she was using was a raggedy loaner she had gotten from the shelter, and this one was much nicer.

After that, they got to chatting. Sam told everyone a little bit about his life. He was working as a UPS man while he studied for the foreign medical exam; his dream was to go back to practicing medicine.

"When I lived in my country," he said, "I worked in a small clinic that was a lot like El Centro. When I first went there, it reminded me of what I like to do."

Charlotte thought about what Sam was like during Chaki's birth. He would be such a wonderful doctor . . . just the kind of person she would want to work with.

"It's going to take a long time," he said. "But I plan to work very hard until I fulfill my dream."

After they had all eaten lots of Flo's pork barbecue and LeAnn's chocolate-chip cookies and Mary Louise's homemade triple-chocolate cake, and they were all sitting back on the white couches feeling very contented, Flo said, "Well, I guess this is as good a time as any to tell you what's going on with the clinic."

Then baby Sam woke up and started crying, and Chaki got up to go get him, although really by now it felt like she (and Sam) were part of the El Centro staff.

Flo had a large shopping bag at her feet, and out of it she pulled the pig, its length of chain snipped off about halfway so that it looked like a pig on a leash.

She took the pig and put it on the glass coffee table with a rattle. Arecely looked up briefly from her book and said, "Wilbur." Then she looked back down at her book.

"Some pig," Charlotte said.

"Well, ladies," Flo said, adopting her official tone, "and, gentleman . . . as you know, the clinic has been closed since the events of last Tuesday, due to cracking of the asphalt in the parking lot. I have been assured that we will all receive our paychecks as scheduled, as this contingency is covered under the clinic's insurance plan." There was a murmur of relief that went around the room. "However, as you all know, there have been many questions about our future that had arisen prior to the events...." Charlotte wished that Flo would drop the manager-speak and just spit it out, but she didn't want to offend her by saying something.

"There a number of issues regarding economics, profits, losses, and the current state of the health care system."

Mary Louise gently cleared her throat. "Um, Flo . . . ?"

Flo frowned a bit. "Yes, Mary Louise?"

"If you could just give it to us on the straight and narrow?"

"The straight and narrow?"

"Cut to the chase?" LeAnn said. She was sitting on the couch next to Sam, studiously pretending he wasn't there. She had barely eaten a bite and had been uncharacteristically silent this whole time. "You know, just tell us what's going on."

"Okay, ladies," Flo said. "Here's the dope. First of all, Mrs. Wetherill is doing better. I spoke to Benjamin yesterday. She's back at the home and apparently okay, just a little droopy on her left side, and her speech is a bit hard to understand, but all in all doing fine and in good spirits."

A smattering of applause ran around the room, and as if in solidarity, LeAnn reached over to take a lemon square from the plate that Charlotte had brought.

"He was able to speak to her about the clinic, and this is what she said. Apparently the clinic was on rough times, and the board of trustees just didn't think it was going to bounce back. The Communicare clinic over in Oxford was competing directly with us, and our patient load was going down."

"Going down? Are you kidding? It seems like we were crazy busy all the time," Charlotte said.

"I know, but apparently we were not getting a lot of new patients, and most of the ones we have, as you all know, do not have health insurance. Communicare has been taking all of the patients who have health insurance, and leaving us with the ones who don't."

"Well, and who's going to take care of the patients who don't have health insurance if we don't?" Arecely said, apparently listening in spite of the fact that her book was still open.

"So Communicare has been negotiating with the board for a while, but the board was refusing to sell the clinic unless they agreed to continue seeing patients on a sliding-fee scale."

"Unless?" Charlotte said.

"Unless?" Mary Louise added.

Flo continued as if she hadn't heard them. "And then, with the subpoena for the pregnancy test results, they were going to have to pay for a legal defense, and that broke the camel's back."

"Flo, what exactly do you mean by 'broke the camel's back'?"

"There was an emergency meeting of the board, Communicare met their terms, and so they agreed to the takeover. . . ."

For a moment Charlotte was so stunned she didn't know what to say. She thought about Patricia Lynch, about the bucket of white paint. She thought about El Centro, where she had spent seven years of her life, missing Julie's soccer games, coming home late for Charlie—it was almost like she had poured some of her life right into its worn-out carpets and peeling paint. She didn't want to cry; she had been holding it together, holding up fine, but this was a loss—one more loss that she didn't think she could take. El Centro really was the center, the center of everything she had built her life around.

Arecely let out a loud sigh, so long and mournful that it stopped the buzz of conversation. Everybody turned to look at her; then they all gathered around her and started patting and clucking.

"It's going to be okay, Arecely," Flo said. "You're experienced and bilingual. Communicare will definitely hire you right away. And we have the authorization to continue paying you for several weeks while they clean the water out of the basement and decide what they're going to do with the building. . . ."

"It's not that . . ." Arecely said.

"What is it then?" Charlotte said, worried that maybe Ricky had run off again, or that she was having a problem with the pregnancy.

"It's Anna . . . Oh, didn't she see . . . ? Life is absolutely never as bleak as all that. . . ."

Charlotte saw *Anna Karenina* lying closed on the sofa next to Arecely, and she got it . . . but the rest of the ladies probably missed it, because just then Chaki came back into the room carrying baby Sam, who looked adorable in the brand-new jeans outfit that Charlotte had gotten him from BabyGap.

After that, Flo filled them in on the details. Communicare was planning to build a new facility in Kennett Square, and they were going to have several departments—women's health would include prenatal care, and they would also have a family-practice wing. They would continue to see patients on a sliding-fee scale. . . . In fact, they were going to form some kind of profit/nonprofit partnership, taking over the assets from El Centro.

"Assets," Charlotte said. "What assets? I thought that was the problem . . . ?"

"The property," Flo said. "Right there on the Maryland Pike. It's worth a mint now. You'd be surprised."

"Oh, no," Charlotte said. "No, they can't sell the property. They can't."

Then Arecely said, "What about the pig? Didn't Dorothea Wetherill tell us to put the pig there for a reason? Didn't we name it Wilbur for a reason? Why don't we open it? You just never know."

Everybody started saying, *Yes, yes, let's open the pig. You never know. You just never know.* Mary Louise went to get a knife from the kitchen.

She cut into his big plastic belly, and a few coins and crumpled dollar bills came out; then she cut a bigger hole and started grabbing with her fists.

It was actually pretty impressive. There was $757.38 in the pig, part in the form of a check for two hundred dollars from Linda Rodriguez, and only Arecely knew that the two crumpled one-hundred-dollar bills hadn't been there for a while, when she'd used them to buy things for Chaki Gibbons, and that she had slipped them back into the pig the night that Ricky arrived, a wad of cash stuffed in his pocket.

So they all sat and stared at the pile for a while, but then finally Flo said, "According to Benjamin Wetherill, the piece of land that the clinic is on is worth over a million dollars." And that pretty much put it in perspective. All of the sweaty coins and bills that had been dropped in that pig by kind, anonymous people trying to do the right thing—it still wasn't going to turn out to make any difference.

Once they had all settled into the silence of resignation, Rosalie Saxton, who hadn't said much until now, stood up.

Charlotte still had trouble recognizing her. Apparently Mary Louise and she spent all their free time shopping. She had a nice perm, and was wearing an attractive navy blue suit, nylons, and blue leather spectator shoes. You might have taken her for one of the members of the board.

"I would like to say something," Mrs. Saxton said. Nobody said anything, so she continued. "I am going to make a donation of two million dollars."

There was a little moment of stunned silence, and then a bunch of *What? Come again? What exactly did you say?*

Then Mrs. Saxton continued. "I'm going to make a no-strings-attached donation of two million dollars."

Charlotte didn't know whether to believe her or think she was soft in the head. "Did you actually say two million dollars?"

"Yes," she said. "I've made up my mind."

It wasn't exactly tactful, but Flo apparently couldn't keep her mouth shut. "Mrs. Saxton, are you positive you have that much?"

But Mrs. Saxton just tittered and waved her hand at her. "Oh, my dear, you must not realize that I'm Mrs. Rosalie Millstone Saxton."

It was starting to dawn on Charlotte, but the rest were still shaking their heads.

"Our farm had been in the family for nine generations, but you know, I had no use for it, and it wasn't commercially viable for farming, so I just wanted to share it with some nice young families. . . ."

"Millstone Estates," Charlotte said.

"Millstone Manor?" Flo asked.

"Millstone Meadows?" LeAnn said.

"I know, I know. Ridiculous, isn't it? All that land, just sitting there. Now I drive by and see all the nice houses with play sets out back and children riding on bikes in the street and it makes me happy."

"You owned half of Westville?" Charlotte asked.

"Oh, no, dear, it wasn't half. It wasn't much more than a quarter. . . . Oh, and the old bats, all the horse people, the foxhunters, they were like to kill me. Furious. They wanted all that land in conservation so they could ride to the hounds through there. New money. All of them. Our family were Quakers, and we were original land grantees from William Penn. Quakers are practical people. I wasn't about to save it for snobs with their horses and hounds."

Finished with her little speech, Mrs. Saxton sat down again, and Mary Louise gave her an encouraging smile and patted her on the knee.

But Charlotte could feel hope bubbling up like freshwater in a spring. "Two million dollars . . . Oh, Rosalie, it is so incredibly generous, and certainly it means . . . it must mean that we can keep the clinic doors open."

But Mrs. Saxton frowned. "Oh, no, dear. Your clinic is in dreadful condition. It's too small, and it doesn't provide a full complement of services. Communicare is proposing to build a beautiful new state-of-the-art facility that will provide many more services to the community. That is where my donation will go."

Charlotte was stunned. "You mean . . ."

Rosalie nodded. "As I said, I'm a practical person. I only invest when I see a sound proposition."

There wasn't much more to say. Flo explained to the staff that they would likely be able to be employed by Communicare, although they might have to work in another site, at least until the new building was finished.

"Just one more thing," Flo said. "About the money from the pig. Mrs. Wetherill wants the staff to be able to donate that money in the name of El Centro, and we get to decide exactly what we want to spend the money on."

Everybody thought about it for a moment, and then Arecely said, "I don't know if this is what she was talking about, but if nobody minds, I actually have an idea."

As they were walking out to their cars, Charlotte grabbed Arecely and asked her, "What did Linda Rodriguez give you?"

"It's about college," she said. "There's this program for women at a place called Bryn Mawr College. She said she went there, and she thinks I can go there too. She said she'd help me fill out all the forms and stuff. And it doesn't matter if you got out of high school and did something else for a while, or even if you have kids. The program is designed for people like that. I want to study English and maybe become an English teacher. That's what Linda Rodriguez studied, and she said all you do is read lots of books and write papers about them, and I think I can do that."

Charlotte gave her a hug and said, "You can do whatever you set your mind to. I've never had the slightest doubt about that."

Forty-nine

Charlotte and Charlie weren't really talking to each other, and Charlotte knew that one of them absolutely was going to have to break the ice.

Secrets. It seemed silly that secrets had come between them. They had known each other since they were teenagers, but maybe that was part of the problem.

Charlotte wasn't quite sure what to do with the information that Deirdre's baby had been Charlie's. Somewhere in the back of her mind, Charlotte had always known that there was a possibility, perhaps even a probability, that the baby was also Charlie's. But they had just left it alone and moved forward, and she wasn't even sure that had been such a bad thing.

That baby was born at twenty-four weeks, and though Charlotte would never be 100 percent sure, it was likely that it had never drawn a breath, although she had always been haunted by the possibility that it might have been born alive, and she assured herself that she had never heard anything that sounded like a baby's cry. But even in a hospital, it was too premature, at least in those days, and it wouldn't have survived.

And in the end, that was what had gotten Charlotte out of trouble, that and the fact that despite her parents' threats against Charlotte, Deirdre had refused to press charges, and spent a year at home recuperating under psychiatric treatment. She had come back to the university briefly in senior year, but then she had met the playboy Juan-Luis Saramago at a polo match and run off with him, and then moved to Argentina, and that had been the end of that.

But Charlotte still didn't really know what had killed Ariel Saramago, and so that was why she decided to pick up the phone and call Paul Stone.

He sounded surprised, but agreed to meet her for coffee at Hank's Place, a nearby diner.

Charlotte felt nervous, and also like she was betraying Charlie, even though having coffee with Paul Stone wasn't exactly breaking her marital vows.

When she saw him, she was surprised. He was lean and slight, and had a more pronounced receding hairline than she had remembered. Hadn't she thought he looked like Charlie? Now she couldn't see the resemblance at all.

"Good job on that flood baby," Paul said. "And congratulations on the merger with Communicare. Looks like it's going to be a great setup for the community."

"Thanks," Charlotte said. She had come to realize that everyone was right, and that the new community health center was going to be much better than El Centro, but she still hadn't picked up the phone to call them. She wasn't sure if she would even have a job, and for some reason, she wasn't sure she wanted to either.

"There's a reason I wanted to talk to you, though," Charlotte said. "I want to know if you know anything about the Saramago girl."

"Other than the fact that she's dead?"

Charlotte winced, but nodded.

"I do know some," he said. "What do you want to know?"

"Cause of death," she said.

"In a nutshell?"

Charlotte nodded again. The waitress came and set a carafe of coffee down on the table. Charlotte poured some into each of their cups, then busied herself peeling the foil lid off of a container of half and half.

"Somebody accusing your daughter of something?"

Charlotte was taken aback. She looked at him searchingly. "No. Why would they?"

"They wouldn't," he said. "Classic Good Samaritan. She found her passed out and tried to get her to the hospital. . . . That's the only version of the story I've heard."

"So what did happen to her?"

"Cause of death, officially? Hemorrhage."

Charlotte took a hurried sip of the coffee. Scalded her tongue. *I can handle this,* she thought.

"Hemorrhage from?"

"Ruptured ectopic pregnancy. Undiagnosed. Apparently."

Charlotte didn't say anything. She tested her sore tongue against the roof of her mouth.

"But what about . . . ?" Charlotte started.

"The cocaine?"

"Yeah."

"How'd you hear about that?"

"ER doc couldn't keep his mouth shut. But that was all I could get."

"Well, it's not a pretty story at all. An old horse guy, guess he used to be something back in the eighties. Rode in the Olympics or something. He worked for the mom, training her horses, and I guess they were lovers. He was down on his luck. No money, nothing. And she was supporting him—big stables, the whole nine yards. But then apparently, dumb fuck, he started sleeping with the daughter, and the mom found out. Yanked the whole thing away from him, sold the farm, and moved up here."

Charlotte nodded.

"So, anyway, that's where the girl was. Presumably he's the one who got her pregnant, and she went up there—he wouldn't talk to her. Wanted to wash his hands of both of them—he was so mad at the mom for pulling the plug. But he was a bit of a cokehead, and so she went back up there with ten thousand dollars' worth of coke and they partied for a week. Then she came back home again."

"Why'd she come home?"

"That I don't know . . . but I do know that she was half-dead already when she got to the hospital—they transfused her like crazy, but it was too late. There was no hope for her."

"I saw the obit in the paper, but it didn't say any of this. Are you gonna run this stuff?"

"Oh, yeah, we're gonna run it. We're just waiting for Bruce to get arrested. The girl was a minor. Only sixteen. They're picking him up for statutory rape—probably already got him by now. It's a great story, if you go for that kind of thing. Mom's back in Argentina. From what I hear, she's always been completely nuts. Family keeps her in a sanatorium most of the time. The girl—apparently she was only close to her dad—was real broken up when he died. Polo accident—he was in his sixties, apparently."

Charlotte took a few more sips of her coffee while she thought about everything that Paul had just told her. Such a sorry story all the way around, but it didn't sound like there was much anybody could have done to help.

"She's actually eighteen," Charlotte said.

"No, sixteen. Her mother sent over a birth certificate."

Charlotte opened her mouth to say something, then thought of a fifty-year-old man having a cocaine party with a pregnant eighteen-year-old. She shut her mouth again. It sounded like he was going to get what he deserved.

"What about the baby? Did anyone ever figure out anything about that poor dead baby in the Dumpster?"

Paul shook his head. "No, and the DA lost interest when it became clear that it was going to be really tough to figure out who did it. It could have been anyone—a transient, someone who just happened to be driving by. I don't think they'll ever know. One thing they did find out, though."

"What's that?"

"Well, the poor housekeeper . . ."

"Maria Lopez?"

"Yeah, that wasn't her real name, but I don't remember what her real name was. Anyway, apparently she had received a telegram from Mexico just a day or two before she killed herself."

"A telegram?"

"The story I got—and I think it's reliable—is that she had left her baby in Mexico just a few days after it was born, to come here to work. Well, the baby got sick and died, and that's what the telegram said. Harsh, huh?"

Charlotte nodded and felt tears stinging her eyes. She thought of the girl who had left a newborn baby behind and come all this way to look for work. It was a terrible, tragic story.

When they were finished with their coffee and ready to go, Paul said, "Charlotte, just one more thing."

"What's that?"

"Do you remember that night at the café? You thought you knew which paintings were mine."

Charlotte remembered. The three modern Madonnas, so like the girls at El Centro, poor, struggling trying, kind of like Chaki—and the one . . . the one that had reminded her of Deirdre. They were haunting images that had stayed with her.

"I thought you might be interested to know who did paint them."

Charlotte shook her head. "No, really, I . . . I'm not in a position to buy a painting, or anything like that."

"An incredibly talented painter. His name is Charlie Hopper. I thought you'd want to know."

Charlotte blanched. "Charlie doesn't paint anymore."

"Charlotte. The gallery—it's mine. I'm just doing the reporter thing to earn extra money to support it until it takes off. Believe me, Charlie paints. He is the most talented guy I know."

He seemed as though he was going to stop talking, but then he cleared his throat, like he wanted to say something else.

"I'm one of those guys who wants to paint more than anything—only I'm not very good. And Charlie . . . he's the real deal. He's got what it takes. And he's got a beautiful wife too, and I guess for a little while I got to thinking that if I didn't have his talent, I might be able to take you away . . ." He paused, scrutinized her, but Charlotte could no longer see whatever it was in his face that had drawn her to him.

"But it's obvious. You're not available for the taking."

Charlotte was left with nothing to say. Paul waved her away when she tried to chip in for coffee, and they walked out together quietly.

"See you around," he said in the parking lot, and Charlotte realized that he was nice enough, the kind of person you might be friends with, and that there was nothing more than that.

Fifty

They were skirting around each other like ghosts. Talking to each other without talking. Julie had to be driven to and from school because of her cast, and they discussed grocery shopping, and sat together at the table at meals as though nothing were wrong, but still, there was no point of contact.

But that night, after her coffee with Paul Stone, Charlotte knew it was time to break the silence, and so when Julie said that she was planning to go over to Kayla's after school, Charlotte was heartened. Julie had been sticking very close to home since the accident, and she wasn't talking about it much. This was the first time she had suggested something like a normal activity, and Charlotte was hoping that that meant she was starting to recover.

The clinic had been closed for just over a week now, but so far Charlotte had managed to keep herself busy—the shower, the funeral, and yesterday she'd been able to stop in for a brief visit with Mrs. Wetherill, who was in the assisted-care part of her retirement home, and she seemed to be doing well. She wasn't sure what Charlie was doing with himself. The pain rested between them like a curtain.

So that night Charlotte made steak and asparagus, and even made his favorite, the no-flour chocolate cake. She set the table nicely, and took a shower and put on some makeup.

When he came in around seven, Charlotte turned toward the door and saw him there, worn flannel shirt, blue jeans. . . . He was wearing his hair a little longer now, since he'd lost his job, and it was odd how sometimes he could still look so much the way he had looked when they had first met.

She could feel her heart pounding as he stood there looking at her, taking in her makeup and catching sight of the silver and crystal that was gleaming in the flickering candlelight in the dining room.

The moment that he stood there at the doorway seemed to last too long—like it stretched over all the years they had been together, through all the ups and the downs, from Julie's birth to the moment he lost his job, and coming to a screeching halt at the moment she had admitted to him that yes, she had been pregnant, and she had never told him, and she had lost the baby, and he had stormed out the door.

The longer the moment held, the more Charlotte started to let resignation set in. She had not been able to save the baby in the Dumpster, or help Ariel, or save the clinic, and now it was clear: She was not going to be able to save her marriage either. She had pushed it too far, broken the trust—some things, once done, can't be undone.

"I just thought . . ." Her words jumbled awkwardly into the silence. But only for a moment, because then one more moment, and everything had changed and the lights went back on. Charlie stepped into the room, and folded her in his arms, and they stayed like that for a very, very long time.

It took them a while, but they did eventually sit down to Charlotte's dinner, and slowly, in broken fits and starts, they started to discuss all of the things, like individual bricks, that had started to build a wall between them.

"Why didn't you tell me you were painting again? I saw your paintings at Paul Stone's café. They were amazing, Charlie. They stopped me in my tracks."

"You saw them?" he said, obviously surprised. "I didn't know you knew Paul."

"He interviewed me about the dead baby in the Dumpster. He didn't let on that he knew you either. . . ."

"Nice guy," Charlie said. "Can't paint at all, but his café/gallery is great. I hope it's going to do really well."

"Why didn't you tell me you were painting?"

Charlie didn't answer right away. Charlotte noticed his pause, and took the moment to refill his wineglass with more Bordeaux.

"I was . . ." he said, then stopped and took a sip of wine. "I was afraid to tell you."

"Afraid?" Charlotte said. She was mystified by this remark, but then she thought about it—all the times she had encouraged him to stick with corporate graphic design, even though she knew he hated it. She had not supported his art. It was time to be honest with herself.

"I knew I needed a new job, and I didn't want you to think I was wasting my time."

"Oh, Charlie," Charlotte said.

"But I did find another job," he said. "That's the part I didn't tell you. That's the real reason that I left. I went up for an interview, and then they called me back for a second interview, and I had to stay."

"Charlie, that's great. I'm so happy for you."

"But, Charlotte, it's not around here. We'd have to move . . . and it's, well . . . it's not in graphic design, so frankly the money is not as good."

"What is it, Charlie?"

He looked up at her as though he wasn't sure what she was going to say. "Art teacher in a boarding school. In New Hampshire. They'll give us a place to live, and I'll get to use the studio in my free time. It's . . . it's just the kind of job I've always dreamed of. I can work and paint at the same time—oh, and Julie can go there for free, and it's a private school, really top-notch." He hesitated. "But you'd have to leave El Centro, and I'm not sure how you'd feel about that."

"Charlie," she said, "El Centro is closing."

"No kidding."

"And, I . . . I actually think it's for the best."

They ate chocolate cake and drank more wine, and a soft feeling settled over the room. Finally Charlotte screwed up her courage.

"Charlie, about the baby . . . I'm really sorry. I realize now that I should have told you. . . ." She trailed off; she could tell she was going to start crying, remembering afresh the pain, the disappointment she had felt.

Charlie reached across the table and took her two hands in his. "I should have told you about Deirdre's baby too. That's why I don't want us to have any contact with her. Ever. Charlotte, I'm convinced of it. She's an ill wind."

Charlotte shook her head solemnly. "I promise," she said. "Never again."

"Just one more thing," Charlie said.

"What's that?"

He stroked her hands between his. "We're still young, and I'd really like to have another baby. Do you think we could keep trying?"

Then Charlotte burst into tears, and Charlie came around to her side of the table, and he folded her in his arms, and that was how they were when the door slammed and Julie came in, beaming from ear to ear, and hurried to join in the hug.

Fifty-one

One year later

The sun was shining, and it was a perfect October day when the ladies of El Centro gathered in St. Patrick's cemetery. Nobody wore black. A few people were wearing scrubs, and others were wearing their day clothes as they gathered around the small black granite marker that was covered with piece of white gauze and surrounded by bright orange and yellow mums.

They had asked Flo to officiate, and so she carried a piece of paper in her hand. She looked different now that she was sporting a dark Florida tan.

"We have gathered here today . . ." Flo said.

Charlotte took a moment to look around the assembled group, the faces as familiar as a worn pair of shoes, and yet everybody looked a little different.

Arecely probably looked the most different. Her hair was cut into an easy-care pageboy—gone were the long lacquered curls, and instead of wearing pink scrubs, she was wearing jeans and a long-sleeved turtleneck. Zekie was getting so big—he stood next to her, gripping her hand, sober as a little man, and Ricky held the baby, wrapped in a pink blanket. Charlotte noticed that Arecely still had a book clutched in her other hand, but she couldn't see what it was. She knew that this entire service had been Arecely's idea—her plan for what to do with the money from the pig.

Mary Louise was wearing teal scrubs. Charlotte had driven down from New Hampshire yesterday and stayed with Mary Louise the night before. Mary Louise was now chief medical assistant at the Communicare clinic, and while Charlotte was there, she told her all about how she was studying to become a doula. "That's a person who helps people while they're in labor, and after they have a baby," she said.

"Well, you've sure got a knack for that," Charlotte said.

"I know," Mary Louise said proudly. "People tell me I'm a natural."

Sam actually looked the least different—he was wearing his UPS uniform. Charlotte would have been surprised, but Mary Louise had already told her: He had been offered a job to work as a medical assistant at Communicare, but he turned it down. "UPS pays better," he said, "and this way I can get to my goal a lot faster."

Chaki kept having to leave the crowd to chase after baby Sam, who was as quick as greased lightning—he kept breaking away from the crowd. She looked completely different too. Her face had filled out, and there was something. . . . Charlotte realized it was the fact that now she had teeth. She must've gotten caps. She looked young, and pretty, and just like any other mother. She had a job working at the Giant in the checkout line, and was living with the girl Crystal, whom she had met in the shelter, and they were sharing babysitting.

Mrs. Wetherill looked well enough. She usually used a walker, but had come out to the grave in her wheelchair. She gave Charlotte such a friendly smile that Charlotte scarcely noticed the droop on the left side. It was nice to see her looking so well.

The only one who wasn't there was LeAnn. She had a class then and couldn't get away. Mary Louise told her that Sam had shamed her into it—insisting that she go back for her teaching credentials when he found out she had a college degree that she wasn't even using. "You don't know the opportunity you have . . . you can't waste it," he'd told her. They were still dating, but Mary Louise wasn't sure how serious it was.

Charlotte breathed it all in—the familiar group of women, the beautiful fall day, and the small black granite marker in front of them, dignified and simple, and somehow just right.

Little Sam squirmed down and ran off, and Chaki whirled around to catch him; then Flo cleared her throat and continued.

"We are gathered here today," she said, "to mark the passing . . ." Arecely's baby started crying, and Ricky started jiggling her. ". . . of a small baby who came into our midst when it was already departed."

"That's beautiful," Mary Louise murmured.

"Damn straight," Flo said. "And I wrote it myself. But let me finish, 'cause it sounds like baby Linda is getting hungry." As though to emphasize the point, Arecely's baby let out another cry.

"The baby, poor soul, was thrown into a Dumpster, and by whom we will never know. It was thrown by an unseen hand."

She paused portentously, allowing them to remember the blurred white hand on the video, the closest they would ever get to a solution.

"And that baby would have lived or died, unknown except by its mother, were it not for a twist of fate—and that would be when Charlotte backed her car into the Dumpster and it fell out. And so, gathered friends, we all feel that this baby . . . well, it wanted itself to be known."

"Hear, hear," Mary Louise said, and it seemed like an appropriate sentiment, so they all echoed the same thing, "Hear, hear."

Just then Linda Rodriguez hurried up, saying in a loud stage whisper, "Sorry I'm late," and then slipping into the crowd next to Ricky, promptly taking the baby from him, and starting to coo over it.

"And so with the money from the pig," Flo continued, unperturbed by the interruption, "we decided that we would not let this baby's passing go unnoticed, as it were, and so we have purchased this plot and this stone so that the baby's memory can stay with us in eternal remembrance."

It was supposed to be a somber occasion, but with all the gathered old friends and the bright sunny day, somehow nobody was feeling too somber, and so they all burst into hoots and cheers and whoops of joy.

Then Flo shushed everybody and said, "And now it is time for the unveiling of the stone." She whisked the white cloth off the small stone so that they could all see the engraving.

IN MEMORY OF
THE UNKNOWN BABY
FROM THE WOMEN OF EL CENTRO
AND MAY HE REST IN ETERNAL PEACE.

They hugged and clapped and whooped and hugged babies, until they all started looking at watches and saying they had to go.

On the way out, Charlotte caught up with Arecely. "How's school?" she said.

"Hard," she said. "There is a lot more to reading books than I thought."

"But you like it?"

"You know what, Charlotte? I feel really lucky. . . . I didn't know I could do it, but it turns out I can. Oh, and I switched my major to biology. I'm going premed." Charlotte gave her a big hug. "My dream is to come back here to work someday to serve my own community. They need a doctor who speaks Spanish. . . . No offense," she hastened to add.

"No offense taken," Charlotte said. "Of course, you're right." And for the first time in a long time, she remembered her patient Maria Lopez, but now, at least, she felt more at peace with the memory.

"How 'bout you?" Arecely asked. "You still working?"

"Oh, yeah, pregnant teenagers. I'm working in a hospital clinic doing prenatal care." Charlotte smiled. She thought of her current crop of young moms. A couple at least would probably go into labor while she was gone.

But they didn't have much more time to chat. Arecely had afternoon classes, and Charlotte had one more stop to make before she headed on the long drive back.

She got a little lost trying to get to Paul Stone's café, but when she found it, it looked exactly the same, except that she was heartened to see that the patio was full of people drinking coffee and eating brunch. It appeared that the place was thriving.

She went in the door, and a waiter with a nose ring—he looked like a young art student—said, "Table for one?"

"No, I'm just looking for Paul Stone."

Paul came out a moment later and gave her a big hug. "Charlotte, you're looking well."

"Thanks," she said. "But actually I'm feeling a little queasy. I'm three months pregnant."

"Congratulations," he said. "Okay, come on around to the front and I'll show you."

He led her around a half wall and a bank of tables, and then there it was . . . hung up high on the stone wall, it appeared smaller, but no less powerful.

Charlotte felt tears in her eyes, and she mumbled something like a little prayer to herself, about thanks for the way everything had turned out, plus asking for a little blessing for the baby inside of her.

"Was it difficult?" she asked.

"Nah, not at all. After the protesters went out with the signs that said, 'Save Our Lady of El Centro,' there wasn't much to it. I just went out there with a blowtorch and cut out the drywall."

"Who painted it, anyway?"

"You know, that's the funny thing. Nobody seems to remember. Someone from the youth group. I asked around. Apparently the painting had been there for years, and nobody seemed to know exactly who painted it."

"It's beautiful, though." Charlotte said.

"It is that," Paul agreed.

She bowed her head, then gazed up at Mary's kind eyes for another moment. As she stood there, she thought she smelled the scent of roses, and when she opened her eyes, she saw that there were a couple of yellow rosebuds in a glass vase on every table in the room. Then she gave Paul a peck on the cheek, went out to the parking lot, and got ready for her long drive north, toward Charlie and Julie and home.

Photo by Paul Sirocham

Elizabeth Letts, a practicing certified nurse-midwife, trained at the Yale University School of Nursing. The author of one previous novel, *Quality of Care*, she lives with her husband and four children in southeastern Pennsylvania.

Visit her Web site at www.elizabethletts.com.

Family Planning

ELIZABETH LETTS

This Conversation Guide is intended to enrich the individual reading experience, as well as encourage us to explore these topics together—because books, and life, are meant for sharing.

A CONVERSATION WITH
ELIZABETH LETTS

Q. What was your inspiration for Family Planning? *Do you know a clinic like El Centro?*

A. The spark of the idea for this story came from a real mural of the Virgin of Guadalupe painted on the wall of a health center where I worked. I'm not sure who painted it, or why it was there. But at one point the boss decided that it wasn't appropriate to have a religious image on the wall, since we were a secular organization. So a plan was made to paint over the painting. Except that things kept happening to prevent it—once the person with the can of white paint got in a minor car accident on the way over to the center, and once there was a big thunderstorm and the road was closed. . . . Pretty soon, people started to attribute all kinds of mishaps to the plan to paint over the mural—half joking, but not altogether joking. . . . And I thought, Well, if this were in a book the women would find a way to band together to save the painting—in real life, I'm sorry to say, the white paint won out.

As for El Centro, it doesn't represent one particular place; it's more of an amalgamation of all of the places where I have worked over the years. I've worked in not-for-profit health centers in California, New Jersey, New York City, and Pennsylvania. I also spent some time working for the migrant health services in Colorado, working with families who came to the area to pick cantaloupes. It has always amazed me how similar these not-for-profit health centers all are in some ways: run-down, overcrowded, and with an astonishing diversity of people working in them—too many patients, not enough supplies, never quite enough money. But there is always a thread of real caring and compassion running through them. That was the world I was trying to bring to life when I wrote about El Centro.

Q. You are an advanced practice nurse, like Charlotte in the novel. Have any of your own experiences inspired incidents in the novel?

A. When I write, I don't draw from specific experiences that I have had, but I do base my writing in real medical situations and the way I have found that people tend to respond to them. I've been working in women's health for about ten years, and so I think I've probably seen almost everything at least once. I have dealt with people like Darla Beckwith, Chaki Gibbons, Maria Lopez, and Ariel Saramago many times.

Q. Family Planning *is told in the third person, with a close look at Charlotte, but also glimpses into the personal lives of other El Centro women. Why was it important to reveal so much of the other women?*

A. I think the story of El Centro told only from Charlotte's point of view would be quite different. The way I thought about it, El Centro was a building, but the women who worked there were its soul, and it would be hard to get a full picture of the place seen only through the eyes of Charlotte. Charlotte is a middle-class woman who does not face the kinds of daily hardship that the patients and some of the other women who work in the clinic are facing. I think she feels compassion but doesn't always understand exactly what they are going through.

One of the things that is interesting about El Centro is what all the different people bring to the mix, and also how people's perceptions of others are not always accurate. Arecely, who is working as an underpaid assistant, is actually a brilliant student. Osama, who drives a UPS truck, is really a doctor. Rosalie Saxton, who seems poor and isolated, is actually quite rich. But in spite of their differences, they all manage to get along, and that is one of the really important parts of the story for me. I think you get a better sense of that—of people's perceptions and misperceptions of one another—when you see the story from several different points of view.

Q. The novel is an emotional ride, from miscarriage to the tragedy of the dead baby in the Dumpster. You tackle huge issues that women are forced to reconcile. Did you have these ideas in mind when you began the novel?

A. When I began the novel, I had in mind the idea of a group of women who work in the field of "family planning" but who seemed to find that their own families were not that amenable to planning. Starting from that point, I started to imagine the kind of situations, both at work and home, that these women faced. What I found was that as women we are confronted with a lot of choices related to pregnancy and childbearing and parenting—and that sometimes the choices we make may not seem to make a lot of sense to others.

The extreme example of this is when you read in the newspaper that a baby was born and then abandoned somewhere—in a Dumpster or something equally sordid. And the universal response, as it should be, is horror, along with wondering, But how could someone possibly be driven to do something like that? There are so many alternatives available that it should never be possible that someone would leave a baby in a Dumpster, and yet we know that occasionally it happens. So that's what I was thinking about—why would someone hide a pregnancy and then deliver a baby in a dormitory room? Why would a bright young girl who doesn't have much money and dreams of going to college get pregnant by accident when she works in a family-planning clinic, and why would a married woman in her late thirties hide a pregnancy from her husband? From the outside, it's easy for us to judge these acts as ridiculous, or inexplicable, or wrong. What is it about our fertility that makes seemingly rational people act in ways that seem so irrational, and why are we so quick and opinionated to judge others about their decisions? These were the questions I had in mind as I wrote this story.

Q. The relationships between the mothers and their children lay a foundation for this novel, and explain so much about the characters. Was it diffi-

cult to create "bad" mothers? Were there any characters in particular who were tricky to write?

A. This is a very interesting question. I believe that the desire to be a good mother is really one of the fundamental desires of women who have children. I'm not just a women's health care provider, but also the mother of four, and I must wonder at least once a day if I've screwed up somehow with one of my kids—I forgot to launder the skirt my daughter wants to wear to a party, I've spoken harshly to my son, or told the kids "just a minute" half an hour ago because I was lost in my work . . . But I'm incredibly fortunate. I have a wonderful husband, a loving family, a clean and safe place to live. Many of the young women I see have none of those advantages, and yet their desire to be good mothers is just as strong as mine is. But sometimes the external pressures—an abusive partner, or poverty—become so overwhelming that they are battling extreme odds. In my book Chaki is trapped in an abusive relationship and she can't quite figure out what to do, but she tries, and Maria Lopez is forced to leave a newborn baby behind to go off to look for work in another country. The one person who doesn't face any of those obstacles is Deirdre, and I think that's what makes Deirdre so terrifying—she's the mother whose only obstacle to being a good mother is her own nature.

Q. In the conversation guide for your last novel, Quality of Care, *you expressed the importance that "several of the characters face situations that are beyond their control." Did you intentionally create similar situations in* Family Planning?

A. Well, it's interesting that you point that out. I don't think I saw that as such a crucial element in this novel, but I guess I do think in general that medicine is an area in which our belief in the rational and scientific comes into direct conflict with the fundamental mysteries of birth and death that are not amenable to our control. I'm interested in that territory where the scientific and the spiritual intersect with each other—in my opinion that is the stuff of good fiction.

Q. What did you hope to achieve in writing this novel? What do you want your readers to take from your writing?

A. I hope that this novel gives the reader a little window into my world. Like Charlotte, I live in a middle-class community, and yet I work among impoverished people who live right in our midst. Every day I see a Chaki with no front teeth, or a Maria Lopez who left her baby in Mexico to work as a housekeeper, or an Ariel, who has got plenty of money but no parents to show her what to do. And in the health center I work in, just like in countless other health centers all over America, there are women just like the women of El Centro—underpaid and overworked, and yet doing everything they can to make the world a better place. So I hope that this story honors all of those women in some small way.

Q. Was the writing process different the second time around? If it changed, what was different about your method or the way you worked?

A. When I think about my writing process, I mostly think about how strapped for time I am! Four kids, a job, and writing novels—you can probably imagine that the main component of my writing process is "write when you get a minute." Otherwise that minute will be filled with something else, like driving to a soccer practice or mopping spilled milk up off the floor or trying to figure out who gets the next turn on the trampoline.

What was different, though, writing *Family Planning* was that the idea for the story was much less clear in my mind at the outset—I had the image of the Virgin Mary, and the idea that there was a baby abandoned in a Dumpster, but the women of El Centro, that wacky cast of characters, they pretty much took over and started running the show.

Q. What writers are particular favorites of yours and how have they inspired you?

A. I have been an avid reader since the day I could read. When I was a kid I read literally everything I could get my hands on, and I mean everything. I went to the library and just read down the shelves—I read old used books, I read brand-new books. I never met a book I didn't like, although if I had to choose favorites, I would have to say that I've never loved a book as much as I loved A *Little Princess* by Frances Hodgson Burnett.

Some of my favorite contemporary writers are Margaret Drabble, Gail Godwin, Sue Miller, Anne Lamott, Billie Letts, Jane Hamilton, Tim Farrington, and Geraldine Brooks. If I were pressed to name the one perfect women's fiction book, I'd probably say *The Stone Diaries* by Carol Shields. I've heard some writers say that they don't read much when they are writing, but that's not me. I've always got my nose in a book, and I discover new favorite writers all the time. Then I call up my mom, who reads just as much as I do, and we talk about the books. That's my idea of heaven.

Q. Have you begun to write a third novel? If you have, will your next novel again explore the world of women's medicine?

A. Yes, I'm still interested in exploring the world of women's medicine.

QUESTIONS
FOR DISCUSSION

1. At the beginning of the novel everything falls apart for Charlotte. Why do you think Charlotte was so hesitant to tell Charlie that she was pregnant? Do you think her miscarriage affected everything else that followed?

2. When Charlotte found the dead baby in the Dumpster it was a horrific sight. But later Charlotte confesses to Paul that "I was meant to find it. . . . Maybe it needed to get out of the Dumpster to let its soul slip free." How is Charlotte able to see such a beautiful moment amid such tragedy? How does this cross over into her own life?

3. When Deirdre moves next door to Charlotte, she is flooded with memories of the events of her college days. Why does Charlotte feel so connected to Deirdre and somehow responsible for Deirdre's losses? Was Charlotte wrong not to cut off contact with Deirdre at Charlie's first request? Do you have an old friend who was once part of your life, but who eventually made you feel uncomfortable enough to cut off contact? How do you feel about this?

4. Why is Paul such a safe haven for Charlotte's confessions? When they kiss is the motivation companionship and solace, or is it more lustful? Does Charlotte owe it to Charlie to disclose their encounter? How might this affect her marriage?

5. Several of the women in the novel are pregnant. Their ages, ethnicities, and economic statuses are so different. Chaki doesn't want her baby, and Ariel is unsure of what she wants to do. Arecely seems ambivalent about being pregnant, and Darla is not pregnant but is so eager to be pregnant that she has false pregnancy symptoms. How do their realities relate to their backgrounds?

CONVERSATION GUIDE

6. Charlotte repeatedly mentions the mural of the Virgin of Guadalupe that is on the wall in the health education room. Why is that image important in this story? Do you think that all of the people who view the painting see it in the same way?

7. How does Dr. Dexter's alcoholism affect the work of the women who work there? Do you think the fact that there are only women working at El Centro changes the environment? How so?

8. Throughout the story, Charlotte is bombarded with everyone else's problems. Does Charlotte seem like a doormat or does she help herself by helping others?

9. Maria Lopez revealed the sorrow of leaving her baby in Mexico. Devastated by the news that her baby fell ill and died, she committed suicide. Why did she resort to such extremes? How does losing a child affect the women of this novel?

10. El Centro is located in Londondale, in rural Pennsylvania near the mushroom camps. The rural landscape of farms and horses creates a picturesque mood. Why is this setting so important to the atmosphere?

11. Deirdre reacts to Ariel's death by taking vengeance on Bruce. Is she acting out of grief in losing her daughter, or is this purely because he caused her pregnancy? How do you feel about the way that Deirdre responds to her losses in this story? Did losing her first child in college scar her as a mother or has Deirdre grown in other ways?

12. How does the title *Family Planning* explain the novel? How do the characters both plan and fail to plan their families? Is this an ironic title?

13. *Family Planning* explores the themes of birth, loss, and recovery. What is the meaning of loss and recovery to the characters in *Family Planning*? Did they recover, and how?